'A quirky tale of love, work and the ...
Company

'A smart, witty love story'
Observer

'Full of laugh-out-loud observations ...
utterly unputdownable'
Woman

'Gorgeous location, dancing dialogue and
characters you'll fall in love with. Irresistible!'
Jill Mansell

'Cheery and heart-warming'
Sunday Mirror

'A Colgan novel is like listening to your best pal,
souped up on vino, spilling the latest gossip –
entertaining, dramatic and frequently hilarious'
Daily Record

'An entertaining read'
Sunday Express

By Jenny Colgan

Mure

The Summer Seaside Kitchen

A Very Distant Shore
(novella)

The Endless Beach

An Island Christmas

Christmas at the Island Hotel

An Island Wedding

Kirrinfief

The Bookshop on the Corner

The Bookshop on the Shore

Five Hundred Miles from You

Little Beach Street Bakery

Little Beach Street Bakery

Summer at
Little Beach Street Bakery

Christmas at
Little Beach Street Bakery

Sunrise by the Sea

Cupcake Café

Meet Me at the Cupcake Café

Christmas at the Cupcake Café

Sweetshop of Dreams

Welcome to Rosie Hopkins'
Sweetshop of Dreams

Christmas at
Rosie Hopkins' Sweetshop

The Christmas Surprise

The Little School by the Sea

Class

Rules

Lessons

Studies

West End Girls

Operation Sunshine

Diamonds Are a
Girl's Best Friend

The Good, the Bad
and the Dumped

The Loveliest
Chocolate Shop in Paris

Amanda's Wedding

Talking to Addison

Looking for Andrew McCarthy

Working Wonders

Do You Remember
the First Time?

Where Have All the Boys Gone?

The Christmas Bookshop

The Summer Skies

Midnight at the Christmas Bookshop

By Jenny T. Colgan

Resistance Is Futile

Spandex and the City

Jenny Colgan is the author of numerous bestselling novels, including *The Little Shop of Happy Ever After* and *Summer at Little Beach Street Bakery*, which are also published by Sphere. *Meet Me at the Cupcake Café* won the 2012 Melissa Nathan Award for Comedy Romance and was a *Sunday Times* top ten bestseller, as was *Welcome to Rosie Hopkins' Sweetshop of Dreams*, which won the RNA Romantic Novel of the Year Award 2013. Jenny lives in Scotland. She can be found on Twitter at @jennycolgan and on Instagram at @jennycolganbooks.

The *Sunday Times* bestseller

JENNY COLGAN

The Summer Skies

SPHERE

SPHERE

First published in Great Britain in 2023 by Sphere
This paperback edition published in Great Britain in 2024 by Sphere

1 3 5 7 9 10 8 6 4 2

Copyright © 2023 by Jenny Colgan

Quotation from *The Dark Is Rising* by Susan Cooper, published by Macmillan in 1973
Copyright 1973 © by Susan Cooper

'The Poorest Company' quoted by kind permission of John McCusker,
Kris Drever, Roddy Woomble; courtesy of Reveal Records

The moral right of the author has been asserted.

*All characters and events in this publication, other than those
clearly in the public domain, are fictitious and any resemblance
to real persons, living or dead, is purely coincidental.*

All rights reserved.
No part of this publication may be reproduced, stored in a
retrieval system, or transmitted, in any form or by any means, without
the prior permission in writing of the publisher, nor be otherwise circulated
in any form of binding or cover other than that in which it is published
and without a similar condition including this condition being
imposed on the subsequent purchaser.

A CIP catalogue record for this book
is available from the British Library.

ISBN 9-781-4087-2615-0

Typeset in Caslon by M Rules
Printed and bound in Great Britain by Clays Ltd, Elcograf, S.p.A.

Papers used by Sphere are from well-managed forests
and other responsible sources.

Sphere
An imprint of
Little, Brown Book Group
Carmelite House
50 Victoria Embankment
London EC4Y 0DZ

An Hachette UK Company
www.hachette.co.uk

www.littlebrown.co.uk

*For Leonid, who has travelled so far and who
is so very brave. We are so proud of you.*

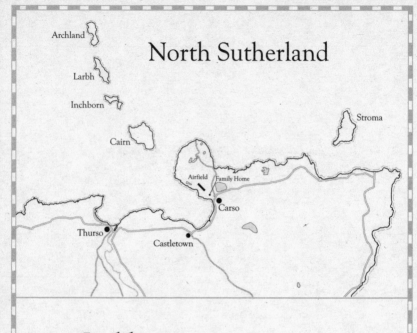

North Sutherland

Archland

Larbh

Inchborn

Stroma

Cairn

Airfield Family Home

Carso

Thurso

Castletown

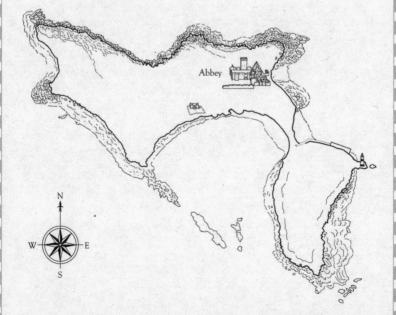

Inchborn

Abbey

N

W E

S

'The moment you doubt whether you can fly, you cease for ever to be able to do it.'

Peter Pan, J. M. BARRIE

Foreword

This is not a book about a pilot.

I know that seems ridiculous, seeing as somewhere on the jacket it probably says, 'Morag is a pilot', and it's definitely a book about a woman called Morag.

In fact, it's so not a book about a pilot, one of the lovely pilots who helped me out with the technical stuff (what pilots do is amazing, I have learned), very sweetly, while gently correcting me yet again one day ('Jen, pilots don't reverse planes. We don't have, like, wing mirrors.'), said, 'You know, it is totally fine if you don't put my name in the acknowledgements.'

And I was like, 'Oh, but you've helped me so much!' and he basically implied that I am *so* bad at flying it would be a stain on his professional reputation 😂. But I am greatly indebted to him nonetheless, and to Captain Colin Rutter of British Airways, who doesn't mind being publicly thanked but also would like it pointed out that there is quite a lot of wrong piloting stuff in here and it totally isn't his fault that I don't properly understand gyroscopes.

This book started last summer. One son took me to the Museum of Aviation in Scotland, which he adores, while my other son was all dragging his heels and like, 'This is fun how?', which if you have more than one child is a scenario you will probably recognise.

I got so caught up in the romance of it – they have a Concorde! And a sea plane! – and what I hadn't realised before was just how much pilots love to fly. That when they're in the air, they are a hundred per cent focused on what they are doing, and any other issues in life seem very distant. So I was interested in that; these days we are so distracted all the time by terrifying news and the internet squawking at us continuously that I wanted to feel that sensation of being deeply engrossed in something cool.

The second thing was the first time I flew after lockdown I realised I had forgotten how, well, basically how amazing it is. That feel of acceleration in your stomach; the astonishing way a heavy metal box full of people simply lifts off the ground; that moment when you burst through the grey old clouds into dazzling sunlight; the excitement of passing another plane. Even when there's lots of queueing and expense and people and fuss, it's still extraordinary, and I had forgotten that.

And finally I wanted to write a little about what flying really represents: the ability to pause and change your life, whether it's temporarily, like going holiday, or for ever, like moving away. To set foot on a new voyage to strange lands. I wanted to dream above the clouds about what your life could be, with the freedom that comes with it; an idea that, if we're brave enough, the world can still be our oyster; that it is never too late; that there are always new horizons ahead.

So this is a brand-new story. And it is not about being a pilot. But I hope you love it nonetheless. (Unless you are already a pilot, in which case, please don't write in. I think you're amazing.)

Jenny

xxxx

Part One

Prologue

Alarm sounding

AIR TRAFFIC CONTROL:	*Sunbird 247*, you have traffic in your ten o'clock climbing no height; read-out showing range of about ten miles.
PILOT:	Looking on TCAS.
FIRST OFFICER:	Not showing on TCAS.
PILOT:	Little out of his way.

'Do you still relive the incident in your head?'

The man from HR was so nice, so desperate to make everything all right. I shook my head.

'No, not at all. Everything's fine.'

'And you did everything correctly.'

'I know.'

'The flight landed safely.'

'Just doing my job.'

We got the bird down, I knew. And I don't know if that made it better or worse. The passengers wouldn't even have realised. It wasn't what you think. There weren't stomachs lurching at that hard lift into the air; nobody screamed. Well. Not on our bird. No trolleys thundered down the aisle. We killed two people, and the passengers barely glanced up from their phones.

It had started out as such a normal day, such a normal run to Alicante with a plane full of cheerful holiday-makers: hen and stag parties who'd been at the airport bar since 6 a.m., drinking holiday pints; families with young children fussing for the beach they'd been promised and furious instead at being strapped into a small seat for four hours; honeymooners, giggling and buying Prosecco from the smiling stews. Normal. Completely and absolutely normal.

ATC:	Do you have visual, *Sunbird 247*?
PILOT:	Stand by.
FIRST OFFICER:	No visual.
ATC:	Stand by. Climb to twelve thousand feet, *Sunbird 247*.
PILOT:	Say again.
ATC:	One-two-thousand-feet, *Sunbird 247*

I was in the right seat, first officer, expecting another routine day. Bob Brechin was captain. Good solid pilot too. Clear skies all the way down. Nothing unusual.

You couldn't even hear their screams as the little plane spiralled down, down . . .

'And are you sleeping okay?'

ATC:	Rescind th—
FIRST OFFICER:	WE'RE VISUAL! WE'RE VISUAL! *(Cockpit noise.)* CLIMB! CLIMB! CLIMB! CLIMB!

Roaring noise.

A month's debriefing for a category two mishap seemed reasonable. And it was fine. I had done four simulator training sessions since then, all perfect, had another medical, no problems.

I wasn't going to be a casualty, I wasn't. I was going to get back in the air, calmly and professionally, and do my job.

CLIMB! CLIMB!

'So you feel you're ready to go back?'
I put on my bravest face.
'Of course! Can't wait! Looking forward to making left seat on the big birds.'
The HR man smiled. 'I see there's no holding you back, Morag.'
I gave what I hoped was an encouraging smile. I saw the whites of the eyes of the pilot of the tiny Osprey, which had broken through a cloud into that vast menacing shadow of an A320. Every time I closed my own eyes.

A crop sprayer, we learned. A sweet young farmer boy. Luis. Showing off to his girlfriend.

We rose. They dived. We slowed to climb. It didn't feel like much from inside. From their perspective, I cannot imagine.

They panicked and went into a tailspin. Luis and his girlfriend. Serenata was her name. Such a beautiful name. Into a field, thank God, outside Yecla.

5

I had done everything right. I had kept my cool. Bob and I had worked well together. We glanced at each other.

Once we were level again, we sat, holding our breath, waiting for the confirmation of the awful news we knew was coming from the moment the little plane had spiralled out of our field of vision.

These days, on our safe, computerised planes, the joke is that pilots are only paid for two minutes a year. But there is some truth in it, and those were ours.

Chapter One

My great-grandfather, Captain Ranald Murdo MacIntyre of the RAF City of Aberdeen Auxiliary Squadron 612, was not a tall man. That was possibly, most people agreed, what made him so damn feisty in the first place.

He was stocky, though, with a bullet head and an expression that almost dared you to defy him and then face the consequences. He was one of those for whom the war was a great time; a huge adventure that broke open his small view of the world from a small town on the north coast of Scotland.

He joined up right away – RAF, back when the life expectancy of those boys was about six months. From the second he took off in a Spitfire, he loved it. He flew fearlessly and into anything, defending the Firth of Forth, and almost entirely buzzing their arch enemies – not the Luftwaffe, as it happened, but 602, the Glasgow Auxiliary Squadron, their west-coast rivals – more than was strictly necessary.

Finally, before his six months were up and the law of averages took him – not that Ranald MacIntyre had any truck with those – the RAF grounded him at Leuchars, and got him to train the next cohort, and the next, which he did with the same exuberant vehemence with which he had tackled the skies. And when the war was over, the chances of him going back to tend the family croft had dwindled to nothing.

He found a little plane, a Cessna, from somewhere – it was entirely possible, word went, that the RAF had given it to him simply to make him go away, as teaching pilots suicidal combat bravery wasn't quite as popular a requirement in the post-war period as it had been before – and immediately started a service flying the archipelago, the majestic chain of islands that run off the north coast of Scotland, which up until then had been connected with only intermittent ferries or, just as often, sail- and rowboats.

The islands thought they had been doing fine on their own, thank you very much, and didn't need this ungodly noisy oily interference in the rhythms of their year, until they started to find it more and more useful to get hold of a paper that was only a day old, or being able to visit a doctor or even spend a day visiting the huge big tempting cities and bright lights of Oban and Inverness. The kirk wasn't pleased, but not much pleased them anyway.

And the tiny air taxi service, which would stop and pick up more or less anyone anywhere, thrived. First for the novelty value, secondly for the convenience of the thing and thirdly for Ranald's complete inability to be put off or fazed by all but the very worst of the weather, and if you are familiar with the north coast of Scotland at all, you will know that that is a formidable talent.

Everyone thought Ranald MacIntyre was married to that plane, so almost everyone was as surprised as he was when at the age of fifty he married pretty Margaret Wise from Thurso and had baby Murdo the next year.

Young Murdo soon became a regular sight sitting up in the cockpit with his dad, and Ranald's old mate Jimmy Convery, who was from the slums of Glasgow, so rough you could barely understand a word he said, and the best and most faithful co-pilot Ranald ever had. Ranald knew that Jimmy had never had a home to go back to after the war, and only the barest bones of one afore it, so when they were demobbed, Ranald brought Jimmy back and they rented the old draughty house not even the curate wanted, and Jimmy never left.

Murdo grew up and went to flying school at sixteen, which you could in those days. Very little can unsettle the pilot who has grown up landing in Scottish weather conditions: frequent fog, sideways rain, snow, hail, all on tiny runways. Inchborn, an island in the archipelago chain without a runway at all, simply had a long beach, so Ranald landed on that at low tide.

At twenty-one, Murdo borrowed the money to buy a new plane – *Dolly*, a brand-new Twin Otter which was his pride and joy – and tried to professionalise the operation a little with schedules, regular deliveries and touring schedules for people's new disposable incomes. But they were never above taking an extra parcel as a favour if they had the weight allowance, or picking up mums and babbies for a very small charge if they needed to get to the mainland for their check-ups, or helping out the air ambulance if need be.

Murdo married young, anxious to get raising the next generations of MacIntyre Air, and young Iain was just as devoted to flying as his dad and his granddad had been.

He was the light and joy of their days, as like Murdo as Murdo had been like Ranald, and excited plans were made to expand the fleet one day – until Iain, told to bring a punnet of red apples from the market, returned with a punnet of green, and the terrible truth emerged: not only was he severely colour-blind but his eyesight in general was also shocking, and the optician in Wick had quite a lot to say about why they hadn't brought the lad in earlier.

For Iain, it was a blow akin to being an injured professional footballer. A maudlin teenager, he took his new, huge NHS glasses off to accountancy school, studied hard and got a job in the finance department of a large commercial airline company based out of Aberdeen, where he got to spend his days in the company of pilots, dealing with the finances of aeroplanes, handling invoices and billing for planes and fuel and cargo, but never ever flying one. It was hard to tell if it were more consolation or torture for the boy who only ever dreamed of being able to fly.

But there was always the next generation. It's not that Iain MacIntyre asked very pointed questions about the eyesight of every woman he dated, but when he met Katherine Trawley, bonny, red-haired and better than twenty-twenty, it was pretty much a foregone conclusion, and when Jamie came along, the scene was set.

Whereupon Jamie cried and wailed whenever he was put to the skies on those long summer days up in Wick, and couldn't understand why people were constantly trying to strap him into a terrifying and noisy metal tin can when there was an entire beach outside with sand and sea and crabs and birds and shrimping nets and wildlife and all the beauties of nature that happen at the glorious top end of Scotland. He made such an infernal fuss that eventually the family gave up and turned reluctantly to their next best hope, babby Morag.

And, well, that was me.

My great-grandfather Ranald's medals lined the shelf of the big old draughty house in Carso, the northernmost town in Sutherland at the very top of the Scottish Highlands, with its tiny airfield and old grey stone houses, the wind blowing all the time, where the North and the Irish Seas met. I remembered him, just, as a crusty presence, firm in demeanour, given to occasional bursts of hearty laughter at jokes I didn't get and a fondness for launching into very long stories that most people had heard before.

Margaret died young of breast cancer, when Murdo was twenty – one of the reasons he wanted to get married so young, my mother thought – and Ranald had carried on, living with his best mate Jimmy Convery all his life. Jimmy didn't say much, but punctuated the anecdotes with throaty laughter fuelled by Woodbines. I remembered him dimly as a whiskery, slightly unnerving presence, but Murdo – Gramps – worshipped him, and I worshipped Gramps, so I figured he must have been okay.

The joy in that house – we lived outside Aberdeen but spent many weekends and all our summers up in Carso – when I showed an interest in flying was extraordinary to me. Ranald passed away the same year, Jimmy not long after, and there was a family superstition that he was somehow reincarnated in me.

I was used to Jamie being the centre of attention as he was an unusually pretty child, red-haired and grey-eyed. I had wild curly black hair that apparently Margaret had shared, but gave me, personally, nothing but grief, as I grew up at the height of GHDs and pencil-thin brows. At school, they called me Morag Grobag, because it looked like I'd been planted in one.

Jamie was clever, sensitive and a wonderful artist. I was quiet, terribly shy and, as the first girl in three generations, felt more or less inadequate. Until I clambered up in the cockpit of the Twin Otter.

It was immediate: the entire family's pride, and what felt suspiciously like relief. Everywhere we went, every summer, I was their little lady pilot, Morag, saviour of MacIntyre Air. People would stop us on the street, talk about flying to me, while Jamie stood sullenly to the side, clutching the sketch pad that was never far out of reach, waiting to vanish at the first opportunity to the nearest burn or tree.

I remember taking my options at school but not as if I had much choice in the matter – maths for reckoning; physics, geography, obviously. Raising money for flight school felt like a full family operation – it's *really*, really expensive, even if you do have a guaranteed job at the end of it. So expensive. Everyone made sacrifices, and I felt that, very much. But I did learn to fly, and there was no stopping me. This sounds terrible, but as soon as I realised it got me more attention than my lovely, popular brother, I was in absolutely full bore.

I was such a shy, nervous child. My mother had to peel me off her when I went to nursery or primary school. I had precisely one friend, Nalitha Khan, who was the opposite of shy, and let me scurry along in her wake. But then, when the family hit upon me following into the family business – well, then everything changed. The chatty gossipy town where my grandfather lived – which normally intimidated me as the old ladies

12

chivvied me to 'speak up then, yon wee Morag, och, you're so peely-wally; it's a shame, with Jamie so bonny' – became somewhat easier to handle.

I kind of thought that it would all get even easier when I started flight school. In fact, the first thing ninety per cent of people said to me was 'oooh, you're surrounded by those hand-some pilots all the time, lucky you', which is obviously, you know, durr, very, very sexist and also rather disappointingly not at all the case. It was mostly men, but they saw me and the other couple of women in the class as mates, honorary lads practically. They were all off chasing the beautiful blonde drama students next door just like everyone else. Which is good, you know. I like being treated as a professional. Of course I did. They were just very, very, possibly too professional.

It was fine, being one of the guys. I was a good student, and good at what I did, and I was never excluded from anything. And I did like discussing engines and windspeed over a couple of pints of lager, of course I did. And talking about cars.

Then Jai and Abdul and Connor would all get into their very fancy cars and drive off and pick up other less technical girls for nights out, and I would just go home to the little newbuild flat I had rented because it was near the airport and not too expensive, no other reason. It was just a place to lay my head between shifts.

I dated a couple of engineers and that was fine, but once I graduated from flight school and moved into a proper job, well, I was just away all the time. So basically, I was a bit too square for the people who were used to people being away all the time, but a bit too exotic for people who weren't. For example, with men, either they were a bit intimidated by my job and never mentioned it ever, but talked a lot about how good they were at fixing cars, or they would ask me loads about crashes and terrifying things which, up until extremely recently, had never happened to me or anyone I know – it's really, *really* rare. Or they'd kind of pretend to feel sorry for me, asking me if it wasn't incredibly boring, mixing the reality of their bad travelling experiences with my wonderful job.

And I didn't know how to explain, not exactly, the feeling when you are just, *just* on the very tip of lifting a huge bird off the face of the earth; the exact second when you go from trundling along the ground, earthbound, to lifting up, up, then suddenly bursting free the chains of gravity; soaring up through the clouds, bursting through, even on the greyed and dullest of days, the poor commuters left far below, endlessly beetling through traffic in the rain while you join the great route of kings, the blue sky stretching ahead of you, the darker curve beyond all yours, laid out in front of you, the clouds soft cushions you wave past and even the snow-topped mountains cowering beneath your dominion.

Which is my way of saying that normally I really, really love my job. Or at least I used to.

But when it comes to dating, I won't lie, it's a conundrum. For me, anyway. Some pilots solve it by having women or men dotted about in busy airline hubs all over the world, but I found to my horror that despite being a millennial I am just not cut out for that kind of thing, although in theory it's cool, obviously. Not many people that did as much maths and engineering as I did at school are cool. My mum says it was because I was a very busy career girl. But she is my mum, and actually uses phrases like 'career girl'.

Anyway. My phone rang the second I left the HR debrief room, when I was queueing at the coffee stall. I definitely needed coffee. Or maybe just something warming and comforting to hold in my hands.

'How did the meeting go?'

'Gramps! It was fine!'

'Course it was,' he said with satisfaction. 'That's my girl.'

'I just need to wait for them to shut the incident log, then onwards and upwards . . . '

'But you're cleared to fly?'

'There's a few hoops to jump through yet, but . . . I think it will be all right.'

My voice was not wavering. Absolutely not at all.

'So,' he said with relish, 'you'll have a bit of time off.'

'Gramps,' I said in a warning voice.

He had never given up hope that I'd come back north. It didn't matter how much I told him about the fact that I was not a bad person for giving up the freezing cold for flying all over Europe, for somewhere where a clothes shop wasn't Mrs-now-Ms Haglye's divorce project, which she proudly called a boutique and had the very latest in matching beige twinsets on very generously proportioned dummies and still did early closing on Wednesdays. That a life of bottomless brunches and sunny trips overseas were what I felt I should probably be aiming for (it certainly was high on the list for all my pilot mates), and wouldn't he want a swimming pool if he had the chance?

'Why would I need a swimming pool?' he said, genuinely mystified. 'The sea is *right here*, bairn. I mean, right here.'

'You should come to civilisation more often,' I said. 'Honestly. You might like it.'

'I've been to civilisation,' he said. 'It smells terrible.'

'People like toilets on their planes, Gramps, it's perfectly normal.'

There wasn't a toilet on the Twin Otter. None of the flights were further than an hour, so you pretty much just had to hold on.

'It's disgusting.'

I couldn't argue with that, especially some of the stag parties we brought home, bleary and extravagantly unpleasant on Sunday mornings.

'Come on up,' he said. 'Come on. The daffs are flowering.'

'They're over here.'

'And everyone's asking after you.'

'Yes, that's exactly the problem! "Oooh, wee Morag wouldn't say boo to a goose!" "Ooh, wee Morag and that frightful hair!" "Ooh, Morag, remember that time you peed your knickers at the Mercat Cross?"'

'That was funny though.'

'It was not funny! Jamie had a pet grass snake and put it down my neck.'

I shivered.

'Aye well, it's no' his fault you don't like animals.'

'I don't *not* like animals; I just prefer useful things. Like aeroplanes. And restaurants and civilisation and roads that go places and don't just peter out in a field.'

'Aye, it's the big shiny life you have now, Morag.'

'Don't pull that one on me.'

'You've forgotten your roots.'

'I haven't!' I said, not for the first time nor, I knew, the last. 'I just found ... a bigger world out there.'

'That smells.'

'*Gramps!*'

His voice lowered.

'But, Morag, you're absolutely sure ... you're sure you're over your near-miss?'

I looked up just then, in the sterile aircraft building. The HR manager who'd taken our session had just joined the coffee queue. Huh, that was a bit weird, I couldn't really imagine what these people did when you weren't in those little rooms with them, painted in soothing colours. A bit like when you're a kid and you see a teacher out of school. Just having lunch seemed a bit normal, like choosing a chicken sandwich or a salad. I noticed he chose a salad.

I thought he wouldn't recognise me, but he glanced up and clearly did. I found myself rethinking the muffin I'd been planning on. Maybe a muffin, instead of a nice sensible salad, would make me look needy and sugar-addicted and emotionally unstable. Perhaps I should order decaf. Or maybe that would make me look neurotic.

Gramps's voice was still booming out of the phone.

'Because when it happened to me, I was a wreck!'

'That was a stealth bomber cutting you up though,' I pointed out, knowing the oft-told story back to front. 'You were the wee guy. We were the big guys.'

I was trying to keep my voice quiet, but the HR man had moved up the queue and could hardly avoid hearing.

'Nobody's a big guy at thirty thousand feet,' Gramps said. 'We're all tiny in God's eyes up there.'

'I'm totally and completely fine,' I said in a voice that suddenly sounded to my own ears entirely unconvincing. 'All my loads of friends and happy and well-balanced social life think I am completely fine ... uh, fresh juice please.'

'That'll be four forty-nine.'

'*Four forty-nine? For juice?!*'

My grandfather was still astounded as we said our goodbyes. I put my phone away and suddenly realised that whoever else

17

had been waiting for coffee had stepped away and there was only the HR man and me left.

'Uh, go ahead,' I said awkwardly, trying to get my phone back in my bag.

'CARROT AND GINGER JUICE!' yelled the girl.

'No, please,' he said, gesturing. I smiled, feeling uncommonly flustered. Flying a five-hundred-tonne ramp weight A380 does not fluster me. HR kind of does.

'Just getting my, uh, juice. Totally normal juice,' I said, as if testifying my movements in a court of law. I vowed never ever to use the coffee stand in the HR department ever again.

He smiled as if he didn't know what to do with that. He had sandy hair and a blue shirt and tie; he looked like a quite cool teacher. Probably had a nice wife and 2.4 kids at home and coached the kids' football team and had basically a perfectly organised life. I remembered how kind his voice had sounded, actually kind of attractive. Get a grip, Morag, I said to myself. Things were already quite complicated enough.

'Hi there!' said the voice behind the till to the HR man. 'No bacon sandwich today then?'

I glanced at him in some surprise. He went rather pink.

'Uh, no, thanks.'

'What about your Twix?'

'I . . . uh, don't want a Twix.'

'But you always have your Twix!'

'I . . . Just the salad please.'

He pinged his card as I scuttled off with my juice, feeling oddly cheered.

It was a tick-box process you had to go through – the captain I'd been co-piloting with was going through it too – and two days later I found myself back in the little bland room with the pot plant, steeling myself. I understood the process: they more or less asked you the same questions to check for veracity while they checked the plane logs and the aircraft while checking on you.

The sandy-haired man smiled as I walked in. He was sitting behind his desk; I had to perch on a chair.

'Hello, First Officer MacIntyre.'

'Uh, hello . . . '

He'd told me his name before; it was something weird, but I'd forgotten it.

'It's Hayden. Hayden Telford.'

That was it. It was kind of like a girl's name but also kind of pretty.

'Sorry,' I said, realising I had gone a little pink. 'I normally have a good memory for small details! Part of my job!'

He wasn't, I'd noticed, wearing a wedding ring. Maybe he took it off for work. Morag, I told myself sternly. Stop being stupid.

'It's okay,' he said in that nice voice of his. It had a faint trace of an accent I couldn't place. I gave myself a shake. Being here – it was so important. Whatever box he had to tick on his computer, he had to tick it today.

'So have you been a psychologist for long?' I found myself babbling regardless.

He glanced up, smiling pleasantly.

'Oh no, I'm an HR specialist,' he said.

'Oh, so you're not, like, a doctor or anything?'

He looked at me. 'No, I'm not a doctor.' He smiled reassuringly.

'Not that it would matter,' I said quickly.

This was getting worse and worse.

'Well, no, why would it?'

'It wouldn't,' I said. He looked at me curiously and I couldn't read it at all. Oh God, maybe he just thought I was crackers.

I fell silent.

'Okay!' he said. Then he skidded his chair a bit closer to me.

'Uh, Morag, it's okay to be nervous,' he said. 'I understand. I deal with pilots and first officers in your situation a lot. If you feel you do need to see a therapist, I'm here to refer you, that's all.'

'No, I'm fine,' I said quickly.

'I'm just doing my job. It's just so we're all safe up there. Okay?'

There was something really reassuring about his voice. I couldn't help it. I liked him.

He paused for a second.

'I quite like you thinking I'm a doctor though. Maybe I should put that on my door. Bit more interesting than being an HR suit.'

'I think your job must be very interesting,' I said.

'Well, it's no flying a plane,' he said. He returned to his desk and pulled up something on his computer.

'Okay. Sorry to do this, but – can you tell me about it again?'

I had hoped that it would help, running through it the second time. But it didn't. It was the awful loss. The shock of seeing it right in front of your eyes.

'Did you have any hesitation in telling the captain what was happening?'

'No.'

CLIMB! CLIMB! CLIMB! CLIMB!

'No concerns that he wouldn't listen to you? Would you have done anything differently?'

'No.'

The dot on the radar. Gone.

Hold it together, Morag. He's not a doctor but he's probably even more powerful. One click on the mouse and this whole thing could just go . . .

'We followed procedure,' I said, making my voice robotically dull. I spoke more slowly. I had learned from bitter experience that it made people – and when I said people, I really meant male passengers who thought having a female pilot was hilarious – calmer. 'The outcome for the small plane was very disappointing. I wish they'd filed their flight plan. I wish things had been different.'

I wish I could sleep at night.

Hayden was nodding.

'Okay. Thanks, First Officer . . . '

'Morag is fine,' I said, trying to sound confident.

He put the mouse down and smiled encouragingly. He had a nice smile; his incisors were slightly wonky, which gave him a kind of schoolboyish charm.

'Okay,' he said. 'Honestly, I don't think you have anything to worry about.'

'I'm not worried,' I lied.

'And what are you thinking about next? Are you wanting to move to left seat?'

That was the standard career path: co-pilot, then captain on short haul, then co-pilot on long haul. That was what was considered to be the goal, at any rate. Some pilots couldn't bear it – like Gramps, for example. He loved taking off and landing (the most exciting parts of any flight) and sleeping in his own bed at night. He had no interest, he often said, in spending years of his life flying over Siberia, or the Sahara.

But I had been thinking about it. And it had been a bad, an insidious thought. Something I couldn't tell anyone about.

If I went to long haul – well, I could co-pilot for ever. Buy a little time. Or at least for however long it took me. I could even take third chair long haul. I would barely have to fly except in a simulator. I would be safe. And the flaming, glorious sunsets on the Sahara were something to see too. Nobody could possibly accuse me of being scared if I was ascending the ladder, moving on with my job. Just until I got better. Because I would get better, wouldn't I?

It was a terrible plan. But it was, at this moment, the best I had.

I tried to make my voice light.

'Actually, I fancy getting some time in on long haul. Some big shifts on some lovely new birds.'

'Ah, off to Dubai, are you?'

It was a joke how many pilots moved there. Tax-free, sunshine and right in the centre of the world. It was a different airline, obviously, but I could work my way up. I shrugged. 'Maybe,' I said.

'You're going to move up,' he said admiringly, and I was amazed with myself, that my ruse had worked. That what was so transparent to me – my fear and my pain – could be so easily covered up, even from a professional.

I tried not to feel guilty. I failed.

'That's the plan,' I said boldly. 'Put it behind me.'

'Or beneath you,' he said, then winced. 'Sorry. That was a terrible dad joke.'

'Ha, you look like a dad,' I said.

He frowned. 'Do I really? I'm not one . . . '

We were both suddenly conscious that the conversation had strayed into the personal. He glanced swiftly at the clock.

'Well, thanks again for . . . '

I jumped up and he stood up too, which I wasn't expecting. He reached over and shook my hand. He held on to it for just a second, I thought. No. I was in an emotionally wrought stage. For sure.

'Well, this is probably the last time I'll see you,' he said.

'Hopefully!' I said stupidly.

'Well, yes, hopefully, yes, I suppose.'

He took his hand back. I felt my cheeks go pink again.

'I wish you all the best, Morag,' he said, and I thought, Well, goodness.

'Bye then,' was all I managed.

'Happy flying!' he said, then visibly winced at himself again, as if he'd said something very dumb. If only he knew in my situation how dumb it was.

Chapter Two

Over the next couple of weeks there were more simulations, as well as a joint debrief with the top brass and engineering staff which I thought Hayden was at – I might, in fact, have packed a Twix in my bag that I thought I might give him just as a farewell joke or something, no biggie. Anyway, he wasn't.

But Bob and I were more or less on our way to getting back in the air. Every day felt more frightening, but I had put my application in for first officer on the long-haul route. I had done it. I would get over it in time, I would.

And then it would be more money – and who knows? Maybe I would fall in love with the sunshine and the 'good life' my fellow pilots went on about, out in places where the sun shone all the time and you had a swimming pool as opposed to where my flat was on a tiny estate of identical boxes near the airport under a grey cloud. I hadn't really been attracted to that lifestyle; was slightly intimidated, to be honest, by the girls in bikinis with amazing nails and big lips. But everyone (except Gramps) was so excited I was applying for it; it seemed so obvious to them. All my pilot mates were excited about huge airbuses, and new massive fuel economy and the future of aviation and just wanted to get in the air, and I tried to join in, and I tried to feel the same, and I almost convinced myself, sometimes.

There is a secret bar round the back of the airport – every airport, actually – where pilots drink. There is a direct line to a cab company that doesn't charge you airport collection fees, and a free car park where you can leave your nice car overnight for free, so for obvious reasons I can't possibly tell you where it is. It's also very good at accepting that sometimes if a pilot has come off a ten-hour shift and feels like it's 8 p.m. and they would like a pint with a friend, it may not technically be 8 p.m. by official GMT, but they can have their pint anyway.

Bob Brechin and I headed there to debrief on the last simulation. It was weird, coming in to work to do various bits and bobs but then not actually taking off anywhere. The bar was half-full of foreign pilots on their layovers as well as ground crew and staff. There were some women but not loads, but if I were to get intimidated by large groups of men, working in aviation would have seen me off a while ago.

He ordered a pint; I went for coffee. Really, I wanted to drive home.

'So, what next for you then?'

I told him about my long-haul co-chair plans and he frowned.

'Neh,' he said. 'You don't want to do that. You should take on a short haul as captain. Obvious, innit? And don't you have an airline sitting right there?'

'You make it sound like a family firm!' I said. 'It's one creaking Twin Otter landing on sand and a prayer!'

He grinned.

'I met the old man once, did I tell you?'

'Murdo?'

'Heck of a pilot. I was just a rube, running up to Glasgow. He told me some stories.'

I smiled.

'I bet he did.'

'You don't want to take over that route? That's real flying, that is.'

'You sound like my grandfather.'

'Ouch,' said Bob. 'Well, I didn't really have you down as a Dubai type. Don't all you Scots burst into flames in the sun anyway?'

'Shut up please.'

I glanced around the room. Standing in the corner talking to a couple of people from the HR department was Hayden Telford.

'Oh look,' I said to Bob, indicating Hayden. Bob looked over and waved, completely unconcerned.

'Oh yeah, the HR consultant. He seemed all right, didn't you think?'

'He's a consultant?' I said, suddenly interested. 'You mean, he doesn't work for the airline?'

'Why?' said Bob, grinning avuncularly and taking a long pull of his pint.

'No reason,' I said as Bob gave me a suspicious glance. I never ever talked about my personal life at work. Partly to keep professional, partly so it gave me an air of mystery and partly because I didn't really have one.

Hayden saw me and, to my surprise and delight, smiled broadly and motioned me over. Bob had tuned into a conversation about football with a group from KLM at the bar, so I wandered over.

'Hello,' I said shyly.

'Hey,' he said. He grinned again, showing his incisors. Normally I am terrible at signals but I did think it: this man is pleased to see me.

'Hayden's leaving!' said one of the other HR people, a bubbly young woman who looked to be quite drunk.

'I was only here for a couple of months,' protested Hayden. 'I'm just a consultant.'

'But we liked having you here! We liked having him here,' she said to me, grasping me on the sleeve to make her point. She had a glass of Prosecco that seemed to be at risk.

'He's leeeavvving uss,' she protested, running her free hand up his sleeve and, to my absolute surprise, towards the buttons of his shirt. I had always considered that this kind of thing was exactly what HR was meant to prevent.

Hayden was obviously thinking the same thing as he caught my eye for a moment, winked imperceptibly, then said loudly, 'Ah, First Officer MacIntyre, I'm so glad I caught you ... Can I have a second of your time? Excuse me, Rosie.'

He disengaged Rosie's hand quite gently. The girl pouted.

'Don't be long!' she said.

Hayden followed me to the other side of the bar.

'Excellent HR behaviour, I see,' I couldn't help remarking.

'Oh, they work hard,' he said, glancing back. 'Everyone has to decompress sometimes. Don't report me to HR for saying that.'

He looked pointedly at my coffee.

'Not you, though.'

'I just don't fancy getting a cab. Also, I don't really like getting tipsy with people I work with.'

He lifted his beer bottle.

'Ah,' he said awkwardly, but he didn't seem in the least drunk.

'So you're leaving?' I said. He nodded.

'Where are you headed?'

'Actually, there's a few possibilities on the table … waiting to see. Life of a consultant.'

'Is that what they call gardening leave?' I said suddenly.

'Uh, no, just a job finishing. You're not on gardening leave either.'

'No, I know; I just like the phrase.'

'You like gardening?'

'Ha! No, I never go outside.'

He looked at me curiously, and I found myself blushing again. This is ridiculous, Morag, I told myself. He just has such a kind smile.

And he wasn't my doctor, I reminded myself.

'So you have, like, technically nothing to do with my case now?' I said quietly. I wasn't quite sure where I got the confidence to say that. Maybe because I was moving on soon too. If this went horribly wrong, well, we would never see each other again.

'Done and dusted,' he said. He glanced down at his beer.

'I can't garden either,' he said suddenly.

'Uh-huh,' I said, staring at my fingers.

'I mean, if you wanted to give it a shot sometime …'

'Won't …?' I swallowed. At least I should find out now. 'Won't your girlfriend or … whatever … mind?'

'Well, in complete contrast to what I just told Rosie, I don't have a girlfriend just now. Or a whatever.'

It felt like the rest of the bar had suddenly gone quiet. He couldn't have been more upfront.

'Well,' I said. 'That ... that might be nice.'

Chapter Three

'And you're absolutely sure he's not a serial killer?' said Nalitha. 'Because who else would *do* that? Just *ask someone out* in *person*?! *Oh my God!*'

We were on the phone. Up where she was, it was still snowing. Down south, there was warmth in the sun. I could hear the wind rattle around her.

'Lots of people meet other people like that.'

'They do *not*,' said Nalitha. 'They go on apps and make themselves miserable for months and months and then settle for the first person they meet that has most of their own teeth.'

'Well, maybe he's not on the apps,' I said.

'Did you check?'

'Not fussed.'

I was too terrified.

'Oh my God, you lying hound! I'm going to check. It's an unusual name.'

'*Do not check!* OMG, I can't bear it.'

Airport Tinder is a deeply terrifying viper pit you want no part of, ever. Vipers who, like, even the other snakes have requested not to hang out with because they're so super-mean, even for snakes.

I sniffed.

'It's just an actual date that actual people go on,' I said. 'We're just going for a walk.'

'It's so, so weird,' said Nalitha.

'You're weird!'

'I can't believe you're not coming back here. We had a litre of cow sperm to transport this morning and apparently if you spill a drop it's basically liquid gold and we'd have to sell the plane.'

Nalitha and I had been friends all through school and when she didn't want to move to the city, I suggested working the route to her and Gramps, and they both took to it right away. She was everything: check-in, security, door staff, runway safety and admin. She could have had a much better paid job with larger companies, but she loved Carso – all her family and friends were there and she could have a lovely large house rather than a rat-sized, rat-infested cupboard in Aberdeen or Edinburgh.

'Stop it!'

'And nine documentary filmmakers all trying to get the same shot for their piece entitled *Lost Scotland* which means we probably, like, aren't very lost, thanks very much?'

I laughed. I did like what went on up there. My day-to-day was usually just taking tired, grumpy people who had waited a spectacularly long time in security queues over to Malaga and back.

'When do you get cleared to fly again? And when do you hear about your new job?' said Nalitha.

'All in good time,' I said, crossing my fingers that they would be soon enough that I wouldn't be roped in to flying anywhere for MacIntyre Air. Because Hayden was something new, and quietly exciting. But he didn't take away from the actual problem I had: whether or not I could still do my job.

It was an unusually pretty spring Sunday morning and the park was absolutely heaving. Toddlers zoomed past on scooters at terrifying speeds. Men who were old enough to know better were even worse on electric scooters, which turned me into a slightly tutting old maid. There were cycle path and non-cycle-path altercations, dogs on leads and dogs not on leads making a beeline for small children who were holding ice cream cones at strategically dog-nose height. It never failed to amaze me, whenever we took off, how crowded the south-east of England was. The endless houses, the endless cars. As if the entire country had been held up, and everyone had simply slid from the top to the very bottom.

I saw him first: Hayden was wearing chinos, a blue shirt and desert boots, exactly the dad style I'd noticed him in first time round. Proper dad core. I didn't mind it at all. In fact, I found it rather attractive, like I was out with a grown-up, a proper adult who didn't waste their life playing computer games. Someone that would have views on eating properly and making organised decisions. I found it sexy in a way that ten years ago I'd liked blue hair and tattoos.

I waved and smiled, and he smiled back, his cute incisors showing, his face friendly and open. Dating in daylight was a completely preposterous affair, I had decided that morning.

Dating stone-cold sober in the clear light of day was an absurd development.

But here was the thing: from the second he beamed, came over and said 'Morag!' as if I was the best thing to happen to him all day, but didn't attempt one of those awkward cheek kisses, it felt somehow easy.

It was so surprisingly easy, in fact, that I slightly suspected him of using some secret HR voodoo on me. He bought me an ice cream, and we walked, and he asked me about my job, but not in the slightly sarcastic awed tones some men used.

And I asked about his, and found it genuinely interesting. He'd been a psychology major, and he came from Hull – his vowels flattened out the more we spoke, just as I stopped flattening out my lilt, all things you have to do down south, or even in the air, particularly when you're speaking to air traffic control. And I found out he'd moved down with his girlfriend from university, but it hadn't worked out, so he was renting a friend's spare room and thinking about his next move.

And then it made sense to stop at a park café, and, well, they were selling rosé, and we could watch the world go by – the literal world, it felt like. It was still absolutely heaving: football games and barbecues, and some amazing Indian dancing, and a troupe of young parkour kids trying to bounce off the trees. After the rosé, we laughed a bit about how unbelievably nice it was not to have to go to work tomorrow, and well, we weren't *so* far from my little apartment, and I normally wouldn't have moved quite so fast, but here I was, with time off, with a nice man in a blue shirt and a Hull accent and an ability to smile every single time a toddler butted him on the shins with their scooter and their parents didn't actually look up from their phone – and a bottle of rosé.

It was more than that. It was the very real sense that we looked like every other couple in the park that I had passed so many times as I'd come off one shift or been heading for the airport at an ungodly hour, thinking, God, wee nerdy Morag, why can't you ever just be *normal*?

So even though it wasn't like me at all, not a bit, we grabbed another bottle from the corner shop and hopped into an Uber, and when we got back to the flat, I kissed his wonky smile and unbuttoned his square shirt (and let him fold it up on the chair) and enjoyed myself as much as I had done in a very long time.

I could get used to this, I found myself thinking the next morning, even as we smiled awkwardly at each other and he asked if he could nip out and get us coffee and I had to explain that actually I lived on a housing estate absolutely miles from anywhere and you couldn't just pop out, you had to drive for fifteen minutes to get a pint of milk from the big Tesco, and he looked in my cupboards and said, well, he would love to make me breakfast, but . . . ?

So I had to own up to the fact that I was never there, and I didn't really cook anyway – 'You live on airline food?' he said, eyes wide, and I winced and said yes, more or less – and that I'd trained myself to drink my coffee black if I had to and he said fine, and we made some coffee, black, and went back to bed.

'There's no pictures or anything,' he said, smiling. 'Do you really live here or is this a show flat you broke into so you could have your wicked way with me?'

I grinned.

34

'No ... I just like things tidy and minimalist, I suppose ... ' I looked around. The only thing I'd done was to hang black-out blinds so I could sleep whatever time I got in. 'Like my cockpit.'

'Well. Have you not been here very long?'

I shrugged. I didn't want to admit the truth: four years. But it didn't really feel like home.

'I'm moving on anyway,' I reminded him.

'Oh yes!' he said, sipping his coffee and wincing. 'Me too.' He looked at me intently. 'Which, I am now starting to think, seems a bit of a shame.'

I leaned over. His hair was thick and curly on his chest, though you couldn't tell when he was clothed, and he had a bit of a paunch. I liked both of those things about him. I was scared of anyone with rock-solid abs who was going to make me go to the gym and drink protein powder, or shaved all over.

It became a little gift, that early sweet spring.

Both of us, nothing to do but wander about, holding hands. I wondered somewhere very deep down, if someone as gentle as Hayden might be the answer; that he might make me better. I suppose a therapist would say the only answers to anything are within you. But he was so kind, such a good listener and so interested in my work. I almost told him about my deepest secret fear. I came very close.

We went to see *Top Gun* with all my pilot mates, who gave me a fair amount of ribbing, but not too much, distracted as we were by complaining about inaccuracies and scoffing at their constant breaching of Health and Safety regulations while genuinely loving it and Hayden didn't complain or shush; he laughed along, and was cool with everything and even made a couple of not-bad dad-style jokes. He fitted in and, oh, I felt such a fizz of pleasure at some of the important people in my life liking and accepting him.

There was no ghosting or ignored dates. No weird stuff. He called when he said he would and didn't mess me about and if, as Nalitha said, he sounded like a fifty-five-year-old and had his pension completely sorted out, well, maybe I liked that about him. Maybe I liked dating a grown-up for once. And Nalitha would like him too when she met him. Everyone did. He was just that kind of a person.

And even while I knew at some level that one day my leave was going to be over and I was going to have to face up to flying again; even if sometimes he caught me staring into space and asked me what was on my mind, he was still the very best distraction.

We were sitting outside one night in a packed and heaving Covent Garden, almost giving up on hoping for service. Hayden had needed new trainers and we had come up to the big city and shopped together, that thrillingly intimate thing to do with someone for the first time – the sense of getting to know each other inside out, the likes and dislikes – and we had laughed at the trendy styles and about how hopelessly untrendy we both were with the happy knowledge of people just on the wrong side of thirty who don't really care that much.

'I am so unglamorous,' he said as we eventually slumped to a free table spotted after a long hawk-like stakeout along with other couples nearby. 'I really am. You have such a glamorous life. I'm so dull.'

I looked at him.

'What?' he said.

'I am trying to decide,' I said. 'What would make you happier right now: if I said, "you're not remotely dull" or "I happen to like dull"?'

He frowned, his chestnut hair falling over his forehead.

'Ooh. Conundrum. How about "not remotely dull"?'

'You aren't, to me,' I said. 'I like talking about shoes, and work, and day-to-day stuff. Maybe I'm dull too.'

'But you're a pilot!'

'But that's good! You don't want a really groovy exciting pilot, I promise. Hysterical, super-dramatic, mega-fun people are absolutely terrible pilot material.'

He smiled at that.

'Of course. Oh well. Good.'

We finally got a waiter's attention, and he surprised me by ordering Champagne.

'Well, that isn't remotely boring!' I said happily.

'I hope not,' he said. Ordering Champagne obviously upped the level of service somewhat, because a bucket of ice and two glasses materialised out of nowhere. I looked at them.

'I genuinely didn't think you were dull. But I will say it more often if this is what happens.'

He waited till we had two glasses poured out then turned to face me. I had absolutely no idea what he was going to say, but inside I was fizzing more than the wine.

'Morag,' he said, 'I have to confess: I liked you from the moment you walked into my office, even though I am not supposed to. I was so glad to sign you off. I really, really, really hoped you'd walk into that pilots' bar one day. I went there all the time.'

'Really?' I said, astounded. He nodded.

'And I was dead chuffed when you did.'

I blushed. I didn't hear stuff like this very often. In fact, I did not think ever. I was more used to people who worked unusual shifts texting me at 2.30 a.m. in case I was in the same time zone.

'And I wanted to ask you something. Would you mind . . . ?' He looked at the Champagne, then back up at me. I liked his open, untroubled face. I liked it very much.

'Well. Here's the thing. One of the jobs I applied for is in Dubai. And they want me to go over there and see them. And they haven't officially offered it to me but . . . I think it's mine if I want it.'

'Oh my God,' I said. 'That's amazing.'

'Your next job has a lot of Dubai layovers, yeah? You might even move there?'

I shrugged. 'There's a way to go yet . . .'

'But . . .'

'But . . .' I said.

'If you get it . . . we could kind of hang out there together?'

'We could.'

'I could . . . come over and put milk in your fridge?'

I smiled.

'Nothing boring about doing responsible grocery shopping in a timely manner.'

'And I would kind of . . . be your boyfriend?'

'Are you allowed to have boyfriends in Dubai?' I mused. 'I thought they frowned upon that kind of thing.'

'Well, we could keep it a secret. And maybe that wouldn't be *at all* dull.'

A smile erupted on my face, bubbling up from the inside. We chinked glasses on the muggy, overcast London cobbled plaza.

Inside, I felt fireworks; excitement bursting out of me. There was a future. There was something happening. Something normal in my life which had always been slightly off the axis of normal. I couldn't stop grinning, or feeling that things were going to be okay. That with Hayden in my life, I could do it. That this man was going to ground me and make me fly all at once.

Chapter Four

The phone rang, again and again. I groaned and turned over. Hayden was there, his back reassuring. He was keeping a carton of contact lens fluid in my bathroom cabinet. It made me feel very mature, having my boyfriend's contact lens fluid. I might actually have said in Boots, 'Ooh, I can't remember what brand my *boyfriend* uses; are they all the same?' to the lady.

I fumbled for the button. It wasn't that early.

'Moooraggg?'

It was a wobbly voice I almost recognised.

'Moooooraggg?'

'Yes?'

'It's Peigi.'

Peigi – pronounced Peggy – was the widow who 'did' for Gramps. Or rather, she had moved into his house when her own husband had died, theoretically to help cook and clean in return for bed, board and pocket money, but in fact we were reasonably convinced she was madly in love with him and had been since they were both at primary school together. Gramps didn't appear to have noticed, to be fair.

'What's up?' I said, immediately worried, getting up quietly and moving into the little sitting room-cum-kitchen. 'Is it Gramps? Is he okay?'

There was a long pause and I felt my stomach drop to the floor like an express lift.

'Peigi?' I said. I felt my way to the sofa and sat down, steeling myself.

'Och no,' she said. 'It's just the flu right enough. But you know it's going around.'

'Everything is,' I said, the relief in me so overwhelming I felt completely lightheaded. When I glanced at my left hand, it was clutching a cushion tightly even though I had no recollection of grasping it at all.

'Well, you have Erno?' I said. Gramps's co-pilot didn't care much for flying, but he was a hell of a pilot. Trained by the Finnish navy, nothing fazed him. 'He must have a mate available.'

'Nobody,' said Peigi. 'It's coming into Easter. Everyone's busy, start of the season. Well, anyone you'd trust with *Dolly* ...'

Even though she was making perfect sense, I genuinely didn't see what was coming because I am an idiot and one whose mind was elsewhere.

'... he's asking for you.'

'What do you mean?'

'To come up and fly the route. Just for a few days.'

'But ...'

Peigi didn't say anything.

'I'm at work ...' I wasn't really, of course.

'Och aye,' said Peigi.

41

'I mean, I'm waiting to hear about a new job, and getting the all-clear . . . '

'Och aye,' said Peigi again. It wasn't that she didn't believe me; I could tell from the tone of her voice that she absolutely and completely didn't believe me. She had known me since I was a wee girl and she'd always happened to be round the house when I was there – her poor husband, it occurred to me to think now. Anyway. There wasn't much she didn't know about me.

'So, what, he wants me to drop everything and just come up, like, now?' I said.

'He's really no' very well,' said Peigi.

'For how long? The weekend?'

'Aye, well. A week mebbe.'

My phone beeped. I held it up. Oh, for goodness' sake. Fate.

It was an incoming email. The results of the enquiry. I glanced towards the bedroom. It felt like the little bubble Hayden and I had built together was being attacked on all sides. The real world was poking in. My shoulders slumped.

'Can I phone you back?'

Peigi sounded as if I'd said, 'Can I kill your dog?' She sniffed.

'Any time you can spare to take on your own grandfather's bookings would be quite the thing right enough.'

My hands were shaking as I said goodbye, then opened the email from the airline. I could barely make out the words, but I saw somewhere, slightly blurred, 'completely exonerated . . . cleared to resume active service immediately . . . promotion to first officer . . . long haul approved . . . report for additional simulator . . . '

And there it was.

I collapsed back in my seat. It was all right. I should be happy.

Everything was saved. Everything was fine. The exultation lasted less than a second.

I had . . . I had fooled them, I supposed. This made me feel unusually grim. They thought I was ready. Hayden had thought I was ready. Bob's immediate exuberant text left me under no impression that he thought we were both ready to get going again. Gramps wanted me up to fly. The airline wanted me.

At that moment, I realised something with absolute clarity. The fact that they considered me fit for flying didn't mean anything. I had thought it might; had thought them having confidence in me might change what I felt about myself.

It did not.

And the guilty, sneaky way of applying for a second chair job was not going to work, not for a second, and I must have been temporarily crazy if I'd thought it would.

I couldn't take the job if I couldn't fly a damn plane. It wasn't safe; it wasn't legal. What if I froze? What if I froze at the worst possible moment?

I couldn't fess up now. It had gone far too far. The man who had cleared me was literally in my bed right now. Oh God. He would lose his job too.

I told myself not to panic. Because the solution was right here: I would go and do one thing I knew how to do, something I had been doing since I was sixteen years old. I would go and fly for my grandfather.

Chapter Five

'It's just for a few days,' I said the next morning.

Hayden smiled. I loved waking up next to him. 'I think it will be great.'

I shrugged. He was going to Dubai to talk to his new employers and look at flats to rent. I had been slightly hoping he'd take me with him. It hadn't come up – he was far too sensible to get us moving so fast. On the other hand, I could get a seat on a plane for nothing and, well, it might be worth showing my face at the hub there . . .

'But I wish you were . . . I thought you might . . . Well, I was going to ask if you wanted to come with me.'

I beamed.

'Well, I would have said no and played hard to get.'

'Would you?'

'Totally.'

He followed me over to the coffee machine.

'I'm getting used to drinking it black, you know,' he said,

resting his head on mine. I smiled. Then I thought again about what I had to do.

'How old is your grandfather?' said Hayden, frowning. 'He must be getting on for a pilot.'

Face it, Morag, he's getting old. This is just the start of it. He'll get sicker and other things will happen, and—

'He's only sixty-three!' I said. 'He's totally fine.'

His voice was gentle. 'Huh. That's quite old for a pilot.'

'Well, he'll find someone else.'

'You're sure you don't want to go?'

I looked at him boldly.

'I absolutely don't,' I said, and it was true. I didn't want to leave him. But I had to. For now.

He kissed me.

'What's he going to do when he retires?'

'I am choosing not to think about it,' I said. He could sell the corridor, the take-off and landing slots. Sell it to a big tourist operator who would charge as much as they could get away with and make people cry when their luggage was a kilo over the limit and you charged them £60, leaving them stranded without mercy. I didn't want that to happen either.

It was bittersweet, us travelling to the airport together. In such a short space of time, I just liked Hayden being there all the time.

On the other hand, there was something lovely about it. My boyfriend and me, at the airport. We walked hand-in-hand down the corridor to staff screening and my friends and colleagues were friendly and smiling. It was cool. And then I got to do what I saw people do at airports every day but had never had the chance to myself: be sad when kissing someone goodbye; lingering and watching them walk away. Yes, it was bittersweet, but with the emphasis on the sweet. My future, walking ahead. And I was going to be with him. Soon. Just this one thing to get over first. I left international departures and took the little bus to the domestic terminal.

I called my dad to check on Gramps. He couldn't be too bad; my dad was full of pride on the phone.

'It'll be nicer up here off those big jets,' he said. 'Perhaps you'll stay.'

'I got my offer, Dad!'

'Yeah, yeah.'

I flew up Saab 340 at 5.40 p.m., a nice little engine. I sat in my favourite seat – 4F, right-hand side – just out of habit for my love of the beautiful London views it gave if you had to circle, which you often did, depending on who was up for missing their time slots that morning. As I went to turn my phone off, I saw a message confirming my mandatory simulator retraining the following Thursday, my first day back at work. And then, everything else.

Nalitha drove to the little airfield to pick me up, beaming furiously.

'How's Gramps?' I said, and she looked away from me, which worried me straightaway. 'What? Is it more serious? What's up with him?'

'Oh no . . . he'll . . . It's just a cold.'

'Peigi said it was flu.'

'Peigi just wants to confine him to bed and look at him in his pyjamas.'

There might have been something in that.

'So tell me everything about Hayden.'

I smiled to myself.

'Oh, he's . . . he's lovely.'

'I've never seen you like this,' said Nalitha, who had been listening to a litany of his many qualities for weeks now. 'This is serious, isn't it?'

I tilted my head.

'I think . . . I think it might be.'

She shook her head.

'Well. A classic English gent.'

'I don't know about that,' I said. 'He's not posh or anything.'

'Have you met his parents?'

'Not yet, but it's imminent. He talks about them very nicely.'

'Are you *sure* he isn't too good to be true?'

'He likes Coldplay.'

'Oh okay. Nobody's perfect.'

Nalitha looked out of the window.

'So, the near-miss . . . I mean, I know this bloke is a big thing in your life, but how's that been? It sounded so scary.'

I so wanted to confess to her, tell her how utterly awful it was, had been, still was. She was my oldest, closest friend, but also she might have to report me. And should she? I told myself I was going to start sitting second chair with Erno; I wasn't piloting the plane. If I felt too nervous or started to flip out or anything, I would immediately recuse myself, immediately step off the plane, get out of there. Then I would work my way back up to it.

I couldn't tell – I genuinely couldn't tell – if I was scared of being able to fly. I knew I *could* fly; I knew I was safe. Or was I scared of ruining my future – this new, exciting future that had Hayden in it, and moving, and promotion, and all sorts of things? Was I overthinking it, until I couldn't go through with it? I had never felt like this before. Our jobs required us to be so safe, so in control – and what if the incident had changed me? What if I wasn't either of those things any more? What if I couldn't trust myself?

'Oh, it's okay,' I said cautiously.

The little plane, spiralling down and down through my dreams.

Peigi opened the door, followed by the absolute love of her life (after Gramps): the world's ugliest spaniel, Skellington, who had red-rimmed eyes, black and white markings, spotty jowls and droopy whiskers, and always, always had mud trailing off his ratty hair and the general sense of having a miserable time in this world despite in fact being the world's most spoilt and pampered dog.

When they realised Peigi was always somehow there when they popped in, my parents had asked her politely how long she might be there, and then Skellington squit on the carpet and Peigi bustled around to clean it up and make some stew, and in the end it was just easier to let her stay for ever and not have anyone mention it again. In due course, she took over all the cooking, although Gramps hadn't quite capitulated to the final embarrassment: the laundry. He hadn't seemed any more likely to succumb to her charms than he had before, but oddly they rubbed along not too badly, except for Skellington, who was more or less a price worth paying for a grey and flaccid roast dinner on a Sunday complaining about how people didn't take as many papers as they used to after a bouncy morning flight.

It was a rambling grey detached house, which anywhere else would be worth about a zillion pounds but here was seen as more of a liability as it was single-glazed and slightly crumbling, and most people preferred the newbuilds with heat pumps and triple-glazing and low energy bills. To insulate the house properly would cost – well, we'd have to sell the plane, probably.

The entrance hall had a wee porch for shoes, laid with nice Victorian tiles, and a coat rack on the side which still held my great-grandfather's flying jacket. It was wildly sentimental, but there it was, still hanging. The sheepskin was grubby now, of course, the leather cracked and faded, but there was still, amazingly, a faint scent of Woodbines about it. It should probably have been in the National Museum of Flight but then so should *Dolly* and so should Gramps and basically that was not a road any one of us particularly wanted to go down. There was a fresh pile of bills on the mat, I noticed.

To the right was the staircase that led up to the bedrooms – the steps still had linoleum on them, which was freezing and slippery in wintertime. I'd love Gramps to replace them with thick, soft carpet, but comfort had never really been his priority. Still, I thought it would make all the difference: I was absolutely terrified he would fall down them one day. But never mentioned that out loud.

To the right was the parlour, which was a rather gloomy north-facing room, with old upright chairs and antimacassars

49

my great-grandmother had made, a very long time ago. Unless the fire was lit, it was rather a cheerless place. The kitchen, however, was large, cluttered and warm from the stove, and just off it what was once the pantry was now the official office, covered in paperwork and file boxes on the shelves which once held jars and jars of chutneys, jams and pickles.

It felt surprisingly good to be back. The patina of decades of life, unchanging, happily going on its way were in this house: jolly Christmases and early-morning starts and lines of the height of my dad drawn on the wall and the sense that as soon as you walked through the doors, you could be completely yourself; that you were wanted and accepted here. Except by Skellington, obviously.

'I'll just head up and see Gramps,' I announced to Peigi, feeling rather ridiculous that I had to answer to someone.

'He says not,' said Peigi. 'He needs his sleep.'

'It's just me,' I said. 'I'll just pop my head round the door.'

'I don't think so,' said Peigi, and Skellington farted loudly as if to undermine the point. I sighed.

'Okay, well, can I go and put my stuff in *my* room?' I asked slightly petulantly.

It wasn't my room of course, but it's where Jamie and I had slept every summer, with a pile of water-damaged Harry Potters in the corner, only one plug socket, which we fought over for our Nintendos fairly relentlessly, and a sink, which we were forbidden to use on pain of death, the reasons for which had long since left my memory. Straight ahead of the house was the airfield, *Dolly* either lined up to go or sleeping in her hangar, and beyond that, the very northern tip of mainland Britain, and the sea and the utter north. Today, a grey cumulus was scudding across at high speed, topped by a zippy little white cirrus. Would make a cheerful hippity-hoppity day for a fly, I found myself thinking. Then: good. Good. Just a fly. Just a trip on *Dolly*. Nothing to worry about.

I turned away before I stared too fixedly at the hangar, unpacked my few clothes – jumpers mostly: it was spring, which was pretty nice down south but up here could mean anything, from so many daffodils it dazed the eyes in the brightness, to an ice storm – and went to put them in the wardrobe. It was in there, hanging up.

'Gramps!'

I couldn't help it. I knocked and went into his room, even though I could hear Peigi sniff from downstairs. Then I lowered my voice; there was a form under the old eiderdown, and an abandoned copy of the *Racing Post* on the bedside table. I backed out.

'Morag, is that you?' came the familiar growly voice.

'Sorry!' I whispered. 'I came in about . . . '

It was a uniform my mum had made for me when I started getting my pilot hours in for Gramps, when I was seventeen. I couldn't imagine I would still fit into it now, despite all of Hayden's protein powders, but it was so thoughtful of him to put it out for me.

'Aye, aye,' he said. 'Don't come in, lass: if I gie it to you, we'll all be in the hospital and there'll be no use for any of us.'

'Okay,' I said, backing away.

'You can post your flight plan under the door in the morning though.'

He couldn't be that sick if I still needed to draw vectors on a route he'd flown seventy billion times.

'I will.'

51

Chapter Six

Waiting for Mum and Dad, who were coming over, and Jamie to arrive for dinner, which I very much hoped was going to be fish and chips down by the harbour and not Peigi's grey and watery stew, I wandered out to the hangar. There was a lock on the door but God knew where the key was; nobody had seen it for years. The Carso airfield was used a lot by military and oil rig transportation planes with much bigger and fancier hangars than ours. I supposed Gramps thought we were rather further down the list if you had to rob an airfield.

I pulled back the huge doors with that satisfyingly rusty rattle.

And there was *Dolly*, large as life! A Twin Otter: one of the best and most reliable planes ever built. They ran for ever; simple, clean, clear planes. It was so funny seeing one after flying A320s for so long, like going from an HGV to a Mini. She was so dinky! Her little legs were like a toddler's, splayed out to the side as they looked at a book; her tyres were the size of a car's, if substantially tougher.

She had steps on the inside of her two doors – front and back entrance, very fancy. Once inside, you couldn't stand up unless you were very, very tiny. There were six rows of three seats: two on one side of the aisle, one on the other. To get on as a pilot, you rather undignifiedly had to crawl your way past passengers' legs. I smiled again, remembering Gramps setting me up there.

The day of my first solo flight, he hadn't told me that's what we were doing. We'd done the usual things: full aircraft check, loading flight plan, checking the fuel lid was shut, spoken to ATC, and then, at the very last minute, he had whispered, 'It's the day,' and pushed me forwards.

'What?'

'You're ready. Off you go. Circle Inchborn twice, buzz the gulls, put her back down here. See you in thirty minutes.'

He hadn't wanted me to panic about it, to lie awake worrying about it. He wanted to remind me that I was perfectly competent, that it would be fine. He didn't even glance around as I got into the cockpit by myself, nineteen years old, running through the checklists in my mind over and over again, checking and checking until I got the okay to taxi from the control tower . . .

That feeling. The runway – comfortingly long, even though a Twin Otter is second only to a Harrier Jump Jet in terms of how much runway it needs – stretched till the parallel lines seemed to touch, a wobbling haze in the distance. The pre-flight checks were done, everything happily clunking into place. Starting up the motor, the propellers had begun to whirr comfortingly with their reassuring clatter. It was odd the first time without Gramps beside me. He normally sat quietly without saying anything nor touching the throttle for hours of flying time, just patiently and quietly sitting for take-offs and landings, take-offs and landings, filling in flight plans, tallying up flying hours, happily discussing cloud structures, wind speed, cross-currents, airspeed and engine maintenance and every inch of the plane.

But we had discussed other things too: the way the sky was never still; how it danced and moved with the wind, the clouds building up and tearing over the world; how you could see weather moving in from miles away, and could avoid it easily enough by flying around it or over it; how you could watch the sky change from black to navy to a fresh dawning blue, to building great castles of grey and white, or watch the sea dancing with white tips, or flat and pale as a distant Caribbean on long golden sands. You got closer and closer to the little dots of the islands, like charms in a charm bracelet, all in a line, looking very clearly like exactly what they are: a mountain chain which broke the surface of the water millions of years ago, only a theoretical line between land and sea, and all of us, clinging to the edge of it. The radar beacons which guide our way and give us our map of the sky tend to follow the pattern of lighthouses, because before we had radar that's how the very first pilots navigated, lighthouse to lighthouse, so it made sense, when higher tech came along, to carry on doing things more or less the same way.

The moment, though, when everything changes, when you feel the plane, which wants to fly and wants to be up there, quiver with the engines and lift, free from the tethers of gravity, your world turns, it feels like, from two dimensions – you, flat on the ground, always the same height from the earth, meandering along a line – into three or more, with the whole of the world around you in every way, the plane free to soar into the element in which it was born to do so and, I sometimes feel, the element in which I was born to be in too. Sailors yearn for the sea, and I can't see a cloud without wanting to examine it.

The sensation that first day – of power and control and everything working as it should be – had an odd effect on me. And without my grandfather's weight too, the plane handled and felt completely different. All the nervousness and shyness I normally experience on the ground day-to-day, the way I hid behind my frizzy hair and ignored the teasing about doing too much maths or being a swot or thinking I loved myself because my grandfather had a plane: none of that mattered any more. All that mattered was talking to ATC and checking my radar, my speed and my height. There was no room in my mind for anything else. I read, much later somewhere, about something called 'flow' which is when you are so engaged in what you are doing, the rest of the world falls away. Musicians get it, and artists, and I felt it too – I was part of the plane, the two of us one single unit, doing what we were both designed to do.

It's a little harder these days on the bigger planes, flying by wire, when you know the computer – the many, many computers – are second-guessing your every move. But it's still there. The heart-soaring lift, the all-encompassing concentration.

I hadn't lost it. I couldn't lose it. Surely.

Chapter Seven

Dinner was good: fish and chips which tasted of home – soaked in vinegar, warm in my hands – from the shop by the shore. Mum as usual was joshing me about my love life, and finally – because it was better than thinking about flying tomorrow – I told them shyly that I'd met someone, and they were delighted and had a load of questions. Jamie tutted and rolled his eyes. But then, because Mum was so dazzled by her handsome bi son's colourful and varied love life that she got herself too tied up in knots to ask whereas usually with me there was tumble-weed, this was something new. Her face fell a little when she found out he was English, and she took news of my new job (I emphasised how much I'd be back in and out of the UK and how many free flights they'd get) with a brave smile. But it was a nice evening, the four of us together. Dad went up to talk to Gramps and even took him some fish and chips, so we could more or less assume he was on the mend. And Peigi circled and made comments that actually there was some stew on the stove (everything Peigi cooked could more or less be termed stew, which Gramps didn't seem to mind).

But I slept badly in the old upstairs room. Jamie's pictures of birds were still pinned to the wall. Hayden had landed and was sending me pictures of the ugliest apartment blocks he could find to make me laugh. But it was reassuring too: he was sending me everything. He wanted me involved in his decision-making for ... well. He wanted to build a future, it seemed to me. And my job here was to make sure I could take part in it.

Gramps still wasn't up when it was finally acceptable to rise – about 6 a.m. Skellington howled at me as if he'd never met me before in his life and I was a burglar, and when I went to let him out he gave me an affronted look, as if I was depriving him of his God-given right to pee in the corner of the larder.

It was a good day for flying: sunny and brisk, light winds coming in from the west but nothing to trouble the horses. It would be fine, I told myself. Fine.

I felt a bit cheerier helping myself to the salted porridge Peigi had left out. I never ate it down south; it didn't fit right. Here, with the thick creamy local milk from cows who ate the richest green grass, endlessly lashed with rain, it was just about right, I thought.

Then I looked at the bowl. And I didn't feel like it at all.

I sighed and grabbed the manifest. Mainland to Cairn, largest island of the archipelago, which had a large settlement and a primary school, then skipping Larbh today, and a drop-off – hmm, this was unusual – on Inchborn.

Larbh to Inchborn is the shortest scheduled flight in the world, but more people than you might think come to do just exactly that one. I remember from when I was very small, many

57

men – I don't know why they're always men, seriously – had come here, announcing they had taken the longest flight in the world – New York to Johannesburg then; it's London to Perth now – and had come to do the shortest. I suppose as hobbies go it's easier than climbing Everest.

But it's a shame they're not very interested in disembarking, because they're missing out. The islands on the archipelago have some of the oldest settlements in the world. Thousands of years ago, if you lived in one of these underground huts, which were carved out of the earth and lined with stones, eating seaweed and seals and sheltering from the wild storms in front of the fire, telling stories to your neighbours, you probably had one of the highest standards of living in the world. People had lived in the settlements continuously for hundreds of years. They must have been relatively safe and unmolested. They had time to make jewellery for each other, beautiful carved bone sculptures. Once, they lived like kings.

Inchborn also hosts the remains of an old abbey, the most northernly in Scotland; it's in ruins but they're surprisingly well-preserved. There's a daily boat that goes in the summer season and it's always mobbed. There's the abbey, but there are also World War Two defences, including a tunnel you can run through from end to end that disappears through the hill-side, which children absolutely love. The island comprises of two hills with a low spit of a double beach, bright gold, in the middle of it, with the abbey perched on the north spit. It always gets a lot of sunlight, I think, but that might be simply because I always used to notice, flying over, whenever a stray shaft of sunlight hit the ancient tower. It's compellingly lovely.

Inchborn is a bird sanctuary too, and I know there are people who live there all year round, looking after everything. It is the loneliest job I can imagine. But you'll see the most astonishing array of birdlife everywhere: puffins, stumbling over the rocks, huge cawing gulls, gannets, of course, and even kestrels. You're more alone there than you are on the international space station; there are no manned lighthouses any more, but there are manned islands. A tiny dot at the end of the world, Antarctica has more going on than you.

Every six months, Gramps flies the caretakers in and out. Mostly it's men, sometimes couples, most of whom are well used to this kind of thing, although he says once or twice they have come back with a very frosty way of looking at one another, which doesn't really surprise me. Presumably there is a very real possibility of driving each other mad, especially in the winter, when there aren't anything like as many tourists there; mostly ornithologists up to study birds. Nobody can stay overnight on the island except for the island keepers, so even the ornithologists' company isn't for very long, which is good for them as they're working, and they need a lot of peace and quiet. Then it's back to the mainland, which feels like a bustling metropolis by comparison, with its cafés and paved roads and street lighting.

Not a heavy load by my standards – if I was popping about central Europe, I could easily hit four different countries in a day. But I was only first officer here, I reminded myself. Erno would be doing all the work. All I had to do was fill in the log, do the checking, do things I had done a million times before in a plane I knew better than my Fiat 500. It would be fine. Fine.

I was miles too early but I set out to walk to the airfield. There was a chill in the air, though the sun was out, and I rather enjoyed the feel of the cold wind. I spent so much time in air-conditioned, pressurised spaces, where the temperature was always the same whether you were inside or out, and everything was white and glass wherever you were in the world, and where floor-polishing machines working ceaselessly, whirring away the footprints of the dust of a million passers-by, was the background noise, not the cries of gulls. I walked briskly, partly to try and get my fears and worries to sink further down into my mind; partly to avoid anyone in town who knew me as Gramps's granddaughter (i.e. absolutely everyone) and would be incredibly curious as to what I was doing in my uniform.

The town was sleepy at this hour at any rate, the little whitewashed bakery the only place open, the scent of heavy pan loaves being pulled out of the oven. It's hard to explain a pan loaf if you don't know it. Think a hard, salty crust and two fine layers of bread that you can tear apart, which when toasted is the perfect holder for soft, salty, melted butter ... I almost felt hungry, then with a lurch remembered what I was there to do; my hunger passed and I carried on. Past the Co-op and the tiny newsagents that used to get in two copies of *Pilot Magazine* every month so that Gramps and I could each read it then discuss it, then send one on to Dad.

There were now only a few cirrus and cirrostratus clouds in the sky. Anywhere else, it would be a glorious day. I mean, it was a glorious day here too, as long as you were wearing your thermals. I followed the cobbled road down past the old grey senior school where Nalitha and I had sung in the school choir because we were madly in love with Connall Alton, not that it did much good at all as Connall Alton liked Patricia Murphy, or rather he liked the car her parents bought her for her seventeenth. I couldn't imagine getting given a car. On the other hand, my parents had bought me what they bought me for my sixteenth, seventeenth, eighteenth, nineteenth and twentieth – flying lessons, carefully saved up for, handed over with such loving and expectant expressions.

I turned and trudged up to the little airport building. It was just a tin shack really. The Civil Aviation Authority was trying to build it up as the 'Airport of the Highlands and Islands!', 'The True North!' the way they'd rebranded the North Coast 500, but it hadn't much taken beyond having a bit of whisky in the gift shop, and then they'd had to immediately dissuade people from opening and drinking it when they saw the size of the planes they were expected to climb in to.

Nalitha came out when she saw me, shaking her head at me wearing the uniform.

'Come back for good,' she said crossly, like she always did. 'You're never here.'

'That's because my job involves flying away. You know. To places that totally aren't here?'

'Yeah, yeah, whatevs,' she said. 'That's very boring.'

'And I'll take you to Dubai for free.'

She gave me a squeeze and looked in my face, frowning.

'Your hair looks very smooth.'

Nalitha is the only one allowed to have very straight shiny black hair like a mirror; it's the rules.

'Yeah, yeah.'

'And you're too thin.'

'*You're* too thin!'

'I am a huge heifer.'

Traditional schoolgirl greetings exchanged, I said, 'I don't

61

think I'm going to be able to get the plane off the ground.' Then I glanced inside the hangar at the little queue.

'Ugh,' she said. 'Yeah, I'm getting to them.'

'Where's Erno?'

'Asleep in his car.'

'Good, good.'

My confidence wasn't high to begin with but my captain being sleepy wasn't a bad thing as it happened. He obviously had no doubts about flying with me at all. The only underslept person on this flight was going to be me. This helped. Also, Erno was a very sleepy person in general. Nalitha headed back to the check-in.

There was a large, dark-haired stubbly man checking in looking aggravated. Nalitha was giving him the kind of smile I knew only too well meant 'I am being nice now because later on I will be poking pins in a voodoo doll of you'. He had a huge mound of luggage and was gesticulating about it.

'Who was that?' I asked her as we headed up to the plane.

'A dickhead,' she said. 'Who thinks I've never loaded a microscope onto a plane before.'

I snorted. Coming up against Nalitha is rarely a wise thing.

'Maybe he's the Inchborn drop-off,' I said.

Nalitha frowned.

'Oh, maybe. Why can't he just take the ferry like normals?'

I shrugged.

'Fraser McLintock is coming back, so I suppose it makes more sense.'

'Oh God,' I said. 'I haven't thought about him for years!'

'You'll be pleased to know,' said Nalitha, 'that regularly spending six months completely alone in the winter on a solitary island has changed him more or less not at all.'

I smiled at the memory. Fraser was the kind, solitary type forever much more interested in birds, rocks, earth, books – almost anything, in fact – than people. He had been, it was rumoured, the last of the monks on the island, and I could believe them: he was tall and skinny and practically ageless; you couldn't imagine him young. The one thing he didn't like, famously, was water. He always flew in and out.

'Do you think,' Nalitha asked for the hundredth time as the large man crossly heaved his own stuff through the tiny hole in the wall which served as our baggage conveyer, 'that people who are dickheads at airports are dickheads all the time? Or do you think they go home and, like, kiss their children goodnight and stuff?'

I shrugged.

'I think people get anxious travelling.'

'Why does that make them dickheads?'

I frowned. 'They're not all dickheads. Most of them are lovely. Some of them get a bit nervy and lose their boarding passes.'

'It's forty metres from the check-in desk to the plane.'

'I know. I'm just saying. Also, you did take on a customer-facing role,' I said, almost apologetically.

'Yeah,' said Nalitha. 'A customer-facing role, not a *dickhead*-facing role. I should have a dickhead exemption. For medical reasons.'

'What medical reasons?'

'Pain. In. Arse.'

The man, who was now sitting in the 'refreshments' area of the airport – i.e. a slightly less draughty side of the metal construction with a deeply horrid coffee machine – glanced up like he'd heard every word, and I turned my face away; our chat was very unprofessional. But even so, it was a tonic to see Nalitha; she cheered me up.

'Ssh,' I whispered.

Nalitha didn't even ask me if I was going to be okay. That's how confident in me she was.

I stood outside. Erno was up, checking the exterior plane, as I'd already done. He smiled when he saw me.

'Hey! Sweetheart! I hear you were terribly brave.'

'I didn't do anything,' I said. Erno shrugged. 'Did you do the right amount of nothing?'

'Well, I'm cleared to fly if that's what you mean.'

'Want to take her up today as captain?'

'Nooo,' I said, too quickly.

He shot me a quick glance.

'I mean, I'm fine,' I gabbled. 'It's just it's been a wee while.'

'Uh-huh,' he said, looking concerned. 'So you want me to do all the flying?'

I looked at him. As usual, even in his uniform, Erno looked like an unmade bed. He was so out of shape for a pilot that he must drag himself through the medical every six months. He hated flying. The only reason he stayed with us is because Gramps loved flying so much he almost never let Erno take the rudder, and that suited Erno just fine. He liked puddle-hopping too, the shorter the better. He was just a very lazy man.

'I've never seen you fly,' I said, smiling to show I didn't mean it. He sniffed. 'That is because flying is boring. Compared with watching television.'

I had never seen a TV show that could compare with breaking clouds at dawn on an early flight, but I didn't mention that.

Nalitha came out, heaving bags in a dramatic way which implied that we must help her poor fragile self immediately, and so we did.

'What on earth is this?' I said, picking up a badly wrapped effigy of what appeared to be a cardboard pirate ship. 'Lifeboat in case things go wrong?'

'Ooh! It's the drama company!' said Nalitha, glancing back into the terminal.

I frowned at her; I didn't know what she meant.

'They tour the islands, play in little community halls.'

'Huh.'

Sure enough, as I completed the pre-flight checks with the door half open so I could chat to Nalitha, I heard them before I saw them, as boarding opened and Nalitha shuffled people on. She was going to come with us to check Fraser on and anyone we were picking up in Larbh, which appeared to be back on the flight plan. I looked at the sky. The cloud cover was thickening, but nothing too serious. I felt a huge pit in my stomach. No. Don't be silly. Nobody was even asking me to fly.

What if I never could again? I asked myself. What if this was it for me?

I sat in the cockpit on the right-hand seat – the pilot sits on the left; co-pilot on the right – and filed the flight plan and did the cockpit checks to calm myself down.

The rest of the flight was filling with typical people at this time of year: ornithologists, clasping their binoculars tightly; some tourists who looked like they were slightly regretting picking to go so far north in Scotland as they watched the fresh rain pelt against the porthole windows and fingered their new North Face jackets carefully; and locals who treated the plane as a school bus and knelt up on the seats to chat to their friends and neighbours, strew shopping everywhere and, on occasion (although not today), try to bring their livestock on as emotional support chickens. Without bamboozling you with very technical aeroplane knowledge, the fewer live chickens one has squawking about an aircraft, the better, in general.

I could really hear who Nalitha meant now, as a small group approached, led by a man with a beard and a bellowing, highly enunciated voice. He popped his head around the aircraft door.

'Well, look at THIS little adorable mini plane in which we are all going to die in a fireball ... Is this thing real?' He frowned. 'I wonder who'll come top of the obituary list. Probably you, Netflix boy.'

A very pretty young man behind him, with slender, delicate features, smiled wanly. He looked like he was dying of consumption in about 1834, though he was faintly recognisable too. There was also an incredibly beautiful black girl with long thick braids, who was rolling her eyes and standing still out on the tarmac.

'I'm not getting on that,' she said in a loud northern accent, standing stock-still.

I glanced at Nalitha. There were a few people, who had come through other modern clean white terminals and were used to airbuses – the EasyJet planes, the ones that join cities all over the world – who found sixteen seats and small prop engines a little bit unnerving, especially on a fairly woolly day like this one was becoming.

Nalitha has several ways of dealing with them, ranging from simply taking the piss – 'a big lad like you?' – to soothing and helping particularly the older ladies understand that they are perfectly safe, and that statistically the most dangerous part of their day – driving to the airport – is now over.

This girl was planting her feet.

'You never told me it was going to be a tiny tin can!'

'What did you think, that they take a 747 up there every day?' said the bearded man again loudly. He seemed to think everyone onboard was delighted that they could hear him. I glanced at my watch, worrying I was going to miss our slot. But then I realised that that kind of thing matters at Gatwick but here, not so much.

'I thought we were getting on a *plane*, not a *hairdryer*.' The woman was standing, smiling but with a very adamant look on her face. 'Nuh-huh. No way.'

'Come on,' the older man boomed. 'They do this flight every day, don't you?'

Nalitha nodded brightly.

'Well, they might have a death wish; I certainly don't,' said the woman, turning to go back into the terminal.

Gramps did get the occasional refusenik, but it was mostly people being frightened on board when we were underway and hit turbulence, and Nalitha was very good at calming people down in a no-nonsense head-girl type of way, which she had found through trial and error was absolutely the best way to deal with things. If you were too lenient, she'd explained, people thought that they had a point and there really was something to worry about. If you were too stern, well, hysterics.

So she adopted a bluff jolly hockey sticks tone which wasn't her normal voice at all. It also had an unfortunate side effect of making men who'd been to boarding school fall immediately in love with her, which she brushed off with a cheerful charm that worsened the situation if anything. There was a man oversupply up in the islands since there were so many jobs in agriculture, forestry, animal husbandry, fishing, oil and gas, wind farms and shipping. And transportation, in fact. Me excluded, obviously. So Nalitha was used to declarations of love and took them in her stride, knowing she had Asif, who was a stone-cold mega fox, waiting at home in their cosy house in Carso, happily feeding their adorable two-year-old while holding down a high-paying job in IT he could do without ever having to fly anywhere.

I was doing my last few checks and very much hoping that this was going to sort out my nerves – although when I glanced at the woman on the tarmac, she was still looking entirely ada-mant, though she shouldn't be standing there – when a head peered through the cockpit door.

'Hello!' he boomed. And then: 'AHA! A LADY pilot! How wonderful.'

I haven't met any actors so I don't know if they're all like that. I'm sure they aren't. Anyway, this one definitely was. Very much so.

'Can you step back, sir?' I said quickly. I didn't think there was much mileage in hijacking an island-bound-hopper, but we were trained to expect absolutely anything. 'Step back now please.'

Erno glanced up, less perturbed than I was, but probably more persuasive-looking.

'Yeah, stand back, man.'

The bearded face fell.

'Sorry! Sorry! I am SO, SO SORRY! I promise I'm not a terrorist!'

'What did you say?' I said.

'No, no, I didn't mean it! Don't say the T word. So sorry, so sorry.'

He backed off, his hands comically large waving in the air. He had gone bright pink, but was rather ruddy already.

'Leopold, for Christ's sake.' The elegant young man behind him was sighing. 'We'll all get turfed off.'

I glanced at my mirror to look back into the cabin. Normally a flight being held up on a commuter route would make everyone tut and sigh and roll their eyes and complain. Here though, people were generally happy enough that a flight hadn't been cancelled by bad weather to mind too much.

'I just wanted to ask,' came the voice from several feet away. It carried perfectly, even on the noisy plane, 'could my young colleague possibly meet you first? She's a nervous flyer.'

'I'm not a flyer!' came a carrying voice from the tarmac. 'Because I'm not going anywhere!'

'As you see, we are a travelling party of players, highly strung but ready to entertain the wonderful people of your islands!'

I frowned. We weren't some kind of jolly sub-species.

'Excuse me?'

'We are the touring players! Performing for your delight and delectation at the very edges of civilisation.'

I frowned again. I mean, *I* could say that about the archipelago, but he couldn't.

'Not, of course,' he boomed, 'that you aren't obviously in the very flush of white heat of technology!'

I gave him a look and he gave me a wide grin.

The woman on the tarmac was looking resolutely moored to the ground, and our departure time was ticking ever closer. I glanced at Erno, who shrugged.

'You should do it,' I hissed.

'I would,' he said. 'But I don't care.'

Annoyed, I stood up and moved towards the door, smiling nicely and squeezing past Nalitha.

'Just lift her and carry her on if necessary,' Nalitha hissed at me, keeping her perfect smile beaming at the other passengers. 'If I don't get back in time for Gymboree, I'm going to shank her.'

'You're not going to shank anyone,' I hissed out of the side of my mouth. 'No shanking.'

'Break both her arms,' said Nalitha. 'Oh *hello*,' she said in a totally different tone of voice to one of our regulars boarding with his diving gear in a large bag. 'So lovely to see you, Georgie! How are you today?'

The man grunted. Wreck divers off the islands were common; we had thousands of boats down there, from the wars to people looking for the North West Passage all the way back to the Vikings. People braved the icy waters to go take a look at them – I mean, I couldn't do it; it gave me a shudder even to think of it, going down into the icy black waters. There was a legend on one of the smaller islands, which were near Scapa Flow, home of sunken and scuttled ships, that if you were there near dark, you would hear, very faintly out on the water, the tap-tap-tapping of Morse code, a desperate cry for help going out long after all possibility of rescue had vanished beneath the icy sea.

I descended the aeroplane steps. The wind blew strongly across the runway.

'Hey,' I said to the striking-looking woman standing there.

'I'm not getting on that, no way,' she said, not even looking at me or the plane.

I smiled.

'I can't believe you're dissing *Dolly*.'

'Who's *Dolly*?'

'That's the name of the plane,' I said proudly, turning to look at the old girl.

'She looks like she's falling apart.'

'She's passed all her tests and checks,' I said fondly, not mentioning that my grandfather was the chief aeronautical engineer, mechanic and general dogsbody. 'She's a great wee runner.'

'I don't want a great wee runner,' said the woman. 'I want a sleek, very safe jumbo jet, and I don't really even want one of those. I just want to go home.'

I changed tack.

'You're an actor, right?'

She nodded.

'That's amazing. What are you meant to be doing?'

She shrugged.

'We're doing *Peter Pan and Wendy*.'

'Oh, I love Peter Pan!'

'It's not Peter Pan; it's kind of ... a grown-up interpretation. But kids can come –it's not grown-up grown-up. It's really cool.'

I nodded.

'Who are you playing?'

'Uh ... Wendy.'

'Oh!' I said. 'That's ... I mean, that's going to be a bit tricky for everyone, isn't it?'

'Hmm.' She shrugged.

'You know,' I said, 'the children who live up here ... you know, they never get to a funfair. There's no local theatre. Musicians never tour up here.'

I was laying it on a bit thick, I knew. There were loads of local musicians, and every child played something or knew how to give a song if required. And every time they did a survey, the results came back: the free-range, unspoiled open-air children of the northern isles were by far the happiest in the UK.

'I cannot imagine,' I went on, struggling to be heard over the wind, 'what it would mean to the children to see you perform. I mean, you could change their life. Isn't that why you got into touring theatre?'

'No,' she said. 'I got into touring theatre because I failed the National audition.'

I smiled.

'There are loads of wee faces who are just going to think you are amazing. Awesome. Life-changing.'

'The show's not that good.'

'I bet it is! Anyway, even if it sucks, the kids won't notice as they have nothing to compare it to. You could basically pretend you're *Wicked*; you'll be the most impressive thing they've ever seen.'

'Not if I'm at the bottom of the sea I can't.'

A particularly stiff gust took hold of her hair and threw it up around her face. She stared at the plane. I turned and looked at it too. I didn't know how to tell her that I shared her fears. But I had to believe it would be okay, and she did too.

'I know she doesn't look like much.' I was saying this for myself as much as for this woman. 'But she is completely airworthy, I promise. And you will bring so much happiness to everyone.'

She looked at me straight on.

'Do you promise?'

'No,' I said, smiling. 'I haven't seen you. And, you know. The National.'

'I was just having a bad day.'

'Okay.'

'I've got kids,' she said. 'It would be very, very bad if I was to die in a plane crash.'

'You're right,' I said gravely. 'Whereas I have no spawn and am completely dispensable in a plane crash.'

She looked at me for a second, then her face cracked into a smile.

'Come on, Boona!' the bearded man was shouting from the top of the steps. 'You can do it!'

'And you're the pilot?' Boona asked me.

'I'm one of the pilots.'

'And you're going to get me home to my kids?'

'Do you like them?'

'What?! Yes!'

'Well then. Definitely.'

Erno looked grumpy sitting in the left chair rather than slouching in his usual co-pilot right. From a flying family – his father had flown for the Finnish air force and then for Aeroflot, and never crashed one, quite the bragging right – he was expected to go into the family business from an early age, so he started during his national service. He had absolutely hated every moment. Unfortunately, having better than twenty-twenty eyesight, an aptitude for mechanical skills, astonishing twitch responses and stunning hand–eye coordination meant he was an absolute natural. They hadn't built something Erno couldn't fly. Unfortunately, again, he didn't want to fly anything.

It was lucky for Gramps though. Erno only wanted to do it because we had the shortest flight anywhere to be found, thus limiting the amount of time he spent in the air, which he found extremely tedious. Also, being from Finland, he found the climate of the northern islands of Scotland pleasingly warm and dry.

I glanced back at the aircraft cabin, which was now full. Boona was sitting next to the bearded man, who was patting her on the hand while she stared down. I gave her a grin, though she couldn't see me, and heard a large sigh from somewhere further down the cabin. The man with all the luggage was sitting there with a hardback book in front of him. He had beetle brows, which were furrowed, and he was glancing at his watch and sighing loudly.

'Are you late for something?' Nalitha asked him, sounding sympathetic although I knew from long experience that she was actually being incredibly sarcastic. There was absolutely nothing happening in the archipelago that wouldn't wait for you.

'No – but are we leaving soon?' he muttered, looking extremely cross. Nalitha glanced at me and I was instantly annoyed with him. Yes, lots of people weren't scared of flying. So what? It wasn't a character flaw to worry about getting in a small plane, was it? Couldn't he think for two seconds about what it might feel like to somebody else?

'Well met, fellow,' bellowed the beardy man from across the aisle, leaning over to shake hands. The grumpy man looked at him, aghast. 'What brings you to our small cabin of miracles in the sky?'

'It's not a miracle,' I interjected quickly, glancing at Boona. 'It's a fine example of modern engineering which will obey all physical laws.' At any rate, the grumpy man ignored him. He was going to be without human company for the next six months; he seemed to be getting into training early.

The spattering rain had cleared by the time ATC okayed us to go – there was another plane beside us, the much larger, thrice-daily shuttle to London. I noticed Boona give it a longing glance out of her window. Erno pootled out onto the runway, which was truly far bigger than it needed to be, as if we genuinely did expect an airbus to start dropping by. We juddered along like a toy. It felt both familiar and strange, like revisiting your childhood school, remembering everything about it, while marvelling about how small it is at the same time.

Business-like, Erno set the plane along the central line without glancing at it. I did the final checks and listened to the murmurs of ATC reassuring us in our earpieces. Nalitha was checking everyone was belted in. I glanced in my mirror. She was patting Boona on the hand, and shooting the brown-haired man evils. Par for the course.

Dolly zipped faster and faster over the smooth tarmac and even now, full of fear and worry about the future, I couldn't deny the feelings of elation and fleetness which happened every time the wheels left the ground when a land-locked vehicle shook free, defied itself, did what humans had always longed to do, yearned to do, dreamed of – heading straight up for the clouds like the birds did. A ray of sunlight illuminated the metal hangar below, making it shine as it fell beneath us, and the cares, the worries of my life below – all of them down there, falling away, nothing here but the reassuring sweet roar of *Dolly*'s engines.

As Erno banked beautifully on the port side, and we prepared to head north-northwest (I thought I heard a faint gasp from

Boona as a view of water filled her porthole), I remembered the conversation I'd had with Hayden the previous evening. He was on a layover, splashing about, it sounded to me, with several high-pitched female voices behind him. I'd tried to tell him how I was feeling, how anxious I was. Surely you can tell the person you're nearly engaged to, right? The person who means everything to you? You shouldn't have any secrets from them.

'Darling,' he said, 'once you're up there, you'll be fine. You're being daft. You have a perfect record. You're cleared to fly.'

He didn't say 'get over yourself', but he might as well have done. I could sense his impatience down the line. Someone threw what might have been a beach ball.

But up here, I could breathe. The steadying rumble. The radar and the map beneath my fingers. Erno glancing at the course, frowning, carrying steadily on as I drew our route on a paper map. Paper maps have long disappeared from large aircraft. Gramps doesn't a hundred per cent trust iPads. Erno looked back at me.

'You are all right?' he said.

'I'm fine,' I said, and it was true. I had been nervous the night before – but of flying myself rather than of being in *Dolly*. Up here, I was happy.

It was twenty minutes to Inchborn, the first pearl in the chain. Its dual golden beaches shone in the spring sunshine, the ruined abbey lit up. Erno circled the island to gauge the winds. The tide on the leeward side was far out, the golden sand rolling on for miles. He flew one more circle, getting lower and lower, pulling back, decreasing the speed so we came to rest gently on the sand, like a marble rolling down a spiral chute.

'That was a greaser,' I said, smiling.

He looked at me. 'You can do the next one.'

I shook my head. 'Come on. I'm on R&R.'

He nodded as if he didn't believe a word of it.

Outside, Nalitha had set the chocks and was now helping the grumpy man with his luggage – or rather, she'd opened the luggage compartment and was letting him haul out his own large boxes while watching him with arms folded. He was doing it in bad grace.

'Who even is that?' I asked Erno, who frowned and shrugged. Some Sassenach probably. I wondered if he knew what he was letting himself in for. One spring, years before, Gramps and I had picked up a married couple who'd wintered there together, and there was so much tension in the tiny cabin – they put themselves at opposite ends of it – that everyone just kept very quiet all the way home in case they kicked off. This guy would be all by himself, but it didn't look like being by himself would be very good company.

Coming up the beach with just one small box, I spotted the lanky figure of Fraser McLintock. I had liked Fraser a lot when I was little. His connections ran back to when Inchborn had been all religious, a place of pilgrimage for holy people. Well, holy people went there now still, but it was mostly people who worshipped birds. Although they hated it when you called them that.

'You're welcome,' I heard Nalitha say as the grumpy man walked past her without saying thank you. Fraser stayed below, as was traditional, to help unload the provisions for the next three months. We could land in the interim, obviously, but it was expensive, and it was more likely that the day-trippers would bring something.

The ferry that brought tourists, birdwatchers and school-children had a wee bar which sold crisps and chocolate bars so if you had a nice word for the captain, you could keep fairly well supplied. Good luck if you fancied a takeaway pizza though. The thing is, he could be as grumpy as he liked on Inchborn, but on the wider archipelago, this wasn't going to work at all.

You got it quite a lot: people arriving thinking that the archipelago was a haven of peace and solitude. Which it was, to a certain extent. If you were looking for no noise louder than crashing waves and chattering birds, you could definitely find it. There were no sirens, ice cream vans, rumbling tube trains, nightclubs or cars blasting out loud music.

But you had to interact. On an island like Larbh, for example, without a hospital, you rely on one another. When weather can often make it impossible to deliver vital supplies, you can find yourself entirely reliant on your neighbours for practically everything: food, warmth, advice. There is a massive skills exchange on the archipelago (I should know; I've been fixing people's bicycles since I was seven). It is a completely interdependent community. So while there is solitude, I have known people be a lot lonelier in the middle of big cities and towns. Here, you'll get to know your neighbours; they'll be turning up with a black bun before you've unpacked your crockery. Back on the housing estate, I hadn't met a single neighbour.

And even Inchborn, where you'd be by yourself for three months – well, I supposed, you would be and you wouldn't. Even out of season, people like to visit. Historians, pilgrims, bird people (of course), school parties – he'll have to greet them every day, answer questions, sort out any minor first-aid issues. I think it must be a bit what going to the Antarctic is like; it attracts rugged individualistic people who want to get away from everyone, only to put them all in very cramped living arrangements next to each other for months on end. But here, once the tourists were gone, it was just you alone, day after day, night after night.

Well, the grumpy man got the job, so I suppose they must have figured he'd be all right. Loads of people apply for it, I've heard. I watched his figure head up the beach to fire up the old Land Rover that belonged to whoever was working there that season.

Fraser, by contrast, came up the steps, waving a cheery hello to everyone who waved a cheery hello back until it became blindingly obvious that he had a collection of fish and bird bits and bobs around his person, and I suppose when you're living alone, surrounded by wildlife, it's probably a bit hard to even notice whether or not you smell worse than a seal, but I can tell you quite conclusively that he smelled worse than a seal.

I frowned at Erno.

'Do you think we could fly the next leg with the cockpit windows open?'

Erno shrugged.

'Can you fly and I'll take a quick nap?'

'No! Erno, it's half an hour in the air – even that can't be too long for you.'

'It's far too long for me.'

'Literally the shortest scheduled flight on earth!'

He sighed and we started our checks again.

In fact, as it turned out, that flight was too long for everyone. The aircraft had got warm on the longer trip from the main island, but the cabin was so small that there was a concentric circle of people flattening themselves away from Fraser as he sat down, beaming at everyone.

'Well,' he was saying, 'it's so nice to be indoors with so many faces again! What's been happening on *EastEnders*?'

There was a radio on Inchborn, but no telephone wires or

internet obviously, and you couldn't get a phone signal. Fraser had tried to encourage people to learn Morse so they could send him the *EastEnders* updates, but there had been relatively few takers so far and he wasn't allowed to jam the waves all night listening in to somebody's TV set on the mainland in case the coastguard needed it.

'This and that,' said Boona, who was closest. Fraser stared at her for a long time. She looked uncomfortable and still very tense, leaning back from his fishy stench and ridiculously unkempt beard.

'Fraser!' said Nalitha sternly, as she'd pulled up the door. 'You absolutely *stink*! Leave the poor woman alone.'

But Fraser was beside himself.

'*You!*' he said, eyes wide. 'You were in *EastEnders*!'

Boona looked embarrassed.

'Not really,' she said quickly, as the rest of the cabin turned round to look at her.

'You were! You're one of the market stall keeper's assistants!'

'It was a very small part,' said Boona, clearly blushing. 'I'm just an actor.'

Fraser shook his big craggy head.

'You're a star,' he said in awed tones. 'I'm sharing a plane with an actual star. Can I have a selfie?'

'*Sit down!*' said Nalitha. 'I mean it.'

'But she's *famous*.'

'So will you be, fish-face,' said Nalitha, 'for being thrown out of a very small plane.'

But she smiled at him, because it was Fraser. He shook his head in innocent disbelief as he did up his seatbelt.

'Well, well, well,' he said. 'Wonders will never cease. A famous person. On Murdo's crappy old plane!'

'Oi!' I said.

'Oh, come on, it's a rusting heap of junk.'

Boona gasped audibly.

'It is *not*,' I said. 'And if you want off this island, you'll take that back, then sit quietly.'

He did what he was told, but craned his neck to stare at Boona in a mixture of wonderment and disbelief.

'Don't worry, hen,' he said, noticing she was nervous. '*Dolly* hasn't ditched us into the sea yet. Of course, there's always a first time.'

'Fraser McLintock, I will absolutely ditch *you* right off this plane!' I hollered and finally there was silence.

It was clouding over as Erno taxied back onto the long stretch of beach, nose pointed directly out to sea. The grumpy man still stood there, I noticed, all his bags beside him, the island Land Rover parked up next to him with – let us hope – the keys still in it, plus I was reasonably sure a fairly pungent aroma of Fraser McLintock left behind too. The house would probably be even worse. He looked a little shell-shocked as he grew tiny behind us, and *Dolly* took to the sky once more.

The purple sky had turned back into rain, which streaked across the cockpit windows in long lines. The winds were picking up, crossing here and there, but I could see a little line on the landing strip ahead. It was the entire island – it had to be, there were only forty-nine of them and they were all there. I smiled, looking down. Normally you'd think people would be starved of Netflix or restaurants or being able to play their Xboxes or get Amazon deliveries, but it looked like they were genuinely starved of community theatre. Well, there you go.

Erno bumped the landing as if we were going down steps. It was absolutely the safest way in weather like this – down a bit, down a bit – but I could hear from the strangulated screeches on the other side of the door that this wasn't going down particularly well with Boona, or anyone else. You could do this, I told myself. You could do it fine.

Still, once Donald – who, among about nine part-time jobs also looked after the airfield on the island, and took his responsibilities very seriously – had cleared the tiny runway and checked for security – there was the entire island, cheering.

'Aha!' said the man with the beard smiling. 'Dare I say ... is this our adoring public?'

'It is!' I said, smiling in return. 'We'll be back to pick you up in two days.'

Boona stood up, beaming. 'Oh my goodness,' she said. 'I haven't ever been met on tour before.'

'They're so excited to see you,' I said. 'Everyone's here.'

'Everyone?' said the young lad. 'How on earth are we doing three performances then?'

'Oh, everyone will come to all three,' I predicted confidently. 'They'll be word-perfect by the end. Have a good one!'

And the cold, tired, touring actors descended the door staircase of my wee plane, waving like Brad Pitt coming down the steps of the Palais at the Cannes Film Festival.

Chapter Eight

Gramps was no better when I got back; he didn't get up for supper, which was a bit concerning. I had made it through the day though: I had been fine in the right chair.

But I thought I would have been able to fly. I thought I might have managed. Yet, at the time, all my nerves and self-doubt came crashing in again. Erno had grumbled endlessly about having to fly everywhere when I knew he hated it, but I simply couldn't get rid of the uncomfortable frozen feeling in the pit of my stomach.

Hayden had a night out with his new team, so I couldn't talk to him. Nalitha headed back to get her boys and invited me round, but I couldn't . . . I just wasn't in the mood for her lovely happy family that night. I thought of the grumpy passenger we'd dumped on an island by himself for six months. He was obviously impervious to loneliness. That night, I wasn't.

The next morning, I was up early again. Nalitha had left me a message on my phone. Late March, and we were delivering a sheep. It sounds absolutely ridiculous that an airline would deliver a sheep, but this wasn't just any old sheep. This was Ramsay McRamson, apparently, a very famous ram that had been bought at considerable expense due to the extraordinary quality of his wool, and apparently twelve hours on a ferry was considered too much for his delicate personality, and therefore Gramps had said we were taking him. Everything first class for Ramsay.

Nalitha was wildly contemptuous. 'I'm not taking him tea,' she sniffed.

'He's not coming in the cabin,' I said. 'He's going in cargo. Very precious cargo. Uh, right?'

He was indeed precious cargo; the farmer had asked if we would keep the heating on for him. Apparently Ramsay was going to live a life of luxury up on Larbh: kept in a centrally heated pen, nothing to do but eat delicious grass and have sex with about a thousand lady sheep. I had wondered aloud as I reached the airport if this wouldn't make some of the next generations of sheep inbred and the dealer had sniffed and said honestly, it wasn't genuinely a sheep's mental agility you were after. Then I had sniffed back and said, like most aeroplanes, *Dolly* didn't actually have central heating for the cargo area. Erno was keeping well out of it, saying if he had to fly the bloody thing it could be swinging beneath the undercarriage for all he cared.

'Are you sure you can't have him in the cabin?' The dealer was being surprisingly insistent.

'A sheep?' said Nalitha.

'This sheep,' said the dealer grandly, 'is worth more than your plane.'

'That's hardly a surprise,' said Nalitha.

'Shut up!' I said. As usual I was terrified Nalitha was going to leave Gramps for taking rich Americans to golf resorts on Gulfstream Aerospace. Although fortunately for me, I think private jet companies take a fairly dim view of stewardesses who are relentlessly sarcastic towards their customers.

'I can't let Ramsay out of my sight,' said the dealer.

'Well, you can't travel in cargo,' Nalitha said.

The dealer sighed. 'Do you have a first class?'

Nalitha smirked.

'Uh, sure, flat bed okay for you?'

'Really?' The man realised he was being wound up quite quickly, and pretended he had known all along. 'Only kidding!' he said loudly.

'So do you accompany many exotic animals around the world?' said Nalitha as they figured it out and she was printing out his boarding pass.

'Only the best,' said the man, patting Ramsay on the head. The ram wasn't to go into his cage till the last possible moment, it had been explained, in case he got upset. There was already a small trail of sheep surprises across the shed floor which indicated he was already quite excited and Nalitha was point-blank refusing to clean them up, saying she already did all the sick. I would have argued but she had a point.

It was quite a day. We also had the very sweet-faced Mrs Fletcher, off to visit her sister on Larbh. Nalitha smiled as she checked her in.

'Staying for the weekend?' she said kindly.

'Aye, aye,' said Mrs Fletcher. 'I've brought her some fancy knitting wool from the mainland. Rainbow, would you look at that! She won't believe it! She'll be so pleased now. Will be delighted to see me right enough. Good old Lizzie.'

We watched her bustle up the steps.

'Have we got a spare seat on the return?' hissed Nalitha.

'What do you mean?'

'They always have a huge bust-up about half an hour after she gets there. She's meant to pay for a new ticket but she always calls up and pleads. And I say, just get an open return and she says there's no need, they'll have a lovely time next time.'

'What do they fight about?'

'Apparently Lizzie can't handle her big city swanking ways.'

'From Carso?'

I glanced in the direction of the sweet little town, which I was fond of but at the end of the day only had one main street and just about stretched to a Co-op. The big dream was that one day they might get a Greggs.

'I'm just saying. She'll be sobbing and slagging her off and asking why we don't do whisky miniatures.'

'Okay, good, good,' I said, making a note on the manifest.

I should have predicted it, and no doubt Gramps would have, but Ramsay at the last minute suddenly got an official email out of nowhere with a doctor's name on it, proclaiming him to be an emotional support ram, and therefore allowed to travel in the main cabin. To make matters worse (and my entire cowardice was on show here), I offered to keep half an eye on it. Erno would far rather fly a plane – easy – than deal with a rampaging eighty-kilogram rump of masculine fur, so accepted easily. Mrs Fletcher was delighted and patted Ramsay as he took a seat next to her. Ramsay bared his teeth. The handler patted him too.

'Can you at least give him a sedative?' I asked, feeling nervous as we taxied to the little strip.

'You are asking me,' said the dealer, 'to put chemicals into this perfect specimen of organic ... sheeponomics? This peak of perfection? Sheeperfection, we call it ...'

Ramsay kicked his back legs into the dealer's face. I glanced at Erno, but he was completely unfazed. Knowing his history, he'd probably unloaded a bear or two in his time. Thankfully the only other people on the flight were our usual consignments of lovely American and Canadian tourists, who thought everything was adorable and full of lovely local colour even when we were trying to literally wrestle a boy sheep to the ground and I was trying to remember which day of pilot school they made me pick up dung pellets.

Thankfully, Ramsay got out early doors. At Inchborn, we had flown straight over and I wondered how the grumpy man was getting on – very, very badly, I hoped – and I watched Mrs Fletcher and her sister run into each other's arms on Larbh, cuddling as if they'd been apart for months. Nalitha must be wrong.

Larbh had a young woman, quite pregnant, huffing on board, who was involved in a major argument with the well-scrubbed young man following her onto the plane.

'You can't say you want to live a free life at the end of the world, then decide you instantly need medical gizmos all over the place!'

'I want to live somewhere clean and beautiful, but not if I have a baby with an arse for a face or at least if I do I want to know about it in advance.'

The man had blond dreadlocks and quite a lot of colourful scarves.

'And getting on a *plane*! I mean, kudos for sustainability, Sycamore.'

'Actually, you can just call me Jill, *Simon*, it's my name.'

'And mine is Spirit – how many times?'

They sat down and I smiled politely from the cockpit, filing the plan as Erno complained about having to take off in direct daylight or something.

'And they'll probably tell you what they think the sex is!'

'I might want to find out,' Jill replied.

His face was horrified.

'No *way* are you imposing gender on this baby. *No way.*'

I thought about Hayden. He did not seem the type of person who would want a woman to give birth in a field in the middle of nowhere without medical intervention. Then I realised I was very much getting ahead of myself vis-à-vis us, and found myself blushing.

It didn't get much better when, sure enough, we got a request later over the radio to pick up Mrs Fletcher, who marched up the tarmac, her face like fizz.

'Ungrateful bloody wretch,' she was muttering. 'I don't know why I waste my time with that woman, I really don't.'

She sat down in one of the tiny seats and glanced at the couple.

'Oh, how nice!' she said, perking up. 'Is it a boy or a girl?'

The next morning, the village postmistress, Callie, popped her frizzy head round the shed door.

'Uh,' she said. 'I have some poste restante?'

I frowned.

'No, Callie, don't make us.'

Gramps took mail sacks, that was no problem. Someone on each island was designated to post them out. But this was different: you were meant to go into the post office and show ID to pick up poste restante. But obviously that was a heck of a round trip for people to do on a whim, and some people couldn't do it at all. Normally, for the Inchborn fraternity, he or Erno would just drop it off if they had five minutes in their schedule; sometimes cargo came off quicker than they thought or it was just a quiet day.

Callie held it out to me imploringly.

'I'm handling the Royal Mail,' I said grumpily. 'This was literally a capital offence until about fifty years ago. Like, literally being hung at the neck until dead. Interfering with the post.'

'You're being very dramatic,' said Callie. 'It's just a box.'

I wanted to complain more but we were hardly overloaded that day, just a clutch of birthday cards for lucky Lucas Croan on Cairn. And we had a small bunch of extreme mountaineers which meant a quiet flight. They were going to climb Ben Garrold on Larbh, a famous challenge if you are interested in the world of making yourself very cold and miserable. They weren't quiet because they were frightened, which was fair: it is a huge hook of rock that appears out of nowhere, like an alien deposited it there. There's a round hole in the bottom of it, then it just teeters up into nothing. It looks like an upside-down needle and is absolutely terrifying to climb, just a solid pinnacle of rock. And, which slightly worries me, if one of them falls off the bloody thing for no other reason than the fact that they have a completely stupid hobby, Erno and I will have to go and fetch them if the MEDVAC helicopter is busy. Gramps has lifted more than a few broken backs and pregnant ladies off at short notice, but I was very much not in the mood.

Anyway, the mountaineers all have jutting jaw lines and

look like they're pretending to be contestants on *SAS Are You Tough Enough?*, eyeing each other up suspiciously. They don't weigh anything because they are all skinny as whippets and carry ultra-lightweight bivouacs, so they're fairly easy clients all round. Occasionally, one of them will come up to us and try to insinuate that we are doing something wrong with the engines, asking a few technical questions to try and catch us out, bless them, because they just can't help themselves, but other than that they are mostly no bother.

'Okay,' I said. 'But I'm not happy about it and I want it on the record. For when I'm in jail.'

'I think,' Nalitha was saying, 'if I wasn't married to the world's best man, I think I would happily do one of those climbers.'

We were watching them sort themselves in the cabin, making very clear to us that they were frequent small plane flyers and knew they had to distribute themselves by weight.

'Really?' I said. 'So intense. And not in the good way.'

'Maybe in the good way,' she said. 'I appreciate people who take the time to learn how to do difficult things properly.'

'You have a point there,' I said.

'Plus so wiry! Good upper body strength.'

I wrinkled my nose.

'They'd make a big point of throwing you around and watching their own biceps flex in the mirror.'

'Mmm,' said Nalitha, twining a rope of her thick black hair. She glanced at me. 'Anyway, you're off the market, yes?'

I bit my lip.

'I've never seen you like this!' said Nalitha. 'Oh my God. You're so loved up.'

I shrugged.

'Honestly. I didn't . . . It's moving quickly, eh?'

'Oh no, it's just. Well, he'll be in Dubai for work, and I'll be there a lot . . .'

'Yes, and if you're in Dubai together you need to be M-A-R-R-I-E-D!' said Nalitha triumphantly, drawing the word out emphatically.

'You don't,' I said quickly.

'Oooh, you checked! You checked!'

I coloured. That's the thing about old friends: you love them dearly but they remember you as the person you were. Shy, awkward, Morag the Grobag (my hair grew a lot one summer. It was a mean nickname, shut up. I'm not even bothered about it at all now). I think Nalitha was used to having all the boys fancy her and me being her nerd friend. This was new territory.

'Whatever,' I said.

That's the other thing about very old friends: they can read your mood on a dime. Nalitha spun round.

'I'm only teasing,' she said, patting my arm. 'I'm so chuffed for you. That's what they say: when you know, you know. And if you both know at the same time; well, it's easy.'

It could, I thought, be this easy. And I felt warm inside.

'CAVOK?' barked one of the men in the front row. The other men nodded, looking annoyed that they hadn't thought to ask that first. I avoided rolling my eyes – Nalitha didn't – but they were just asking for a weather forecast in the most macho way they knew how. I would play nice.

'Absolutely,' I said. They all nodded as if they all knew this and were experts on everything and that this was the only thing that was going to save them from falling off a mountain rather than their incredibly expensive medical insurance which meant that Jimbo (the helicopter pilot, who was unbelievably handsome, unbelievably dumb but fortunately unbelievably good at flying helicopters) or I would in fact have to come out and save their arses. Nalitha had pointed out that our bonus for rescue missions on privately insured clients was so astronomical it would totally be worth our while if we cut some of their guy ropes or something. Then, when one of them barked a question at her about altitude wind speed, she threatened to do it for free.

At any rate, they were light and not too badly behaved as show-offs go, so I agreed with Callie I'd take whatever the stupid poste restante was. It was for Inchborn, just as I'd thought.

'Great!' Callie had said. She vanished, reappearing with, to my extreme displeasure, a trolley with a large heavy-looking box on it.

'What!' I said. 'That's our trolley!'

'It's not my fault,' she said slightly peevishly, 'that your grand-father runs an entire airline that only has one trolley.'

I scowled.

'We had *eight* trolleys,' I said. Which was true at one point. Then we had an unusually icy winter, and there were some slightly guilty-looking Carso children and lots of crashed trol-leys at the bottom of Tigh Na Bruach Road.

'And how heavy is that thing? It's mad.'

It was an old steamer trunk, festooned with shipping labels, made of wood and covered with fabric. Solid brass clasps held it together, with leather straps banding around the body.

'That is completely ridiculous,' I said, bending down. I couldn't help but admire it though. It was a thing of beauty:

a piece of furniture from an age where travel had nothing but adventure and glamour attached to it; where a voyage would be undertaken not in hours but in weeks, or even months. It seemed to speak of far-off lands and strange spices.

'He probably got it in TK Maxx,' said Nalitha, sniffing. But I bent down. It was real, all right.

'What's in it?' I asked.

Callie pursed her lips. 'As postmistress, I couldn't possibly say.'

'Oh, *now* you're being all law abiding,' I said, frowning. 'Thanks, *postmistress*.'

'We should charge for this,' said Nalitha. 'It's going to weigh a lot more than those racing snakes onboard.'

'I know,' said Callie, looking beseeching. 'I should hold on to it. He was very bad not to take it before. But it's taking up my entire storeroom. There's absolutely no space left. It's getting in the way, I keep barking my shins on it and there's no response to texts telling him to come get the bloody thing because—'

'—no signal,' I said. That is a problem, when the entire world can't imagine you not having an internet signal to do banking, parcels, anything else. You're considered such a freak without one.

I glanced back at *Dolly*.

'Okay,' I said. 'Sling it in and don't tell anyone.'

Callie grinned.

'You are *so* my favourite pilot,' she said. 'I'm so glad you're back.'

'I'm not back!' I said. Or the pilot, I thought privately to myself.

Erno was in the cockpit already. He was tightening up a nut, writing in the log in his tiny, cramped hand and eating a bacon sandwich, all at the same time. Massive slob, helluva pilot.

'Erno! Could you not?'

'I could not not. Could you fly this damn plane?'

It was a clear, bright, cold day up there, absolutely gorgeous, the horizon stretching way, way beyond, curving gloriously, the last dying specks of pink and yellow beneath the broad blue. You could tell it was cold just by touching the windshield. But it looked as beautiful as the world can. The islands stretched into the distance like pearls on a necklace, so many completely uninhabited except by the birds. It felt like the world was mine: empty and clean, the skies wide open. Just take it, I told myself. Just do it. Just ...

I glanced over at the throttle. I felt it in my body, that sickening lurch as we had risen vertically up, doing our best to get away, to stop what we could not stop, the endless spiralling down of a plane the size of this one ...

I sat down definitely on the right-hand chair as Erno grumpily finished his bacon sandwich, and set about the instruments with greasy fingers, and I tried to put the fears to the back of my mind as he took off and we soared, wheels clunking smoothly into place behind us, the ground fading away, and we were over the wide-open sea, the world unfolding before us. All my senses were focused and alive; my coffee forgotten as I checked our course, the weather fax, the radar. On my distant left, I could see Inchborn, with its distinctive outline of the ruined abbey clear against the tufted heaths behind it. There was the great northern cliff, white with the guano of all the gulls and puffins. Then, looming up as we carried on over the broad waves, a cargo ship or two crossing depths;

they were so much slower than we were as we ascended the glorious heights – although I know people of the sea that feel as strongly about their own element as I do about mine, and I am sure they have an absolutely equal disbelief that I can feel sorry for them. To me, though, they are losing their way over the ocean as I zoom and soar and see the sun bounce off the tip of every wave, the shadows of distant clouds turn the water a thousand colours from aquamarine to darkest midnight, and then all vanishing beneath my wings. Usually all mine, and looking at it I felt a flame leap in my heart: it never grows old or tired, day after day.

We dropped the mountaineers in record time as I knew we would; they were all very keen to show how easily they could swing their fluorescent backpacks onto their shoulders and jog away from the terminal, and then there was probably some stupid race up the mountain as well. Obviously, I didn't want anyone to fall over because that would have been terrible.

'I hope they all fall over,' said Nalitha peering over my shoulder as we listened to them shouting bro noises to one another, 'and bounce down and we have to come and rescue them individually and get paid per flight from their big city insurance each time. On a Sunday.'

'You don't,' I said.

'I so do! I had to sit back here. Do you know what they were all talking about? What pains in the arse their wives and girlfriends were being about them coming out over a weekend. And then they were all laughing and talking about how their women were much more fun before the baby came and now they were really boring.'

I screwed up my face.

'Okay, maybe some twisted ankles,' I said.

'Grim and grisly death,' said Nalitha. 'I'll show them wives and girlfriends.'

I glanced at my watch.

'At least we're making good time.'

There were only two people on the return leg: some women who were heading to the mainland for the week and were quite giddy about it.

'Don't forget we have to drop that poste restante,' said Nalitha.

'Oh lord,' I said, clambering back aboard. 'We agreed to carry a package on this flight and we don't know what it is. Gelignite? Cocaine? Dinosaur DNA?'

'Stop with the dinosaur DNA,' Nalitha said.

I was slightly regretful about heading south, which I took as a good sign. Inchborn was so much fun to land on: the beach with the pale blue water pounding on one side, and the whispering dunes on the other with sand of palest gold.

I felt the crosswinds under the flaps as Erno shifted position and we relinquished the sky, giving ourselves up to the pull of the land once more, where we would not be this magnificent, bouncing eagle in the sky, but a pointless hunk of metal as gravity-bound as anybody else.

Still, what a place to land. Erno brought her down so carefully that the nose tilted gently, gently, and I had a strong feeling of the wind settling beneath the wheels as we touched down on the sand, gradually letting *Dolly* run slowly along the beach, which reached ahead of us for miles, until she came to a spot perfectly in line with the dunes. If Erno had been doing my Malaga run, he'd have got a round of applause from the hen parties.

It was odd there being nobody there to greet us. I frowned. 'I'm just going to toss it out the window. Honestly. He's on an island where nothing ever happens, he wants us to bring his big stupid box, a *plane lands* and he just ignores it? Rude bugger.'

I jumped down to help Nalitha. The wind was clear and fresh and everything was very cold and bright; the air tasted incredibly good, but it was freezing out there.

'I am not,' I said quite firmly, 'going to go to his house to deliver it.'

After a couple of seconds, however, we saw a dark figure traipse over the dunes. It was entirely unhurried, clad in a long dark coat.

'Yeah, all right, hobbit,' I grumbled. 'Got nothing else to do today.'

'Well, you don't,' said Nalitha irritatingly. 'You won't come to mine. You're just going to go home to watch *Married at First Sight* by yourself.'

'That's *something*,' I said crossly.

Gradually, he came into focus. He was wearing the same faintly peeved expression he'd worn on the plane, and had a hat pulled down over beetling brows. He wasn't as old as I'd first thought; he couldn't be much older than me. Goodness, what a weirdo.

'What?' he roared into the noisy wind. 'What's wrong?'

'We have your stupid parcel for you!' Nalitha roared back, her voice getting caught by the wind and ripped away. He held up his arms, not understanding.

'Oh, for goodness sake,' I muttered, freezing cold and unwilling to put my coat on. 'He ordered the damn thing.'

Nalitha lifted the box again. There was no way she could get it down the steps on her own; it looked heavy and was very unwieldy. Erno was still in the cabin, almost certainly grabbing a nap. I harrumphed again and picked up the other end of the box and together we manhandled it down from the hold.

'Oh!' he said, looking at us. He didn't dart forward to help.

'Sorry,' he said, as we collapsed on the sand. 'Is that for me?'

'No,' I said. 'It's for all the other people who live here.'

'I'm so sorry ... I didn't ... I thought the post office would keep it for me: it's a post restante.'

'Well, yes,' I said. 'But the post office is the size of a cupboard and they didn't want this cluttering up the tiny amount of floor space they have.'

'Oh,' he said again, staring at it. 'I didn't think of that.'

We all stared at it, then, following his lead, turned and looked over the dunes. Sure, it was a tiny island but it was still at least half a kilometre to the abbey and, next to it, the rather fine grey house that served as island keeper quarters.

'What is it?' I asked.

He frowned and didn't answer.

'I'm more concerned about getting it there.'

'Well,' I said brightly, glancing at my watch, 'you have plenty of time to drag it!'

'Hmm,' he said. Nalitha gave me a side look for being rude.

'Where's the Land Rover?' I said.

'Needs fixing,' he said. 'Fraser had been driving it on a flat. Fish hooks all the way through it.'

'Figures.'

We stood around for a while.

'Well, do you want us to take it back then?' I said eventually, with bad grace.

'I really don't.'

This didn't get us much further on. I checked the sky but annoyingly it was completely clear so I couldn't even make up a storm that might be coming in. We carried on standing there, looking at each other. I was genuinely annoyed. We had done this guy a massive favour and he was acting as if we'd ruined his day.

'Shall we just leave it on the beach then?' I said in sulky tones.

'Well, my house is . . . '

He indicated roughly in the general direction but without doing what a normal person would have done: one, either not asked us at all and figured it out; or two, begged us for a favour and been extremely lovely and promised chocolate cake which we happened to know he had because one of the boxes that we had personally loaded for him had been labelled as such.

But no. He stood there like all of this was *somebody else's problem*. Even Nalitha began to look like she regretted this entire thing, and Nalitha never regretted anything.

Just as it couldn't get any more awkward, and everyone was absolutely freezing, there was a black smudge to the left of my field of vision. I turned round, unable at first to see what I was looking at. The smudge gradually resolved into many little smudges which then revealed themselves to be people – or rather children, mostly, in brightly coloured parkas.

'What the crap is that?' said Nalitha.

'Have you been keeping lots of children prisoner here?' I said. 'And they've suddenly found their chance to escape?'

'Damn it,' he said, not listening to me, but staring at the group.

'Oh yeah, they did escape,' I said to Nalitha.

'The boat must have come in. I should have been there.'

He frowned, then waved as the children came towards him.

'Mr MacAleese! Hiya, Mr MacAleese!'

'Aye, aye, hiya,' he said, frowning again.

'Seriously,' said Nalitha. 'Are you … training a junior militia for the end times?'

'It's the school group,' said the man crossly. 'The boat's arrived, and clearly I missed it because someone dumped a plane on my beach.'

'Yeah, *your* beach,' I said.

'Well done on wasting all that fuel though,' he said.

I glanced at Nalitha, astounded he was being so rude.

'Next time, we'll just drop it, shall we?' she said.

The kids were upon us now.

'Is that your plane, miss? Is that your plane?'

'Can we see the gulls, Mr MacAleese? Are there baby puffins? Can we play with the puffins?'

'Aye, naw, you can't. You cannae touch any of the birds, yeah?'

They sighed.

'Can I touch your plane?' said one of the boys.

'You can't do that either, I'm afraid,' I said. 'Also, we were just leaving.'

'The noise and the fumes are really bad for the birds,' said the man and I genuinely wanted to kick him in the knees at this point.

The children nodded.

'It's environmentally unsound,' said one little girl in a hand-knitted scarf and I slightly wanted to point out to her how grimy the diesel ferry that had brought her there for literally no other reason than a day out was, but I felt being horrible to children wasn't really something I wanted as a personality trait, so I just smiled tightly.

'Now,' said Mr MacAleese, 'before we do the tour and go visit some seals, who wants to help me carry this box?'

'Yay!' went a dozen tiny voices, and they came forward

determinedly under the eye of a friendly-looking teacher, shouldered the box with much kerfuffle and shouting, and then the little party bore it away cheerfully, chattering at the tops of their voices, like exotic birds in their brightly coloured jackets and hats.

'I am never,' I said as I clambered back into the very welcome warmth of the cabin, 'doing anyone a favour ever, ever again.'

'Well, it got sorted,' said Nalitha practically. 'I mean, we delivered the box and it got taken away.'

We glanced out of the window where the line of children was just visible on the crest of the dunes, bearing the box aloft in a jolly fashion.

'What *was* it?' I said.

'I don't know,' said Nalitha. 'Not a clue. The label just said "Equipment". Probably some ... bird folder.'

'They fold birds?'

'I don't know, do I?'

Erno was doing all the pre-flight checks. I had had a quick look at the tyres and the fuel cover before I'd come back upstairs. Just to be sure.

'Maybe it's a treasure map. Maybe they *are* his secret gang of child soldiers,' said Nalitha.

'Or he is just a very bad-mannered graceless individual,' I said as Erno started to push the plane gently forward.

As we circled round to head further south, I glanced down. The little ferry, the *Mary Lise*, was in the tiny dock that led up to the double beach and the monastery on the south-west side, opposite where we had landed. You could see the dimin-utive crowd of smalls, now sitting politely on the sand, as a dark figure, presumably Mr MacAleese, was gesticulating at something.

'What's he doing?' I said, fighting the urge to tell Erno to fly lower for a closer look.

Erno looked down.

'I don't know,' he said. 'But the children seem very excited about it.'

It was true, the little coloured jackets were hopping up and down. The man, by contrast, appeared just to be standing still.

'He must be beguiling them with his intense wit and charm,' I said.

'He's probably got an otter,' said Nalitha.

'I hope that's not a euphemism,' I said, as we banked and made for home.

Chapter Nine

It hadn't gone that badly though, I told myself as I walked back to the house up the cobbled street from the little airfield. The air was cold and fresh in my lungs, and I stopped in at the bakery and bought three French cakes. If Gramps wasn't well enough to eat a French cake, well, he really was sick and I could start worrying. And probably eat his French cake.

Peigi opened the door, Skellington scowling at me from her ankles.

'Oh, there you are,' she said, as if I'd nipped out to the cinema for a couple of hours. 'There's someone waiting for you.'

Hayden! I thought instantly. He's realised how I feel, how lonely I've been, how terrified I am about losing everything. He's dashed back from Dubai! I prepared my face into a beaming smile.

'Oh great.'

'Oooh yes. A man,' she said, her voice imparting heavy meaning. 'For *you*. I got out the fancy biscuits. Also he was very interested in Skellington. I told him all about his kidney disease and he was very sympathetic.'

Skellington in no way had kidney disease; that dog was vetted every single time he had a mild cough. It was Peigi's excuse for his vindictive pissing in other people's houses, and his ugly yellow eyes.

'Hiya!' I yelled cheerfully, striding into the parlour, the room at the front of the house which we never used, which would definitely be where Peigi had sent him. 'Hey, sweets!'

I marched in, full of relief.

There was a strange man standing there, staring at the fire – or rather where a fire would have been had we laid one. He wasn't looking at his phone, which I thought was the default of every single person in the world. Instead, he was standing, not stooped, just looking. Like a horse, I thought.

He was tall, with fair hair, a large nose and rather plump lips, which looked rather incongruous. He was also wearing a ridiculous yellow North Face jacket, which he had (wisely, to be fair) not taken off.

'Um, hi?' said the man with a mild Scandinavian accent. I swear I could hear Peigi snicker from outside the door.

'Oh!' I said, completely deflated. 'Sorry, I thought you were someone else.'

'I know,' he said. 'I heard some gossip and ... well ... sorry, I hope you don't mind me dropping by.'

'Mr Frost?' I said. It was the CEO of the large airline that wanted the route.

He nodded.

'I hope you don't mind me popping in,' he reiterated. 'I wanted to look at the terminal building, so ... '

'It's hardly a building,' I said, still out of kilter.

He turned round, taking his time. I wondered if he really was a slow person or whether this was some kind of management technique he'd learned in some weird culty leadership lesson.

'Captain MacIntyre—'

'Morag is fine,' I said.

'Okay,' he said. 'I very much hope your grandmother's dog is feeling better.'

Oh, my goodness, cheeky old Peigi. Well, I couldn't be bothered to correct him.

'I'm sorry,' I said firmly. 'I think there's been a mistake. My grandfather – Captain MacIntyre, the real one — isn't well. He can't see you.'

The door of the parlour swung open.

Peigi already had filled the old teapot and had looked out two matching mugs, which was something of a miracle, even if they did both advertise fuel companies. She had cake too; she generally had a fruit cake on the go, as Gramps liked it (or, if he didn't, had obviously mentioned it once long ago, and she had made one a week ever since). She had cut us a couple of slices and put the whole thing down on the polished wooden table Gramps only ever used at Christmas.

Mr Frost took off his ridiculously expensive North Face jacket to reveal an equally expensive suit underneath, although this was dark grey. He looked very odd in our scruffy home. I put my hands round the tea to warm them.

'So,' he said, smiling, 'this is the base of the great operation of MacIntyre Air.'

'I don't think you need to be sarcastic,' I said icily. He looked up from his tea, startled. It was weird. I would never normally have given Callum Frost a moment's thought. But now I was here – now I was back at the family base, standing on the very flagstones where Ranald had sat over long nights, working out payloads and fuel costs with Jimmy, where he'd built the entire thing up from scratch before people up here had telephones and before many of the islands even had electricity. It was extraordinary what he'd done. An amazing achievement. And this arrogant sod in his stupid North Face jacket just wanted to snap it up, turn it into a column on a spreadsheet. I was suddenly incredibly cross. How *dare* he?

'I wasn't,' he said, blinking. 'I mean, your great-grandfather... he was a legend. My dad met him. Said he was a very tough SOB.'

He smiled. My eye wandered to the picture of him on the mantelpiece, standing next to my great-grandmother Margaret, looking young and handsome. Callum Frost followed my gaze.

'Then when Murdo took it over... I always wondered, why he didn't expand? All that pioneering spirit?'

I shrugged.

'I mean ...' he continued, 'we started going to Norway, Iceland, Sweden ... We've added five new routes in the last two years alone.'

'Good for you,' I said. 'I especially like the way if the flight is cancelled you just dump the passengers and don't bother getting them home. Or the nine euros you charge for a sandwich.'

'I'm so touched you've flown us!' He smiled.

'Well, Murdo doesn't see it that way. He's not in the business of just making money.'

Frost tried not to cast his eyes round the shabby room, and failed.

'He sees us as a service; something the island people need. A lifeline to his own communities, not some kind of global takeover project.'

Callum shrugged.

'Couldn't you be both?'

'No,' I said. 'We don't make enough money. *They* don't make enough money,' I added quickly.

'That's because you don't have enough planes or think big enough. You should be bringing loads of people up here.'

He walked towards the rattly old windowpane. From the side of the house, you could see down towards the cliffs, bright in the evening light, the sky over them pinkening, the water below brightly flecked with gold.

'Look at it,' he said. 'It's so beautiful. And wild, and empty.'

'Well, not if you have your way,' I pointed out.

'Don't you think more people deserve to see it?'

A perfect V of swifts passed overhead in full formation, like an air show squadron.

I frowned.

'Well . . .'

'Look at the North Coast 500.'

He was talking about the motoring route that ran from Inverness through Sutherland, Caithness and John O'Groats. It was absolutely lovely and had proven wildly popular from the start. Which meant, in practice, that the entire area was overrun with cars, slow camper vans, littering, traffic jams and people letting their dogs out in areas with sheep.

'Yeah, what about it?' I said.

'Look how much money it's brought in.'

This was also undeniable. It had been such a huge success from which everyone along the route had benefited. I still didn't think we should be chartering massive jets to overboard the routes even more though. Which was probably wrong, of course. It was a terrible thing to have a country as beautiful as Scotland and want to keep it all to yourself, I found myself thinking.

'But that's the whole point of the archipelago,' I said. 'It's because people don't want to be inundated. They don't want to have loads of tourists coming to look at them. They're not tourist attractions! They're working people!'

'Yeah, working people who like money as much as anybody else.'

There was a silence and I felt very tense all of a sudden, though I didn't know why. I mean, it was hardly my concern. I was moving to Dubai with my lovely boyfriend.

'So, what did you want to talk to Gramps about?' I ventured in a more conciliatory tone when he calmly sipped more of his tea and ignored the fruitcake. But deep down, I knew.

He looked around the house once again, and I could see him taking in the chipped cupboards, the rattling windows, the sheer shabbiness of it all.

I think it was guilt that was making me so cross about it. Because on one level, if I was being completely cynical about it, it was the right thing to do. Sell up, get Gramps a nice big wodge of money and relieve me of any guilt about not coming back here. Surely it suited everyone. But it wasn't what Gramps wanted. Knowing what he did want – for me to come back – and that it wasn't going to happen was making me truculent, ill-tempered and defensive.

Callum Frost looked up at me.

'I think,' he said, 'we might be able to make your family an offer on the route.'

'Yeah.' I folded my arms. 'Why? There's no money in it. And Gramps . . . Murdo is perfectly happy doing what he's doing.'

'For now,' he said. 'But, Morag, can you imagine: brand-new planes, low noise, low fuel, environmentally friendly?'

I snorted.

'And more of them! Bringing high-spending visitors to share in all this amazing vast beauty up here. School parties and university tours—'

'—and oil prospectors and people who want to steal birds' eggs,' I said. 'And charging old grannies forty quid when they can't figure out how to print out their boarding pass. And calling hand luggage a tiny evening bag.'

' . . . and land conservationists and environmental people. You know how tight money is,' he said, looking at me. 'What's to stop the government selling off one of those bird sanctuaries or stopping farm subsidies? Or stopping your subsidy. What will you do then?'

'They won't,' I said boldly. 'This is a service to these islands. They're needed.'

'Don't you think it might be really helpful if they had more than five flights a week?' said Callum, and just then I hated his smug face. 'And a plane that doesn't fall apart if you get two icy days in a row?'

'That is so not fair,' I said. 'There's nothing wrong with *Dolly*.'

'She's older than dirt,' said Callum. 'And you know it. What are you going to do when she finally kicks the bucket – lease?'

'Something will turn up,' I said grimly.

'So your grandfather is absolutely not at all interested in selling the route?'

'Absolutely not.'

'There would always be a job for you.'

I looked up at him.

'I have a job! With a—'

'—real airline,' he finished, smirking at me. 'Well, you could turn this into a real airline.'

'I don't think so.'

'And this is what your grandfather thinks too, isn't it?'

'He knows what you do,' I said. 'You take every single piece of joy and wonder in flying and squeeze it for profit. You take a beautiful world and turn it ugly as hell; stressful, uncomfortable, miserable. You take something amazing humans invented and make it a dismal experience, all so you get to be a tiny bit richer than you could possibly ever need to be. You cram people in and charge them a fortune for bags and dump them miles away from where they want to be. Would you take any responsibility for weather? If we can't fly, we take people home the next time we can. You just make them buy new tickets and pay for their own hotel accommodation.'

Callum frowned.

'We run a business millions of people happily use every year.'

'They don't happily use it! They use it because they can't afford to use anything else.'

'No, they choose to fly as cheaply as possible. It's up to them if they want to buy a really expensive muffin or not. We have a perfect safety record and a punctuality record that is notably better than yours.'

'We greet half our passengers by name.'

'That sounds terrible.'

We sat there in uncomfortable silence.

'It's just an air slot,' I said. 'We don't own the sky. Why not apply for the same route and run it yourself?'

He harrumphed. 'It's hardly Heathrow to Berlin. You fly down light all the time. If we don't get the government subsidy, there's no point doing it.'

'I see you've been keeping a close eye.'

'Of course.'

'Anyway,' he said, 'we'd undercut you by fifty per cent and

chase you out of business in a week and a half. I don't want to do that. We'd want to form good relationships.'

'With my grandfather?'

'Well . . . that would be rather up to him.'

I looked at him.

'You aren't desperate to keep good relationships,' I said. 'You don't want the plane. You don't want the route, otherwise you'd run it already. I know what you want. You want the government subsidy. You'd promise to bring in new jobs and snaffle up all the tax breaks for every other bit of your business, all the fat lucrative Glasgow runs.'

He blinked and stood up.

'No,' he said. 'I want to run a wonderful airline, which goes to wonderful places.'

I stood up too, feeling ridiculous and upset. I think of myself as quite a calm person normally – it's kind of part of the job – so feeling my stomach churning and my throat tightening making me unable to speak out loud was very upsetting. Direct one-to-one confrontation was absolutely not my style, especially seeing as it clearly hadn't bothered Callum in the slightest; he was completely unruffled as he put his expensive coat back on, and placed his card on the table.

'Just in case . . . ' he said, smiling politely.

'How much?' said Hayden patiently. 'I mean, will it keep your grandfather happily in the lap of luxury for the rest of his life? I am struggling a bit with why this guy is evil, to be honest.'

There was a splashing happening behind him again.

'Where are you?' I said.

'Oh my God,' he said. 'I didn't want to tell you but ... the new office. It has pool parties.'

'You are kidding me!' I said.

'I know!'

I could hear girls squealing.

'This is a complete HR nightmare!' I said. 'What if someone's bikini top falls off?'

'It's three o'clock in the afternoon.'

'Hmm,' I said. 'Are you surrounded by scantily clad lovelies?'

'Not really,' he said. 'Mostly it's Pat in processing wearing a really large muumuu.'

'Well, that cheers me up.'

'There's one scantily clad lovely I am *very* interested in seeing, so can you just sell out to a millionaire already?'

I looked out of the window. A stark ray of sunlight was hitting the archipelago, the distant islands looking like picked-out jewels on a chain. The wind blew the grass in the sparse front garden, revealing shiny pieces of glass in the rockery my great-grandmother had built long ago.

'You'll see when you come here,' I said. 'And I'm not scantily clad today. I've got my thermals on.'

'I hope I will,' he said. 'Soon.'

Something splashed very near him that sounded like a beach ball.

'Uh-huh,' I said, smiling.

'So what did your grandfather have to say about it?'

My heart leapt. Someone cared about what was going on in my family.

'He still hasn't got up. Quite a nasty flu.'

'Oh no,' he said. 'God, I hope he's okay.'

'I miss you,' I said, meaning it deeply. He had become such a part of my life, so fast. And I wanted him to see us, to see Carso, to meet everyone. Well, maybe not that ram. But suddenly, I felt desperate.

'Well, it's all here waiting for you.'

There was more squealing. Yes, I thought. But I want you here.

I looked around the old kitchen, Skellington asleep in front of the range, letting out noxious farts. He had a hideous habit of sleeping with his red-rimmed eyes hanging open, which was entirely disgusting, and his black and white hair was matted from the mud his lower body had slunk through that day. There was a definite Eau de Wet Dog permeating the air. Outside, even through the watery sunlight, people were leaning into the wind to walk up the streets, their coats pulled around them.

'So you're flying tomorrow?'

'I'm on the roster.'

'Good luck. You're going to smash it.'

If Hayden believed in me, if Gramps believed in me, I must be able to do this. I definitely could.

Chapter Ten

I didn't sleep much. Perhaps it was obvious and Hayden was probably right: *Dolly* was getting older; Gramps was getting older. But for now that was further down my list of worries.

I stared out of the window. Old habit: I never closed the curtains. I just liked looking at the sky, always had. When I was little, in the summer I could drift off to the sky turning pink towards 11 p.m., slowly bringing in the shortest and sweetest of nights, and I'd wake up to wonderful sunshine bouncing off the water. In the winter, I liked to be cosy, bundled under my duvet and the old floral eiderdown I'd inherited which had been made by my grandmother and her sisters as a dowry when she got married. I'd look up at the stars, one or two of them occasionally blinking, revealing themselves not in fact to be stars, but little parcels of people in the sky heading out towards far-flung places such as Reykjavik, Bergen, Stockholm, Archangel. I felt comforted to see a plane pass in the sky, knowing that the pilot would be sitting, carefully watching over their snoozing passengers, saying good evening to air traffic control, handing over from Shanwick Oceanic Control to Scotland, drawing long sparkling lines of light on the great dome of the dark blue sky, our playground. Normally, though, I fell asleep instantaneously.

Tonight, I did not. In fact, I was terrified. What if Gramps thought I'd come up for five minutes to cover his sick leave, decided I knew best and more or less just let Callum Frost in? Encouraged him. Like I thought Gramps was over it, past it, that everything had to go, that he should just sell up and leave it, he was too old. But then to be the person who ended the dream, the great ambitions, of Ranald and Murdo, of all the MacIntyres – could I really take that responsibility? That I sold out their dreams for money?

And I still had to do the job. I could do it. Gramps believed in me. Hayden believed in me. I just had to believe in myself. I remembered suddenly, flashing back to Hayden's office – before I knew his name was Hayden even – he had asked me, glancing down at his file, if I wanted a psychologist or a counsellor. And I had wanted to impress him, had wanted him to think I was the cool tough pilot girl. And I'd said no. What an idiot. A further thought struck me, a terrifying one. What if the airline found out I couldn't fly and blamed Hayden for not getting to the bottom of it? That was his job, after all. What if he lost his transfer and it was all my fault? I screwed up my face. Oh God, oh God. How could I even tell him? Would he have to go back and tell the airline?

Okay, I told myself. Calm down. A few days up here, helping out, saying no to Callum, then back, take the final simulator test for the airline – and it was all ahead of me. A new life in the shimmering desert. With a man who made me the best version of myself. Everything was out there for the taking. All I had to do was land a plane I knew as well as my own hand.

'So you're going to fly today?'

Erno looked pink and very grumpy this morning.

'Uh . . .' I said. And stopped.

I couldn't answer. Say yes, Morag. Say yes, Dumbo.

Erno looked me up and down.

'This is just a holiday for you, isn't it?'

'No,' I squeaked. 'I came up to help.'

And then I said it. I let myself down. I couldn't help it.

'To co-pilot. I'm a first officer!'

'Not on this plane.'

I swallowed hard.

'Honestly, Erno.'

'I heard about your trouble,' he said, and I flushed immediately.

'That's not it,' I said quickly. Nalitha was hustling that morning's passengers up into the little cabin. I busied myself with the checks, refusing to move from the right-hand seat.

'Uh-huh,' he said, sitting down heavily and letting out a great sigh.

Okay. No. This meant everything. I could do it. I could. I had to. The thought of Hayden getting into trouble resurfaced. I couldn't let him down, even if I was letting myself down.

'Okay,' I said suddenly, surprising myself. 'I'll do it.'

He looked at me and stood up.

Today we had a full hen party which had taken every seat on the plane and I got up to check everything was okay. They had conga'd up the tarmac in full regalia and were now imploring both Nalitha and me to take a wee glass of Prosecco, a formidably dangerous idea, though that hadn't seemed to occur to them.

'No, thank you,' I said politely.

'But you have to! It's bad luck if you don't toast the bride-to-be!'

The bride-to-be was a generously proportioned maiden from Glasgow with thick ropes of blonde hair, wearing eyelashes that curled round and practically touched the top of her forehead, like an affectionate cow. Her upper lip was blown up like a bicycle pump and thickly covered in pink lipstick. I could kind of appreciate it without ever feeling the need to show up one day and get someone to put a needle right into your lip – and paying money for that to happen. I wondered if lots of girls did that in Dubai. Cor. They probably did. I hoped it wasn't a legal requirement.

'Okay,' said Nalitha.

'No!' I said. 'Sorry, girls, but we are so thrilled to have you onboard and congratulations!'

'Yayyyy!' they all yelled.

'Also, you should see him!' said someone dressed up as a bridesmaid. 'He's lush!'

They started showing pictures of a scrappy-looking skinny guy who, next to the glamazon he was marrying, looked alternately dumbfounded and delighted, like he couldn't believe his luck but was also slightly terrified of it.

'Lovely,' I said. I couldn't stop smiling: their simple optimism and joy and slightly squiffy excitement was infectious.

'He is *so lush*,' the bride confided. '*And!* He has his own garage.'

I smiled.

'That sounds awesome.'

'It is,' she said, wobbling slightly. Her mates, looking slightly fearful, got her sitting down and belted in.

'It is very, very awesome.'

She beamed.

'Are youse married?'

Nalitha nodded, whereas I kind of shook my head and, as my eyes widened, I was suddenly aware that I must look absolutely ancient to them.

'You should make more of yourself, you know. You're no' sae bad.'

I blinked.

'Thanks,' I said. 'Okay, just off to fly the plane.'

'YAYYYYY!'

Normally I would have been insulted by this. But whenever I thought of Hayden, tiny fireworks went off in my stomach. I wouldn't have a hen night like this though. Then I told myself to stop being so ridiculous by getting ahead of myself.

The girls all cheered and started pulling small bottles of Prosecco and straws out of their bags. I glanced at Nalitha, who smiled – they could have a drink on the flight, it was only a hop and they were cheery, not inebriated.

I slipped my hand into my pocket to turn off my mobile before I entered the cockpit. It wasn't that it interfered with the navigation systems – we only tell you that to be annoying. It was just so drummed into us that it was banned when I was in training that I never even questioned it; it was automatic. The mobile got locked away, except for dire emergencies.

Just as I picked it up, it rang. It was Hayden's number. I smiled.

'Sweetie! I have a plane to fly, you know?'

There was a crackle on the end of the line.

'Hello?'

Nalitha looked at me, frowning. We were close to schedule and it was just about time to take off. It didn't matter locally: nothing else was up and about today, but the 09.40 Helsinki to Reykjavik passed fairly close by and we didn't want to get in their way. And people had things to do, as evidenced by the rowdy noise of the girls in the back – they were being picked up by the seal bus on Larbh which did exactly what it said. Although the seals were unlikely to hang around for terribly long if they kept the noise up. Even as I thought this, someone started a wobbly rendition of a Celine Dion song. Perhaps they shouldn't be allowed to open the Prosecco onboard.

All these thoughts went through my head as I waited for the phone to connect.

'Hello? Sweetie? Hayden? Hello?'

The phone line crackled and the connection held.

There was a thudding noise that I gradually realised was music.

'Hey, babe,' came a voice. Hayden's. Oh, thank God.

'Darling?' I said. He didn't normally call me babe.

'Hey, babe,' he said again, and because I am such an idiot it had taken me that long to hit me.

He wasn't talking to me. He'd pocket-dialled.

He sounded drunk. That wasn't like him at all: he liked a nice glass of wine but he wasn't a massive party rage monster. Sensible.

'So you work for the airline?'

The voice sounded young, European – German? Swedish? I couldn't tell. My heart was thudding so loudly I was sure it would attract attention.

119

'Yeah.'

I froze in place. I knew I should throw the phone down as if it were a snake or a scorpion; it was equally bad for my well-being. But I couldn't move. I literally couldn't move. My brain would not compute. That was Hayden, mild-mannered, gentle Hayden, with his flat Hull accent I absolutely loved.

'Tell me about the worst thing that ever happened.'

'Well . . .' He didn't sound like himself at all. He'd adopted a slight drawl. Who was this guy? 'We were flying over Spain once, and this tiny crop duster . . .'

My mouth dropped open.

'Nalitha . . .' I croaked. She dived over, grabbed the phone from my hand and put it to her own ear. Her expression showed me that it was indeed just as bad as I thought. She nodded briskly, then hung up the phone.

'That's him?'

I nodded mutely.

'I thought he was English; he sounds Canadian or something.'

'I know.'

'What's more, he was telling that girl what happened to you like it happened to him.'

I nodded again. She whistled through her teeth.

'Shit.'

Nalitha pushed me, more or less, into the cockpit and nodded her head to move Erno from the right- to the left-hand seat.

'Erno, you're taking off.'

Erno lifted his hat off his moustache with a surprise grunt.

'Huh?'

'You're flying this leg.'

He sighed.

'But—'

'Do it.'

He moved with bad grace as Nalitha went and did the safety briefing for the passengers, who sung along heartily, and I sat down, going through the pre-flight checks automatically, barely conscious of what I was doing.

What the hell? What was he up to? I had ... I thought ... I mean, he was so normal. So ordinary, with his tidy haircut and the intention – shared by both of us – to one day join the National Trust and go see more films at the NFT and learn how to do cryptic crosswords and oh! All my plans. All my silly, silly plans.

I stared straight ahead. It was a brilliantly still day, the sea like a pond beneath us, reflecting the early spring sun. It was lovely outside, a glorious day for flying, as long as you had your strong sunglasses on, but heading north that wasn't a problem. No problems, nothing unexpected, a totally regular day in every other way. Except my heart, which had only just come alive after years of work and study and doing what was expected of me, my late-blooming heart had been pulled out by the roots.

We took off, Erno flying low. I could see a beautiful long-legged heron unfold itself on a completely empty beach we went over, taking to the air with a grace and beauty that put even *Dolly* to shame. They never cared, I thought. Birds didn't care. They didn't need transponders or gyroscopes. They were born being able to dead reckon. And they didn't care about stupid boyfriends doing terrible things when they were away, who you were meant to be able to completely and utterly trust. A tear trickled down past my sunglasses. Pilots shouldn't cry.

Erno landed on Larbh, not a crosswind in sight. He tactfully didn't say anything to me, barely mentioned it, as a cheer went up from next door, and a song of 'Hooray for the lady pilot!' started up. Nalitha went through to sort them out.

Standing at the door of the cockpit watching them disembark was tough. The bride, her long fake blonde locks streaming behind her, with the veil and the silly frilly dress on the bright golden sand in the sun suddenly looked absolutely beautiful. She kicked off her shoes at the bottom of the stairs and ran delightedly across the sand, her friends laughing and photographing her. Yes, I thought. She was beautiful.

I swallowed hard.

'Oh God,' I said. Nalitha slung her arm round my neck, didn't say anything. Didn't have to.

The island was deserted; there wasn't even a place within walking distance to have coffee. I saw that already the boatman was there to pick up the girls to go look at wildlife. There was a tiny, scattered settlement but it was two miles down the road. And today we were going back light; nobody was coming home. The girls were camping at a beautiful tree lodge and we'd get them again tomorrow. So it was just us watching the birds and the girls all charging down the beach now, laughing, shouting, free.

I envied them as they ran away from the plane, from responsibilities or the fears that had crept up like fast growing vines, choking my windpipe. There was pretty much no one else on this island; they owned it completely and so were letting out war whoops and kicking off their shoes and running their city pedicures into the frigid water, laughing and splashing, not a care in the world – to my eyes anyway. I would have given anything to be one of them right at that moment.

We had some time before we had to turn round: there was a large amount of silage piled into the back, which, although light, is not very nice to travel with. Luckily, it was warm enough to leave the aircraft open, give it a bit of an airing.

On any other day, the bright fresh air and warm sun streaming in would have been absolutely delightful. Today, it felt mocking, even as the laughter of the young girls faded into nothing and the birds were the only creatures you could hear once again. I felt very far from home. I felt like I didn't really know where home was. Because I had, I now realised, begun to think that it would be where Hayden was. That he was home.

Nalitha sat me down in the front row and brought me a cup of coffee; Erno went out to smoke one of the nasty little dark cigarettes he liked, while Nalitha gave me a cuddle. I stared at my phone like it was a living thing I was too terrified to touch.

'Are you going to call him?' Nalitha said. 'There might be an explanation.'

'What do you think?' I gestured. 'Maybe he was talking to that sheep-pig Babe.'

'And the sheep-pig Babe retired to Dubai,' said Nalitha, nodding. 'It's possible.'

I hung my head.

'Oh God,' I said. 'Oh God.'

'There's loads of guys,' said Nalitha, trying to be encouraging, but that made it worse. Far worse. That assumed that it was over, that it was dead. That we were already over. I started to cry again.

'I want that one,' I said.

'So you're just going to ignore him telling massive lies ... I mean, he is in HR, isn't he?'

I nodded.

'And isn't impersonating a pilot a crime?'

'Only if you try and fly the plane,' I said. 'I think you're allowed to just drop it into casual conversation.'

I sniffed loudly.

'Oh God,' I said. 'He's so interested in my job all the time. I thought he was interested in me!'

I remembered how excited he'd been to go see *Top Gun* with a load of pilots and I thought – oh my God, what an idiot! – I thought he'd been excited to see my friends, to hang out with me. I shook my head in disbelief.

'Oh God, I've been just a great big fat *fool*,' I said.

'You haven't,' said Nalitha. 'He's just . . . he's just showing off.'

'To impress girls!' I said. 'So he can sleep with them! While he's in Dubai and I'm not!'

'I never really saw you in Dubai anyway,' said Nalitha. That set the tears off again.

'Oh lord, I'm sorry,' said Nalitha. 'Do you want me to hack into the instruments and bring down his return flight?'

'Kill an entire passenger load just because he's in it?'

'Yeah, you know. Collateral damage always a risk in vengeance.'

I swallowed.

'I thought . . . I thought he might be the one, Nalitha.'

'Maybe he's concussed?'

I stared at the phone.

'Are you going to call him and give him a chance to explain?'

I was still staring at the phone. I couldn't do anything just now; I was hysterical and worked up and deeply, deeply wounded. And my brain was working overtime to find a simple, innocent explanation, and coming up short.

We fell into silence, and I watched a sandpiper on the beach, not afraid of the huge metal bird, chirruping happily to itself as it dipped its long beak into the sand, poking for food, completely happy, sun on her feathers.

'Oh lord,' I said.

'Come on,' Nalitha said. 'It's a short day. Let's get Erno to fly us back, then we'll go have a couple of glasses. Hammer it out. You'll be fine.'

Nalitha spread out on the front row seat and refused to put her seat belt on, but we ignored that and Erno took off south-south-east, the plane gathering more speed than she needed. We had so little weight on board, we could have practically taken off like a Harrier Jump Jet. She was a light thing of flashing metal and silver wings, born to be in one element; to be in the air like fish were meant to swim.

People complained about flying being unnatural with these miles of cabling and riveted aluminium, but being in the air was the only place *Dolly* wanted to be. She would even flap and twist a little on the ground, hating driving or reversing, wanting nothing more than to be soaring up to the clouds. We were up to two thousand feet today, with not a cloud in the sky so the air was clear and sweet. There she was free to do what she wanted to do and feel the air across the top of her wings.

I looked out of the window. There was chatter on the radio of an incoming weather front moving swiftly. I frowned. Clouds were building up out to the side, like Lego blocks towering and turning themselves into a city in the sky. Erno groaned in irritation as I craned to see it. Then he groaned again and I turned round. Erno wasn't, as he normally was, calmly holding the control column, watching the instruments and his watch and exuding vibes that he was very much only counting down the minutes till he could be back on solid ground again, looking for his next meal. Nalitha had once said if you could teach a wolf to fly a plane, that would more or less be Erno.

He groaned again.

'Erno?'

As I looked closer and Nalitha got up, it was clear that something was wrong. Erno was white and dripping with sweat, his eyes closed.

'Erno?!'

Nalitha dropped to her knees and loosened his tie.

'Can you hear me? Are you okay?'

'I feel very, very bad,' said Erno, his voice a moan.

'What did you eat for breakfast?'

'Usual.'

'What is usual?'

'Four sausages, four bacons, two hash browns.'

Nalitha and I exchanged glances.

'Well, that would do it,' said Nalitha.

I didn't think about how my life was falling apart, how bad things were, my confusion about Hayden, my nerves, fear and worries. I didn't think about any of that. All of it vanished, and everything I had ever learned kicked in.

'Erno, assuming control,' I said, banking the switches and pulling forward the rudder before I even knew what I'd done.

Dolly bounced slightly beneath me, but it was straightforward enough. I felt a slight tremor of wind and checked the speed. Sure enough, something was blowing at us.

Erno was breathing hard; Nalitha was talking to him. We

were about thirty-five minutes out of Carso. I glanced at the pair of them; I would have to radio something to the tower.

'Tell me where it hurts,' Nalitha was saying.

'I can't feel my left ...'

Suddenly, he slumped. His belt held him in the chair, unmoving, but he had clearly lost consciousness.

'Bollocks,' we both said at exactly the same second.

Chapter Eleven

Squeezing into the tiny space – it's about the size of the front of a very small car – Nalitha had unbelted Erno, who had slumped gracefully to the floor despite being a big, heavy man. But surely any heart issues would have come up in his medical? He was still breathing. I picked up the radio.

'Mayday mayday mayday,' I said into the radio. 'MacIntyre Air pilot incapacitated. Now below minimum crew complement. Aircraft . . . '

My throat went tight. It used to be you could fly this plane single-handed. Not these days.

'Aircraft under control. Stand by for further instructions.'

The tone of the air traffic controller's voice didn't change an iota. With utmost calm, he simply said, 'Clear for immediate landing; Inchborn INB cleared MacIntyre Air.'

I didn't have to pull up the charts to see; I knew exactly where I was. Halfway down the archipelago, past Larbh, with Inchborn hard ahead on the starboard side, before the mainland. Below, the waves had got choppier than the flat calm they'd been that morning, but it still looked bright ahead. Behind was the worry.

'We're too close,' I said. 'We don't have time to do a proper descent. I'll have to bring her round.'

'Can't we fly him to a hospital?' said Nalitha. 'He needs to be in hospital.'

I shook my head. 'Can't fly with one pilot, Nal, you know that. Absolutely not. It's the law. I have to put down the first suitable place I can. Which is here.'

The hospital was a further forty minutes' flying time, plus the airport. It wasn't legal or safe.

'But we might lose him!'

'I'm sorry,' I said. I'd have to go round until I could find a good angle to land at. I could do it, I could do it, I was telling myself.

'Request air ambulance to Inchborn,' I said into the radio, so they could scramble the helicopter immediately.

Nalitha was trying to bring Erno round. He looked a terrible colour, a nasty grey, and she was incredibly worried that he might remain unconscious.

'He could go into cardiac arrest at any point,' she said. 'Erno! Erno, come on!'

The radio crackled to life again to confirm they had the helicopter en route and confirming that *Dolly* was cleared to make an emergency landing on Inchborn.

'But I'd get her down quickly,' said the voice. 'There's a cell on your tail.'

He meant the storm, and he didn't have to tell me that. I could feel it.

Nalitha tried the Inchborn radio frequency a few times but

there was no answer to warn the grumpy man we were coming in to land, and sooner rather than later.

'He's probably just ignoring us,' I said, concentrating hard on everything I needed to do to land safely.

'Well, he won't be ignoring us in six minutes,' said Nalitha. 'Oh God, Erno, come round!' She lightly slapped his face. 'He should be lying in the recovery position.'

'He can't,' I said grimly. 'We're coming in to land, and it's going to be choppy. He has to be buckled in.'

I started going down. But we were far too close, and it was still far too tight. The beach was too short. There was no way I was going to make it. I tried to calm down. There was no way anyone could make it.

Abruptly, I pulled up the nose and pushed us into the air. I'd go round and give us another go. That was fine. Perfectly normal behaviour. Anyone would have done the same.

My hands were trembling on the control wheel – but I had her. And then we came face to face with what had previously been behind me.

The clouds were now skyscrapers; vast black tower blocks rising up on all sides, overwhelming. You can't hear thunder over plane engines, but we both saw the jagged flash of lightning.

'Buggeroo,' said Nalitha.

The speed of it coming on was unexpected. I'd seen the forecast that morning: it should have been a hundred miles north, miles away from us, cracking over Iceland. It shouldn't have been here. Not now.

Normally you can run from a storm front; duck or weave underneath or over the top of it; simply divert. There was no diverting. We had to set down as quickly as possible, with a vengeful God blowing before us.

Dolly stuttered and dropped through an air pocket, the collision of the warm and cold air. We were jolted up and down immediately, Erno bouncing off his chair like a doll.

'Crap,' said Nalitha.

There was nobody there to land this plane. Nobody but me.

Chapter Twelve

'Buckle in,' I said to Nalitha. Her face was set. ATC was jabbering at me, telling me, I knew, to get my bloody wheels on the ground ASAP.

'Should we jettison the cargo?' said Nalitha.

'No,' I said shortly. We couldn't even if we wanted to, which we didn't. Nalitha was brilliant, but she didn't know planes like I did. We were bucking in the air. It felt like a giant hand was scooping up the tiny plane and playing with it. I pushed back, feeling us tilt unsteadily. The forces on the metal were getting stronger by the second; the roaring of the wind was audible even over the headphones. Nalitha was still trying to raise the Inchborn man, with no luck. I had to turn out of this wind before it pushed me up too far; before I couldn't get back to earth at all.

I banked at well over forty-five degrees. *Dolly*'s old joists didn't like it, but we had to get round and face the right direction; we had to lose the height. Bringing her into Inchborn was bad enough; I certainly couldn't risk Cairn, where there were houses and barns.

It was strange, but I didn't think of being afraid. Not like I had been before. I didn't think of Spain a tiny bit. I was entirely focused on what was going on and what I needed to do, the years of training kicking in.

We were too fast; we were too full of fuel to be where we were. *Dolly*'s alarm started to sound; she didn't like being this close to the ground and was telling me to pull up. I desperately wanted another shot, another go to get round and bring us in in spirals, but now the entire sky was a huge black bundle with a great, flat wall of pounding rain. I couldn't risk the crosswinds behind the clouds, which were flickering with lightning. They could pull us in and spit us out, a tiny ball of metal.

Nine hundred feet, eight hundred.

It was closer now every second, the expanse of the normally golden sand turned grey and ominous because the sun was blocked by the vast monstrous shadow which seemed to be taking over the world. The storm was the world now.

The alarm grew louder, but I was committed to landing now. Erno was unconscious beside me, Nalitha behind me somewhere, as quiet as she had ever been.

Bring her down, Morag, I said to myself. Bring her down. And suddenly nothing else mattered: not my fears, not the job, not my future, not Hayden. Not Gramps, not the airline. Not every stupid problem in my life. Nothing but this – me and *Dolly* – versus the world, versus the elements.

Three hundred feet, two hundred. We were too fast. Too close. I could do this. I could. I could . . .

I eased the throttle, pulled back steady, steady, steady . . .
BANG!

133

The wheels hit. Too fast and too heavy. I could feel it. The plane flapped, protesting, bouncing high off the ground. She wanted to be flying again. She didn't want to be dealing with the pull and drag and physics of the two-dimensional world and the unforgiving flat earth. I completely understood. I didn't want to be there either. We smashed back down furiously, still moving. I wanted to close my eyes. I couldn't.

A vicious crosswind caught us, pulling us off centre, almost pushing us into the sea. I over-corrected too quickly, swore and spun us at full force almost into the dune. Stones pinged off the wing, and Nalitha swore quietly under her breath. If we pinioned too quickly, we could spin right round or even tip. But in fact my problem was more pressing: we were running out of beach.

I glanced at the instruments. I had two choices: to pull back, speed up and take off again – which wouldn't help the situation one iota – or to slam on the brakes with all my might, keep a steady course and close my eyes and hope to God we didn't end up smashing into the cliff at the end of the beach.

'Bollocks,' I said again, but quietly, under my breath.

I jammed on the brakes, smelt the burning asbestos as we churned up sand, *Dolly* squealing in protest. There was a banging noise and I realised sickeningly that we had burst one of the tyres. Now I had even less control.

'Come on,' I said. 'Come on. Come on, *Dolly*. You can do it. You can do it.'

Nalitha's eyes widened as the cliff face filled the windscreen, towering up above us, huge and merciless. We barrelled towards the grey monolith, seemingly powerless to stop, as the huge machine, so graceful in the air, so unsuited to the terrain it now found itself – with much exhaust pumping and a huge yell of effort from me – gradually, agonisingly slowly, finally brought itself to a stop, the tip of her nose practically touching the cliff.

There was silence for a second. I felt the thudding of my heart, sweat under my armpits. The grey stone filling the cockpit windows made it feel like it was dark, still; the entire plane trembled in the rising wind. But we were down. We were down.

'Bloody McArseholes,' said Nalitha, but quietly. I could only nod. I breathed slowly in and out, mouth, nose, mouth, nose. Inside, I felt jubilation rising. I'd done it. I'd done it. We were there.

I jumped up, out of my belt, looking at Erno. Together, with shaking hands, we unbuckled him and got him into the recovery position. He looked terrible – deathly white and sweating – but he was breathing and he had a pulse. Nalitha ran to the first aid box and took out the oxygen canister, fitting it over his nose and mouth. I radioed again, to be told that they hadn't been able to despatch the air ambulance because of base conditions of more than force six but the smaller helicopter was coming and so we should keep monitoring Erno and giving him oxygen.

Then I stepped up and opened the door.

It was as if we had landed on the moon, or a distant, violent planet that didn't want us there. The wind whipped into my face immediately and, despite it being four o'clock on a spring afternoon, the sky was completely black. Sand blew up from the long yellow beach in stark waves of its own. The sea was even worse: a toiling, smashing wild animal with a billion claws, roaring at the world, a beast of inestimable power that wanted to churn, to consume in its fury. It was a hell of a storm. I worried suddenly how far the tide would come in. How I would get the plane turned around.

One thing at a time, I told myself. I walked around the

bottom of the aircraft, unable to hear myself think, rain lashing my face.

Finally, I could make something out over the tearing noise of the rising storm that shrieked in my ears. It was a *flip flip flip*. I glanced up. A helicopter was trying to chop its way through. Bright yellow, it was a sturdy thing – not the air ambulance, but a navy search-and-rescue job, designed for high winds and for winching sailors from the high seas. I realised suddenly that I was freezing. I hadn't even noticed before. But now I relaxed a little bit. Real professionals drove those things; they'd manage from now on. Though even as I was thinking that, I saw the helicopter veer this way and that and attempt a couple of different ways to side-swing onto the beach when I realised that of course landing on sand was hard for them too; they would be looking for a safer spot. I ran to the top of the dunes, where there was a stronger surface of flat rushes and seagrass, and waved my arms in a cross, noting a large enough flat area for them.

The helicopter followed my waving arms, and I got well out of the way as it managed to set down without too much sand rising up and engulfing the entire craft. The pilot stayed at their controls as the paramedic jumped out. There were no time for niceties.

'Patient?'

Getting Erno out of the plane was tricky – he was a big, big fella. The paramedic, after checking him over and congratulating Nalitha (who beamed) on her first aid – took the head of the stretcher while Nalitha and I, as carefully as we could, took Erno's legs and we all carefully manoeuvred him down the narrow steps, which suddenly seemed as steep as a mountain, and into the maelstrom.

'I can only take one of you,' he shouted. Nalitha and I looked at each other.

'Don't be daft,' I shouted over the storm. 'I have to stay with *Dolly*.'

'But you could fly out and fly back with reinforcements ... ?'

'I can't fly out in this; don't be daft. You need to send someone back. Anyway, I've got a burst tyre. You'll need to get it ferried up here before I can move the plane. You'll need to wake Gramps, get hold of it, get it out on the first ferry, okay?'

Nalitha nodded and we loaded the stretcher into the helicopter. I patted Erno on the forehead. He was so clammy.

'Go well,' I said. Erno muttered something in Finnish. Nalitha held his hand.

'Come on,' said the paramedic, looking at the sky. Far away in the distance, there was a skinny flash of something that had to be more lightning, fast approaching.

'We have to move.' He looked at Nalitha. 'You've done well.'

Erno, under the oxygen mask, was indeed stirring. I took his hand.

'You're going to be okay,' I said, giving it a squeeze.

'He is if you get out of his way,' said the paramedic, but not unkindly. The pilot was motioning them urgently, and I waved them off. Erno even managed a tiny wave, or at least a lifting of his hand. Nalitha gave me a thumbs-up and I gave her one back, then a quick hug. Her heart was still beating as fast as mine was.

I finally stood back from the dune, hand over my eyes to avoid the sand thrown up by the helicopter getting in them as it vanished. Having spent the minimum time possible on the ground, it disappeared into the dark clouds. That was when I began to think about the clear and evident predicament I had found myself in.

Part Two

Chapter Thirteen

I looked around, frowning. There is, by the way, lots of training – lots – about how to get a plane safely down on the ground, or onto water. There is absolutely nothing that tells you what comes next. Once you've got the plane down and everyone more or less safely out of the aircraft, there's not much after that. Presumably you're meant to be set upon by cheering hordes who hoist you up on their shoulders.

I pulled out my phone. There was no signal here on an uninhabited island at the far northern edge of the world, nothing at all. Of course. Nothing but birds and the oncoming storm.

Well, there was one person here though. I was tempted, in fact, to retreat to the plane, turn on the power and bed down there. And surely Nalitha had left some muffins somewhere ...? But I was going to need that power for other matters. When someone came back in the morning with new tyres and, well, ideally, my grandfather if he hadn't been ill in bed. I sighed, clambered back up the steps, grabbed Nalitha's waterproof from inside the door and radioed our status back to ATC and the base.

Much sympathy was given, along with the rather depressing news that the storm was turning into a three, possibly a four. I sighed. Well, Nalitha would let everyone know we were safe: *Dolly* and me.

I felt unnerved about having to go back out in the storm, which was now throwing handfuls of hail against the cockpit windows. Visibility was absolutely terrible, even without a cliff in the way, but I had to look for this man here, wherever he was. I tried to remember exactly where the house was. It wasn't far, I knew, just the other side of the dunes. The island was small enough you couldn't get lost for that long, surely? We had a large storm light in the locker, and I took it out.

Why hadn't he heard or seen the plane land? It was, after all, a huge machine descending from the sky. I tried the radio again, all local frequencies. Nothing at all. This was very bad of him: he should be manning it, especially on a day like this. What if I was a boat about to smash up on the rocks? I thought crossly. Or, even worse, a plane making an emergency landing? I could have needed him out here with beacons. And he was ignoring his post. Stupid mainland idiot, he had absolutely no idea how much we all relied on one another up here; how much you depended on your neighbours and friends and colleagues. The archipelago was interconnected – that was the whole point of it. It wasn't a holiday home for hermits.

I realised suddenly that I had thought 'we' as if I were a part of it too. Well, for now I was.

I know it sounds ridiculous to be scared on an island smaller than some people's back gardens – like those explorers who die just out of sight of their shelter, only feet away. But the visibility was so awful. It was absolutely impossible to see anything outside, barely a hand in front of your face. The wind was going to try and blow me over.

On the other hand, it was impossible for me to stay here if that lazy fecker wouldn't answer his radio. The plane was listing too, restless sitting on the sand where she wasn't designed to be for long periods of time. The burst tyre was making her unstable, and although I knew the tides for the normal landing section of the beach, this section I didn't know about. Whether the water ever came all the way in I had no idea. I couldn't even examine the sand, try and catch a clue, see if it was covered in seaweed or not. The wind howled; the thunder bellowed overhead. I sank into my waterproof and told myself that it would be completely ridiculous to cry at this moment. My phone sat there like the worthless hunk of plastic it was.

Okay, I told myself, standing up. Come on. Let's go. Slowly, almost dragging myself, in the pitiable hope that the storm would recede, I shut down the heating, the lighting – all the systems. Secure and off. I flinched as I felt a huge wave of rain and hail hitting the side of the plane.

It was so stupid. This dumb old plane we'd all been teased about, which I had left behind so long ago for my huge new horizons – now she was like a dear old friend, rattly windows and all. Her familiarity had grounded me – literally. And while everything was awful, there was also relief cascading through me – that I had been up to it. That we had landed, however shonkily.

'You'll be all right,' I said, hoping against hope that I was right. Then I pulled the lever and twisted open the great door, the howling night throwing itself straight back at me with all its might. I set my jaw and stepped out.

A line from an old Susan Cooper book rose to my mind: 'tomorrow will be beyond all imagining'. It was beyond imagining outside. The sheer force. I had flown over and around storms, and occasionally caught the tail-end of something that hadn't moved quite as predicted. I didn't mind a bit of turbulence; it was what we were trained for, even though I knew the punters didn't like it. I found it exhilarating, controlling the plane, trying to find the smoothest path, and I was endlessly intrigued by how the air whirled and found its own way from high to low, from warm to cool, clashing, taking up space. Since air is invisible, we cannot see it move. I think Van Gogh did though. The first time I saw *Starry Night* I could see he was painting the air, and the wind, and how everything around us is moving all the time. We just ignore things we can't see, then get surprised by rain. But if you follow the glorious ebb and flow and push and pull of weather patterns, tugged this way and that across the sky by the sun and the moon and the tides, you see it. And sometimes you can't avoid it.

At the base of the steps, I stepped into icy water. I was wearing ridiculously unhelpful shoes: the flat black lace-ups that were part of my normal uniform, which I'd adopted here. Though I was wearing two pairs of socks: my feet always got cold flying. Gramps wore flying boots all his career, and so should I. I swore as the wind whipped my hair and my hood back and spray stung my skin.

I looked at the burst tyre. The rubber had of course flown off completely, leaving the metal rim which now was thoroughly stuck in the mud. There was absolutely no moving this aircraft

144

now; it was as if we had buried an anchor. I shone the torch at it, trying to stay out of the way of the waves. Bugger it. Bugger bugger bugger. I should come back with reinforcements when the storm retreated ...

I looked into the terrifying blackness of the roaring water and high waves. One splashed me up to the waist, then another one came which looked as if it would hit the top of the steps. I had to get off this beach, and quickly: this was incredibly dangerous.

I ducked under the fuselage, something I never ever do – it felt like bad luck, even then – and scrambled up the height of the dunes with my wet feet. Getting out of the water was made notably worse by suddenly being in the full path of the gale's fury.

Suddenly, a huge light swept over me and I nearly collapsed with relief, thinking someone had come to rescue me. The next second, I dimly realised that in fact I was out from the shadow of the cove, and what I was seeing was the lighthouse, turning its automated eye on me, before going back to warn those still at sea. There were no other lights on the island at all, apart from the thirty-second sweep of the lighthouse's great beam. At least, I thought, I was not at sea. At least I was not, like Erno, en route to the hospital. There were poorer souls than me at large tonight.

I pulled my now drenched jacket closer round myself, cursing for the thousandth time my stupid shoes, and looked out to see where the hell the building was. Suddenly a horrible thought occurred to me. Not answering his radio even though he was legally required to have it with him – no lights on? I mean, what did I really know about this guy? I didn't even know his full name. Was he actually there? Perhaps something bad had happened to him. Who knew why people took this weird job? I remembered the story of Archland, one of the furthest islands of the archipelago. People had gradually moved south to more populous islands, with schools and post offices and so on, until there was only one person left: the old shepherd who refused to leave his hearty flock, who lived in an unheated stone bothy with no electricity or running water so he burned peat and grew potatoes and vegetables and made his own cheese. He had lived for fifteen years as a hermit, until one day one of the geographic ships were visiting the island and found him dead by one of his stone walls. Gramps had told me the story when I was little as a positive tale, saying that when he flew over it he could still hear him whistling, happy as Larry. He said that he remembered the huge flock of sheep and would occasionally fly low, drop the hermit some chewing gum or give him a wave. The old shepherd never wanted him to come down, never seemed to lack company.

'Happiest man I ever knew,' Gramps always said, but Jamie and I had found the story completely terrifying, the idea of the hermit sick ... getting sicker ... imagine knowing you were going to die ... all by yourself ... then still haunting the ground you walked on, the same patch, the same tiny island, for ever and ever, and if you ever went to his little ruined hut – it was still there, you could fly over it, although the government had taken it over for possibly nefarious purposes so you weren't allowed to land – and went inside, would you hear a *tap tap tap* from a shepherd's crook at a window, as a pair of fierce, burning eyes shouted that he wanted to be ALONE?!

I shook myself. Things were bloody bad enough without scaring the crap out of myself with made-up stories. There would be a perfectly simple explanation, of course there would. And in the meantime, despite the jacket, I could feel myself shiver, my teeth rattle. It was freezing up here.

I screwed up my eyes. Bloody lighthouse light didn't swing round long enough for me to see where I was going. Every time I picked a direction, I couldn't see a damn thing. The roaring of the wind was crazy too. I took a deep breath and tried to remember roughly the way I'd seen the man storm off before, when we'd dropped off the box. And I tried to remember if I had ever seen, years before, lights in the dark mornings of winter. We must have done. It was on the west side of the island, I was sure of it, near where the two beaches met like a curving spine made out of gorse.

I marched on, keeping the lighthouse on my right, terrified of walking in circles, trying not to think about the waves lapping at the foot of the plane. There was no point in shouting; nobody could have heard me even if I was standing right next to them. Visibility meant it might as well have been night time though the dark was heading in anyway. It was as awful as anything I had ever been out in, and all I could do was keep my head down and march on.

I thought back to the books I had loved as a child: stories of Antarctic adventure and disaster. Was this what it was like, trudging on and on through the dark and storms? I looked up again, but it was pointless: I could see nothing, and my torch-light was already fading, the batteries not quite up to it. I sighed.

'CRAP!' I howled into the wind. 'CRAP CRAP CRAP! BUGGER IT!'

And at the very next minute there came a noise and I jumped out of my wits.

Chapter Fourteen

It was a throaty chuckle, strangely perceptible even through the storm. A terrifying, goblin noise. It was the laugh of a man who had stayed behind when everyone else had gone; who had been driven mad by the solitude, or who was mad before and needed a place to come and express his madness ... The deep chuckle came again, out of the dark, and I suppressed an urge to scream.

'Who the hell is that?' I shouted pointlessly. 'Where are you?'

My heart was beating so fast I felt like it was jiggling up and down. Suddenly I broke out into a cold sweat all over, my teeth chattering as I swung my torch wildly.

'WHO IS THAT?'

The howling wind, the thrusting rain, the quiet chuckle. My eyes blinked as I tried to widen them: was he going to attack me? Was he laughing at my predicament before leading me off into the dark, into his outhouse, to do God knows what ... ?

My torch finally pointed towards the ground, and I jumped, full up with shock and then a gushing relief so warm and so profound that I felt tears pricking my eyes and a sudden intense urge to pee. A chicken was standing at my feet, not looking up at me, just gobbling, as if asking furiously for an explanation as to why the world had turned so black and strange and horrible.

'Oh my God! Chook, you gave me a shock!' I said, blinking back the lump in my throat. 'Jesus.'

I spun around. Chooks didn't wander too far from where they got their meals, in my experience, so I waited for the light-house's flash once more and saw, just barely, the grey outlines of a house over the headland, about fifty metres away.

'Oh my God,' I said, then remembered something I'd read about chickens. 'Don't look up into the storm,' I said. 'You'll just fill your beak up with water and drown.'

I bent down to pick up the animal, who squawked loudly in alarm and juddered away from me. Not quite knowing what else to do, I followed it.

I realised my mistake as I reached the door, a sopping, dripping, deafened, terrified, bedraggled mess, the chicken squawking crossly at my heels in the hope that I would have food for it. This was the back of the house. It was a huge, solid, flat-fronted manse-type structure of grey stone built, I would say, when the Victorians were still getting over the Georgians and before they started to put twiddly bits everywhere (I am not an archi-tecture expert). That said, it was beautifully built too, possibly as a home for the head monk, or for the priests who came and went from there. The last of the monks hadn't left till the 1850s, possibly lured by the bright lights and fleshpots of Oban, but there had been priests there, and the island had been a place of pilgrimage with religious meetings and conferences right up till quite recently, when the Church of Scotland had finally turned it over to the heritage and bird people. The house remained more or less habitable, by the looks of things, although dark and closed up from here. There was a shed leading to a coal cellar, and what appeared to be several outbuildings with spades and wheelbarrows left around.

I inched my way around the side of the house, my eyes mostly shut from the driving rain, until my fingertips hit the outside of a large bay window – and thank God, there was a warm light beaming from it. I looked in – only to be confronted with the sight of a large hairy man, who immediately screamed his head off.

I have never killed anyone – I realise that's not a statement most people ever have to make out loud but sometimes as a pilot you just do – but I would say the closest I got to it was just there and then specifically. I screamed back of course – I didn't know screams were contagious, but they are. And then I realised that, from a different perspective, somebody was having a cosy night sitting inside on an uninhabited island when a terrifying black figure with tendrils of long dark soaking wet hair had suddenly appeared at their window.

By the time I had done enough pointing at the door and pulling down my hood to reveal I was not in fact a serial killer or the spirit of a long-dead ghost and he had opened the door, he was bright red and aghast, and I was absolutely mortified.

'Jesus H. Christ,' he said, staring at me wide-eyed. The warmth of the house was instantly appealing; I was desperate for shelter, desperate to get in as the wind and the thunder beat at my back.

'Can I come in?' I said quickly.

'But ... who are you? Where did you come from?'

We were howling at each other over the noise.

A huge sluice of rain went down the back of my neck.

'Can I come in?!'

He frowned.

'I don't know. Are you a ghost or a murderer?'

'No,' I said. 'Although if you don't let me in, I may have to turn into a murderer.'

He came back to himself then, stood back and ushered me into his hall, which had a stone floor I immediately started dripping onto.

'But where did you *come* from?' he said plaintively. 'Oh my God. Is there a shipwreck? Is there a boat washed up? Are there more?'

He plainly didn't recognise me, which showed just how desperate it was out there.

'There could be,' I said. 'But how would you know, seeing as you *haven't got your radio on*?'

He frowned again as I bent down and took off my shoes. More rivulets ran over the grey stone. I started to shiver.

'The radio's broken,' he said. 'Fraser just left it. I've sent away for a part, which is hard to do when you ... have a broken radio.'

I blinked and pulled off my jacket.

'So I have written a letter to the manufacturers and was waiting for the next time the ferry came to take it with them or the plane— Oh!'

151

He had finally recognised me.

'Oh my God. I know who you are. You're the pilot. Oh my God! Have you crashed?'

'No,' I said rather stiffly. 'Thanks to my excellent handling, I landed the plane perfectly well, thank you.'

He looked out into the early darkness.

'Are there more people out there?'

'Just me. We had a medical incident. The helicopter managed to get them out ... Seriously, can you just not hear anything in here?'

I paused to listen. But then I understood immediately. All I could hear was the wind rushing round the house, rattling the ancient window frames. The rain and hail were mixing up and throwing themselves against the glass. And then underneath the wind, rain and hail, there was the crackle of a wood fire and strains of some soft sweet music playing in a distant room ... It sounded like Neil Young.

He shook his head, and then collected himself.

'Oh my God, come in, come in! I'm so sorry ... I didn't mean to leave you dripping. Get out of those wet things ... Would you like a bath? There should be enough water ... ' He thought for a moment. 'Yeah, there will. I try not to use it but it is there. And are you hungry?'

'I'm guessing you have eggs?'

He frowned again. 'How did you ... ? Oh God, are the chooks all right?'

'I wouldn't say they're delighted,' I said. 'But I only saw one.'

'Oh, that will be Barbara. She's always moaning and wandering off.'

'That sounds about right ... '

He was wearing an old checked shirt with missing buttons,

very old moleskin trousers and a Fair Isle sweater which was almost as much hole as sweater. His hair needed cutting and his beard was out of control – he was, I found myself thinking briefly, the complete opposite of Hayden – and his face looked as cross as it had when I saw him on the plane.

He caught me looking at him.

'I wasn't expecting company,' he said defensively.

'I'm sure I don't look my best either,' I said.

He snorted, which I felt was unhelpful.

'Morag,' I said.

'Gregor,' he said, and turned and walked back up the hallway.

The interior of the house was old and very, very shabby. It was only inhabited by passing visitors, I supposed, who didn't much care if things looked nice or not, or were smart or not. There were stone floors throughout, and dust and spiders' webs on the ancient light fittings. The lights had brass fixtures, half hanging out of the wall on wires. There were no pictures on the walls; the entire hallway was cold and cheerless.

He caught my look of disdain immediately.

'I'll show you into the east wing then, shall I?' he said.

'What?'

'Oh, you just looked like you were disapproving of the house.'

'It's just . . . ' I looked around. 'Sorry. I suppose it always looks so grand from the outside.'

'Aye, well, there you go,' he said. 'No, amazingly, it's not considered a luxury posting.'

'Well, I suppose it doesn't matter too much if I drip all over it then.'

'Oh aye. Right.'

The bathroom was absolutely hideous, with avocado units that were decades old, and freezing, ripped linoleum on the floor. There were odds and ends of pink soap around and a large frosted window which was rattling ominously in the storm.

I minded a lot less, however, once Gregor switched on a ridic-ulously old-fashioned and almost certainly incredibly dangerous electric heater set in the corner of the ceiling, which glowed an alarming orange. On the other hand, it heated up the room incredibly quickly.

The large towels were many times washed and patched up, but this had made them soft. The clawfoot bath, to my utter surprise, filled up incredibly quickly with steaming hot water. I suppose when you didn't have to share your water pressure with anyone else . . . Also maybe he didn't bathe. I knew Fraser wasn't a fan.

Gregor left me to it, then a few minutes later he knocked gently on the old bathroom door – it didn't have a lock, priests presumably not requiring that type of thing – and smiled apol-ogetically, carrying a large pile of clothing.

'Sorry,' he said. 'I had a look. There's loads of clothes in the house but they're kind of all like this. They were left here.'

'So they belong to . . . what, a dead monk?'

'That could probably be an artisanal selling point in the city.'

I half smiled at his joke and accepted the clean, old, faded pair of striped pyjamas and a large, soft, grey knitted jumper, and he retreated again. My body slowly ceased shivering, and the nerves at the ends of my fingers started to spring painfully back to life.

Oh, that bath. That bath. When I get to the end of my life and have to relive it, it will be that bath where I will want to be.

Firstly, I had opened the large medicine cabinet – not to be nosy, just by sheer force of habit. Okay, of being nosy, but even so. Who doesn't open medicine cabinets?

To my surprise, it was filled with a bathing gift pack. I squinted at it. That couldn't be right. For a second, I wondered if Gregor lured women here in the rain, suggested they have an innocent bath ... Then I realised how unlikely it was that he would have somehow poisoned Erno from afar on the off-chance that I'd be flying over his island ... And then I looked at the gift pack more closely. It was so old, the bath cube had crumbled into nothingness. Probably left over from one of the couples' attempts. Maybe they thought they'd have lovely bubble baths together, before they'd degenerated into long silences and month-long huffs.

Anyway. They weren't here and if anyone accused me of stealing their bubble bath, I'd do my best to replace it. I uncorked it – there was suddenly a heavenly white magnolia scent – and poured the entire thing in, where it bubbled and steamed ridiculously.

There was a bookshelf in the bathroom. Actually there was, I found out pretty smartly, a bookshelf in every single room in the house – at least one – as well as books piled up everywhere where the surface was more or less flat: books on the stairs, in the stairwell, under the beds, beside the beds. I glanced through the bathroom shelf and fell with delight on an old Jilly Cooper which had somehow slipped in between the *Ornithological Guides to the Northern Archipelagos*, and a Wisden's from 1974.

Stripping off my wet clothes and putting them under the terrifying industrial-red heater to dry, I sank my exhausted, aching, adrenalised body into that deep, scalding, scented bath – yes, it is up there with one of the nicest things I have ever done in my entire life. The bubbles covered me like a huge fluffy duvet.

There was another knock at the door.

'I'm in the bath!' I shouted.

'Okay,' said the voice. And a hand sneaked round the doorway and left a large tumbler of whisky on the floor, just in reach.

Chapter Fifteen

Coming downstairs after my bath in the flannel pyjamas and the old sweater – my underwear had amazingly dried out by the heat lamp in no time; I didn't want to think what it would do to the generator – and fortified by the whisky, I felt sleepy and very slightly woozy.

Everything was a disaster, I knew that in my conscious brain. Everything tumbled into my mind like small planes spiralling down into disaster. But, I told myself, we hadn't been that. We hadn't been the small plane that didn't make it. I had done it. I had piloted her through and, God willing, Erno would be okay. It didn't stop me thinking about it though, as everything hit me all at once. Oh God. And there was nothing – absolutely nothing – I could do about it.

The storm whipped on, its fury apparent in every window frame. I couldn't let myself think about everything that was happening. Right now, my phone was a useless block of plastic and there was nothing outside this strange house that I could do a single thing about, at least until the storm had passed. I knew there was a lot coming my way: I was going to have to sort out the plane and the parts and my job and, OMG, Hayden and my life, and kick into professional gear. It was a lot. But right now, at this precise moment, I couldn't do a single thing. There was nowhere I could be, nothing I could possibly be working on. It was a strange feeling, and I would have been wrong to think it could last.

I knocked shyly on the sitting room door, but it was empty. I slipped inside, feeling sick.

This room – the old parlour – was wonderfully cosy. The curtains were closed now around the bay window, presumably the best way to stop any more terrifying rain or soaked monsters emerging from the storm.

Of course this room was lined with books up to the ceiling on ancient built-in bookshelves, which were sagging in the middle, each stuffed two or three deep. I suppose if you were stuck here for the entire winter season reading is exactly what you would do – Netflix was out of the question.

Gregor was still nowhere to be seen. The music, I saw, was playing on an old-fashioned record player which scratched, and I was briefly mesmerised as I watched the vinyl go round and round. Gramps still had one too but I'd never seen him actually play it.

I sank into a surprisingly comfortable old horsehair armchair, still holding the dregs of the whisky in my hand.

And to my surprise, I was so exhausted that I almost fell asleep – but then, just as my head was drooping, there was a great rattle of thunder outside as lightning flashed, and like a shot of adrenalin I sat bolt upright, remembering it again. Oh my God. Oh my God. What was going to happen? Was Erno all right? Was he *dead*?

I tried to hold on to the wave of his hand, the way he had been talking to Nalitha, the relative lack of concern of the paramedic. He was going to be okay. This time, my traitorous brain said no – or tried to. He'd be tucked up now, safe and warm in his bed. Nalitha too.

Then I thought of *Dolly*. Oh God. What on earth was going on out there? The thunder was still crashing; the rain still pouring. It was almost impossible that so much water could possibly invade such a tiny space, but it was going for it regardless. In my mind's eye, I could see my poor plane. I imagined her just sitting there, sinking deeper and deeper into the sodden sand, the wind blowing one way, silting up her legs and tilting her further and further until she fell, tipped into the waves. They would gently start to carry her out to sea, and she would go past the seals, past curious whales and creatures of the deep. Perhaps she'd be as curious to sail on the swirling dark waters as she had always been to fly, and coral would build on her wings and eels would be indistinguishable from untethered floating seatbelts—

Oh, for goodness' sake, I told myself. You're being ridiculous. I had never ever in my life felt this way about a plane. Airbuses – A320s – they had different characteristics, and I certainly preferred some to others. But I didn't have an emotional connection to my planes. They were just a job, that was all, like a laptop or a toolkit.

Dolly though. I remembered being tiny, running out across the bright yellow sand, Gramps yelling behind me, telling me *never* to cross the runway and taking my hand to lead me up to what I then thought was a *huge* gigantic plane ... I had a vivid sense-memory of mounting her steps, pausing carefully at each one before reaching the cockpit and dangling on the leather seats, my feet not touching the floor, which was good, because we *never ever* touched the steering pedals.

The thought of her, my Gramps's pride and joy, alone, drifting on a dark sea, ruined along with the company, our dreams, our plans, was terrible. Oh God, how was I going to tell everyone? They were going to think it was all my fault. Maybe even that I'd done it on purpose to get out of working for the company, to get Gramps to sell up. Word would have got around now, that Callum Frost had been there.

I gulped, and tears started in my eyes. I was stuck here too, with no radio, no phone— No, Nalitha would tell the ferry – or rather, everyone would immediately know the second they'd scrambled from the helicopter, and they'd all come for me tomorrow. I told myself to calm down, but I didn't appear to be listening to myself as I was shaking and trapped in a loop of panic.

The door was pushed open and Gregor entered backwards. He was, I noticed, carrying two plates and a handful of cutlery.

He caught sight of my face as he turned around.

'What's the matter?'

'I'm worried about my plane,' I said, unable to keep the wobble from my voice. He frowned.

'But you're all safe?'

I nodded.

'But . . . I'm worried about the plane.'

His brow furrowed even more.

'Is it . . . a magic plane? With a soul?'

'No!' I said, stung.

'Right then,' he said. 'So every person is safe?'

'My grandfather's company might be ruined!'

'But you're safe?'

I shrugged.

'I'm not sure.'

He looked down. Then he proffered a plate of food.

'I can't get sad about metal, sorry. Eat.'

I followed his gaze. The plate was slightly steaming and smelled amazing. There was brown rough-hewn toast dripping with melted butter under a huge pile of gleaming yellow scrambled eggs, with two pieces of salmon over the top.

'Are you a vegetarian?' he asked as I looked at it. He seemed slightly sullen, as if he was going to fall out with me if I was after him making me another plate of food.

'No,' I said.

Weirdly, my body seemed to know it wanted food. I found myself grabbing a forkful, realising I hadn't eaten since breakfast. Turns out there's nothing like a terrifying emergency landing ahead of a storm to bring about an appetite. Slowly, I found my panic receding as I took one mouthful, then – almost immediately – another.

The salmon was rough-smoked, salty and chewy, nothing like the slimy pink stuff you get at the supermarket. The eggs were full-bodied, liberally sprinkled with salt and very creamy. The bread was nutty, and the salted butter had melted on it just exactly enough.

'Oh my God,' I exclaimed. 'This is amazing.'

'Sorry there's no lemon,' he said. 'I think someone tried growing some in the greenhouse, but it's not having any of it.'

I shook my head.

'It doesn't need it. That's just to hide the taste of cheap salmon. It's ...' I put down the fork. 'Did you smoke this yourself?'

He shrugged and tried to look modest.

'Aye, well. There's a smoker here already. This isn't my first season.'

'It's very good. And are those from the …? Are these Barbara's?'

He shrugged.

'Aye, maybe. And Karen's probably; she's a great layer.'

'Did you give them those names?'

He scratched his head while I kept eating. It was absolutely one of the most delicious things I had ever tasted, simple and plain as it was.

'You baked the bread?'

'I baked the bread.'

'Have you got a bread-maker?'

'Is this an examination of some kind?'

There was only one more ingredient on the plate. He looked at me and I looked back.

'Not the butter?'

He shrugged.

'Like I said, I've been here before. I've had some time on my hands.'

'You have a cow?'

'Of course I don't have a cow.'

I put the toast down slightly gingerly.

'What is it then?'

'Lindsay grazes his sheep here sometimes,' he said quietly.

'Is he meant to do that?'

'Keeps the grass cropped. Easier than mowing.'

The Lindsays, I knew, farmed Cairn, the next island south on the archipelago.

'He brought sheep over on a boat?'

'They like it. It's a day out.'

'Is it though?' I said, frowning. 'So they cut your grass and you milk them?'

'They eat my delicious grass,' he protested. 'Feels like fair exchange.'

I put down the toast.

'Och, don't be weird.'

'I'm not being weird!' I said, feeling weird.

'So you can land a plane on a beach in a storm but you're scared to eat butter that came from a sheep even though you just ate a hen's periods *and* the actual flesh of a fish.'

I didn't have an answer to that, and I knew I wasn't going to be able to resist finishing the toast anyway; it was so crunchy and delicious. I closed my eyes as I took my last bite of the salty, rough salmon, the smooth, creamy eggs and the nutty toast all together. It was heaven, and I looked at the empty plate regretfully.

'Thanks,' I said, for more than the food.

I got up after eating with a groan, offering to carry the plates through to the kitchen.

'Ah, just leave them,' he said. I frowned.

'It's no trouble,' I said.

'I'll get them later.'

I put them down on a table, then found myself watching them. I really did just like everything neatly put away.

'Do you have a dishwasher?' I asked politely. He snorted, then picked up a heavy book, put on a pair of round glasses which looked older than he was, and rather like they came with the house, and went and sat under a lamp.

'You can sleep in the second room on the left upstairs,' he said. 'It's made up.'

'Uh, thanks,' I said. 'But I'm going to have to have a look at the radio. Let people know I'm all right.'

'It's missing a part,' he said. 'I told you, remember? I'm waiting on a part from the mainland.'

I eyed him severely.

'I cannot believe they gave this job to someone who can't fix a radio. You can make butter out of a sheep but you can't fix a radio? Surely that should be on the job description list?'

He pulled down his glasses.

'I have a joint undergraduate degree in history and biosciences, fifteen years' experience in the field and a PhD in avian science from the University of the Highlands and Islands.'

'And you can't fix a radio. Are those even your glasses?'

'What has that got to do with anything?'

'Nothing. Can you tell me where your radio is?'

He sighed.

'Is rescuing you from the storm and providing you with food and shelter not enough?'

'You mean, not leaving me outside to die?' I said. 'Do you want a lollipop? Also, I think fixing your radio is probably quite a good way to say thank you.'

He gave me an unimpressed look. I had actually been ready to gush my gratitude for the bath and the food, but he was treating me as if I was some total rando and acting as though he did this all the time. Or that I was a total inconvenience. I mean, clearly I was both a rando and an inconvenience, but he didn't need to make it so obvious.

Normally I wouldn't be so chippy though. I mean, I had had a hell of a day and had a lot going on and, frankly, men were not at the top of my agenda of favourites at that moment. Then, glancing down at my striped flannel legs, it hit me. Another reason I was feeling bad – obviously I am a very cool professional pilot and all of that, etc. – was because I was genuinely cross that I

164

had turned up looking such a fright that he had taken me for a creature of the night. Which is ridiculous, but then I had caught sight of myself in the mirror before I got into my bath, and my dark hair looked like a witches' brew, and I had mascara down my cheeks and my eyes were bloodshot tiny holes and my lips were pale and cracked from shouting and screaming and running about in the cold, and so on. Honestly, I looked like Haggis McBaggis in the very worst way. So I was pretty annoyed that I had met this man – who was completely unattractive and covered in beard – in his old stupid jumper with holes and his stupid furrowed brow, and he'd decided that *I* was a daft old crazy-looking bint that wasn't worthy of *his* time.

Is this how Hayden saw me? Some bedraggled, plain creature, barely worthy of notice, just dull old Morag, compared to the blonde Amazons? I had now fleshed out the girl he had been speaking to when he'd pocket-dialled me so that in my head she was Scandinavian, about six foot tall with perfect skin and a perfect figure and shiny blonde hair.

If even this monstrous weirdo, who lived all by himself as a hermit in a house at the end of the earth – literally on the tip of the world – if even *he* didn't respond to me as a woman in any way ... well, was it a surprise that Hayden was a bit distracted? Had I been an idiot all along even to think it was possible?

I had a lot more important things to worry about of course but ... Well, I had noticed. Because of course I wondered ...

'Just let me see your radio,' I said in a humbler, more resigned tone.

He barely looked up from his book.

'Why don't you believe me?' he said. 'Did you really think I'd just popped out to the cinema instead of answering your SOS?'

'No,' I said. 'I know this will come as an amazing surprise to you, something you could never really have imagined before, but some girls can fix radios.'

He blinked. Then he took off the glasses – he saw my gaze follow them – and stood up.

'Might as well take this through while I'm here,' I said, picking up my dirty plate.

He looked at it.

'Sure,' he said finally. 'Want me to put your name on the lease?'

Then he turned round and left the sitting room, and I followed him, annoyed with myself for spoiling the atmosphere. But I had to let people know I was okay.

Chapter Sixteen

As soon as I left the range of the cosy wood-burner, the house suddenly felt freezing, in marked contrast to when I'd first arrived and it had felt warm. Now, though, I tugged the old jumper around me more closely and shivered.

We walked up the stone corridor to the kitchen, which was at the back. It reminded me of Gramps's kitchen, with its big stove which gave out a dim orange light, burning all the time. There was a large dresser with crockery and an open press filled with ancient-looking tins, soap powder, treacle in tin jars and pickles, jams and preserves in old glass dishes, signed and dated with stickers. It was dark, but not cheerless.

Gregor led on, however, through a door at the back of the kitchen. It led to what at one time must have been a wash-house. It was strange to think that the priests and monks who had first lived here must have had servants to do their laundry and cook their meals. Men of God, but also men with useful women around to do their dirty work. There was still a large butler's sink as well as a washing machine that looked more or less dismantled and hadn't worked for years. And, on a shelf, a radio that looked like something from the last war.

'You are kidding me,' I said in my most sarcastic tones.

'What?' Gregor said, scowling.

'This is your radio?'

'I have absolutely no idea how you were born on the archipelago and keep expecting people to have state-of-the-art satellite systems,' he grumbled.

'They do on Larbh,' I said.

'All I have to do is okay the boat to come in, and very occasionally you guys,' he said. 'Nothing ever happens here. That's the whole point. Apart from the school trip once a week when the boat docks, which really interrupts my work.'

'You want to stop *children*?'

'They throw eggs.'

'You have one source of human interaction a week and you're trying to ban it?'

'Well,' he said. 'Believe it or not, some people quite like peace and quiet.'

'*That doesn't mean that you let your radio run down.*'

I was genuinely cross with him. I suppose I was cross with everything, and he was bearing the brunt of it.

'You are on a tiny rock in the middle of the North Atlantic,' I said. 'Pain is the name of these islands. They were the last stop for any sailors looking for the North-West Passage, or going to the North Pole to explore, or to look for whales. Every square inch from here on out is running with blood. There are hundreds – thousands – of wrecks of ships beneath the waters of the archipelago. Even now, it's really dangerous to live up here, clinging to the northern latitudes. I don't know why you're so

168

blasé about it. You can see what it's like. If you hadn't been here, or I couldn't find you, *because your radio wasn't on*, I wouldn't have lasted the night. And this is *spring*. I would have *died*.'

He looked a bit guilty but didn't say anything.

'What if one of the children hurt themselves?'

'Well, that would certainly solve my visiting children issue.'

I made a Marge Simpson noise, walked up to the radio and turned the most likely-looking knob. Actually, I recognised it straightaway: Gramps had had one when I was small. Normally families with a large working radio system spend a lot of time telling children not to touch them. Not in our family, of course. We were generally encouraged, though Jamie wasn't interested in the slightest.

But I was. As I touched the old Bakelite knob, felt its weight in my hand, wiped away the dust and felt it hum to life, I remembered again how strange it was to move along the dial and hear snatches in foreign tongues, which were sometimes harsh-sounding to me or like shouting or singing or speaking very fast and excitedly, or slowly and slurred. None of them I understood, but I was enthralled every time. And in between the voices there was of course the crackling which I thought was the water of the seas between nations, until Gramps explained to me that it wasn't. It was air, electrons even, bouncing around everywhere, which the radio picked up. Everything, he explained, had a sound. Everything hums. Nature is never silent; it's just that normally we can't hear it. Some of the static is other things too: microwaves and other radios. Some of it, Gramps explained, is background radiation from the Big Bang, from the very dawn of time.

I had been immediately transfixed, spending hours trying to hear things – even aliens might make noise, if it was all atoms in the universe. Or sometimes a voice would appear out of the blue – once, there was a loud 'Jeremy, what *are* you doing?' in a very affronted tone, but then I could hear no more of that conversation.

We are just fish at the bottom of a sea of air, Gramps always used to say. All of us, marching along the dark, heavy bottom of the sea, so immersed in air we never think about it. And only those who fly, he impressed upon me, could escape it, could reach up and get closer to the sun. But to move through the air, to dance in it, you first had to understand that it was there, for ever crackling with life. I knew I wanted to get up there to be among it.

I smiled slightly as I pulled on the cracked leather head-phones. They felt familiar. Only a sniff behind me reminded me that Gregor was still there.

I turned the knob. There was nothing but static; crackling electrons from every corner of the universe. Nothing else at all, not even the distant ping of a ship passing or a pattern of beeps.

'The power's still on,' he said, 'so I don't know what's up with it. It's lighting up. I just can't find anyone.'

'You had it on FM,' I said.

'Really?' he said.

'No,' I said. 'Not really.'

I pulled the headphones off.

'Did you check the antenna?'

'Uh … no.'

'Where is it?'

'Uh … '

I tracked the line up the side of the lean-to with my eyes.

'Oh,' he said.

'You didn't check when you arrived?'

'I have checked,' he said shortly, 'for thirty-nine species of nesting tern.'

I gave him a look.

'Are they good at fixing radios?'

I stepped away.

'Okay, well, there's no point going up to look at the antenna now. Did it seriously not ever occur to you?'

He shrugged.

'I was going just about to write to the manufacturer.'

I was about to make a tart response about getting Finn to solve all your problems till I remembered that Finn had been running that boat for twenty years and there was absolutely nothing he didn't know about fixing anything, not least radios, and it was probably an entirely sensible plan.

'But ... what were you going to do if you broke your leg?' I said.

'Lay out a big help sign with pebbles,' he said. 'You'd have flown over it sooner or later.'

I considered this.

'Okay, well, what if you'd broken it inside?'

'Set something on fire.'

'Huh,' I said. 'Is there not ... ?'

I glanced around.

'There must be.'

'What?'

'You must have a Morse code set here.'

He shrugged. I looked up at the old dusty shelves in the lean-to. What looked like old washing machine parts – ancient rusty tools and boxes of nails and other things that looked like somebody thought they might be useful at one time – littered the area.

'You can't do Morse?'

'No,' he said. 'Once again, I am—'

'You have a PhD, yes, yes, very good.'

'I don't understand why I have welcomed you into my home when you needed help and you're genuinely being so rude,' he said quite mildly.

I prickled immediately: I didn't realise I was being rude at all.

'Am I being rude?' I said.

'Well, it's slightly better than the cannibal ghost I thought you were when you first turned up.'

I thought about it. Outside, the wind was still doing its best to knock us over.

'But you're not prepared,' I said. 'When I fly, I have to check everything a million times because it's so dangerous, and because I have to keep people safe. And it just seems that you don't even care about keeping yourself safe.'

'People lived without radios for a very long time,' he said.

'No, they didn't!' I said. 'They had terrible accidents and lay in ditches till they died of tetanus.'

He blinked.

'Look,' he said, 'can't you just accept that you're stuck here for, like, a few hours? And that it might be ... faintly inconvenient?'

'Not really,' I said. 'How much does the tide come in on the north side of the beach?'

He frowned.

'Where I landed the plane ...' I elaborated.

'Oh. Well. Not too much ...'

'Right up at the top end?'

He shrugged. 'I don't know. I don't really go up there. And in weather like this ...'

172

'Well, that's why I'm asking. Seriously, I'm trying to find out if I'm going to lose a plane – an entire plane – and enquire after my seriously ill colleague, and let my family know I haven't been killed in a storm, and you act as if . . . I'm demanding a hot tub in my room.'

'I realise it's been difficult,' he said, his face full of irritation. 'I'm just saying that however much you tinker with other people's stuff in here, you're not going to be able to get a message back to the mainland tonight, so we might as well hunker down. There's plenty of food. Get a good night's rest and try again in the morning.'

'Just give up, you mean,' I said.

He looked at me, clearly infuriated, then threw up his hands.

'Oh, fine, you do whatever you like,' he said.

'Well, I could hardly make things any worse,' I retorted, my fear and anxiety spilling over into genuine irritation now.

He turned around to go, and I turned back to the useless radio – and just as I did so, all the lights went out.

It was pitch-black in the lean-to. Pitch-black, locked in a cupboard, can't-see-your-hand-in-front-of-your-face dark.

I froze.

'What the *hell* did you just you do?' came a strangulated voice which sounded very much like it was trying to keep itself calm.

'Nothing!' I said. The static on the radio jumped and suddenly stuttered to a halt as if to contradict me.

'You've shorted the whole place out! By messing about with the radio!'

'No, I haven't! I didn't!'

'Oh God, that's all we need. Was it not enough for you to be stranded – did you have to make it worse for me too? Teach me a lesson about, what . . . my poor radio management skills?'

'Well, I was just saying your radio should be— No, of course not!' I said. There was a massive crack of thunder right above us, and a vivid flash of lightning briefly illuminated the fact that we were both still standing exactly where we had been a moment ago: he was trying to get out through the door, his face set. It felt a tiny bit like a horror movie.

Nobody spoke for a moment. The static had cut out with the power. It was extraordinarily, spookily quiet. I didn't want to have to ask this question, but I had to.

'Do you know where the fuse bo—?'

'No!'

His voice sounded embarrassed now. I fumbled in my pocket and, thank goodness, there was my phone. Useless as a phone, obviously, but ...

I turned on my phone torch. Thank God it still worked, and there was light. I blinked and followed it around.

'Good,' said Gregor. 'Let's get back to the sitting room, where I can at least see and be by the fire.'

'*You* go to the sitting room,' I said. '*I'll* find the fuse box.'

He appeared to consider this.

'Fine,' he said. I lit him fumbling his way back through the kitchen and into the hallway, then resumed poking around in the lean-to, without success. I then felt my way along the walls until I found the fuse box under the stairs. So that was something.

Unfortunately, turning the breaker on did absolutely nothing. It wasn't the fuses. It must be the generator. It probably had water in the windings.

Slowly, I straightened up. It looked like Gregor had been right all along, which was absolutely infuriating. I slowly made my way to the sitting room, turning off my phone torch as soon as I could since there was barely any battery left. And of course nowhere left to plug it in.

Inside, the warm glow of the fire had been augmented by several candles – ecclesiastical, by the look of them – dotted here and there. Gregor was sitting, back to his book and his glasses, and barely glanced up as I came in.

'I think the storm must have flooded the generator,' I said in a more conciliatory tone.

'I'm sure you're right,' he said, folding his arms.

'Well, I can take a look at it in the morning.'

He nodded.

'You can sleep in the second door to the left at the top of the stairs ...' he reminded me. He stood up and lifted a candle. 'Here.'

'I'm sorry about your generator,' I said.

'Well, you shouldn't have touched—'

'It wasn't me touching the radio!'

'I'm sure someone will come and rescue you in the morning.'

'I'm sure they will.'

I took the candle and turned around crossly, marring my exit by stumbling on the doorframe on my way out. I have never wanted to get away from somewhere faster in my entire life, and I've taken embedded winter mountain flying.

Chapter Seventeen

There was no doubt about it: the bedroom was creepy. The hallway was creepy, the stairs were creepy – and creaky – and the landing was creepy. There was a faint scent of the pretty white magnolia on the air, which my front brain knew was just the old bath oil I'd found in the bathroom cabinet a couple of hours before, but to my now overtired and feverish imagination, it was the trail of a ghost ...

No, stop being an idiot, Morag, I kept telling myself. You're a scientist and an engineer, this is ridiculous. And there have been too many scares tonight. The lightning, the near-crash, that bloody chicken.

I peed as quickly as I could. There wasn't much I could do about my teeth, but I rinsed my mouth out – there was plenty of water, thank goodness for small mercies.

Then I tiptoed, utterly freezing, across the unheated hallway. There was linoleum underfoot, slippy to my bare toes. There were several closed doors off the corridor. I hoped I would get the right one. Second to the left. Off the stairwell. That was it. I tried a rattly old round white handle, heavy in the large door. It opened with a click.

The room inside had a chill to it, that strange sense you always get when a place has had nobody in it. Which logically would assume that people leave a trace, which led me back to ghosts again – but I banished that thought as quickly as I was able to; I was completely overwrought.

It was a plain room, barring the now inevitable lines of bookshelves. They smelled musty, but it wasn't an unpleasant scent – quite the opposite, in fact. The house itself, although cold, wasn't as damp as I'd feared.

The bed was a small brass double, with an incredibly old-fashioned counterpane on it, fringing hanging down from it. Underneath were actual sheets and blankets, no duvet, tightly tucked in as if it were a hospital.

I went to look out of the window. Oh God. My own hollow-eyed reflection, lit only by the candle behind me, was frankly terrifying. I realised, ridiculously, that I was too scared to carry on standing by the window, just in case I saw another face peering in at me despite the fact that this was the second floor. This was so stupid. I dived into bed, pulling the counterpane around my shoulders to stop from shivering. Inside, the bed felt as cold as outside.

Beyond the window was endless nothing. Normally I did not mind the erasure of the boundaries between land and sky. When I could see nothing but sky, with the occasional cloud wafting past far, far below me, I felt completely happy, plough-ing through my element, at one with the air above and with the ground below me.

Here, though, in front of my eyes was a churn: an unhappy

maelstrom of three elements – air, earth and water – all at war with one another, wrestling for territory, demanding and striking one another. You could not see where the ground began, or see if the rain was coming from up, down, left or right. There were no glimpses of the moon or stars through the fast-moving clouds. Only the regular forks of lightning zapping through showed any direction in the madness.

I was tiny; I could feel it. A tiny dark blob on a tiny island, which was the tiniest speck in the middle of the sea in the middle of a bunch of other specks. All over the great wide curved earth, people were living perfectly normal lives, getting up, going out in the sun, going to work, kissing their loved ones.

When I was at school, we were taken to an exhibition called 'Field for the British Isles'. It took up rooms and rooms with thousands and thousands of little terracotta figures, which had holes for eyes, looking up at you. I don't know what the exhibition was meant to make you feel. Our art teacher, Mr Bricketts, said it was something about conformity or uniformity or something. But I didn't think that at all. I loved it. The little figures were so hopeful and optimistic. Of course Garry Robinson tried to steal one and we all got into a massive row and Flora MacGowan threw up on the coach home and the school announced it wasn't going to do any more visits if people didn't behave themselves – but I still remembered it fondly.

I felt that sometimes when I was flying; the idea of little people, safe and warm and tiny, turning their little eyes up towards me. Most people in the world cluster along just two lines: west to east from New York through Europe and North Africa; and north to south through China and India and the countries of the east. Elsewhere, there are great vast swathes of absolutely nothing. Siberia goes on for hours and hours under a plane; the Sahara too. Australia is vast and practically empty. And here too there's water everywhere and only tiny little islands.

From forty thousand feet it's amazing, astounding that humans have found a way to live there. You can't fly over northern Scotland – or Greenland or the Norwegian fjords or anywhere far away from the bustling conurbations of the world – without feeling a little in awe of the pinprick settlements of people in a nearly empty universe.

There wouldn't be a plane passing overhead tonight; everyone would be diverted around Iceland or grounded, not risking getting tangled up with a force nine.

I felt suddenly alone without the endless map I carry in my head. It consisted of flight paths that crisscrossed every empty sky above me and vapour trails that reassured me that someone – many people – were up there.

The lightning lit up the startling landscape outside. The house faced south, I saw now, whereas we had landed on the east beach. Ahead was yet another shore, and there was a neatly tended rockery garden, it looked like, with pebble paths leading down to a stone wall with a wrought iron gate in it which in turn led you out to the machair, the dunes, the wind-flattened grass. Beyond it was the roiling sea. I saw all this in flashes here and there as bouncing lightning skittered its forks across the waves. I wondered briefly if we were the tallest thing for miles around, if we'd attract the lightning ourself. But then, the abbey was behind us. That still had its bell tower half intact. Okay, it was a thousand years old and a national treasure, but I'd still rather it caught on fire than we did. Also, if it had managed to stay up for a thousand years, I rather suspected it could manage another eight hours.

The weather was beautiful, too, I supposed. Everything that happened in the heavens was interesting to me. If I hadn't been so far from home or if I wasn't terrified – partly for Erno, partly for *Dolly* – I would probably have loved watching it. If I had been safe and warm in my bedroom in Carso.

That was odd, I mused. You would think that my first thought of being somewhere safe and warm would be the tiny flat, but all I could see out of the windows were more and more houses, on and on, each mild variations on the original, and you couldn't see the sky at all really; just in slices. The roof was so low, the ceilings so small. You could go out in the garden, I supposed, lie on your back and stare straight up. But someone would probably phone Neighbourhood Watch. Even so, there were so many outdoor 'carriage-style' lamps it wasn't even clear how much you would see, not including the great lights of the city just beyond.

I hugged myself in the cold sheets to get warm. Eventually, I put my socks back on again, and the overshirt, and that helped a lot. I was just considering perhaps adding a towel or two from the bathroom when suddenly my overhyped brain must have switched itself off, because I don't remember another thing. I hadn't been expecting to fall asleep: I expected to lie awake worrying for a long while, or at least be kept awake by the rattle and crack of the storm and the racing waves, which made everything in the old house creak and move like we were at sea.

I think now of guilty men in prison cells: the police say they always sleep because the worst has happened and there is nothing else to be done.

Chapter Eighteen

It took a little while the next morning to remember exactly where I was, and why I was completely twisted up in a massive counterpane. But eventually it struck me, and my heart plummeted into my stomach as I remembered the entire awfulness all over again. Oh my goodness.

A second thought struck me – that although it was daylight in the room, outside it was still blowing a gale with rain and hail still throwing themselves at the windows. This storm was going absolutely nowhere; I thought it would have blown itself out last night when it was screaming at the top of its voice but no, it was still flexing its muscles.

I got up, ran to pee, once again wincing at how cold it was. I remember my dad talking about how they never had central heating when he was small and that we were all spoiled, etc., but I'd never really imagined it. Without the heater on, it was absolutely Baltic in the bathroom; I was popping out with goosebumps even as I tried to pee as fast as I could.

I came back into the bedroom, which in the daylight now had an unloved feel to it. There was a cupboard there but it was empty. I kept my pyjamas on and loaded up the layers with a jumper.

Downstairs, the fire had been built up overnight and was still smouldering, thank goodness. With trembling fingers, I added peat and stoked it into a warming blaze. I had optimistically tried the light switch, but no joy. It had been a silly idea anyway, but you never knew. Any minute now, I would go into the kitchen and try and light a kettle – any minute now – but instead I found myself rotating in front of the fire, trying to get warm all over. I built it up even higher until it was roaring.

The view outside was completely grey, like a black and white photograph, waves leaping up over the grey stone wall I had seen through the flashes of lightning last night. There was a wrought iron table and several chairs in the garden, now tossed to the side like dolls' playthings. The beach looked to be an absolute mess and the dune grass was completely flat on its side. Rain still threw itself hither and thither.

'Bollocks,' I said. I knew I should shut the curtains – they were thick velvet, double-lined, excellent insulation, and the single-paned glass was absolutely freezing to the touch – but I couldn't face it. There was barely any light, but there was some at least, and it was all I had.

Coffee. Please could there be coffee! Deciding to venture to the kitchen, I picked up an old knitted throw from the ancient sofa – it smelled musty and bookish, but not in a bad way, rather in a kind of slightly doggy kind of way. A dog, I thought, would have been really helpful at this point. A big hairy one you could use as an electric blanket. Even Skellington would have done.

I padded through to the kitchen, feeling the cold through my socks. I didn't know how much heating oil the Aga still had, but I was going to have to hope it was enough. There was a warmth coming from the stove itself, but, as I looked around, I could see nothing that looked like a coffee machine. I nearly hit my forehead: of course it wouldn't work anyway if it plugged in. No freshly ground espresso for me.

I saw a stovetop kettle with some relief, filling it with that cold, clear, icy water from the tap. I had a glass of it, straight, and felt breathless and knocked out by its freshness. It woke me up better than coffee could, but I still turned on the hob, using a match, and placed the kettle on it, then looked in the cupboards to see what supplies I might find.

I kept my hands as close to the kettle as I could while it was boiling the water. I had never in my life thought of myself as spoiled, but it felt barely better than being outdoors. Then I quickly opened the back of the kitchen door, just to see if it was perhaps better out there. The howling, freezing maelstrom outside changed my mind very quickly and I pulled the door back straightaway so that it slammed – so hard that it shook the entire house, or felt like it.

Oh God, I had only just realised – the fridge would be off. I opened the door and sure enough it was – but the temperature in the kitchen had to be low enough? I sniffed the small enamel jug of milk. Sheep's milk, of course. I wondered if he had any long-life out the back. He must do, or someone must have got some in for emergencies. I didn't fancy my coffee – or tea, I supposed, if he had bags – with either sheep's milk or long-life, but beggars very much couldn't be choosers.

'What the hell are you doing to my kettle?'

I started and turned round, clutching my woollen blanket around me like some eighteenth-century fishwife.

'You scared me,' I said.

'Okay, we can probably stop scaring each other now,' Gregor said. 'We're the only two people on this island. It's either going to be you or me— Bloody hell!' And he dashed over to grab the kettle, but too late: the bottom had melted. There was a bad smell in the air, now I realised it, and it wasn't just old house, it was melting plastic.

'Oh God,' I said. 'Sorry. I thought it was a stovetop one.'

He stared at me. There was now a hole in the bottom of the kettle.

'I thought,' he said slowly, 'that you were meant to be, like, the sensible practical engineering radio-fixing one.'

'Oh God,' I said again. 'I'm so sorry. I'm just a bit drowsy . . . '

'It's an *electric* kettle,' he said, looking at me with an expression of total disbelief. 'I thought you knew all about electrics and fuses and so on.'

'Okay, I said I'm sorry,' I said, now more irritably. 'I was just trying to make coffee.'

'By melting down a kettle?'

'Oh, you're not going to let this go, I see.'

He stalked past me. He too was wearing the old-fashioned pyjamas that could not possibly have been his to start with, plus two jumpers. It was impossible to tell what he looked like behind the beard and the misshapen clothing; in fact, he looked like he was wearing a potato sack. As did I, I supposed. He took the ruined kettle and put it in the sink to cool down, then opened a window to let out some of the black smoke.

Then he calmly went to a cupboard in the dresser and took out a tiny steel coffee pot with a black handle, filled it with water and set it down on the stove. He then took out a bag from a larger cupboard and I was absolutely delighted to smell immediately that it contained coffee beans. He took a small handful and tipped them into a grinder.

'Wow!' I said.

'What?'

'Nothing. I'm impressed. What else do you have? Secret wind-up Netflix?'

The coffee grinder made an incredible noise as he cranked it, but the smell of it filling the air was absolutely heavenly. I closed my eyes.

He ignored this, peering outside. 'I think it's clearing up.'

'It really isn't,' I said. He did something with the little coffee pot on the stove, which started to whistle. The smell was mouthwatering. He glanced up at the sky.

'Neh, it'll pass.'

'Well, obviously it will *pass*,' I said. I wasn't too keen on a man trying to tell me what I didn't know about weather patterns. 'But right now, it's *here*.'

He poured out two tiny cups of coffee.

'Milk?'

'I'll take the powdered,' I said, holding up the unopened tin I'd found. He frowned.

'What, over the fresh goat's milk?'

'Fresh *what*?! I thought this was sheep . . . '

He ignored me. ' . . . which reminds me . . . '

And then there came a knock on the door.

My heart leaped. Someone had come! It must be the ferry: Nalitha must have got word back and Finn had come straight out, braving the weather to come fetch me! Amazing! I turned round, trying not to catch my blanket on anything. Then I jumped back. Butting the back door, in the howling storm, was a large head with great curling horns coming out of its head and terrifying snake-slit eyes ... I leaped backwards as Gregor chuckled.

'Aye aye, all right.'

He headed towards the door.

'Don't let it in!' I blurted out, not really meaning to. Animals were not my bag, not at all. I preferred my creatures made of steel and aluminium.

'I think,' he said, opening the door, 'Frances has a bit more of a right to be here than you do. She's invited.'

The creature clip-clopped in. She had wiry hair and a curious face that looked like it was perpetually smiling. She bent her head into Gregor's hand, who scratched behind her ears affectionately.

'Aye, aye, lass,' he said. 'I'm coming. She gets her breakfast then we get ours,' he said to me, downing his tiny cup of coffee in a one-er. I didn't follow his example, but sipped at mine. It was warming and woody and good.

Then he pulled down a thick tweed cap on top of his unruly hair, picked up a bucket and disappeared into the storm, Frances clicking along by his side. What an infuriating man. On the other hand, I *had* rather melted his kettle. I sighed.

'Clothes?' I shouted out behind him.

He turned round, frowning again as if I just wouldn't stop demanding ridiculous things.

'Try the chest in the linen cupboard,' he said, flapping his hands as if I were a particularly annoying distraction. Which I supposed I was. But I had problems of my own.

I didn't expect the chest to be much use, and I was right. It contained a collection of clothes people must have discarded over the years, including – and I could not say I wasn't tempted – monks' robes, plus an old priest's surplice with a rather fabulous fiery staff embroidered on it. I wondered what had led to that being left behind. There was a strong smell of camphor – to keep the moths away, I supposed – but it was not unpleasant.

At the bottom, though, was a large and roomy pair of dungarees which I instantly decided would do me absolutely fine, as well as a large thermal vest in a granddad style, a large fisherman's striped top and a bobbly jumper. Thankfully, there weren't any mirrors. Presumably the religious men thought they were encouraging the sin of vanity.

There was, it turned out, a tiny square of mirror – for shaving, I supposed – just above the sink. I looked strange without impeccable make-up; I had washed off the mascara that had run down my face. I wished I had my falsies on. I realised I hadn't gone out without a full face of slap in . . . well, it had been a long time. I studied my face carefully. I didn't actually look hideous, although my hair was climbing the walls without my GHDs. I was used to seeing those curls as my mortal enemy, to be ruthlessly burned out of existence, but actually they weren't too bad. And my skin looked, well, a lot less tanned. But it wasn't *bad*, strictly speaking. A bit pink in the cheeks, but that might just be the cold. I fumbled in my bag and grabbed my Dior lipstick and smeared it on to see if I could look a little more like myself. I didn't. In the dungarees, it looked totally ridiculous. I sighed, and wiped it off again in the cold water.

I glanced out of the window. Irritatingly, it looked like Gregor had been right after all: there were breaks in the clouds and, while it was still raining, it wasn't hurling like it had been. It was quieter too. The noise had died down. The storm was abating.

I went back downstairs in search of some more coffee – there wasn't any, and even better the plasticky smell had gone – instead there was a beautiful loaf of bread, warm from the oven, cooling on the top of the stove. It was too hot to touch, even though my mouth watered just looking at it. Nearby, I saw an opened jar marked 'Marmalade 2022'.

I closed my eyes. Toast was one of my definite no-nos. Really. There's a lot of sitting down being a pilot, and irregular mealtimes, and all that airline food. And then I'd been in a new relationship which meant lots of lovely meals out and nice wine and nights on the sofa and oh my God, I was *not* going to think about Hayden right now. Absolutely not. Okay. But still, I have to try really hard not to gain weight, the single most totally absolutely boring thing in the universe.

So I mostly (with many failures) tried to avoid bread and potatoes and rice and basically absolutely everything I like. Love, in fact. I bent my face closer to the loaf. Oh my God. It just smelled absolutely divine: a small, puffy thing of beauty, steam still coming off it, with a honey-coloured crust . . .

Oh, he wouldn't mind, would he? He was hardly going to eat an entire loaf of bread himself. I glanced around but he was nowhere to be seen. I supposed he was very busy with his best friend, the goat.

Okay. I would heat up some water for tea and if he hadn't reappeared by then . . . I mean, he couldn't deny me breakfast – it was a human right, surely.

I didn't feel up to tackling the coffee pot, but found a large box of teabags and boiled the water in a pan. It took for ever, and I was still very wary of the milk, so black tea would have to do.

I took one more look round – then greedily tore into the bread with my hands, unable to locate a bread knife.

It was still hot, the steam rising from it. I took a pat of the butter from the non-working fridge, and it melted straightaway. Then I plunged into the marmalade. I couldn't even remember the last time I'd eaten marmalade. I spread it thickly on the warm golden loaf and lifted it up to my nose to sniff before I sank my teeth into it. Just as I did so, a weak, watery shaft of sunlight finally made it out from behind a cloud, lighting up the little messy kitchen and showing off a large picture of the Last Supper someone had hung up on the opposite wall.

'This bread has been anointed by God,' I said to myself. 'He wants me to have it.'

And I took a huge bite.

I wish I could have savoured it. I wish I could have eaten it slowly; that time could have stilled. All I know is, when I am old, grey and bedbound and everything else has gone, I will still remember how good it tasted.

As fast as the first slice vanished, I found myself pulling more off, slathering it again with butter and marmalade. To stop myself turning into an wild animal, I physically hauled myself away from the stovetop. I had to leave some behind. Obviously. I looked at the piece remaining. It was so small, I thought, gobbling it up, that it was a bit pointless leaving it, really. I mean, he must make bread every day. I mean, it might as well not be there at all when you thought about it. Maybe he'd even think he hadn't made one if I removed all evidence. Or maybe I could suggest that the goat had come in and eaten it. That might do it.

Nearly half a pot of marmalade was gone, just like that. I felt terrible. I devoured the lot – not entirely unlike a goat come to think of it – before I managed to pull myself away. I mean, now the storm was clearing, obviously we were going to get help pretty soon, but even so, I felt rather guilty.

There was another room off the kitchen, separate from the lean-to larder where the radio was: it was a boot room, I discovered, full of Wellingtons and jackets. I chose a set at random and, glancing back at the scattered crumbs rather shamefacedly (it had been a Very Small Loaf to start with, I told myself), I pushed open the door and stepped out into the yard at the back of the house to see if I could figure out just when I was going to get off this rock.

Chapter Nineteen

Everything was mud to begin with. Mud and unidentified objects. It felt like the world had been picked up, shaken and thrown back down again. The wheelbarrow was on its side, as were most of the plants.

The second thing took a moment to notice: the wind had stopped. It had fallen quiet. You could still hear the waves, but they were normal waves, not terrifying crashing feats of nature.

And you could hear the birds again; the gulls were also chattering loudly to one another, complaining again as they normally did. They had been silenced in the storm, presumably diving for shelter like everybody else. I tugged the huge coat around myself, but it wasn't even that cold any more. It didn't feel like the same place. I pulled down my hood and glanced at the sky. The huge scud of grey clouds was moving out, north-north-east; off to upset our Norwegian cousins, I supposed. And behind them there was a bank of clearest blue, almost cheeky, as if the entire sky was protesting innocence about ever having caused a storm, no way, not me. I'm used to ducking and weaving around storms and often they come in and out of grey clouds or damp days. Sometimes, though, it's just like this: as if a curtain has closed over the sky, then opened again to a new scene, clean and fresh and a blank slate for the day. I couldn't help smiling; it really did feel like utter cheek from the weather.

I looked around, feeling the mud pull at my Wellingtons.

The austere grey house didn't look nearly so intimidating in the watery sunlight. I could see more clearly the large, solid two-storey building, which had been built with confidence in a world where travelling by ship was the fastest way to get anywhere, so living on an island was hardly the drawback we'd consider it today. I could see the bathroom window frosted above, and somewhere that must be my bedroom. Ivy grew up the ancient-looking black pipes and spread across the back of the house; it was the very light green of spring and rather fetching.

There was a grey stone path leading from the kitchen door, which I moved down, and on either side, even though it was covered in debris and sand, there was a clear layout of a kitchen garden, with high walls down either side to protect the tender seedlings from the worst of the North Atlantic weather. The little plants didn't look too bad. I was no expert but they looked like rows of carrots, potatoes and cabbages, still safe and warm in their beds. I saw the gate I had stumbled through too, askew on its hinges and in bad need of a coat of paint. I had to go see *Dolly*, check on how she'd fared. But I didn't want to.

I moved forwards, turning back once more to look at the house. There was no aerial on it, nor a TV aerial or a radio mast. I frowned. Then I realised: there must be one on the top of the little outhouse addition. I walked round the other side of the building and sure enough, there it was, fallen from wherever it had started. It was fixable enough, I supposed, though it still probably wouldn't power the radio, as it was too old to take batteries even if Gregor had any, and I didn't think I could trust that he did. I would have to radio from the plane.

I walked further on, then was distracted by a noise around my feet. Glancing down, I saw a chicken – the same chicken, entirely possibly, who had come to my rescue the previous night.

'Hello,' I said crouching down. 'Are you meant to be here, around the kitchen garden?'

'She very much *is not*,' came a growly voice. Looking up, I saw beyond a gate, which had been practically pulled off its hinges – presumably why the chicken was free to wander hither and thither.

'BARBARA!' Gregor shouted. 'Get over here.'

The chicken fixed me beadily.

'You're all right,' I said as she squawked at me.

I moved through the broken gate.

The coop was a mess, with steps collapsing and the wire fencing showing several massive gaps here and there. Gregor was standing with a toolbox, looking absolutely bamboozled.

'It's a mess,' he said.

'Well, yeah,' I said. 'It's local weather; they must have warned you.'

He frowned.

'It's hardly my first time here. But I've never seen it this bad,' he said.

'Where are you even from?'

'Glasgow.'

'Ah, you're a city boy.'

'Yeah, yeah.'

'So you know what you're doing with the coop?'

He shook his head.

'Not really. They just pointed me at the chickens and said, "You know about birds: get on with it."'

I put down Barbara, who immediately made a bid for freedom back towards the vegetable garden. Several other chooks, seeing she was up to something that looked like it might be fun, went to follow her. Gregor groaned.

'Oh my God, what a pain in the neck.'

I was conscious I was taking on a snotty tone again, but I said, 'It can't be that hard to fix.'

'Oh yeah, I forgot you know everything and I'm useless.'

'I don't know everything! I was just thinking: banging a couple of bits of wire in front of the gate to stop the chooks escaping until you can figure out how to fix it properly might not be the worse idea!'

He still looked helplessly at the toolkit.

'Then we can watch a YouTube video on it,' I said. 'Here. You do this; I need to go see my plane. Where's the extra wire?'

He gestured rather pathetically and it made me really cross with him. There were outhouses all over the place and he'd been here before: hadn't it even occurred to him to check?

The weird thing is, they advertised this job from time to time and it got picked up by the national press – could-you-live-on-an-abandoned-island? kind of thing. They always got loads of applications. I mean, let's assume a certain amount were from totally crazy people, but even with that they should surely have had plenty of candidates to choose from?

Although I was desperate to get to *Dolly*, I was equally still

194

putting it off. What if I found I'd ruined her beyond repair? What if she was on her side, or worse, not even there?

I could feel the March sun warming through my jacket. It felt so good – even before the storm, the weather had been fairly grim from the moment I'd arrived. 'In like a lion, out like a lamb' isn't a saying we use much in Scotland about March; normally it's in like a lion, out like an even more annoyed lion, who is also drunk, but sometimes – just sometimes – the sun does come properly out and it feels like a benediction.

So I marched round several of the outhouses, which were filled with the most peculiar old junk. I suppose once anything got to Inchborn, it just had to stay here; bringing things on and off was so difficult when you couldn't drive. So there were all sorts of strange things: ancient desks and odd pieces of machinery, a broken sundial, three sinks, rolls of linoleum and – at the back, behind two broken hoes – a roll of fine wire.

I pulled it out in triumph.

'Okay, this will get us started,' I said. Gregor didn't look particularly happy about it.

'It doesn't need to be perfect,' I said. 'It just needs to be *done*.'

And weirdly, because I was kneeling down and hammering, I got so unbelievably hot that I ended up having to take off first the big jacket and then the itchy jumper. It wasn't actually difficult, nailing chicken wire, and soon Gregor was helping me by unfurling the other end. Barbara squawked and made her displeasure with the arrangements perfectly clear, but I ignored her, and got engrossed in what I was doing, right up to the point where someone stuffed their nose in my ear.

I jumped up yelping, completely shocked. There in front of me, nuzzling up to me, was the pale cream and grey goat, with a long beard and that same clever, inquisitive face.

'Frances!' I said. I wasn't *quite* as freaked out as I'd been when she'd come into the house, but nonetheless she was very disconcerting. I'd rather expected her to smell, but she didn't – or rather she did but it was just of perfectly clean mud.

'She recognises you,' said Gregor, looking over. 'Goats are clever, you know.'

As if listening to what he said, Frances butted me again with her head, but gently.

'What's she trying to do, eat me?'

'How would that work then?'

'I don't know, do I? Maybe she'd start with the socks, then go toe by toe.'

'Okay, well, no, she just wants some affection.'

'How do *goats* want affection? They're wild mountain animals!'

She butted me again. Against my will almost, I scratched behind her ears. The goat nuzzled me happily.

'I mean it! How could she even learn it?'

'From her own mother,' said Gregor, looking at me like I was an idiot. 'She's a living creature. Of course she likes affection.'

'I thought that was just humans. And dogs, I suppose.'

'Why?' he said. 'That's a bit human-centric of you, isn't it? Why shouldn't animals feel everything humans feel?'

'What, like ... mild disappointment at their Wordle score?'

'Emotion belongs to every living thing,' he said severely. 'Hey, Frances.'

The goat turned round and trotted to him affectionately.

'You *trained a goat*?' I said, astounded.

He shrugged, taking a snack out of one of the many pockets on his coat. Frances snatched it from his hand with a happy snuffling noise. I watched them curiously. 'You're not really an animal person?' he said.

I shrugged in turn.

'Not a lot of goats where I live. I normally deal with machines, that's all.'

He nodded.

'Where do you live?'

'Near Heathrow.'

He looked at me. 'That's a place?'

'Obviously.'

Although the funny thing was, it kind of wasn't. It was a place between places, really. A liminal space, somewhere you went through on the way to get from where you were to where you were going. Which made me feel sometimes that I was liminal too; that I lived in airports, that I too was only a stop on the way to places; that I was in transit. But all of that was changing.

'I'm thinking of moving . . . or, my job is moving.'

'Uh-huh.'

'To Dubai.'

He raised his eyebrows.

'That's quite a change.'

'I know,' I said. 'I think it will be amazing.'

He looked up into the freshening air, the streaky sunlight slowly waking up the water-sodden grass, the wind now a light breeze through the leaves, as if ashamed of its early behaviour.

'Och aye,' he said.

'You don't like the sound of it?'

'Not a big concrete fan,' he said. 'Not a big air-conditioning fan either.'

'It's a better climate than here.'

He looked at me.

'You're kidding, aren't you? It's exactly the same except that instead of not being able to leave the house because it's cold you can't leave the house because it's hot. And you can't really deal with that by adding extra clothes.'

'Well, it's interesting.'

'I'm sure it is.'

'Have you been?'

'No.' He half smiled. 'And I don't think I want to get in a "have you been" competition with an airline pilot.'

'Especially when your entire world is four square miles.'

He glanced around him as if he hadn't thought of it like that.

'Well, maybe it is,' he said, and he didn't look terribly upset by the idea.

I straightened up. The barbed wire fence wasn't exactly what you'd call a professional standard job, but it would keep the chooks in, till the next storm anyway. I caught Barbara going for one final charge at the last spot and picked her up.

'Sorry, sweetheart,' I said. 'I'm afraid it's back to chokey for you.'

'Oh, you can let her go,' said Gregor dismissively.

'I've literally just fixed your coop,' I said.

'I know,' said Gregor. 'Most chooks like being safe and having their own spaces and their own place to roost. But Barbara hates it. She wants to be free. You can set her free.'

'Won't she get eaten?' I said.

'No foxes here,' he said. 'Seals wouldn't get to her; beavers don't want her. She'll be okay.'

'Haven't you got eagles up here?'

'Eagle would take her from the coop easy as anywhere else,' said Gregor. 'Won't make much difference.'

'Oh,' I said. 'Oh.'

I glanced down, looking at Barbara who was pecking furiously and giving me occasional side-eye.

'Well then,' I said to her.

'I don't know why you keep being weird when you pick her up,' said Gregor. 'She won't bite you.'

'She might peck me though!' I said. 'I don't want that either!'

'Why, worried about your manicure?'

'Sure,' I said. 'That's why I've been messing about with a hammer and barbed wire for the last half-hour. In *your* garden.'

Barbara fluttered her wings furiously as I bent towards her but, conscious of Gregor's eyes on me, and a sublimated competitive streak, I reached my arm down, stuck it under the bird's stomach and hauled her up as she protested furiously. Then, as I put her down, fluttering, on the other side of the barbed wire, she immediately stomped off towards the beach as if she had some terribly important business I'd been keeping her from.

Speaking of which.

I straightened up, dusted off my hands and returned the toolbox to the shed. All of this, Gregor simply watched. Which did very little for my mood.

'Where are you going?' he asked finally.

'Well, I know you think I crawled up from the depths of the ocean, but there was, like, an actual aircraft that crash-landed here last night?'

'Oh yes,' he said. 'Want me to come?'

'You literally just told me you don't know anything about machines, can barely use a hammer and hate modern civilisation. So, no, I'll probably manage.'

Plus I didn't know this person well at all. He might be the kind of man who liked to stand around broken things, sucking their teeth and making very stupid suggestions. I have met more than a few of those.

'Suit yourself,' he said, but without rancour.

Okay. I had to get to it. There was nothing else for it, nothing else to put it off. I had to get back to my plane, find out the worst.

But presumably by now someone would be missing us? Nalitha would alert everyone. There would be a ferry arriving any minute. Yeah. Every step I took towards the dunes lightened my heart. The sky was a clean washed blue and there was a breeze, but there was warmth in the air, that perfect heather-scented promise of summer on a spring day that you feel early in the year up here – it doesn't always last, of course, as winter likes to pop in and out just to remind you that it is always lurking. But on a day like this . . . Even with everything that had happened, I felt something unusual as I marched over the tops of the dunes, the grey stone house disappearing behind me. The end of the island was visible to my left; ahead was the beautiful ruined abbey, no longer terrifying and sinister in the storm, but instead a riposte, something still standing which storms could not destroy: a testament to the human spirit nearly a thousand years old.

I felt present. I knew there were many other things I needed to be doing; I knew everything was going badly – possibly very badly – in my life. But just here, just now, with the sun warm on my back, my belly full – with a sudden stab of guilt I remembered that I had eaten all of Gregor's bread – it was hard to be truly unhappy. It was possible to feel that worries would get fixed, that just like the abbey, life would go on – changed, perhaps, for Gramps and for the company. But we'd get through. He'd be okay.

It was so gentle now, the light breeze, the soft sun. It was going to be okay. Wasn't it? It was. Surely. Everything was going to be all right. If we could make it through the storm. And I didn't think about anyone whose name began with 'H'.

I almost ran down to the beach – I'd completely forgotten about dune-diving. How could I have forgotten? Jamie and I would throw ourselves down the dunes for hours, cascading, toppling or just collapsing into the light, soft sand under our toes; tireless, as my mother sat on the beach, trying to keep the sand out of our packed lunches with no success at all. Tizer and cheese and ham on pan loaf never tasted better, or a packet of Golden Wonder in the open air, then back for more, and there was paddling or swimming if we were feeling brave.

How could I have forgotten all of that? My hair had untwisted itself again and I knew I must look absolutely mad, curly and free. Suddenly I didn't care. I pulled off the Wellingtons and left them at the top of the dune. I shook my hair behind me and jumped off, tumbling, breathless, laughing, skidding on my way down, sand squidging between my toes.

I did not know how I had forgotten it all when I'd been moving in and out of airports all over the world in that sterile, air-conditioned air, a world of Pringles and signs for toilets and taxis and queues and magazines and coffee shops, all identical and hermetically sealed.

I came to a standstill finally, out of breath at the foot of the beach. I had overshot myself the night before, I saw; doubled back and gone round in circles. It now felt like a nightmare, one that disappears in the morning sun like dew.

It will be fine, I told myself. She'll be fine. I rounded the headland of the cove. She'll be okay.

Chapter Twenty

At first, I could just about make the plane out, and I was delighted. She was still there! She'd be okay! And the radio would work!

I could contact Gramps, get them to send out a fresh tyre on the next ferry – he'd have one in his workshop for sure – get it here and I'd be home in absolutely no time, and back in London for my last simulator. It would be fine.

Better than fine, I thought to myself, as long as Erno was okay. After all, I'd landed that plane. I was well. I was over it. I was going to go and get on with the rest of my life. Hayden would throw himself at me and explain that his phone had been stolen by someone who sounded a bit like him, or he'd had temporary amnesia or . . . well, anyway, my life would keep on, keep moving.

I think my eyes didn't really want to see what was in front of me as I got closer. I think I had been put in such a good mood by the weather settling, by landing the plane at all and my successful chicken-cooping – who'd have thought it? – and, surprising as it was, even Frances saying hello.

Last night, everything had been so dark and bleak and frightening and freezing. And today, the world was completely different. I needed to take this as a sign, I told myself, reaching instinctively for my phone to take a photo of the beautiful day before remembering that of course my phone was dead and didn't have the faintest hope of waking up any time soon. I would have to look at the generator too.

Okay. I could do it. It would be a funny story one day, far away from here in my successful life.

As I drew closer, though, it became increasingly clear that something was terribly wrong.

My brain didn't want to take it in at first; it lied to me, told me it was a trick of the light, or the angle I was walking in the sand, but there it was, clear as the bright blue day. *Dolly* was listing. There was no doubt about it. The port side – that's the side with the door in it – was tilting inexorably towards the waves which were lapping around the one wheel that was still in view. The other was deeply embedded in the sand. Her port wing was leaning down towards the muck. My heart stopped and I ran towards the plane as if there was something I could do.

'Oh no,' I said as I ran. I felt sorry for her now as she sat, squat and tilted on the sand. She looked drunk.

'Oh, sweetie.'

I went up to her on her sloping side – I'd left my Wellingtons at the top of the dunes so I splashed through the freezing water in bare feet, but I barely noticed, not really – and tried to push her up again. Planes are light but not that light; I couldn't budge her an inch. The sand was wet and sucked down the burst tyres; it was like she'd come to land in quicksand. The tide had forced sand onto the drooping wing. And even now I could feel the waves gently but inexorably rising up again. I had to move the plane or the wing tip would end up touching the sand.

I took out the key from my pocket and unlocked the airstair, letting it come down gently. My heart sank because, as soon as it started to open, water started to run out down the steps. While the storm had played out, the little plane must have been completely engulfed. Any little crack, any little hole – water will always find a way. And last night, the sky had been one great maelstrom of water. Twin Otters aren't pressurised; we're not airtight. We are watertight, obviously, but ... to a point. And that point appeared to be a gap at the bottom of the airstair where it met the aperture. There must be some perishing in the lining ... She was an old plane, after all. Nothing that would ever have put people in danger, beyond the odd draught, but when a one-in-a-million accident happened, then all hell broke loose.

The water cascaded down the steps. Oh lord.

I stepped inside. Everything was soaking wet. All over the floor were spilled lifejackets, paperwork, maps, checklists, safety cards, all soaking together in a great black muddy jumble. I made my way to the cockpit, wishing now that I hadn't left my footwear behind.

Every instrument was also soaking. It wasn't remotely safe to attempt to turn her on; I'd spark the whole place and perhaps kill myself. I looked longingly at the radio. But it wasn't possible. As I stood, I realised with horror that the plane was wobbling even further with me standing on it.

I jumped quickly over to the other side, jarring my foot hard against the co-pilot's seat, and let out a panicky yelp. The whole structure creaked and groaned ominously. I had to get out of there. Carefully, I retreated and went back down the steps. It was incredibly difficult to pull them up out of the sand and push the door shut; I felt she was going to topple onto me. But I finally managed it, staring wide-eyed. Was I imagining it or had she had moved closer to the sand even as I'd been there? Had I made it worse?

Oh lord. I realised something suddenly: all the mental energy I'd spent defending *Dolly* from Callum Frost, I'd told myself I was nobly doing it for Gramps. But was I really? Or was it because deep down I loved this damn plane?

The sun gleamed off the windows of the stricken plane as she stood there, looking crippled and lost. I suddenly felt very sorry for her, and for myself. And Gramps, and for everyone.

'Oh, *Dolly*,' I said. The plane creaked in the wind in reply.

Okay, I told myself. There was no point in standing here, watching things get worse. I had to get organised. Get back. Everything could still be sorted out. Couldn't it?

I climbed up the dunes, which wasn't anything like as fun as jumping down them, marching up, hot, sad, not even wanting to turn around and watch my little plane leaning miserably towards the waves. To my amazement, back in the house garden, Gregor had barely moved. He was still standing, scratching Frances's ears. I didn't get it, truly. There had just been a terrible storm, and we were without power, electricity, internet, completely cut off, and he wasn't even trying to fix things, trying to get things back to normal, just standing, staring over the fields like a horse.

I walked up, feeling the dejection in my shoulders.

'Hey,' I said. He glanced at me and frowned suddenly. I couldn't quite tell if his face was stern or mock-stern.

'What?' I said.

'Did you eat my lunch?'

I had completely forgotten about it.

'Uh ... ' I said. 'The thing is ... '

He shook his head.

'Because ... I kind of made that loaf to share.'

I looked up at him. Didn't he realised there were slightly more important things to worry about? That there was a huge very expensive aeroplane dying in the sand on the other side of the dunes?

'Is it possible,' I said politely, 'that your goat ate it?'

He glanced at Frances for a minute, who moved her mild goaty face to his and rubbed up against his stubble. I had the oddest impression that this goat was in love with him.

'I don't think so,' he said.

'Oh, so you'll take a goat's word over mine?' I said. 'I feel that's unlikely.'

'Also, the bread was on top of the sideboard. That's too high for Frances.'

'Goats are literally *very famous for jumping*.'

He frowned again, although his mouth was twitching.

'Are you saying you didn't eat my loaf?'

'Oh,' I said, kicking the ground with my Wellington boot. 'Actually, I remember now. No. I did eat it. I'm sorry. It was so delicious.'

His face looked incredulous.

'That was ... an entire loaf of bread.'

'Yeeaaaah,' I said. 'I know.'

'I mean, did Frances get *any* of it?'

That would have been a better shout, I now realised. Now I felt like a pig and a liar.

'No,' I said. 'I'm sorry. I should have told you.'

He gave me a wry look under those beetling brows of his.

'Also, you should have managed to restrain yourself from eating *an entire loaf of bread*.'

'Okay,' I said, stung. 'Are you going to keep going on about this? I'll make you another one.'

'Do you know how?'

'Nope,' I said. 'I was just trying to make you feel better.'

'Does it work, trying to please people?'

'You should probably try it some time,' I said. 'Anyway. There's no time to worry about that now. Where's the generator? We need to get in touch with the mainland.'

'In the outhouse,' he said.

'The power hasn't mysteriously come back while I was away?' I said hopefully.

'No. No one mysteriously baked any more bread either.'

I rolled my eyes.

I waited for him to ask about the plane, but he didn't.

'Aren't you the *tiniest* bit interested in what's happening with my plane?' I said eventually.

'Is it fine and you're about to leave?' he said.

'No.'

'Well then, not really.'

I sighed and turned towards the outhouse. He was really a very vexing person.

'Okay. Great. Thanks. Let me sort everything out then.'

He shrugged.

'I don't think there's anything to sort out. Apart from lunch and it's a bit late for that.'

I frowned at him.

'We're completely cut off from civilisation!'

'Civilisation has a way of sneaking up on you.'

'I have no idea what's going on with my co-pilot and as far as my family knows I'm dead!'

'I thought that girl saw you get off the plane.'

'Yeah, okay, but I *could* have died after she left last night.'

'Well, you could say that about most nights.' He gestured around. 'The sun is shining, there's provisions, it's nesting season, the chooks are laying and we have peat for the fire; I genuinely don't see what you're worried about.'

'Because not everyone lives like an actual hermit!' I said. 'Some people do have real things to be getting on with! We could lose the plane!'

'Real things,' he said, picking up his hoe and moving over to the vegetable beds. 'I just think we might have slightly different opinions as to what real things actually are. You're the one who keeps checking your phone even though there is literally no possibility of there being any pictures of kittens on it. Sorry – helicopters or whatever.'

I sighed with exasperation and walked past him to the shed.

The generator was a large grey Hyundai model, oily and dusty. There was a heavy smell, given off by several tins of petrol on a shelf above it. I checked first, hopefully, in case it had just run out of fuel. That seemed to me very much something Gregor would just let happen and not worry too much about.

But it became clear very quickly that there was plenty of fuel sloshing around so that wasn't the reason it wasn't working. There was also, sloshing around, lots of water on the floor, and on the shelves and in fact on the one thing that should be kept dry at all costs: the generator itself. Bending down, I saw the culprit: part of the door had literally rotted away. It was carelessness, plain and simple, over something that should have been kept safe, and I cursed it.

Sure enough, the generator windings were wet. It's not like if your phone gets damp, or your headphones, and then you dry them out in some rice, and if you're lucky, in a few days they'll start working again. If a generator is on and gets soaked through, they short. I learned this in training about aircraft engines but it's relevant to all engines really. They were burnt out. Gone. Nothing. I glanced around the shed. You'd need replacement parts. In a well-organised place, you'd probably have some but . . .

No, of course there was nothing. Some screws and wires and a random hammer, presumably for hitting the generator if it ever had problems starting up.

How, I wondered, could someone come and live here with so little regard for their personal welfare? All I ever thought all day in my cockpit was safety safety safety, check check check. It had been drilled into me all my life: be safe. I had chosen my sensible safe job and my sensible safe career and my sensible safe boyfriend (or so I'd thought) and this was . . . the opposite of safe. It was careless and could have been life-threatening. Still was, because without it we had no power, no way to reboot the radio batteries and no way to contact the mainland.

I stared at it in dismay.

Of course, I wasn't . . . I mean, nothing really bad was going to happen. We were ten miles offshore; we weren't on the moon. Someone would come, possibly any minute. Any time. The ferry would come. The weather was lovely. Everything was back to normal.

But it was Sunday, I thought, having to mentally check. Which wasn't helpful as ferries normally didn't run on a Sunday but someone would come by, wouldn't they? Or actually they'd probably send a helicopter over, wouldn't they? Maybe I should draw something on the beach. Someone would come and check we were all right.

Sunday. I had to be in London for Thursday. Somehow we'd have to get the plane moved. Oh lord. We'd better contact the insurers, I supposed. They would need to send a boat for it – the sooner the better. Every second that plane spent on that beach, soaking wet, meant that the situation was getting worse and worse, to the point where she might get unsalvageable.

I couldn't bear the idea of telling Gramps about it, that I had taken his baby, and made such a terrible, terrible mess.

I felt tears prick my eyes and went to wipe them away crossly. They wouldn't help. I hadn't done it on purpose.

But I couldn't stop them. Once the first one came, I got an awful pain in my throat and could do nothing about it except sob quite loudly and let them flow. I was stuck in this ridiculous place, we had no power and absolutely everything was wrong. I wanted to trust that Nalitha was going to get help to us, but how could I be sure? She might be stuck at the hospital, or … well … Actually, my friend would normally crawl over broken glass to help me, I was sure of it. So why hadn't she sent the cavalry?

Chapter Twenty-one

After a proper cry – the kind that makes your face dirty, not the kind that would have made you look pretty if you were being filmed – I wiped the snot off my nose with a leaf, which did not work very well, and went in search of a cup of tea.

Gregor was still working in the garden. He looked up at my tear-stained face.

'What's up?' he said. 'I'm not that cross about the bread.'

'It's not about you!' I said. 'You know the generator is completely fritzed? The building it was in hasn't been looked after, there's no replacement parts and everything is falling apart which means no power.'

He shrugged.

'It's okay,' he said. 'We've got candles. And plenty of peat.'

'That's not the point! The point is there is stuff to do, I have to get off this damn island, I have to figure out how to get the plane off and I have to find a set of clothes that didn't belong to someone who's been dead for sixty years!' I pulled crossly at my hair. 'And I can't believe that we've been totally cut off and you don't seem to care.'

He shrugged.

'Oh, it happens all the time in the winter. You just get on with it.'

'Well, *you* do,' I said. 'Seeing as your job is sitting here on your arse doing eff all. But some of us have lives, thank you very much.'

He looked hurt.

'I'm ...'

'Sorry,' I said immediately. 'That wasn't very fair.'

'Not really,' he said, and then: 'I get it though. I'm sorry. I know you are finding it tough and I know you want to get home. But you will get home, Morag. And everything you're finding tough about being here ... I'm telling you, it's just normal. It's okay. You're safe.'

Something about him saying 'you're safe' threatened to unlatch something in me and make me start crying again. I had to fight it quite hard. I hadn't felt safe since. Well. Since the incident. And because I hadn't really been able to talk about that feeling, not with Gramps, or Hayden or anyone, and nobody had been able to say it. That I was safe.

'Thanks,' I choked out, then headed back to the house in case I really did cry again.

I added some more peat to the fire in the sitting room – the sun was warm, but the house still had a chill about it, being so old and dark, I assumed. Except for the kitchen, where the Aga burned on a peep. I wondered how much fuel was left. No, this was stupid. A helicopter was going to come across any moment. Planes didn't simply disappear out of the sky without anyone noticing. They'd be scrambling everything to come find us. I knew Nalitha would be doing her best. But I still had to check.

I went rummaging on back larder shelves and came up with gold: an almost-new roll of gaffer tape. It was covered in dust, but I no longer found I cared. I found a headscarf in the little dark room too, and pulled my now rampant curls out of my eyes.

I took my gaffer tape, went back outside and found a ladder leaning against a shed wall. I glanced up at the roof, frowning. There it was; I could see it. The antenna was obviously knocked over. And not even by this storm; it had been out for a few days; that's why he hadn't answered it during the storm. Honestly, I was amazed he managed to get both legs in his trousers in the morning.

I sighed and carefully placed the ladder against the wall. Barbara was still following me about; I looked at her and she looked at me.

'Well, I have to go up it,' I found myself explaining, 'otherwise I'll have to live here for ever.'

Barbara squawked at me.

'Well, it's all right for you. You can fly!'

I wanted to ask Gregor to come and hold the ladder for me, but he was nowhere to be found, even when I yelled his name. I tested the first step. It was sound enough. And heights don't bother me. Well, so I'd always assumed, given my job. But I found, as I crept up closer to the gutter, a definite nervousness creeping into my stomach. When I was flying, I could control how high I was. Here, I was at the mercy of a creaking ladder, a windy day and a chicken who seemed quite likely to boot the ladder away any second just for laughs.

I made it to the gutter, which was full of leaves, needed a

clean and was wobbly anyway, and sighed. My hands were shaking, which I hadn't expected. On the plus side, a tiny parapet ran round the bottom edge of the roof, obviously for decoration at one point, but now very helpful to me as I took hold of it and swung myself onto the roof proper. The rake, thank God, wasn't too terrifying.

I scrambled up the slate – there were tiles missing here and there – and sat in the warm shadow of the chimney on the opposite side to the way the smoke was blowing, giving myself a moment or two to catch my breath and, although I wouldn't have admitted it, calm myself down a bit. Then, I glanced around. From up here, the island was mine. The view was extraordinary.

Suddenly it became clear where we were exactly: you could see the chain of islands going back towards the mainland with Cairn and then further north, getting smaller and smaller to Larbh and Archland. Or, if you were that way inclined, you could think of yourself sitting on the spine of a great beast, only the vertebrae visible. That was how people thought of it in the old days: something was sleeping beneath the waves, and if you were very lucky it let you live on its bumps.

The water was calm, a million miles away from the maelstrom that had filled the sky and churned the world upside down just a few short hours before; it looked like pools between the islands. Even the mainland didn't look so far – as if you could hop, step and jump to get home.

There were no boats out, I noticed suddenly. This was unusual; I had never flown over the archipelago without it being full of pleasure boats, ferries, people sailing or pootling about; fisherman. Even in the coldest of weather. I frowned. There would be tankers, I supposed, but they passed far to the north of here; shallow channels and unpredictable harbours meant they didn't like to get too close in case they got stuck. But where was everybody else? I realised I had rather hoped to see a flotilla steaming towards us to rescue us.

I was pondering this when my attention was caught by a black shape to my left. I shifted slightly, enjoying the heat of the chimney on my back and the afternoon sun to my left.

Beyond the front of the house, south of the abbey, was a large clearing next to a small copse of young trees. Trees had thrived on the archipelago thousands of years ago, and they were being reintroduced to combat soil and machair erosion, forming a strong interlacing network against the rising seas. Hardy trees too: hazel and rowan and birch. Gramps sent me the local paper from time to time.

In the middle of the clearing stood a figure that had to be Gregor, completely still. Gregor or a scarecrow, I thought, but I recognised the bull shoulders and the slightly hunched, suspicious stance. What on earth was he doing? I was about to whistle, but I realised he wouldn't hear me, and even if he glanced around he wouldn't see me. I stared at him. He was a strange fish, right enough. What was he even doing?

As I watched, frustrated, there came a sudden flash of movement. I screwed up my eyes. Then I saw it: the flash resolved itself into a hawk.

And then I remembered that when we'd flown away, after we'd dropped off that box – I had forgotten all about it until now – the way he'd stood, just like that, in front of the children. Had that been what he'd been doing then? It must have been. We must have missed the fast, brown swoop of the creature. I wished I had binoculars up here.

The bird circled once, twice around the clearing, then gently

Gregor put up a gloved hand, and the hawk immediately came in to land on him.

Even from here, I could see him soothing and crooning to the animal, feeding it something. They looked as if they were all alone in the world, which presumably they thought they were.

Gregor repeated the gesture, let the hawk fly away and then round again, soaring up into the bright blue sky.

For a second, it flew high enough to be level with me and I suddenly wished with all my heart for the hawk to fly towards me so I could get a good look at it – him? Her?

But I held no interest for the bird. It circled away from the house, banking so lazily I could only dream of being that elegant in flight. I could watch the air rippling its feathers as it flew, could see the diagram I knew so well, of airflow and airspeed over the wings. In my world, on a plane, it was comparatively so clumsy and mechanical as it was made of computer design and fuel and force and gears and wires. In theirs, it was an effortless, natural fusion of hollow bones and a pure instinct for the wind.

We, pathetic earthbound humans, fought so hard to attain the ability to play in three dimensions. I watched the creature, fascinated. Gregor's stillness made complete sense. He was the tree the hawk was circling; he was a source of food, of well-being.

The hawk circled again and I wondered how long it had taken to train, whether it had been on a rope of some kind. But there was no tether now: the bird flew, soared, circled the tree-tops, a flash through them which showed the palest of green on their spindly, new-born spring branches, and back to Gregor's side. I could have watched them all day. But I had a job to do.

The antenna was merely snapped, not broken off entirely, thank goodness; the wire still ran. I taped it together as firmly as I could. It wouldn't make it through another storm, but it would do for as long as I needed it – hopefully just today, if we could manage the alternative I had in mind.

I went back down carefully. There was no sign of Gregor, which was irritating as I could have done with some help carrying the ladder.

Then I made my way back towards the lean-to from last night.

'Uh, hello?'

As I went in through the back door, I realised that I was hungry again, even after eating all his breakfast. I would have thought I was too stressed and busy to be hungry, but it turned out the opposite was true: I was completely and utterly starving. There was an amazing smell coming from the Aga and I poked my head round into the kitchen.

Gregor started like he wasn't expecting me.

'Oh, come on,' I said. 'I've been here, like, a whole day.'

'I know,' he said, but he kept staring at me in that slightly discomfiting way. 'I'm just not used to people being about, that's all.'

'Are you making lunch?'

He shrugged.

'Someone ate mine.'

'I think,' I said, but I was smiling, 'you should never ever let that go and bring it up in every single conversation we have until I leave.'

'Will do. Anyway, there's some stuff that was in the freezer...'

'Ooh!' I said.

'Okay,' he said. 'Well, it's only stew. It's heating up.'

'Uh-huh,' I said, thinking sadly of Peigi's horrible stews. But even so I was hungry. 'Can I have some? Please, if I ask very nicely and promise to never steal again?'

He looked at me.

'You sound like you're asking me to reward you with food for stealing food.'

'Noooo,' I said. 'I am asking you to reward me with food because I am going to get us *out of here*.'

I produced, in triumph, the Morse oscillator. My Plan B.

He frowned.

'How does that work?'

'We can attach it to the antenna,' I explained. 'It'll generate a radio signal. Or it should do if the battery holds.'

He frowned as I tried to turn it on. Nothing.

Pulling off the back, I saw to my disgust that the three triple A batteries had corroded beyond repair.

'Are you about to give me a row because I didn't get in special triple A batteries just in case a cross, hungry pilot washed up? And also, you are adorable and everything, but I don't actually need to get rescued from this place which I love and which is also my job.'

I wasn't listening though; I was focused.

'Have you got any batteries? I don't believe you don't have any batteries.'

He did in fact have plenty of batteries for torches, I noticed. But they were all double A.

'There must be triple As somewhere,' I said. Where's your TV ?'

'I don't have a TV.'

'Well, good for you,' I said. 'Are you telling me this *house* doesn't have a TV?'

'Oh no, it does,' he said, thinking about it. He disappeared into the dining room and I followed. It was on a large dusty cabinet, facing the table, which was plainly never used. This room faced north and was completely freezing. The TV was probably older than me; a big fat thing, perched on a huge table, with an integrated video player.

'Wow,' I said. 'Actual videos. Have you got any?'

'I don't know,' said Gregor. But I didn't care about the videos. What I was after were the— 'Aha!'

It was an ancient tiny remote. I crossed my fingers, slid open the back and found two triple As; a transistor radio on the bookshelf which also had to be older than me yielded another two.

'Whoop!' I said. Then I looked around at the bookshelves. 'There must be a Morse code guide here somewhere.'

'I thought you knew Morse code?'

'I do! I'm just a little . . . rusty.'

We turned the house upside down until we did indeed find a little pamphlet called 'Learn Morse code in two weeks!' By the looks of it, very few people had got past page four.

I shot back to the kitchen, pleased at least to be doing something, to be busy.

Carefully, I inserted the batteries and the little machine beeped on.

'Well!' I said happily. 'Look at that.'

I frowned and scribbled something down on paper.

S-E-N-D / H-E-L-P / I-N-C-H-B-O-R-N /
W-E / F-I-N-E / P-L-A-N-E /
D-A-M-A-G-E-D / M-O-R-A-G

Then I had a few practice runs before I plugged in the antenna and went for it.

Gregor looked at me and I swear he almost appeared mildly impressed. Then he went back to stirring the pot. It smelled absolutely heavenly, nothing like Peigi's at all, especially when he disappeared and came back in, slipping the fresh rosemary he'd obviously just picked into the pot. By the Aga – almost in rebuke, it kind of felt to me – was a bowl of dough, rising gently.

```
... . -. -.. / .... . .-.. .--. / .. -.
-.-. .... -... --- .-. -. / .-- . / .- .-.
. / ..-. .. -. . / .--. .-.. .- -. . / -..
.- -- .- --. . -.. / -- --- .-. .- --.
```

Okay. I suppose there was no choice but to repeat it, and just wait and hope someone found us.

```
... . -. -.. / .... . .-.. .--. / .. -.
-.-. .... -... --- .-. -. / .-- . / .- .-.
. / ..-. .. -. . / .--. .-.. .- -. . / -..
.- -- .- --. . -.. / -- --- .-. .- --.
```

I eventually went through the whole sequence four times. Someone would be looking for us, surely? A passing ship that could radio Gramps? Someone with a working mobile phone?

Meanwhile, Gregor appeared to be putting a salad of dandelions and early garden greens together. This perked me up.

```
...  .  -.  -..  /  ....  .  .-..  .--.  /  ..  -.
-.-.  ....  -...  ---  .-.  -.  /  .--  .  /  .-  .-.
.  /  ..-.  ..  -.  .  /  .--.  .-..  .-  -.  .  /  -..
.-  --  .-  --.  .  -..  /  --  ---  .-.  .-  --.
```

'Do you ...?' He indicated the stew. I was about to shush him – it is simply not possible to talk and do Morse code at the same time, or maybe it is if you are much more skilled than I am – but realising what he meant, I smiled and nodded vigorously.

I moved away from the device to eat and oh my goodness! It was just a stew. And I hated stew. But it was like something new entirely, something I had never tasted in my life before. No, even that isn't true. It was the soul of a stew, but the best one I'd ever tasted. The rich thick sauce was the colour of chocolate, and contained the full-bodied flavour of everything: chilli, red wine, herbs. The meat was so soft you could cut it with a spoon; there were carrots and great dark mangetout running through it; and all around the top was a little crusted blanket of salted potatoes – brown and charred crispy, soft and luscious underneath, soaking up all that delicious juice.

'Oh my God,' I said. The salad leaves cut through the lusciousness of the stew with their light astringency, lifting up the flavour and throwing everything into sharp relief. After being out in the open air, and the stress and anxiety of the day and the night before it, this tasted like – it sounds mad – the culinary equivalent of someone putting their arm around you and telling you everything would be all right, which the person who made the stew obviously hadn't the faintest interest in doing.

I slurped it incredibly quickly. I was so used to eating salads from plastic bowls with a plastic fork. I knew I should slow down, savour it and the warmth and comfort it provided, but I couldn't. I had no idea where it had come from, this hunger. Like I had a hole inside myself I didn't know how to fill. That I didn't even know it was there.

I looked up. He was staring at me, looking faintly horrified.

'I haven't eaten all day,' I protested.

'Well, there was that loaf of—'

I started to sing the opening lines of 'Let it Go' and he smiled. I looked around for a napkin to wipe my mouth; it was just so good to be neat. There was a real mismatch between how he seemed and how he cooked. This was such honest, warming food, served by such a diffident man. I couldn't work him out at all.

'Well,' I said regretfully, looking at my empty bowl. If he hadn't been there, I might have licked it. I looked around for more but there didn't seem to be any. I suppose he only froze single portions. I almost sighed aloud. Then something occurred to me.

'So there are lots of frozen things we'll need to eat then?' I said cheerfully. 'I mean, someone will probably come get me this afternoon ... but I could probably help you before then. Ice cream and whatnot.'

'Most things will keep well enough in the burn.'

He meant a small river that ran through the dunes down to the sea. And he was right, of course.

'Cornettos won't keep well in the burn.'

'I don't have Cornettos!'

'You monster!'

He smiled.

'How would I even transport Cornettos? How would they even get here?'

223

I tried to imagine living so far from civilisation that you couldn't bring a Cornetto home. It really was a bit amazing.

'Oh yeah,' I said.

'But you know, there's a van that comes round most afternoons.'

'Is the—? Gregor!'

He gave me a sideways look.

'I thought pilots were meant to be terribly clever.'

'Everyone's terribly clever until they're thinking about how much they want an ice cream.'

I started clearing the table.

'So your bird . . . What kind is it?'

He perked up immediately.

'Och, she's no' my bird,' he said. 'She belongs to herself. But she lets me train her sometimes. Not always, but sometimes.'

'Okay,' I said.

'She's a sparrowhawk. Smaller than a goshawk. She's a good girl.'

I smiled.

'Did you always love birds?'

He frowned.

'I suppose so,' he said. 'I mean . . . they're amazing.'

'Except when they get trapped in the fuselage,' I said. 'I'm joking.'

I don't think he thought it was very funny though.

'Planes are such a . . . ' He flapped his hands as if looking for the right word. 'Such a *vulgar* substitute. When there are creatures in this world who can do it perfectly well. They're such ugly, clunking copies of something that's so beautiful.'

'You don't think planes are beautiful?'

'Huge, noisy machines?' He sounded flabbergasted that anyone could think that.

224

'Huge, noisy, *useful* machines,' I said. Then I felt a little sad. 'Not even Concorde?'

'Concorde?'

'You didn't think Concorde was beautiful?'

'You fly Concorde?'

'Well, no, *durr*, she went out of commission when I was twelve. I was just saying.'

He frowned. 'When you watch a raptor fly, you're watching a dinosaur. On the wing. Understanding every nuance of the wind. Hunting, killing, soaring. Something so wild and free we are privileged to share the earth with.' I didn't say anything. 'No?'

'Well … I felt quite privileged to share the earth with Concorde.'

'Okay,' he said. 'I get that.'

'Well,' I said again, rinsing out my dish. 'I suppose I'd better get back to it.'

I washed his dish too but he didn't say thank you even though the water was lukewarm and there was no washing up liquid, just a scrubby old bar of green kitchen soap.

I sat back down at the kitchen table and sent it again

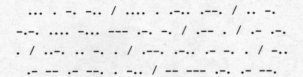

But this time, after I'd repeated it, something happened. The little light went green, indicating a message incoming.

I looked at it in disbelief – first I had to transcribe, then read it back. Twice. Finally, I sent another message: 'Are you sure?'

'Yes.'

'Is everyone fine?'

'Yes.'

'When on?'

They didn't know. They signed their name and I realised it was Donald, in the airfield. Of course it was. Bless him.

'Tell I am fine,' I managed.

'Roger.'

'Is Erno fine?'

'He is fine.'

'Plane is damaged.'

'We know. Watch moon tide.'

Chapter Twenty-two

I turned to Gregor when I'd finished.

'There's no power on the mainland! The storm blew everything out!'

I realised that while on one level it was awful, on another I was relieved: obviously Nalitha had been trying her best for us, but nothing could be done.

'Aye,' he said with no change in his expression.

'You knew about this?!'

'There's been no lights on the headland all morning. Normally you'd see something, especially before dawn. So, I figured.'

'You figured and you didn't tell me?! Save me all that trouble?'

'But if I'd said to you, "All the power is gone on the mainland," you wouldn't have believed me. You certainly wouldn't have taken my word for it.'

'I would have . . .'

Okay, so maybe he had a point.

I sat back in my chair. Goodness. Nobody was coming. Nobody was coming to save us. Me.

'Oh my God,' I said. 'How long am I going to *be* here?'

'I mean, you're welcome, aye.'

'Oh my God,' I said. 'My interview! I have to be back in London for Thursday! I have to be!'

'Well, you might have to swim it.'

He got up.

'I'm going to check the gulls' settlements, make sure they're managing all right.'

'Okay,' I said, dazed. 'Hang on . . . Last time the power went out, how long was it out for?'

'Three weeks,' came the slightly dour response.

'You are *kidding*.'

But he was already heading out the door.

No. That wouldn't happen. That was ridiculous. They knew where I was; they knew I was completely stranded with Captain Weirdo. They would come and get me. Of course they would. The ferries wouldn't be affected by the power cut, would they? Mind you, they needed fuel and if fuel stations didn't have power, well, I supposed everything could more or less fall apart pretty fast.

Oh God. And also, had the storm even hit down south? Who would even know or remember where I was? Nobody would ever believe me. My being stranded on an island without power or internet access was the most rubbish excuse for not making an interview I had ever heard in my entire life. I was like Tom Hanks, only with a stupid chicken instead of a volleyball.

And the plane. Oh my God, the plane.

I ran out after Gregor.

'What did Donald mean, moon tide?' I said.

Gregor frowned. 'Oh aye,' he said eventually. 'We should probably check that out.'

Of course, checking the details on the internet was completely out of the question. This must be how people used to live, I marvelled. Just . . . not knowing stuff. I mean, how did that even happen? You just . . . guessed, or got on with your day?

Gregor went into the sitting room, which now felt incredibly pleasant with the sun streaming through and the fire puttling gently on. I looked around. If I hadn't been so incredibly stressed, after my large lunch and eventful morning, it would have been a nice place to sit down for a snooze. No doubt that's what Gregor had had planned.

I wondered if Hayden was absolutely beside himself worrying about me. I wondered if he'd realised about the pocket-dial. Probably not: there were a million calls flying between us all the time. One more probably wouldn't register. There *used* to be a million calls flying between us, I clarified in my head sadly.

Gregor pulled down a heavy, dusty hardbacked volume from the shelves. 'Almanac' was printed on the side.

'What is that?' I said.

'It'll tell you the tide times.'

'What, for today? Or in Viking times?'

'Well, it should work for now, more or less. They can predict the tides of the future by the tides of the past. That's how it works.'

'Wow,' I said, looking at the book, printed before the internet was even dreamed of. 'What about global warming and rising seas and so on?'

'Well, yes,' said Gregor. 'This tells you when high tide will be. It doesn't tell you how high.'

I felt rather foolish.

'Oh okay.'

'It's based on phases of the moon,' he said. 'It's not that complicated.'

He put on his little round glasses again to peer at tiny little tables of close-printed figures and traced down the page with a large finger.

'Here we are, here we are . . . Oh, there's a note.'

He flicked over the pages.

I was about to make a sarcastic remark about how much faster Google would have been, but strangely it felt rather comforting getting my information from a book written by an expert, decreed correct by other experts and set down in paper and ink for ever. Whereas it was entirely possibly if I googled it, someone would have a remark to make about how tides were fake news generated by the government to hide the fact that the earth was flat, or how you could learn to control the tides by this one trick doctors didn't want you to know, or that tides were problematic now.

'It's a . . . oh,' he said, looking slightly surprised. 'It's . . . well, it's a "chaste moon".'

'It's a what?'

He kept one finger in the book to hold his place and started flicking through the rest of it.

'Here we are. That must have been what the Morse code guy meant. The third full moon of the year, known as the chaste, or the hunger, moon.'

'Moons have names?'

'They do . . . '

'Why the hunger moon?'

'Well, that's obvious,' he said. 'Winter's end, spring just beginning. Nothing to eat.'

'Well, what about chaste then?'

'Because spring is such a pure season.'

'If you weren't reading that straight from that book, I would think you were very clever,' I said.

'But that's what clever is,' said Gregor with almost a wry look in his eye. 'Stuff you learn in books.'

'What else are moons called?'

His finger ran down the page.

'Well, strawberry moons are June.'

'Oh, how pretty!'

'The flower moon is May. The hunter's moon is October. The wolf's moon is January.'

'Wow,' I said. 'I never thought . . . Well, I suppose . . . I mean, why wouldn't you give them names?'

'Well, quite,' he said. 'Native American. Although that's not what it says here. This book is quite old.'

'Well, what does it mean for us, the chaste moon? Why was Donald telling me about it?'

'It's going to be a supermoon. Huge. Very high tides. It's the changing of the seasons,' said Gregor, looking sombre.

Outside it was afternoon, the light already starting to fade.

'What, so . . . ? Hang on. What does that mean?'

I thought of *Dolly*.

'The beach . . . the tide . . . how far up is it going to come?'

'Well, yeah . . . I mean . . . pretty far, I think.'

We both sat in silence for a minute.

'Crap,' I said.

231

As the light fled, the sun of the day turned to a deep low gold, leaching out of the sky. It had been a beautiful day: air fresh as raspberries; the sun warm and forgiving; the sky the blue of violets that weren't even in season yet. But I hadn't had much time to appreciate it all. Instead, we had had to put together a plan.

We both looked at the machine in the garage: the ancient Land Rover, the type that only has canvas on the back and can often be seen in old war films driving men to certain death in the desert.

'Tell me,' I said, 'you can at least drive.'

He gave me a sideways look.

It wasn't the same one I'd seen on the beach. That one could carry stuff, but it didn't have what we needed: a tow bar.

'So it's not even your car?'

'Funnily enough,' he said, 'when you're watching birds and observing them, loud car engines aren't the help you might imagine.'

'I mean, what if the fuel has gone off?' I said. 'If there even is any.'

There was petrol in jerry cans at the back. I'd pointed out that this place was a fire nightmare. What if it had been hit by lightning? Gregor had serenely suggested that as the house was higher and had a weather vane, presumably we'd have gone first, which wasn't as comforting as I think he thought it might be.

'And where on earth are the keys?' I said, remembering the absolute bazaar of bits and pieces that made up the backroom.

'Ah well,' he said, and then I saw that they were in the ignition.

There was a tow hoist at the back, and a large amount of rope. I looked at it.

'You seriously think,' said Gregor, 'that we can drag a plane up a beach?'

'I don't know,' I said. 'But I don't have a better idea.'

'You could say goodbye to your plane,' he said sombrely.

'Come on! Hurry.'

We dressed warmly, then pulled on sou'westers and waterproof trousers. I felt unrecognisable and Gregor was a shapeless mass too. But more importantly, I felt warm and dry, and if the last twenty-four hours had taught me anything, it was the absolute importance of those two things above all else.

Night had stolen over us almost without our noticing, although I had felt the cold increasing in the air. After the maelstrom of the previous evening, it was almost preternaturally still. I looked out over the water of the southern tip of the island; it was as calm as a mirror. And above it, rising gradually, was the largest moon I had ever seen.

It was the kind of moon a child would draw, taking a brand-new yellow crayon and drawing a huge circumference on a navy blue piece of paper. We had barely noticed night come on us: the moon was so bright it was as if it had traded shifts with the sun. It shimmered straight across the water, lighting a yellow pathway that looked like a fairy bridge. Looking at it, I almost felt I could step on it; walk my way back to the mainland on golden steps.

'Come on then,' Gregor said. 'You're the one with all the plans.'

'This is your island,' I said. 'You need more plans.'

'Uh-huh.'

The Land Rover set off down the bumpy track – it wasn't a

road, nothing like it, just a stony track. We barely needed the headlights on; I never saw a clearer night.

We had to approach the beach from the north to avoid sinking into the dunes, and as we got closer, I let out a horrified moan. The waves had been big the night before in the storm but they hadn't crashed onto the cliffs or the shingle or the dunes. Everything had changed since the morning though. Here, despite the fact that the waves were not crashing – it was still so calm, so peaceful and very beautiful – they had come up as far on the beach as I had ever seen. The centre of the beach was still clear, which is where we normally landed.

The corners of the bay, up by the rocks, were a very different story.

We drove the Land Rover as far up the beach as we could, then Gregor killed the engine and we sat in silence and looked at the horrifying scene.

The plane – my family's plane, my Gramps's pride and joy, the little jewel in our family's crown, where I had sat as a child, where I had sat in the cockpit, my feet too short to reach the pedals – was listing further and further as every single wave crept over the wheels ceaselessly, stretching out their white foaming fingers – it was being pulled inexorably further out to sea. I groaned.

'Oh my God.'

Gregor was staring at it. Then he turned the car a full one-eighty on the sand and started reversing towards *Dolly*. I looked at him. I had thought he was giving up and had been fully prepared to fall out with him.

'Come on then,' he said. 'Let's get it hooked up.'

I was quite impressed with him for once, as he jumped into action and leapt out to fasten the rope.

'Okay,' he said. 'Is there something you can tie the rope on to?'

'The wheel shafts, I think,' I said. 'Will you get in the plane and steer?'

He straightened up, as he thought about that. 'Seriously? I think that might be a terrible idea.'

'I'll do my best. We just need to get her tugged up the beach, just to here where she won't be in danger any more. Oh God, why didn't we do this this morning? I know why. I thought she was safe enough to be left for a little; I thought we'd be rescued by now.'

'There's no point in harking back,' said Gregor. 'You just do what you can now.'

I picked up the rope and prepared to head for the wee plane.

'Oh God,' I said. 'Do you know any knots? I can't remember any knots. I don't know any knots.'

His face registered fake shock.

'You're telling me *you* don't know how to do something? I thought you knew how to do everything.'

'There's not a lot of knotwork in the flying trade!'

'You spent your summers up here and never learned to sail?'

I looked at him and was about to make a sarcastic response when a huge swell coiled up and suddenly, under the great white moon, the unthinkable happened.

The little Twin Otter had been shaken free of the sand and was quietly, without fanfare, floating off into the sea.

For a moment, we just stood and stared. It was such a shocking sight. She lifted gently and, after the listing and the slipping, she was now flat again, bobbing up and down gently. The huge wave had pulled her over the shingle, and it got her deep quickly enough that her wheels didn't touch the ocean bed.

She looked almost peaceful out there, bobbing gently under the stars.

'Oh my God!' I shouted. I charged down the beach to the edge of the water and splashed in.

'Hang on, hang on,' shouted Gregor behind me. 'Don't jump in: it's deep! And freezing. Hang on! Let me reverse up the car.'

But he was too late. I plunged into the water. It was unbelievably, shockingly cold, even through my wet weather gear, which instantly sprang a leak, of course. But I couldn't help it: the plane was bobbing away on top of the water and I had to get to her. There was no way around it: I had to slip out of my Wellingtons and start swimming.

'Christ!' I screamed as I flailed in the cold water, keeping my head above it. Every year, people tried to get me to do variations on that swim on New Year's Day when you rush into the freezing water and shout about it. I had never gotten around to it – i.e. I had never felt like doing it – and now I knew why. It was absolutely horrible. I splashed clumsily and heavily towards *Dolly*, my wet clothes dragging me down. Finally, I grasped her huge tail fin and hauled myself out, shaking off water like a dog and gasping.

Astounded, Gregor was standing by the water's edge, holding the end of the rope, looking furious.

Chapter Twenty-three

'You couldn't have waited *two seconds*?' he said. I looked around. The water was calm; at least I wasn't getting swept away. The night was so still, his voice carried over the waves, even though he wasn't shouting.

As I tried to control my frightened, shocked breathing, having been knocked senseless by the icy water, I realised it hadn't occurred to me that *I* would get swept away. It did not occur to me that I should probably have given it some thought before it actually looked like a possibility. My head felt tight and very sore from its dousing.

'Oh, for God's sake.'

He held the rope up again. I attempted to bend my arms into the water and paddle the plane back to shore. This went exactly as badly as you might expect.

Gregor on the shore gave a large sigh, kicked off his boots and lined them up carefully by the side of the water. Then, to my surprise, he pulled off his waterproof jacket and trousers, jumper and T-shirt until he was standing in his boxer shorts. My eyes widened in surprise. He was leaner than I'd thought under the shapeless clothing; his shoulders were broader. Without wasting any time, he dived straight into the freezing sea.

I tried to make an 'I'm sorry' face when he had to dive again into the quickly deepening water. He was with me in two minutes.

'I'm sorry,' I said instead, immediately pulling off my top to give him something to cover himself with.

'It's okay,' he said. 'I swim here most days.'

'You don't.'

'I do,' he said. He was barely shivering.

For a moment, we paused as he found his balance and got his bearings. I looked away, not wanting to appear as though I was staring at the spectacle of a half-naked man sitting on the top of a plane that was floating in the middle of the sea. Apart from the gentle plash of the waves, it was completely silent all around. I gazed up at the sky.

The stars were absolutely ridiculous, like diamonds dripping out of the sky. Orion's Belt hung heavy; it was clearer even than when I flew at night-time. In fact, I felt closer to it down here on the sea that I did miles up in the air. Venus was visible, brilliant and beautiful.

I realised Gregor was looking up too.

'Rare night for it,' he said, half smiling. 'What are you looking for?'

'Betelgeuse,' I said, pointing. 'Look. It's fading. Just there, at the end of Orion. It's a red giant. It's going to explode one day. You'll be able to see it; you'll be able to see it in the daytime.'

'Oh yeah?' he said. 'What, soon?'

'Well, in the next hundred-thousand years,' I said. 'So in astronomical terms, pretty soon.'

He looked at me quite respectfully for the first time.

'Can you dead-reckon?'

I shrugged.

'If I had to.'

'Wow,' he said. 'So you can look at the stars and tell where you are?'

'If I can look at the stars and look at the horizon, and I have a protractor handy,' I said, 'and a bit of time. Mostly it's easier just to use the GPS.'

'But you always know where you are?'

'That's pretty much my entire job,' I said. 'Knowing where I am.'

As he looked at me, I felt a funny chill that wasn't just my wet clothing.

'Where are you now?' he said curiously.

'Utterly lost,' I said.

He passed the rope into my hand. We were sitting on the plane, drifting down the beach towards the Land Rover, and the rope wasn't tight. I looked at it and looked around the smooth top of the aircraft. Obviously, for aerodynamic reasons, planes are built with very few ridges on top or handy boltholes. I didn't see anywhere suitable at all. Gregor followed my gaze.

'Where do you . . . ? Do you still think the wheel arch is the best place?'

I thought about it.

'Probably,' I said.

'Okay,' he said. 'I'm going to dive under and attach it. Then I'll drag her out, okay? And once we're on the beach, you can get in and steer. Deal?'

We were, I noticed, bobbing lower on the water. *Dolly* was obviously taking on a lot.

'We're sinking,' I said.

'We are,' he said. 'I'd say sooner rather than later.'

He was right, of course. And we were freezing and exposed on a bright cold northern night, brilliant with stars and the great huge chaste moon. It was a terrible situation in many ways.

But I couldn't help it: I wanted to stay just a moment longer. It was cold, stark and bad things were happening. But somehow I felt more alive than I had in years.

The next second, Gregor dived off the side of the plane and vanished from sight. I worried briefly, but then realised I would soon have to get back into the freezing water myself, which wasn't a pleasant thought in the slightest, and was somehow worse now I knew what it was going to be like rather than plunging in in ignorance, but it had to be done. I pushed myself off, shouting rather unnecessarily loudly as I hit the water, and gracelessly doggy-paddled to the beach to feed out more rope over the waves.

Gregor didn't resurface for a very long time. I was getting anxious again: how long was he down there? I suddenly was terrified that he was trapped underneath – maybe the weight of the plane had sunk on top of him and had started to crush him? Maybe his leg was caught where the wheels were? Maybe he was twisting, struggling, unable to understand why I wasn't coming for him? He wasn't the most practical of people; we'd already established that. Oh no. I prepared to wade in for the third time, even though I was thoroughly chilled and had absolutely no faith in my instincts to lift the plane or rescue Gregor, but I didn't know what else to do. I could feel the adrenalin shoot through me. Just as I had waded in, curiously numb now to the frigid water, to my intense surprise and relief, Gregor popped out of the waves right next to me, jumping high and shooting up from the bottom.

For just a moment, in the moonlight, he looked like a stark, silvery seal, his dark hair in drenched ringlets round his face.

'Got it,' he said, panting heavily. 'Where are you going?'

'Uh,' I said. I looked down, barely recognising myself. I was up to my thighs in the water, but felt absolutely fine, like I didn't want to get out of the water. Gregor's face suddenly looked worried.

'Come on, get in the car! Till she starts to move.'

I found myself obeying and squidged up the beach, the Wellingtons presumably lost for good. The area around the cliffs was now completely full of water, the Land Rover nearly at the water's edge even though we'd left it far away from the tide. The speed of the sea was absolutely terrifying, the immediate power of it.

I climbed into the car, and Gregor jumped in next to me.

'You keep looking behind, tell me if it's working,' he said. All thoughts of me getting in the plane had gone.

Gregor gunned the engine. It fired up, but when we tried to move forward, it went until the rope was taut and then stopped.

'It's not going to be able to,' I said. 'She's too heavy.'

'It will,' he said through gritted teeth.

'It's an entire plane filled with water,' I said.

'That's floating,' he said. He tried again, gently pushing on first gear and inching along the sand.

This time, I felt this great weight behind us, pulling us back – but then, slowly, it started to budge. We started to overcome it and, bit by bit, the Land Rover started to move across the damp sand.

I hadn't stopped looking behind me. All you could see when we started was the fin and the top of the propellers and the wings. But now, gradually, *Dolly*'s snub nose started to emerge from the waves.

'She's coming! She's coming!' I shouted in excitement. Gregor didn't react, didn't change the infinitely slow speed but continued trundling up the beach to safety.

It was absolutely amazing to watch. Sparking, tossing off water like diamonds reflected under the stars, slowly, slowly, *Dolly* rose from the waves.

'You're doing it!' I shouted out, still overwhelmed with excitement and glee.

'We're not there yet,' growled Gregor, but finally the front wheel – tied with a beautiful knot I noticed – hit the sand. I wouldn't have thought it was possible but Gregor slowed down even more, desperately trying to keep the vessel upright. Water sluiced from every orifice, dripping and sluicing through her.

'Okay,' he said as she continued to inch out of the water. 'You have to go and steer. With the tiller or the rudder or whatever you call it.'

'The rudder,' I said.

'I don't care. Can you jump out while I keep moving? I don't want to stall the momentum.'

I nodded and did so, landing softly on the sand in my bare feet.

I still didn't even feel the cold as I watched the plane emerge. It was an incredible sight under the vast moon, watching a creature appear from the depths; she looked like something elemental, huge and old, lumbering up the sand. I moved rocks out of her way and then, when enough of her had emerged, waved to Gregor to stop. When I opened the door, water burst out at me, cascading down the steps. I let it come out, as much as it could, then marched up the saturated steps.

Inside, the plane was ruined. I almost thought for a moment that I should have left her: she was bad before but now she was plastered with wet paper and rubbish everywhere, the seats completely soaked and ruined. I didn't want to think what condition the electrics would be in. Should I just have let her sink beneath the waves? Well, there was no time to think about that now. I went up to the cockpit, careful of my bare feet.

I could see the Land Rover clear as day out of the windshield, and opened the window to wave that it was all right. Obviously, I was used to seeing bigger planes being winched out onto runways – but not on a piece of rope and not with a Land Rover, that was for sure. The rope held, though, and we went slowly and surely, me simply keeping the joystick tight so we followed the car up the sand in as straight a line as possible, waves still lapping at our heels, up to the original landing place at the top of the beach, where we came to rest with something of a squelch. The water was still sloshing up and down the plane, rendering her a little wobbly.

'We got her! We got her!' I was oddly exuberant and overexcited all the way back in the car. Gregor was quiet, but by the time we reached the house I realised just how very cold I was. The Land Rover had no back, so there wasn't any heating in the car, and I was trembling and my teeth were chattering violently. My head was still very sore.

However, when we stumbled into the house, I was still exuberant. There was, of course, no light, and the only warm room was downstairs, where Gregor immediately piled peat onto the fire and stoked it high until it was roaring, then lit a dozen candles and placed them around the room. They were church candles, thick white things stuck in plates and various sizes and levels, and their smoke plumed, but it was light, just about, more so after he pulled open the curtains and the moonlight flooded in.

'Take your clothes off,' he said brusquely. 'You're absolutely blue. I have never met a woman who spends so much time soaking wet.'

He brought in clean, faded towels. There was no chance of a bath, of course, without an immerser.

'Hey.'

I didn't immediately hear what was being said, so eventually turned my head.

'Hey,' he said again. 'I've been saying your name for five minutes.'

I hadn't realised. I was standing very still in place, staring straight into the fire, shaking, body and soul. I couldn't actually move.

'Oh heavens,' he said.

'I'll ... ' For a moment, I wasn't entirely sure where I was. I felt very peculiar indeed. 'I'll just go upstairs and change.'

He shook his head and took a step forward.

'You will not,' he said, just as I tried to move and all the blood rushed to my head rapidly and I found everything around me taking on a fuzzy white tinge. I felt extremely peculiar and suddenly, without being able to do anything about it at all, I found myself pitching forward into nothingness ... and then, equally suddenly, found myself grabbed by a pair of strong arms.

His voice came to me from seemingly a distance away, slightly distorted.

'Whoops-a-daisy ... Okay, right, there you are. I've got you. I've got you.'

I felt sick, then very wobbly, wasn't entirely sure where I was, but I was still being held up by that pair of strong arms. I could feel a rough fisherman's sweater against my face, and I suddenly felt safe.

'Come on, you're going to have to . . . You're absolutely blue. You're going to have to get out of those wet things.'

I could hear what he was saying but it didn't really make any sense to me. All I could do was lean against this person holding me up.

'Come on, come on . . . Oh, okay then.'

I was led over to sit down, further away from the fire, which I didn't like. I liked even less when he started pulling at my sleeves.

'What are you doing?' I chattered.

'You have to get out of these wet clothes. Now, in fact.'

'Nooo!'

'I'm afraid so. God, stop struggling; this feels awful, what I'm doing.'

'I'll be cold!'

'You're already cold; that's why you sound so mad. Come on, Morag. Come on.'

His voice had turned kind.

'I'm not looking, I promise. I will do this entirely while staring at the ceiling. Which has a lot of cobwebs, I now realise.'

It was easier, I found, just to let him do it. He peeled off my soaking jumper and shirt, unbuttoned the dungarees. He left my bra and pants and pulled a huge soft blanket around me. Then he half picked me up again and carried me back over to the fire, ensuring that the blanket was still tight around me.

'Sit down,' he said, and I followed his lead like an obedient child, sitting cross-legged in front of it, my head heavy.

245

He hauled something sizeable – a duvet, I found out later – and piled it on top of the blanket, instructing me to stay put exactly where I was in front of the fire and not move. I was quite happy to oblige and stared into the flames, thinking about absolutely nothing again. He vanished and then came back with a huge steaming mug of tea.

'Sip this slowly,' he said. 'Don't burn yourself.'

Even holding the cup in my hands was exquisitely painful as the blood started rushing back to my fingers and toes. Electrical light flashes of cold started to zip up and down my limbs, and although I had stopped shaking all the time, occasionally my entire body would burst out into a fit of it. I couldn't seem to get warm.

Gregor seemed to sense this and moved closer to me once again, gently putting an arm around me and rubbing my shoulders and back through the blankets, saying words in a quiet voice that I didn't understand until gradually I started to feel myself come back to life. I don't know how long we sat there in front of the blazing fire, although I remember the pain that came in my newly awakening limbs as they gradually thawed.

'God,' I said finally, sipping my cooling tea. It was the most delicious thing I had ever tasted.

Gregor immediately took his hands off me like I'd yelled at him.

'Sorry,' he said.

'No, no, no, thank you,' I stuttered, craning my neck round so I could see him. 'Thank you. I don't know what happened.'

'You took a dousing,' he said.

'So did you.'

'Yes, but I'm used to it. And I took my clothes off first, so I

246

had dry clothes to put on. Whereas I thought you were going to freeze into the shape of your jumper.'

I shook myself out again, my head clearing.

'I've never been so cold in all my life.'

'That's spring in the islands for you,' he said quite matter-of-factly. He seemed a bit brusque, slightly embarrassed about being so close to me. I nodded, rubbing my arms under the quilt.

'Do you want to get dressed again?' he said. 'I brought down ... '

And he indicated to the side of the fire where he had standing on an old-fashioned clothes horse yet another pair of old priest's pyjamas. I almost started laugh. 'Oh my,' I said. 'This is just the home of fashion right here, this place.'

He smiled back. 'I can't believe they built the Harvey Nicks in Edinburgh instead of here.'

I couldn't believe he'd even heard of Harvey Nicks, but didn't show that I was impressed, merely poked a hand out from the duvet for the in fact deliciously toasty and soft flannel pyjamas.

'Um.' He stood up. 'Are you hungry?'

I thought about it and realised that I was totally and utterly ravenous. Again.

'Yes,' I said.

'Yeah, you normally are,' he said mildly. 'We still have a freezer to get through.'

'Okay, well, I don't want the handles,' I said weakly, and he half smiled and disappeared while I put the pyjamas on. The bliss of being warm was extreme.

What he brought back in was very simple; two long toasting forks, a fat slice of the home-churned butter and a little clay pot full of salt. And in his other hand, a large defrosted plate of yellow triangles. I looked at them before I realised what they were.

'Oh my goodness!' I said. 'Those aren't . . . ?'

'I didn't want to leave you alone to go in the kitchen and make something new,' he said. 'Also, there's no light in there and I'm too scared to cook in the dark. Is this all right?'

'Oh boy, yes.'

The blood was returning to my extremities; I was feeling more like myself again. Gregor eyed me carefully.

'How are you doing?'

'I feel fine . . . I think. A bit beaten up,' I said, testing myself. 'I got really woozy there for a moment.'

'I know,' he said. 'I was worried about you. Hypothermia isn't funny.'

'I didn't have . . . ' I frowned. 'Well, I felt very odd.'

'Sorry I had to order you to take your clothes off.'

I felt myself get a little pink.

'Uh, don't worry about it.'

'Only because you had to get out of—'

'No, no, I mean, I get it.'

I glanced over at the breadboard he was carrying again.

He brought them closer.

'Potato scones!' I said in an awestruck tone. They didn't look like the ones that came in packets though. I glanced up.

'You made these?'

He smiled at my amazed tone.

'It is not, I promise, rocket science to make a potato scone.'

'No,' I said. 'More like wizardry of some kind.'

'Well,' he said, and now it was his turn to look a little pink. 'Let's get them on.'

I couldn't remember the last time I'd had a potato scone. The ones they sold in England were awful.

He put one on each toasting fork and handed one to me. I wasn't quite sure what to do at first, and it was on the point of bursting into flames when he showed me how to gently hold it just above the fire, letting it slowly turn from yellow to gold and brown hues, puffing out and raising on the outside, even as he kept telling me off for wanting to eat it too soon.

'You're too patient,' I said, dabbing at my singed mouth.

He laughed. 'All falconers are,' he said in a slightly sad voice.

'Is that what you are?'

'Oh no, I'm an ornithologist – falconry is a hobby.' He wrinkled his nose. 'One I'm not very good at.'

'Don't you have to be patient as an ornithologist too?'

'Yup. But not as a pilot, I see?'

I had reached out again, and actually burned my fingers this time.

'Oh, well, not really. There's always stuff to do and work – it's the passengers who have to hang around really if there's a problem, not us. We have to be punctual, not patient.'

He smiled. 'That's why you have to be busy all the time.'

'I don't have to be busy all the time!'

'You haven't stopped climbing up on my roof since you got here. And doing stuff with barbed wire.'

'There was a lot to do . . .'

'Nothing that can't keep,' he said quietly. 'There's always work. No need to rush.'

But I wanted to say that somehow there was – there were flying hours to accumulate, exams to pass, specs to memorise, boys to meet, promotions to get . . .

But oddly, for the first time I couldn't quite remember why I felt I had to do all those things, and why I had to do them so fast. Who exactly I was running this race for? Gramps and Ranald? The lads in pilot school? The kids at school who'd called me Morag the Grobag? To make some obscure point to Jamie?

Carefully and slowly, Gregor pulled the toasting fork towards himself and declared that the potato scones were *finally* ready to eat, 'but give it a minute'.

Too late, I had already grabbed at mine. I stuck my fingers in my mouth.

'Don't say that's exactly what you were just talking about,' I said.

He laughed aloud.

'I genuinely cannot believe you have burned yourself three times,' he said. 'Seriously, have you not eaten in years? Burning and freezing to death on the same night is—'

'—probably a very lucrative wellness idea waiting to happen,' I said.

'—a sign someone needs to slow down.'

It was my turn to laugh.

'I think if the universe needed to give me that sign it could probably just have crashed me into a deserted island and let me enjoy the scones.'

Gregor moved to the bookshelves and pulled out a very dusty old bottle of whisky from next to a stack of Waverly novels. He raised his eyebrows at me and I nodded, so he just poured it into my empty tea cup.

'Medicinal,' he said.

The potato scone had finally cooled enough for me to take a bite. Oh, it was heaven. Thickly spread with butter, salt on top of it, crunchy on the outside but smooth in the middle, it was a cardiologist's nightmare but absolutely and totally delicious.

It was so warming and comforting, especially given how long I had lived away from Scotland, away from home, how far I had travelled and, even now, at this turning point in my life, how far I still had to go. This most glorious taste of home, of sweet-scented fireside warmth and cosiness and rest at the end of a long night warmed me from the inside out.

'Do you want another?' he said, smiling as my eyes shut and I nodded fervently. We poured a little water in our whisky and toasted the potato scones and each other, and it was one of the most memorable meals of my life.

'So why here?' I asked when we had finally finished, having gorged ourselves on defrosting raspberries, which had grown wild in such abundance the previous summer they had had to be stored away. 'I mean, is this a really awesome post for an ornithologist?'

He shrugged.

'It's pretty cool. We have puffins, terns ... We had a stork once. Nearly caused an international incident.'

'And you like being by yourself?'

There was a very long pause.

'Well, yes, obviously,' he said.

'Really, though?'

'Really, though,' he said. 'Other people don't like Frances and they eat all my food.'

'Uh-huh.'

'And you like lots of people and being on the move and being surrounded with people all the time and being very go! go! go?!'

I shrugged.

'Not all the ...'

I couldn't really deny it. It was true, that was my life. Or had been.

'Why were you so grumpy on the plane?' I said suddenly, changing the subject.

'Well, don't mince your words,' he said.

I looked at him.

'Well?'

He shrugged. 'Okay. But don't laugh.'

'What?'

'I'm ... I'm afraid of flying.'

'Oh, for goodness' sake!'

'Yeah, all right. They wouldn't let me take the ferry because Fraser needed the plane.'

'Ha! But also, how did you end up here in the first place?' I said.

'I ... It's a long story.'

'I don't know if you've noticed,' I said carefully, 'but there is literally nothing else to do here.'

He glanced at the bookshelves as if confused by what I'd just said. I suppose to him, if he had birds and animals and books, maybe that was everything there was to do.

But it looked like he was contemplating telling me his story. I watched him as he stared into the fire. His heavy brow was furrowed, his eyes half shut. He rubbed his dark beard rather nervously. He didn't have the glasses on; they were on the armchair, I noticed, just next to his latest discarded book, *The Goshawk*, by T. H. White, which I had never heard of. He carried on staring. He was a very unhurried person, and it felt infectious.

I took a final sip of the whisky, which had warmed me as much as the food had, like the duvet had, and the full momentous day finally stopped turning over in my head. *Dolly* was safe, or as safe as could be, and there was nothing – absolutely nothing – I could do in this world right now. No one I could possibly speak to, nowhere I could possibly be, nothing that was on my to-do list, or my run list, or my life goals, or my phone. No beeps, no disapproving reminders. It was nuts, I realised. The one thing – a watch – that had worked perfectly for hundreds and hundreds of years, and had then been supposedly improved to work better. And now I couldn't even tell the time since the watch strapped to my wrist, which counted my steps, had run down too.

'Well,' he said finally, and his musical voice was soft and gentle. 'It'll sound silly when I say it out loud.'

'Sillier than "I crashed my plane here"?' I said.

'Huh. Maybe not. Maybe yet.'

He sighed.

'I had ... a bad break-up. Really bad.'

I glanced up at him. I had managed, I realised, to barely think about Hayden, what with everything that was going on. I'd managed to put him right out of my mind because, without a phone, I couldn't fret. Could only focus on doing what I was doing.

'So you turned yourself into a hermit?' I said. 'Good God, what did he or she do?'

'She,' he said, smiling wryly.

'But a person,' I said. 'Not the goat before Frances.'

'Okay, forget it.'

'No, no. I'm sorry. I am sorry.'

I was. I was making stupid jokes to distract from my own feelings.

'Huh.'

'So you became a hermit because of a woman?'

'I'm not a hermit!'

'What on earth is your definition of a hermit?' I said.

'I'm an ornithologist – I come here and do the spring shift. I don't live here all year!'

'Oh,' I said.

'I didn't . . . get dumped by a girl and live by myself for the rest of my life. I come and cover hatching season. I'm an ornithology lecturer at UHI!'

It struck me as odd that I hadn't even been aware of this incredibly elementary information.

'Oh,' I said again. 'Is that why you don't know where anything is in your own house?'

'You just thought I was a massive weirdo?'

'I'm not not saying that now.'

He chuckled.

'Yeah, all right, Plane Crash Ghost.'

'I'm not a plane crash ghost!'

'That's exactly what a plane crash ghost would say. I've been here by myself for weeks.'

'I think if I was a figment of your imagination I'd have better hair,' I said.

'And wouldn't eat, like, absolutely everything.'

We sat in a companionable silence. It was oddly comforting, I was finding. For someone so prickly.

'So . . . what was she like?'

'Oh well. She was nice. And she left. And I was . . . I was being very dramatic about it.'

'You flounced.'

'Well, she flounced first. Off to travel the world. And I was so

254

fed up with boring my friends and so sick of myself being sad every time I remembered something we'd done . . . '

My thoughts flew to the nights out Hayden and I had had, the cafés, the restaurants. I felt deeply miserable when I remembered those.

' . . . every time I had to walk past somewhere we'd been.'

I found myself nodding vehemently.

'You've been through this?'

A lump stuck in my throat and I couldn't speak. Because Gregor was speaking about something that was old; that was dead. Whereas while I was here, I was in a Schrödinger's relationship: neither alive nor dead. And seeing each other would settle it one way or the other, I supposed.

I didn't say anything, and he smiled sadly, and I realised he must have assumed that I had.

'So I applied on a whim really. But when I came here— Fraser did the interview, I'm not entirely sure he was paying attention. There was quite a lot about psalms, for some reason. Anyway. As soon as I came here, I knew. It was so beautiful. When I was here, dealing with the birds, I couldn't think about anything else. Couldn't dwell on where I'd messed up, or what was going on in the world that I couldn't do anything about.'

'That's how I feel when I'm flying,' I said.

He looked at me.

'Well,' he said. 'Then you know.'

I nodded. I did know.

'And I thought it would be just a temporary thing – a way to clear my head. And then . . . it grew on me. I started to . . . I love it. I don't love getting here but I love how even in this tiny miniature world, every single day is so different. Every single creature changes; no blade of grass stays the same. The clouds break and re-form and cast new shadows and life moves forwards and spirals in the air and I feel a part of it all and . . . ' He stared into his whisky. 'I'm babbling. No more whisky for me.'

'I don't mind,' I said sleepily. I didn't. I liked it. Also, was kind of comforting to know he wasn't *really* a monster weirdo hermit.

'Why were you so cranky?' he said. 'When you showed up. Was it just crashing the plane? You just seemed so furious.'

I leant forwards.

'No,' I said slowly, and for the very first time I began to open up. 'It wasn't just the plane. I had a near-miss a little while ago. And the pilot and the passenger in the other plane died. And I had been . . . I had been scared. Too scared to fly.'

'Oh my God,' he said quietly.

'I'd been co-pilot,' I said. 'Sitting there. Doing charts and checks. I couldn't . . . I couldn't bring myself to . . . '

He didn't say anything, just gave me time.

'Landing the plane . . . I had to. It was the first time I'd flown.'

I'd said it. I'd let it out loud. The air was soft, the fire crackling quietly away. It felt ever so slightly like a weight lifting from my shoulders.

'Well,' he said. 'You did a brilliant job.'

We sat there in silence, and I couldn't say how long it went on for, as the fire burned down and the quiet of the island night settled on the old creaking house. I felt my eyes grow heavier. As if I could finally be calm.

It had been a very long day. My head was nodding forwards when I thought I heard Gregor clear his throat again as if he was about to say something else.

'Well, if we're sharing,' he started. 'After . . . '

But the flames were dancing in front of my eyes and I was so warm and so cosy and so at peace, so that was the last thing I heard.

Chapter Twenty-four

'Hey.'

The fire was nothing but embers, and for a moment I woke up, so cosy and warm and comfortable that I didn't really want to move, but then I realised where I was: wrapped up in a duvet, lying in front of a fire like a dog, and remembered I was on Inchborn, and everything that had happened. The huge clear moon had moved in the wide bay window. Gregor was standing up, which was what must have woken me. His large dark eyes looked kind and tired and sad. He was holding his book, and his glasses were back on.

'You fell asleep,' he said.

'I get that.' I rubbed at my face.

'Bed?'

'What time is it?'

He shrugged. 'Who knows? Dark time. Go to bed.'

'Okay,' I said. I realised I needed the loo. I gave him my hand and he pulled me up, and suddenly I found myself standing very close to him. He smelled like woodsmoke and I remembered again how comforting and strong he had been when I had got in from the cold. I found myself slightly leaning against him once more, a little groggy, still half-asleep, just wanting to lean onto another human being – this human being – after the drama of the day.

'Thank you,' I murmured dreamily, my face nearly on his shoulder. It was, I thought woozily, very comfortable there. I liked being there. It felt good. I felt him too, strong against me. I was half-asleep but it felt that we were almost moving together, gently, softly, me pliant and sleepy, him broad and strong beneath the layers of clothing . . .

Suddenly, he stiffened and jerked back.

'Um, I don't . . . This isn't really appropriate . . . ' he said.

I blinked, startled into full wakefulness, rather unsure exactly as to what had just happened. Realising he had become awkward again, I immediately backed off, horrified with myself.

'I didn't mean . . . !' I said but I didn't know, deep down, if I was telling the truth. What had I meant?

He held up his hands.

'You're very tired.'

'But I wasn't . . . '

It was true. I hadn't been trying to come on to him, not at all. Had I?

But I hadn't been, surely . . . I had just felt safe. Safe and warm, when the last two days had been anything but. That was all. But his face was so horrified, as if I'd given him a lap dance, that I lost the words to explain, or I didn't know how to explain in a way that wouldn't make it sound much worse. To myself. About how, trapped at the top of the world with a hermit, it was me who felt lonely.

'Get some rest,' he said, his face closing up again, and I remembered suddenly that he had been about to say something before, and then I'd fallen asleep in front of the fire. I felt guilty and ashamed, and I wondered what on earth it had been.

He gave me a candle and pointed me upstairs to bed, and I went meekly like a child, still burning up with shame and embarrassment. He stood downstairs, as if to make sure I was entirely gone, just in case I performed a full claws-out sneak jump-attack on him. I grimaced to myself. Oh, for goodness' sake.

I crept to the dark bathroom, trying once again not to spook myself out by catching a glimpse of my candle-lit face and wild hair in the mirror and thinking I was a horrifying ghost, and crawled into the stiff sheets and eiderdown of the old bed, still wrapped in the blanket to help me warm up as quickly as possible. I thought at first that I wouldn't sleep at all. But then I huffed out the candle one second and the next I was awake to a bright beam of sunlight bursting through the window, suffusing the room, leaving bright yellow panes on the eiderdown.

Chapter Twenty-five

It was a dream of a day. I stood at the window, transfixed, staring south out to sea. Something appeared. It started as a grey dot, then became more – a flurry – and even though I knew nothing about birds except how to avoid them, geese in particular, I knew what these were: a huge murmuration of starlings, arriving to land from the warm south. They would be following the sun or magnets or ley lines – who knew what to get home? (Actually, Gregor probably did, but I was in no mood to ask him.) – twirling in the air, like a dancing pepperpot, making three-dimensional sketches in the sky. They were so beautiful and elegant, a vast array in flight. I realised something as I watched them: it hadn't even occurred to me to get my phone and take a shot.

I watched them swoop from one impossible geometry to another, and then stared out at the sea, which sparkled invitingly, despite having done its utmost to kill *Dolly*, Gregor and me the day before. I shook my head. Amazing. And I had given up this life so easily to go to flight school, to go where the big planes were. I'd barely looked behind me.

I was getting reasonably tired of washing out my knickers every night, but hey ho, they were almost dry. This time, the chest yielded an only-slightly-musty grandfather shirt and a peat-smelling, grey-holed jumper which on someone with less crazy hair – or possibly more crazy – might have passed for Hoxton chic. My uniform was dry, but horribly stained and crumpled and the idea of zipping myself into it was less attractive right now than the ancient but very soft and comfortable jumper.

My memories of last night had crystallised. I had been weakened, that was all. I had been tired and a little sick. I hadn't been trying to get off with him. He had to know that. As if, anyway. Stupid beardy bird nerd weirdo loner guy. If anything, he'd taken advantage of me just by being really nice to me when I'd got a drenching . . . Okay, that take wasn't going to fly. Being kind wasn't really a very good reason to launch a vendetta. Still, I needed plausible deniability. Maybe go with confusion? Or I could pretend I'd forgotten all about it?

I checked the lamp by the bed, just in case the generator had fixed itself by magic. It hadn't.

I walked downstairs trying to look dignified, which is quite difficult when you are wearing a sweater with holes in the wrists so your fingers catch in them. I was prepared to act in a mature manner and tell him I had obviously not been doing anything like *that*, and anyway if I had it was because I was very confused (that much was true at least) and I didn't remember a thing and really it was kind of his fault when you thought about it. But, as I descended, I caught the most amazing scent coming from the kitchen and once again all of those thoughts fell out of my head. What was it with me? Why was I so relentlessly starving all the time? Although I supposed potato scones and raspberries, although phenomenally delicious, weren't exactly a rousing supper.

In the kitchen, Gregor was standing with his back to me, patiently stirring a large pot on the Aga. He did, I noticed, everything patiently, everything slowly. Normally I liked – needed – to be careful, yes, but more importantly swift and correct. I had to be able to make decisions quickly; that was part of me.

The constant motion of my work – with teams that changed every day; constant delays and uncertainties and huge buses full of people I would never know or get to know; going to countries I also never got a chance to know beyond the bland lighting of the airport corridors; the coffee shops that barely changed from country to country; the air-con and the duty free – was so quick, and I was part of a machine. I was trained to the highest level so that every pilot I ever flew with – most of whom I'd never met before – would slot right in without either of us batting an eyelid, just becoming part of the huge ongoing maw of a world in perpetual motion.

And this was quite the opposite.

There was a lot going through my head just watching someone stirring a pot, especially when Gregor turned round and I saw it was only porridge, after all.

'Hey,' he said.

'You need to know,' I said, quickly, my voice coming out as a bit of a strangulated gasp, 'that I didn't mean anything last night. I was just tired and I thought we were having a hug. It didn't mean anything more.'

I thought he would apologise too for his rude and hasty

overreaction, pushing me away like I was some kind of lust-crazed Medusa, so disgusting it was absolutely insane that I could have ever got off with anyone – I mean, had the positions been reversed I would probably have apologised – but he didn't. He just nodded.

'Want some porridge? I have honey, or cream . . . some rosehip syrup from the garden. But you have to eat it without making those weird groaning noises you keep making when you eat.'

'Okay,' I said, slightly embarrassed.

'So, do you want some or not?'

'Uh. Yes, please.'

'What do you want on it?'

'I don't know: everything?'

'No, that will be disgusting.'

'Okay, you decide.'

He set down in front of me a large blue and white striped earthenware bowl, slightly chipped, and a large enamel-handled spoon, and I took a spoonful. Mindful I didn't want to give him the impression I was a sex-crazed lunatic, as I apparently did last night, I managed not to make any noise. Anyway, it was only porridge, for God's sake. Okay, so it was smooth with a tiny bit of bite to it, the perfect consistency: creamy and rich but not overpowering, with just the right amount of syrup. But, you know. Anyone could do that. It almost completely escaped my mind that he was sullen, difficult, lazy and had taken ridiculous offence when he thought I was coming on to him, which I wasn't. *As if.*

'Is it okay?' he said, and I realised he was looking – not without a twitch to his lips – at my bowl which was mysteriously empty. I appeared to be scraping a finger around it. I frowned, cross with him.

'It's okay,' I said. 'Where did you learn to cook?'

'It's porridge,' he said, astounded. Then: 'At the Haute Cuisine School de Porridge de Paris.'

'Yeah, very funny,' I said.

'My ex didn't cook. One of us had to.'

I waited to hear if he was going to elaborate, but clearly not. It was hard to tell if he was just being rueful, if he was still hung up on her or whether he simply hadn't had the chance to talk to anyone about her. Knowing men as I did, the latter was entirely probable. Many was the night I had cruised over the plains of central Europe listening to a litany of low-voiced divorce complaints from men I barely knew, who had no one else to tell. I like men, always have, but they can't half be doofuses.

I looked outside through the dirty windows. It really was the most glorious day outside; the sky was washed blue and the new grass was pushing up on the lawn. I had better go check on *Dolly*. And send a message to the mainland, but what was it going to say? Please send out a boat even though you have limited supplies and a crisis on your hands and I appear to be perfectly fine?

'Is there enough hot water for me to have a bath?'

Gregor frowned. 'There's a little bit from the Aga but I don't think it would be a very nice bath. The immerser hasn't got—'

'Power, yup, got it. I just wondered if the fireplace heated water.'

He shook his head. 'I don't think so.'

He poured the last of the porridge into my bowl without me asking.

'What are you going to do today?' I said.

'I'm going to kill a chicken,' he said casually.

'What?!'

'Well, we only have rapidly defrosting veg in the freezer. It's planting season so there's nothing to harvest. We have to eat.'

'Can't you just bake some bread?'

'I can,' he said. 'But we can't live on bread alone.'

'I could totally live on bread alone,' I said. 'And frozen peas. And this rosehip syrup. That pretty much covers all the bases.'

He changed the subject.

'And I need to check on my gull counts and look at nesting pairs, and tend the garden.' He glanced at the weather. 'Grass-cutting, too, probably. And I'm going to pickle anything I can salvage from the freezer, and cut some more peat. Normally I'd have a school party today to show around, and they won't be here.'

'Ooh,' I said. 'That sounds quite busy.'

'What about you?'

'I am going to go up on the roof,' I said.

He frowned. 'I thought you were going to say that. Why? They know you're here. They know you're alive. They'll come when they can and you might even get off this island before you break your neck.'

'I have a really important work thing,' I said. 'On Thursday. I need to make sure someone comes and gets me before then.'

He smiled.

'Ah yes. I forgot.'

'Well. You know.'

His face looked sorry. I felt sorry.

'I mean, much as I'd love to stay and pickle things to ward off starvation . . . '

'Tell me more about the job,' he said.

'It is kind of big and very fancy actually,' I said, wiping my mouth after I realised that I'd left more syrup around it than might be generally considered dignified under the circumstances. 'It's being first officer on a long-haul aircraft. A380s, in fact. Flying all over the world.'

'So what does a first officer do?'

'I'm the co-pilot.'

He looked at me.

'So you're not flying?'

'I'm there if they need me,' I said, turning pink.

'Is that why you went for it?'

'I thought . . . I wasn't going to take it,' I said. 'If I couldn't fly when I came up here . . . I couldn't.'

'Don't they test you before they give it to you?'

'Yes, in simulators,' I said. 'They're all right. That's why I need to be back by Thursday.'

'Wow,' he said. 'You mean something could have happened on a flight and you wouldn't have been able to take over?'

'Something did happen!' I said. 'And I did!'

'So you're cured?'

It was odd: I found myself thinking that I did feel . . . was 'cured' the right word? I felt better. Much, much better. But it hadn't been about taking over the plane; my training and instincts had kicked in immediately then. It had been about telling someone. It had been about telling him.

'Is it fulfilling?' he said. 'Doing the long-haul stuff?'

'I love to fly,' I said. 'Ordinarily. To feel that moment when the autopilot switches off as you're about to descend, ATC rattling out instructions, the weight of the plane behind you, bringing everyone safely down, balancing on the wind . . . I absolutely love it.'

'But long haul isn't like that, is it? Isn't it just lots of sitting?'

'Well, I'm not watching in-flight movies,' I said.

He was right though. It was a lot less of the fun and joy I associated with flying, and a lot more of the airports, the sitting and lots and lots of very similar terrain – going east, Russia takes a long, long time; likewise southbound with the Sahara.

'And it's a promotion,' I said. 'I mean, it's okay if you get a *free house* thrown in with your job but most people don't.'

He nodded.

'I know,' he said. 'I don't even have to pay for electricity.'

I smiled at that.

'It just seems a bit weird,' he said, 'that the stuff you really love about the job, about landing and taking people up and down and being with the wind . . .'

I nodded.

'It seems weird that the more senior you get, the less there is of that.'

'It's the same with any job though,' I said. 'If you love teaching, you'll get promoted to being a headteacher and spend your time doing paperwork. If you love being a doctor, they'll make you head of hospital committees and so on. You'll probably end up a university administrator.'

'Never!' said Gregor. And I absolutely believed him.

Oh, but it was, and I say this despite myself, very heaven to be on Inchborn that morning, stepping out onto the dewy, jewel-green lawn. The daffodils and the daisies tangled themselves together as if in a race to see who could be first to open up to the sun, the green of the lawn was so vivid that it was almost fluorescent and every kind of bird was twittering in the soft air.

Or perhaps, I thought, they were always like that in the spring-time, and sealed inside I simply didn't notice.

Frances came up to me as soon as I came out of the gate and butted me gently.

'It's fine,' I said to her. 'He's all yours. You don't need to be jealous.'

I patted her and gave her an apple from the stash I had secreted in my dungaree pocket in case I got hungry again.

The salt of the sea all around smelled fresh in the air and mingled with the emerging celandines in the borders, as if the entire island was turning itself into a tangle of fresh and lovely new things to attract its winged friends. I almost stopped short when I realised that of course that was exactly what Inchborn was doing: heaven and earth and sea in perfect harmony.

I should realistically have been more anxious about home, today, the second day since the crash. It was now Monday, and time was ticking away. The messages would be piling up on my phone; people would be worried and anxious. There would be so much to deal with.

But somehow, I just couldn't get anxious about that now. It would have to be dealt with later. I was powerless, which meant I simply couldn't be worried or stressed on a day like today. I couldn't answer the phone or handle my emails; I couldn't make any meetings or do any shopping or pick up my dry cleaning or check my direct debits, nor could I do my steps or buy anything especially diet-orientated or weigh myself or go to the gym or call my parents or listen to any improving podcasts or watch the latest television show absolutely everyone had watched except for me or have my eyebrows done or update my Instagram or scroll everyone else's Instagram, or send cute messages to Hayden ...

Being absolutely unable to do any of these things – none of them, at all – was oddly freeing. I felt like nobody knew where I was. I felt ... I felt free. That this day belonged to me, and me alone. That I could choose what to do, and where to be. I had no idea what time it was, though I realised with a start that I'd forgotten about not knowing since there was no way of telling. I couldn't remember the last time that happened.

All of it was mine. And this wasn't a low, heavy, nothing time, like lockdown when scrolling was the only thing anyone could do. Or like waiting to hear about my job, which was fretty and enervating. I had proper, free, open time, as wide as the sea.

I breathed in happily, took a bite of a small, sweet, slightly dented apple and went to explore.

First, I eyed *Dolly* up where she was beached. I opened up her door to let the fresh, sweet air circulate and dry her out a bit. Chances were her superstructure would be absolutely fine; it was designed to get wet and cold. The seats would dry out fine too; they were leather so they might be a little stained. The wings would be fine and the wheel – well, we just needed a new tyre.

The real issue, of course, was the instruments. They'd be fritzed, like if you dropped your phone in the toilet. And, just like dropping your phone in the toilet, it would take a few days before we could see what nick they were in. Otherwise ...

Oh goodness, she was so old now. I patted her dead instrument panel affectionately. At least she hadn't been lost at sea. But Gramps ... he was going to be so upset. I thought about

270

Callum Frost. I didn't know what was going to happen now. This would push a sale, I supposed. It wasn't how it was supposed to end.

We could probably get her on a flatbed truck, and send her back on the ferry. The insurance would pay for that. It would be a sad homecoming for such an adored plane. Maybe not much point taking her back to the airfield; she should probably just go straight to the scrappers.

I was surprised to find a small lump in my throat. I patted her. It felt like sending a dog to get put down. She was only an aircraft, not a person.

'You'll be fine,' I said. 'Bits and pieces of you will go fly all over the world! It'll be amazing!'

But I wasn't even convincing myself.

I left the door open and hopped down so I could stop feeling depressed. Instead, I went to explore the abbey.

It was so peculiar to get the place to yourself without the normal hordes of pilgrims and tourists who disgorged themselves from the daily boats, took photos, huddled into the gift shop to buy Edinburgh rock, fridge magnets and tea towels. Today, I could wander round it at leisure, marvelling at the huge fireplace in the remnants of the kitchen and the massive tools still hanging on the wall. I could enjoy in peace the way each arched window framed a perfect view of island and heavens, like a picture frame. It showed that the monks were not in the least bit impervious to beauty or decoration, however austere their lives were meant to be.

And how austere were they really? Not having to beg or fight or toil for their living in those cruel days – being a monk surely wasn't the hardest of jobs. And when I looked around and pondered the isolation, it occurred to me that of course

271

they were not isolated at all: the quickest way to get anywhere was by boat, the roads were few but available so that living on an island was more or less just living by the motorway. Anyone up in the archipelago, one of the oldest continuously occupied settlements in the whole of the British Isles, would usually pass by; any travellers and sailors between Scotland and the great advanced civilisations of the Nordic countries would pass by here. It was isolated now, though perhaps it hadn't always been.

Perhaps it was a jolly life here, of good fellowship, harvesting vegetables, singing and guiding boats to a safe harbour, far away from tribal wars. The ocean's plenty here to feed you, and you'd be relatively protected from invasion.

On a day like that day, it was nice to think that way. That it was a happy place.

The sun was warm enough to sit in if you kept out of the wind, and I found myself wandering away from the abbey and over to the east beach where there was a nice hummock just under a large patch of seagrass on the machair. I lay down on it and closed my eyes.

It was so lovely that I nearly dozed off. There were puffy little clouds in the sky, and the calls of the birds and the gentle crash of the waves were very soothing. In fact, there was nowhere on this tiny island where you couldn't hear the sound of the waves, and I found it very comforting.

I fell into a reverie when suddenly I heard a cross noise and felt something on my chest.

I sat up abruptly, shocked, as Barbara the chicken, looking equally startled, flustered her wings and tumbled down into my lap.

'Barbara!' I said. 'You are a very badly behaved chicken.'

She borked at me.

'What is it? Is Timmy trapped down a well?'

She borked again, ruffled herself and turned around on my lap in a slightly rude gesture.

'Do not settle yourself!' I said. 'You are not going to lay an egg on my dungarees.'

I was growing quite attached to the dungarees.

Barbara borked in a way that implied she might or she might not, and that is how Gregor found us when he marched over the crest of the machair.

'Here you are,' he said. He had been looking for me. He did a double-take.

'Are you having an argument with a *chicken*?'

'I'm not doing anything with Barbara; she hopped on me. She'd better not be one of the chickens you're killing. Don't kill any of them!'

'I'm not quite sure you understand how food works.'

'Neither am I. I am now officially vegetarian.'

He shrugged. 'Okay.'

'Will that stop you killing one of the chickens?'

'No,' he said.

'Oh, for goodness' sake.'

I thought how awful it was going to be if the scent of roast chicken, with him doing whatever stupid wizard nonsense he pulled off in the kitchen, was going to be like.

'They won't know a thing about it.'

'Yes, but I will!'

'Up to you.'

'How can you love birds and look after them and still kill chickens?'

'How can you have this point of view and, up until thirty

seconds ago, still eat chickens – particularly chickens, may I add – that don't have anything like the most wonderful, free, happy, amazing lifestyle that these ones do, especially Barbara.'

'Nobody is eating Barbara!'

'Agreed.'

He stopped, and I felt as if we were at a bit of a stalemate.

'Anyway, it looks like we have some feathered visitors up on the north rocks. Want to come and have a look?'

I looked at him, surprised he was asking me. I thought he was sick of me, in fact.

'Uh, sure, but I've got a lot of bum-warming work on for Barbara.'

He stepped forward.

'Don't kill her!'

'I'm not going to kill her!'

He skilfully whipped away Barbara, who borked noisily at him, then stalked off in the opposite direction, ignoring us both.

I followed Gregor, scrambling up over the dunes – he walked fast – and past the abbey, up along a ridge and into the darker green mossy rocks beyond which the rocks turned into a cliff and ascended into the austere heights at the northern edge of the island.

I had never been up here before, and I was surprised by how much of a scramble it was, the slippery green moss rendering the rocks treacherous. The sun warmed us as we climbed; I started feeling rather hot and so pulled off my jumper, leaving it hanging on a neat little hook. Gregor was ahead and didn't look back so I had to chase him in a rather ungainly fashion, although, on balance, I preferred it that way than for him to have to march behind my bum as I struggled over rocks. Good cardio, I found my brain thinking, before I told it to shut up.

He stopped at a flat section and sat down in the sun, legs dangling over the edge, squinting into the bright sky. I joined him, trying to cover the fact that I was out of breath and my cheeks felt hot.

From up here, the vantage point was breath-taking. You could see every step in the archipelago in both directions, like giant's footsteps. Down below, *Dolly* looked like a toy left behind on the beach by a careless child. I eyed her sadly.

'What will happen to her?' asked Gregor.

I shrugged.

'I don't know. She might be too heavy for the ferry. And her electrics are fritzed so she isn't safe to fly. The best thing might be for people to come up and dismantle her for parts.' I started to feel emotional again. 'Gramps might do it. Bring a lad up. You'd get decent money for . . . for the bits. Then the skeleton you could bring back, sell it for . . . scrap.'

My voice wobbled then.

'And that will be the end of it?'

I nodded, unable to speak.

'We should have let her sink,' mused Gregor. 'She would have formed coral. Made a habitation for fish. People could have dived down to her. It would have been cool.'

I looked at him.

'Really?'

'Absolutely. That's why they can't move the old oil rigs. Their legs have become amazing breeding grounds for fish and krill and all sorts of things. They're rewilding the ocean.'

I shook my head in disbelief.

'That's amazing. But no. I couldn't . . . I couldn't let her sink.'

'There's a thousand ships round these parts,' said Gregor. 'A thousand-thousand. Longships and warships and everything in between, that didn't make it through the archipelago. It might have been fitting.'

We stared at the infinite turquoise blue spread out around us all the way to the horizon; today it was so calm and peaceful, as if nothing bad could ever possibly happen there. You could see all the way to the mainland too. It was such a clear day, so perfect.

I looked down at *Dolly* again. She didn't look too bad from up here. Her superstructure was fine.

'There is,' I said, a germ of an idea springing in my breast, 'one tiny, tiny possibility . . . '

I stared at *Dolly* intently. I knew never to be fooled by the way things looked from a distance. You had to trust your instruments, not your senses, when you're flying. Your brain thinks it knows which way is up and which is down but it's wrong all the damn time, and sometimes if you don't spot it in time, you'll be too late.

Gregor, in that slow way of his, didn't encourage me; he just waited for me to go on.

'I mean . . . on a really, really clear day . . . I mean, it isn't far . . . Technically, you could try flying it without instruments. Just by looking.'

'Isn't that dangerous?'

'It's unbelievably dangerous,' I said. 'You make mistakes and you can't judge your own speed. If you get in cloud, you could be in a tailspin before you even knew what was happening.'

'So you probably shouldn't do it then.'

'They used to fly like that all the time,' I said, still with my eyes on the little plane below.

'Didn't they used to die all the time?'

'They did,' I conceded. 'They used to die all the time.'

'I feel you've used up quite a few of your nine lives already.'

'You're right. And we'd never get clearance from ATC. Not in a million years. If they caught me, I'd never fly again.' I smiled ruefully. 'I suppose I just have to reconcile myself to doing the sensible thing: talk to the insurance company. Let them come and pick it apart.'

I sighed.

'Do you always do the sensible thing?'

I thought back to last night. Not quite. And also, I thought 'sensible' might be a bit overrated. 'Sensible' was in Dubai, pretending to girls he was a pilot.

Gregor handed me a water bottle and I took it gratefully: it hadn't occurred to me to bring one. The cold fresh stream of water was bracing and absolutely delicious, and I took a long pull, letting my legs dangle over the ledge, nothing beneath them to the water below.

'Come on then,' he said. 'Bit gnarly, the next bit. But worth it, I think.'

He wasn't kidding. The cliff head was steep and required careful manoeuvring. I hadn't done anything like this in a very long time – or ever, I didn't think – and I found locating routes and placing my hands in toe- and footholds tiring but fascinating, like following a jigsaw puzzle. In one or two areas, someone had even hung ropes you could pull yourself up on. By the time we reached the top, I was flushed and proud of myself, and the view was even more astounding than before. Now *Dolly* was a dot far below on a golden sweep of a painter's brush, and the sky and the sea and the warm sun filled the senses, three hundred and sixty degrees around.

More than that, though, was the noise. A great cawing filled the air. There were gulls milling everywhere – we had come up the side of the cliff, thankfully, as over on grassy knolls of the summit were huge amounts of guano, white splashes everywhere. Haphazard nests sprawled with wasted pieces of twigs scattered here and there.

'You brought me up to see some seagulls?' I said. 'Because I have to tell you, they nick my chips almost anywhere in Britain.'

'Nope,' he said. 'Look over there.'

He pointed to the far side of the cliff top, and I gasped aloud.

'Oh my God!' I said.

'Shush,' he said, lifting the binoculars.

Over and away from the gulls, as if they liked to keep to their own neighbourhood, was a tumbling, jolly mass of little round black and white birds, cawing and circling.

'Puffins!'

He looked at me.

'How did they ever let you in the air? They're guillemots!'

Sure enough, these birds were elegant to look at, not round and pudgy like puffins.

'Oh,' I said. I'd never heard of guillemots; I thought that was a band.

'Early this year too,' he said. 'Must be the warm weather. They're breeding, look. See they're in mating pairs?'

I did see: there were little and self-important, presumably female birds, sitting quietly as the males chuntered about here and there and occasionally took off from the cliff edge and dropped like dive bombers into the waves far below.

As I studied them further, I realised that it was such a privilege, such a gift to be allowed to see them and their private, funny little rituals. There was one bird that came up with four fish in his mouth, strutting back proudly to his nest as if showing them off to the other birds, his mate ruffling her feathers.

Even though Gregor was marking things down solemnly in a book and taking film footage with one hand, I couldn't stop tugging on his sleeve to point out when one of them did something particularly amusing or incredible. The speed with which they swept into the sea was extraordinary. They were like blurs.

'There'll be double that many by next week,' Gregor said with satisfaction. 'I'm meant to have tour groups every day from the OI. Well. We will or we won't. The birds don't care.'

'I'm glad,' I said impulsively. 'I'm glad I got to see them and it was just me.'

He looked at me, then smiled, showing off white teeth.

'You're not the only flier on this island, huh?'

We stayed, watching – I was agog and never got tired of it, especially when Gregor lent me his binoculars and I could see them so close I could watch the individual birds communicating with each other. I also saw a couple of eggs – no babies yet – and suddenly found myself intensely invested in how things would turn out, especially for Mr and Mrs Big Fish.

'They're busy,' I said.

'They are,' he said. 'And they flap about everywhere all the time. Just like you.'

'I do not flap!'

' "Oooh, why can't you rewire a house?!" "Ooh, let me build a chicken coop!" '

'Shut up!' I said, laughing.

The sun was moving lower in the sky by the time we finally stood up to go. And I realised that there was absolutely nowhere else on earth I would rather be than under Scotland's huge and ever-changing skies, smelling the soft gorse beneath and listening to the hew and cackle of these amazing creatures.

There was light, air, space and freedom. A place to which I belonged utterly; a place I could breathe. Gramps had been right all along: what swimming pool could possibly, possibly compete with this?

We had to head back eventually, and I was deep in thought. Going down was harder than coming up, and I realised I was tired as I dropped my footing a couple of times. When Gregor noticed, he beckoned me back to the ledge we had sat on on the way up. Now the sun had warmed it through magnificently, and it was incredibly pleasant to rest my weary bones on it. He felt in among the stuff in his rucksack and pulled out a tartan flask.

If you were ever to have told me that I could get so excited at the sight of a tartan flask, I would never have believed you, but the hot sweet tea inside was the best thing I'd ever tasted. Then he pulled out a Tupperware box, opened it and, to my absolute delight, revealed two huge scones, still holding the last breath of warmth, filled with butter and sweet, heavy home-made jam.

'You brought *afternoon tea*?' I said in astonishment. He looked almost embarrassed.

'Well, it's nice,' he said. 'You usually feel like a treat about now. Well, I do.'

'I *do*,' I said. 'I am *so* glad your ex couldn't cook.'

We sat and ate our huge scones and shared the flask of hot sweet tea, and I looked at a sketch he'd made of the large guillemot couple with the most fish. It was very fine, beautifully wrought with just a pencil on a thick sheet of card.

'That's lovely,' I said. 'Can I have it?'

'No,' he said. 'It's an official document.'

'Oh.'

'I'm kidding,' he said. 'Of course. I only do it for fun.'

'Well, it's absolutely gorgeous.'

He set down his whole rucksack, which was now notably lighter.

'How set,' he said carefully, 'are you on this whole "no chicken" thing?'

I frowned.

'Barbara would be so disappointed in me.'

He nodded.

'All right. And how does it extend to fish?'

I thought of all the fish the birds had just brought up.

'I suppose fish are all right,' I said. 'You know, if the guillemots have already been there . . .'

He frowned.

'So you have absolutely no double-standard issues at all?'

'I do!' I said. 'I absolutely won't eat anything that borks at me!'

He laughed at that.

'Okay then,' he said. 'Are you okay with carrying the rucksack back?'

'Uh, why?'

'I have some langoustine pots,' he said. 'Could go check them.'

My face fell.

'Oh no, the poor . . .'

'Well, *I* have to eat,' he said.

'Will you be humane?' I said. 'I feel bad.'

'That's okay,' he said. 'Thinking about what you eat is the right thing to do.'

I thought, rather ashamed, of all the ready airline meals I had scarfed down, barely looking at them.

'Yeah,' I said.

He stood up and took off his top and his trousers. He was wearing swimming trunks. I tried not to look at him, and to ignore the fact that underneath the shapeless heavy garments, he was broad-shouldered, narrow-waisted and lean-muscled. He looked, in fact, exactly like what he said he was: someone who swam in the sea every day. Nevertheless, we were still miles up.

'What on *earth* are you doing?'

'*You* are not used to cold water,' he said. 'As I told you, I am.'

And he handed me the rucksack.

'See you back at the house.'

And simply walked forward and arched himself into a perfect dive off the side of the ridge.

'GREGOR! ...'

But there was no point in calling on him: he had gone. My heart jumped in my mouth. I inched forwards to the side of the cliff gingerly, worried about falling, and saw, what seemed like miles below, a dark head surfacing like a seal, shaking the water from his eyes.

'Aren't you meant to not swim after eating?' I said to nobody. Perhaps that was a myth. At any rate, the figure below me was striking out round the cliff and towards the beach, where I could now see orange ropes tied up at the far end. Goodness. And his was definitely the quick way home. Although absolutely not a route I would take for myself.

I gathered up the rucksack and checked to see if we'd left anything – of course he hadn't – and was about to start out for home when something over the sea caught my eye. It was a glint. I frowned, wondering if something was trying to send something via Morse code again. I should get on to that before dinner.

Then I remembered there were binoculars in the bag, and I rifled through it till I found them. Careful not to look at the sun, it took me a while to figure out where the glint had come from. But with the binoculars it was obvious, and something my brain had probably already known. Coming towards the island was a boat.

Chapter Twenty-six

The silly thing is that my immediate reaction should have been, of course, hooray! Finally! I was going to get off here and out of this place and see everyone and I was going to make my interview and we'd figure some way to get *Dolly* on a ship and it was all going to be fine and go back to normal.

But something else struck me too, to my complete and utter surprise. I found I was slightly annoyed. We were having langoustine for tea! And I had to tell Barbara she was saved, as was I! And Frances might want a cuddle! And how would I know what was going to happen to Mr and Mrs Big Fish? And I had been looking forward to bed that night given how well I slept there, the fresh air knocking me out until I didn't know a thing about anything and slept so beautifully I could have been in the finest hotel in the world.

I was incredibly surprised to find myself ambushed by all that.

I was even more surprised by what I did next.

They wouldn't be coming for us right away, I thought. They

had to go and check on the islands with children. And there were the actors, goodness. They'd be scared. And the hen party, who hadn't been remotely suitably dressed for a stay in a stormy island with no power. So they wouldn't be coming for us for ages. So I hardly needed to mention it to Gregor.

I walked slowly back down the cliff and recovered my jumper, watching my feet so I didn't trip over the rocks. Gregor's route was definitely quicker. The sun was warm on my back as I picked my way up the dunes and past the abbey, no longer sinister, as it had been that very first night, in the bright afternoon glow, but friendly-looking, all the tiny closing daisies providing a glorious carpet over the ancient floors. I picked a bunch. At the gate to the house, Frances came right up to me, butting my hand gently. She was clearly getting used to me. I kindly let her eat the daisies. Barbara was nowhere to be seen. She probably understood every single word of the chicken debate, I found myself thinking, even as the other calmer hens pecked around the stony pathways.

I slipped in through the back door and grabbed a bottle from a jewel-coloured line in the larder of long-ago-bottled rhubarb wine, presumably for the holy men. They wouldn't mind. I also grabbed two glasses and a corkscrew and headed into the parlour, when I heard a sound. I frowned, pushing open the door. It was just as I'd thought. As soon as he saw me, he went bright red and tried to hide it behind his back.

'Christ,' he said.

'I know,' I said. 'Oh my God. I mean, it would have been less embarrassing if you'd been looking at a naughty magazine.'

'Forget it,' he said.

'Uh-uh,' I said. 'I've seen it now.'

We both looked at the guitar he was ineffectually trying to

conceal behind his back. Frances had pushed her way through the door, and now lay down in front of the fire and prepared herself for a nap.

'Oh God,' he said. 'I didn't think you'd be back so fast.'

'Do you know "You're Beautiful" by James Blunt?'

'Shut up!'

'Do you bring it out at parties?'

'It will not surprise you to know that I don't go to a lot of parties.'

'Huh,' I said. 'I'm not surprised; everyone hates Guitar Guy.'

'I'm not Guitar Guy!'

'Do you ever pose in front of the mirror like a proper rock god?'

'No!'

'Don't lie in a house of God!'

He laughed, as if admitting it. I drew out the wine.

'I believe rhubarb 1998 is the perfect vintage to go with langoustine.'

'I have never made an attempt on that stuff. I assume it will be unconscionable. Do you drink, like, all the first-class airline wine?'

I stared at him. 'While I'm *piloting an aeroplane*? OMG, it really isn't just buttons, you know! I barely ever drink at all!'

I opened the wine anyway. It smelled pretty good, rich and fruity, like alcoholic jam. I poured us a couple of small glasses and handed him one.

'What?' he said at my enquiring expression.

'Go on then. Play me something.'

'Oh no.'

'I'm afraid if a guitar has been sighted, you have to play. Those are the rules. Especially in a house without internet *or* TV.'

'I don't really—'

'I don't care,' I said. 'I have no ear for music anyway, so it doesn't matter how bad you are.'

'Well, that's useful,' he said.

It was lovely enough to go and sit in the front garden and watch the last of the golden rays. Also, I would highly recommend spending as little time as possible in an enclosed space that has a goat sleeping in front of a fire.

The grass was overgrown and covered in pebbles and seaweed that the storm had hurled in, but we pulled up a couple of battered old deckchairs. I thought he might get huffy about it, but he'd brought the guitar, so I sat back contentedly. The wine, the sunshine, the physical exercise . . . it had been a good day. I let my eyes droop.

He strummed for a bit, then stopped. I opened my eyes.

'What?'

'It's embarrassing, playing for people.'

'Don't be daft,' I said. 'You can play music. Most people can't. To let them share that . . . It's a gift you can share. You'd be giving me a present. It doesn't matter if it's an amazing present or not, it's still lovely to get. You're selfish keeping all the music to yourself. To open yourself up . . . it means something.'

And for once, I wasn't teasing him. I was completely sincere.

He thought about that.

'Okay,' he said.

I settled back again, and he gently strummed some chords, then, equally gently, started to sing in a low sweet growl:

When I feel like the words
Are breathing in and out of me

And I'm standing beside you,
there's a shadow where a man should be . . .

It wasn't a song I knew, but I was struck by how sad it was,
and how wistfully he sang it.

I would be glad enough
If, wherever you might be,
People would remember
We're woven in a tapestry . . .

His voice was sounding stronger now, as if he'd forgotten I
was there. It had a lovely lazy gruff timbre.

While we steal what we can
In our courage to be free
And I find where I belong –
Among the poorest company . . .

I smiled at that but he didn't look at me.

When I feel like the world
Is ruthless, spinning far from me,
A country on my shoulders, its flag flies from a
     gallows tree
I won't let it get me down.

His voice caught, and he seemed to be having trouble getting
the words out.

I know there are people now

People who have made it through
Who live their lives like I'd want to . . .

He broke off, clearly unable to go on. He stood up, his face distraught.

'Are you all right?' I said, jumping up too.

He shook his head.

'I haven't . . . I haven't sung that song for a while.' He turned away. 'I haven't sung anything for a while.'

'It was nice,' I said, trotting after him. 'I mean, proper good, not annoying party guitarist good.'

He pursed his lips together and went on inside, Frances following along behind.

'Stay outside,' he said. 'I'll get supper.'

I didn't; I followed him in. He was standing in the kitchen, gently frying black garlic in butter. The smell was ridiculously good.

'I'm sorry. It's taken you so long to get over your girlfriend.'

'Oh, I'm over her,' he said. 'I am. It wasn't . . . it wasn't just that.' And he turned away. I remembered that he had wanted to talk about it last night, and muggins here had fallen asleep. I also remembered the boat, which sooner or later was going to turn up and fetch me and take me back to – well, the real world, I supposed. I could see from Gregor's back – I found it very easy now to read his mood – that he didn't want to talk any more.

'Don't be sad,' I said. And then I had a thought.

As he paid attention to the boiling water, I went and put the batteries back in the transistor radio and turned it on. Immediately, pop music came blaring out, the total opposite of his own gentle song. But I didn't care. In fact, I was pleased: he needed cheering up. And also, it was my last night here. Maybe even less than that. So I refilled both our glasses and fiddled with the dial until I found an old 1980s channel, and just as I did so, 'You Make My Dreams Come True' came on.

'Yeah!' I said. 'Now *that's* how you play the guitar.'

He couldn't help it: he turned and looked at me, and then he smiled.

'What? You can't like more than one type of music?' I said.

'So what you're saying is, you get to slag me off for being party guitar guy but you're going to dance to this all over my kitchen.'

'I'm not dancing,' I said, then I realised I'd drunk quite a lot of wine and, as I looked down, my leg was definitely at least twitching. 'Are you saying pilots can't dance?'

'Ornithologists really can't dance,' he said, flipping the garlic expertly.

'Well, let's see,' I said. And barely knowing what I was doing, as the evening beamed pink rays in through the back door, I moved towards him and first we were laughing and doing silly dancing, and then suddenly we were just dancing, and the music changed to 'Alive and Kicking' by Simple Minds, which isn't a silly song at all, it's a lovely and slightly sexy song, and he wasn't anything like a bad dancer.

And that is how Finn found us after he had moored up the boat and had come up to the house, presumably to find out why we were ignoring that he'd landed and why there was nobody waiting for him as he putt-putted up to the harbour.

Chapter Twenty-seven

'Well,' said Finn at the door. 'I see you are all fine and well in yourselves.'

We jumped apart like we'd been caught doing something we shouldn't have. I turned off the radio.

'We're okay,' I said, somewhat embarrassed.

'And the plane?'

'She's round on the east beach, pulled up . . . '

He nodded.

'Aye well, you'll be wanting to get back down south.'

'Yeah, eh, I have stuff to do,' I said. Finn was looking over in the direction of where *Dolly* was, behind the dunes.

'She won't fly,' I said. Finn and Gregor exchanged a look.

'All right then. What about you, Gregor? What are you going to need? The mainland was a right mess; power was out for a couple of days.'

Gregor borrowed a pen and paper from him and, with help from me, wrote down the generator parts he needed as well as the radio aerial. Then we went upstairs and I grabbed my few old clothes and worthless phone. Gregor fetched an entire cheese for Finn, which I eyed.

'It's goat,' he said. 'You won't like it.'

'You really don't need anything else?' Finn said.

Gregor shrugged. 'I do pretty well.'

As it was a golden sweet-scented evening, and I was already deeply regretting the langoustine I wouldn't be eating later, it was impossible not to agree with Gregor's assessment of things.

'Better go,' said Finn. 'We've got a few to check on.'

Gregor turned to me. We were suddenly very shy with one another.

'Well. Safe trip, I suppose,' said Gregor.

'Cheers,' I said. 'There'll probably be people here to strip the plane. Or see if they can load it, whatever.'

He nodded. 'The tourists will be back anyway, soon enough.'

He sounded rather wistful about it.

We smiled and I glanced down.

'This sounds silly but . . . I hate leaving you by yourself.'

He shrugged.

'Fewer people stealing my food. And . . . are you really going to be all right back out in the . . . craziness?'

I thought about it.

'I think I am,' I said. 'I think . . . yeah. I can do it.'

'Just keep busy,' he said, nodding.

'And you . . . just keep not too busy.'

I turned to go, absolutely amazed I felt so torn. I looked at Gregor, then looked away. It was silly. All of it.

He looked back at me as if he were about to say something, and then changed his mind.

'Uh . . .'

'Yes?' I said, but a little too quickly.

'You're ... uh. Well, I think Barbara would probably say you're welcome any time.'

'Thank you.'

'Barbara says you're welcome.'

'No, I mean, thank you ... for everything.'

He didn't say anything, just nodded once sharply. Then he turned to head back into the house – to get ready to meet his hawk, I assumed. He passed the box I'd delivered what felt like a long time ago, and I realised I'd never gotten round to asking what was in it. Well. I don't suppose it mattered now: he had to get back to this strange, lonely life of his, and I had to get back to mine. Or see what was left of it. Our very, very different worlds.

'LADY PILOT!'

Huddled on the boat already was the travelling troupe of actors, which had also been stranded by the storm. They were touchingly pleased to see me, and wanted to tell me in great detail about how they had performed everything they knew, including Shakespeare plays, to the people without power on Larbh, and how appreciative they'd been. And it did sound rather fun, watching *Macbeth* by candlelight. Boona asked me about the plane, and I wished I hadn't told her when I saw her horrified face.

The hen party was down below, having located the little bar, which they had insisted on breaking open. They had obviously found the entire thing the most jolly adventure they could imagine, and they tried to rope us all in; the actors were happy to oblige. Normally I didn't mind being in the middle of noisy groups or parties, but now it felt a little much after the stillness of Inchborn. A lot of noise and fuss to contend with.

Also, on my mind was that I had to go back to explain to Gramps I'd lost his plane.

Chapter Twenty-eight

My heart sank as we approached the dock as the evening was pinkening further, all the heat soaking out of the day. I realised I still had the old man's dungarees on. I supposed I'd have to send the clothes back at some point. Well, no. Maybe not.

Gramps was standing on the dock, waiting for me. Then I made out two figures next to him. Mum and Dad. Of course.

Those suspicions – that I might have died – were confirmed as we stepped off the boat onto the dock and my mum charged over and grabbed me in her arms and squeezed the breath out me, taking me completely by surprise.

'Morag! My darling Morag! Oh my God! Oh my God!'

My dad wasn't quite so gushing, but his eyes were distinctly damp as he came over.

'Those hours when the storm came and we hadn't heard from you,' he said. 'It was ... I can't tell you how bad it was.'

'But Nalitha told you I'd landed the plane.'

'She told us you were right by the cliff! In a storm! And she'd left you there! She feels awful about it,' said my mother. 'She was in pieces.'

'She couldn't do anything else! How's Erno?'

'He's fine, he's fine,' said my dad, waving his arm. Gramps came up.

'Is your flu better?' I said timidly.

He let out a whiskery laugh.

'You daft bint! I didn't have the flu! I just thought you needed your confidence back,' he said. His voice lowered. 'We've all had a near-miss.'

And then he squeezed me tight.

'You didn't!'

My first instinct was to be absolutely furious with him. He'd lied to me and tricked me and got me on that plane through false pretences.

Then I remembered that first flight when he hadn't told me I'd be doing it till the very last second. He knew I had to figure these things out for myself. He knew me better than I knew myself. I suppose that's what family is in the end, even if that is occasionally extremely annoying.

'I would be more annoyed with you,' I said, 'if it hadn't been working ...'

He beamed at me.

' ... well, until I crashed your plane.'

'Not what I heard,' said Gramps, and he patted me on the back. 'Well done, lass.'

'She got a bit of a dousing,' I said. He nodded. 'But I think ... you might be able to strip her down ...'

'She was getting very old,' he said. 'I guess we both are.'

I looked at him.

'Come on, Dad,' said my dad. 'Let's get her home and into some proper clothes. She's had a shock.'

'But!' said my mum meaningfully, and I followed her gaze.

I had been trying not to think about it, trying to put it out of my mind till I got back down there, see where we stood. He'd never even seen where I lived; he hadn't met my family yet.

'There's someone here to see you,' said my mum. And standing at the end of the pier, his hair ruffled, his face grinning widely, was Hayden.

He opened his arms wide.

'Oh my God, darling. I was so worried. *So* worried! You won't believe . . . Well, Christ, there's a lot of messages.'

My mum was beaming.

'He's ever so nice!' she said. 'You didn't tell us he was so nice!'

I swallowed hard.

'He . . . he is nice.'

Hayden walked towards me, his face still in a wide smile. He looked lovely in his smart blue shirt, pressed chinos and the trainers we'd bought together.

He doesn't know, I thought. He doesn't know I heard him. He thinks everything is fine.

'Mrs MacIntyre, do you mind if I kiss your daughter?' he said, arms outstretched, and my mother giggled like a teenager and said, 'Well, on you go then, you big daftie,' like they'd been friends for years. And it was all there, right in front of me. Everything I'd ever wanted. The man I'd started falling in love with. And all I had to do was step forward. Everything could be fine. I could have everything I'd ever wanted – the big job and the nice man and life moving forward, as it should.

I heard a gull cawing on the breeze. I didn't glance behind me. My mother's face. Shy, nerdy little Morag, with all her flying hours, and never a nice man. I froze for a second. A tiny expression of uncertainty crossed Hayden's face.

'Oh, you poor thing,' he said. 'You must be traumatised. I've booked a place to stay. Come and let me look after you.'

'And oh God, your hair,' said my mum. 'You have been in the wars!'

Collectively, they bundled me into the car, my mum insisting I sit in the front. I didn't say anything.

Back at the house, the heating was turned up and Peigi had the fire roaring so I knew this was definitely a special occasion. Dinner was roast chicken, I noted ruefully. I stuck to the potatoes and vegetables.

First off, I plugged in my phone. It binged and filled up with messages as soon as it got enough charge in it to do so. I looked at it almost fearfully. It seemed a lot to take on.

'You were on the news!' said my mum excitedly, pulling something up on her iPad. 'The plane that disappeared!'

'She didn't disappear!' I said. 'She landed perfectly well.'

'They shouldn't have put the location,' said my dad disapprovingly. 'They'll get looters.'

'Looting what?' I said. 'A puddle-jumper with rinsed electrics?'

Gramps was staring at his cup of tea, very quiet.

'She's no' in the water?'

'She was,' I said honestly. 'We pulled her out again.'

He looked at me with some surprise.

'You did, aye?'

'Wow,' said Hayden. I shot him a glance. I was surprised at my reaction but I was furious with him. What was he going to do, store it up for later?

But he looked so normal sitting there, before helping my mum clear away plates. She appeared to be more smitten than I was. This should be making me so happy.

'We did. Gregor and I pulled her out. He's the guy who's looking after Inchborn.'

'Well now,' said Gramps.

'But the electrics ...'

He nodded.

'Aye.'

'You did brilliantly,' said my mum, who couldn't stop coddling me. 'We're so, so proud of you.'

'My little aeronaut,' said my dad, getting slightly choked.

Chapter Twenty-nine

It was strange, having a shower and changing back into myself. I had a really long, hot one and washed my hair and gave it a mask; it was in absolute rats' tails. I moisturised myself all over and shaved my hairy legs and plucked my eyebrows – I hadn't been away that long and yet still everything appeared to have fallen apart. In the mirror, I was a total fright.

I carefully blow-dried my hair straight, then put make-up on. It felt a little weird. I found a dress and a pair of tights in my bag and added an extra layer of lipstick, then headed back downstairs.

'Oh!' said my mum.

'What?'

'Nothing.' She smiled. 'It's just I was thinking how nice you looked when you came off the boat. I love your curls. And your lovely skin. You just looked so fresh and young.'

'And now I look like a terrible old bat?'

'No!' she said, kissing me. 'Now you look like an amazing professional grown-up pilot who saved a man's life!'

My brother Jamie had shown up too, and shrugged his way over, pretending not to be pleased to see me.

'Hey, sis. Quite some showing off there.'

'Hey, I saw some guillemots nesting!' I said.

His eyebrows went up. 'I can't believe you can pronounce that. You're interested in something that doesn't need petrol?'

'Yeah, yeah,' I said. 'It was cool, actually.'

'I know they're cool!' said Jamie. 'That's why I spent nine days in Orkney photographing them for *Outside* magazine lying in the grass in the pouring rain and none of you were remotely interested, remember?'

'Yeah, yeah,' I said again.

It was a lovely evening. We wandered back down to the dockside for an ice cream from the excellent local sweetshop. Hayden went and stood in the queue for us. Jamie didn't mention him.

'How's Gregor?' he asked instead.

'You know him?' I said, surprised. I'd assumed he was an incomer nobody knew.

'Och aye. He's a big deal in the bird world. Did you meet his hawk?'

'I didn't get too close. I met his goat though.'

'He has a goat now?' said Jamie. 'Cool.'

'He's weird!' I said decisively, glancing over to where Hayden was. 'Good cook though.'

'How's he bearing up?' said Jamie. Then he looked uncomfortable. 'I mean, how did he seem to you?'

'It seemed a bit dramatic,' I said. 'Moving to an island to get over a girl. He's quite quiet.'

But he hadn't been quiet that last day, I thought. When he jumped off the cliff in a perfect arc into the water. When we'd danced in the kitchen. Those hadn't been the actions of a quiet man.

'Aye well. He's been through it.'

'Been through what?'

Jamie shrugged.

'Well, if he'd wanted you to know he'd have told you.'

I frowned. Jamie strode ahead, just like he always did when we were small. Some vestigial memory or belief that they'd run out of Flakes.

'He was . . . He did want to tell me something,' I called. Then I was embarrassed.

'Aye?' said Jamie, turning round.

'But he didn't. I . . . I fell asleep.'

'He tried to tell you something deeply personal and you fell asleep?!' said Jamie.

'It was a very full-on couple of days.'

'Classic you.'

'It is not classic me!'

'Aye, it is. Don't tell me: did the focus stray off your amazing career and fantastic being-a-pilot stories for one minute?'

'That's not— That's not what I'm like!'

'Ooh, Hayden! Oooh, Dubai! Oooh, Barbados! Planes planes planes! Everyone pay attention to me! I'm so busy and important.'

He was trying to say it like it was funny but it didn't feel like he was being funny at all.

'That's . . . It's just not true.'

'Oh my God, she has eyelashes and flies a plane! Isn't she brilliant!'

I had absolutely no idea why Jamie was being so cranky with me. I didn't quite realise at that moment that he'd spent seventy-two hours with my parents in utter hysterics at the thought I might be lost, when he regularly took himself off for months at a time to paint emus in the Australian bush. And of course me being the pilot. It's not as if they didn't want it to be him. Not as if they didn't basically beg him to go to flight school, and he didn't want to.

'That is *not* what I think.'

'Here we go,' said Hayden, returning in triumph, his hands full. 'An extra Flake for the amazing famous pilot.'

Jamie rolled his eyes.

Nalitha had been to see Erno. He was fine, in bed at home, grumbling about having to change his diet, but enjoying getting to sleep as much as he wanted.

'So,' she said, as we wandered down the little main street, 'I hear lover boy dashed to your side.'

I looked at her. She was still the only person who knew.

'So what did he say?'

'I . . . I haven't mentioned it.'

'*Rags!*'

I shrugged.

'Nalitha, he's lovely. Everyone likes him. It was one stupid mistake.'

'No, it was one time you overheard him! It could be literally *every night*! He could be doing it *right now* while you're here talking to me! Maybe he's trying it on Peigi – you know what she's like with pilots.'

'You should meet him,' I said.

'I shouldn't,' said Nalitha in a warning tone.

I closed my eyes. I didn't know what to do. To my total surprise, I found myself wishing I was back on the island. Back where I didn't have any problems beyond getting through each day. I wondered what Gregor was doing right now, then shut that thought off immediately. I had a real life here. I had ambitions and plans for my future.

Gramps came with us to the airport to get on one of Callum Frost's cheap jets down south.

'I need to tell you about that,' I said. 'He made an offer, can you believe? Such a bastard.'

Gramps frowned.

'Did he?'

'Yeah. Sorry. A lot has happened. Don't worry: I told him to do one.'

'Did you really?'

'Gramps! His planes can't even land on Inchborn! He's a dick. You don't want it!'

'You seem to know a lot about me, Morag,' he said. 'You seem to think I want to fly down to Dubai and hang out. And you seem to think I'm an idiot who won't know when to give up flying.'

'You're not an idiot,' I said. 'But don't sell up – not to him! He's awful.'

'Uh-huh,' said Gramps. Then he clasped my shoulders. 'I don't think that simulator is going to give you much trouble now, do you?'

I shrugged. 'The whole sky is waiting for me.'

'The whole world,' he said. And he gave me the biggest hug and shook Hayden's hand formally.

Hayden tried to hold my hand on the plane but I was staring away from him, as if I was leaving Scotland for ever, and pretended that I didn't see. I was trying to trace every purple ridge as I peered out for the best view of the archipelago: Carso to Cairn, Inchborn, Larbh, Archland and home again. It was a glorious day out there for a run. Gramps should be off now, taking the mail, making faces to small people with birthdays, reuniting families, wowing tourists. I wondered how long it would take the insurance to cough up for a new plane. I wondered if Gregor would ever look up when it passed, and think about me.

Chapter Thirty

After the freshness of spring in the north, everything down south was rushing on fast forward. It was muggy and grey, the daffodils already done. Hayden was obviously confused by my silence. He had given up trying to hold my hand as I stared out the window, and was obviously putting it down to trauma.

But I wasn't traumatised. As we flew south, I found myself feeling worse and worse. I had gazed at the cumulonimbus, thinning and lightening as we flew to warmer climes, and had found it the opposite of my heart, which felt as if it were becoming more constrained, more getting squeezed into a smaller and smaller box.

'So how was Dubai?' I managed to ask as we drove back to my flat. He shrugged. 'Oh, just work really. Lots of introductions. But I think you're going to love it! Loads of complexes have pools and at night it's lovely and warm and you can go down to the souk and shop, or go to one of the hotels or an amusement park or a water park … There's absolutely loads to do …'

I bet there is, I thought. But the archipelago *was* a water park, full of the most remarkable species and the clearest water I had ever known.

'Are you nervous for your sim?' he said.

I shook my head. 'I don't think so.'

And it was true. The terrible fear, the – well, PTSD, I suppose, though that was a strong word for it – had gone. Crash-landing *Dolly* had seemed to fix it, and possibly even just a few days' breathing space had healed me. I no longer felt frightened to fly.

I felt very, very frightened about what lay ahead though.

It was hot and humid outside, smog in the air, and I was cross and enervated and I couldn't sleep. Hayden had been understanding when I hadn't wanted to have sex with him, and was tidily asleep, his hair over his brow. He didn't snore. Oh, there was so very much right with this man.

I moved into the tiny bare sitting room and sat down at the plastic breakfast bar. I wanted to get things straight in my head, figure out how to handle it. I knew what Nalitha would say, and it would probably involve a pair of rusty scissors. But she didn't know Hayden. But then, did I? Oh God. I watched him sleeping again, my heart soft. Then I went back to the kitchen and found myself googling Inchborn.

Presently, I found myself hypnotised by a documentary about the abbey, full of things I had never known such as fabled kings and queens of Scandinavia and Scotland, who had visited and received hospitality there; great ships – the *Erebus*, the

Terror – that had stopped there on their way to doomed missions to find the Northwest Passage; even, amazingly, information about a settlement that was underneath the abbey. The settlers of 1200 AD not only knew they were not the first to be there, but had respected their forerunners. I tried to imagine the monks of hundreds of years ago, trying in their turn to imagine the impossibly distant travellers who had lived deep in their own pasts.

There was even, to my astonishment, a bird cam set up for the mating pairs so you could watch them live. Obviously it was dark, but there was night vision on the camera. I peered through it, hoping to see my little chonky family, but I will tell you it will take a better bird person than I will ever be to be able to distinguish guillemots in the dark.

Guiltily, almost, I googled Gregor.

I knew before it came up that he wouldn't be on social media. No social media, no Insta, no Facebook even – come on, who didn't have a dead Facebook account from a million years ago? There was a large foxy-faced man in Canada who liked ice hockey and shared his name, as well as an academic in Seattle. But of the quiet ornithologist, not a thing. Too busy reading books and wearing glasses, I supposed. Thinking about his ex.

I felt guilty about even having the search window open, which was also strange, because who cared if I was looking him up? I mean, how could it possibly matter what I was looking at? I stared at the computer sadly, and went back to remembering Inchborn: the way the shadows hit that great empty beach; the way the moon had come down to touch the water; the crackle of the fire and the quiet turn of a page in a book.

That's when I saw the video, right at the bottom of the page. My heart jumped, quite without me having anything to do with it. I clicked on it at once.

There he was. His hair longer, with stubble and wearing a shirt and tie, when I would not have suspected him of owning such a thing. His glasses, though, were just the same.

I took a glance next door, then reached for the headphones, which made me feel even more like I was doing something sneaky. Which I wasn't. I just couldn't sleep, that was all. Just ... you know, consolidating my experience or something like that. I had been through a major life experience, after all, I thought. Any therapist would tell me to process it properly. And anyway, it wasn't like Hayden had any right to tell me who I could pay attention to ...

I shut the thought off in my head, slipped the headphones on and pressed play. He was giving a lecture, obviously to an attentive and quite large audience, and there was a board behind him that was showing a picture of a sparrowhawk – unsurprisingly, I supposed.

His deep burr was so familiar that it took me a while to tune in to the fact that he wasn't speaking in English.

I scowled. Murdo spoke Gaelic, and the new generation was getting it at school. I was the last generation who had been told it was useless, and you shouldn't learn your own mother tongue, but that of the ... well, I wouldn't say invader. Let's say: larger constituency. When I travelled for work, I could order a coffee or a beer in a smattering of French or Spanish or German. But I couldn't speak a word of Gaelic. I was ashamed.

Gregor spoke on, the words playing like music, guttural and sweet and low, more like song than speech. I found myself quite lulled just watching him, feeling warm and safe and closer to sleep than I had been since I had returned. Then I realised there was an option to click for subtitles in English, and durred myself.

He was – again unsurprisingly – talking about the birds of

Inchborn at a lecture of the Scottish Ornithologists' Club at Aberlady, I learned. I couldn't see the audience, but there was a lot of approving throat-clearing and harrumphing.

I watched, fascinated, listening to his voice tumble like a waterfall over the deep, guttural stops and light, shimmering cadences of the language of the Western Isles. I could have listened to him all day. Then I saw what he was saying as he was winding up his lecture.

'*Rainnig mi Inchborn ...*'

'I moved to Inchborn ...'

'... *aonar* ...'

'... alone ...'

'... *cuin a bha mo beatha dona* ...'

'... when my life was bad ...'

'... *agus an t-eilan* ...'

'... and the island ...'

'... *leighis e mi* ...'

'... healed me ...'

I paused the video then, looking at his face. I couldn't stop looking at it. I let the video continue playing, but he went back to discussing migration patterns and didn't say anything remotely personal again, even after he was greeted with warm applause and the video stopped.

I replayed the video, this time without the subtitles. In the chill of the little sparse unlived-in kitchen, in the quiet of the cul-de-sac, where good, kind-hearted people slept in nice John Lewis beds and dreamed blameless dreams, I sat listening to a quiet, unusual man speak about a subject I knew nothing about in a language I did not understand, and felt myself comforted and drowsy, as if I were back there, lit by candles and huge strings of stars, hanging so close it felt they might rattle.

I called Jamie. I know phoning people is not quite the thing these days, but I couldn't get up to see him and I needed to know. I'm not a monster; as soon as it was more or less light, I WhatsApped him before I called him: 'Can I call you about something?' and immediately got a message back saying, 'What is it? Is Mum all right? What's happened? What's wrong?' so I just called him there and then, even though it was six o'clock in the morning.

'Hey,' he said. He didn't sound sleepy at all, and there was wind whistling down the phone.

'Are you outside?' I said.

'There's some nesting mallards in the long willows,' he said quietly. 'I'm trying to sketch them before they wake up and try and break my arm.'

'I did not realise it was such a dangerous business.'

'Yup, you're not the only one at daily risk of imminent death.'

'That's not *exactly* how I'd describe it.'

'What's up?' he said suspiciously. 'You don't sound like someone is dying.'

'No,' I said, suddenly slightly ashamed at such urgency. 'I just ... I need to ... I mean, I was wondering ...'

There was a squawk in the distance.

'Oh bugger, they're up.'

I heard him stumbling away quite quickly.

'Is this a bad time?'

'There are no particularly good times in my job,' said Jamie. 'Of course, I'm not successfully burning nine hundred kilograms of carbon dumping six stag parties in Magaluf.'

'Jamie ...' I said, and he must have heard something in my voice, as he softened a bit.

'Go on then, sis,' he said. Then a rustle. 'Oh, crap, it's going for my easel.'

There was a very loud squawk.

'Oh, I'll call you back ...'

'What's this about?!'

'I just wondered about Gregor.'

There was a very long pause.

'What were you wondering?'

'The thing you were going to tell me. The thing he was going to tell me.'

Jamie paused again before saying, 'I think you should be asking him.'

'I can't,' I said. 'There's no internet and no phone and he's not on social media. I mean, I could write him a letter but there's no plane left to deliver the post ... and his Morse is *crap*.'

'Yeah,' he said.

'So ...?' I said.

Another pause.

'I wouldn't ask if it wasn't important.'

'Important, how?' he said.

'Important for me,' I said in a low voice.

'Are you sure?' he said. 'Because you're my sister and I love you, and he's a good friend of mine.'

Suddenly everything took on a real seriousness and urgency, and I felt my heart beating faster.

'Not like that,' I said. 'I just ... I just wanted to know.'

'You're not going to do anything stupid?'

'What, like running off to art school?'

'Yeah, whatever.'

'Just tell me, Jamie? Please?'

He sighed.

'Okay. He had a girlfriend, Monifa. She was really cool. A doctor. She worked for Médecins Sans Frontières – I mean, super-cool. And they travelled everywhere together. He would look for birds and if he couldn't get funding for that, he would cook.'

'Figures,' I said, surprised at the gut-punch of jealousy that attacked my stomach. 'So what happened?' I asked as casually as I could. Maybe he caught her butt-dialling him while off partying with lots of other boys. I doubted it though: she sounded awesome.

'They had a stillbirth.'

I was so shocked I couldn't speak. Instantly, I wished it was something I didn't know. Something I could take back. The fact that Gregor had been willing to tell me knocked the breath out of me.

'Oh no.'

There weren't even words for it. Suddenly the thought of Gregor, coping alone, surrounding himself with animals, felt close to unbearable.

'Oh, Jamie.'

'Well, you did ask.'

'What happened to . . . ?'

'Monifa? She went travelling. She left. Couldn't bear to be around the sadness. It got pretty bad. Told him she'd only stayed with him for the baby, all of that.'

I thought of his patient, intent face, urging on the guillemots, willing their eggs.

'What's her full name?'

He told me and I immediately googled her on the laptop.

Sure enough, there she was on Instagram, giving a huge wide smile. She was gorgeous: shiny skin, curly hair and looking awesome in a bikini, hanging out in incredibly sunny hot spots. Including ... yes. Dubai. I screwed up my face. God. You can never ever bloody tell from Instagram what people have been through. Never. No wonder Gregor wanted nothing to do with it. That wasn't him being weird. That was basic self-preservation.

'I get it,' I said. 'And he retreated ... '

'Yeah, well, not everyone wants to hop over the globe all the time.'

'No,' I said thoughtfully. 'No, they don't.'

There was another loud squawk.

'Oh God,' said Jamie. 'Can you google "can ducks eat paint?"? I should probably go.'

And he hung up.

Chapter Thirty-one

The simulator centre was at the airport so it wasn't far, but I could feel myself trembling from coffee and sleeplessness. Not the ideal way to land a really large aircraft, even if they weren't real.

But I wasn't really thinking about it. I was thinking about Gregor, and how awful, how unbearable his pain must have been and must still be. The worst thing. Compared to it, a job interview, however taxing, didn't feel quite as scary to me as it might have done.

There were over a dozen unremarkable metal boxes in a row along a metal gantry. I followed my assessor, a quiet, clever-looking man called Mo, along to one of the B777s. After *Dolly*, I had forgotten just how large the cockpit was.

Inside a flight simulator it is completely all-consuming. You absolutely feel you are in the air; every window shows you whatever they want to program (that morning, a foggy day at Birmingham Airport). However tired and anxious I was feeling, the training and adrenalin kicked in – it always does – and I ran through the pre-flight checklist and procedures with ease as Mo quietly ticked things off on his iPad. The captain in training was a beautiful, stern-looking older woman who nodded her hellos in a way that made it very clear that being professional rather than being friendly was the current modus operandi. Fine by me.

I made the flight plan to Dubai – of course, I thought, with a rueful smile to myself. It would be.

I felt the weight of the plane as Captain Meredith taxied out – everything was weighted and organised so perfectly that I could feel every jolt as we moved to the centre of the runway. I made the final checks, and we moved off smoothly. I thought of the jerking, bouncing Twin Otter and smiled to myself. The 777 was a Rolls Royce of a plane, an absolutely beauty.

If Gregor could heal himself, then I could do this.

An alarm sounded just as the wheels took off into the heavy fog. Engine failure on the left side. I was expecting something like this, had prepared for it a million times, and immediately moved into action. The captain was speaking to ATC and preparing to circle the airfield and land again. I couldn't see Mo behind me but I could sense him as he failed the second engine.

Again, it was a case of following protocol. The 777 is full of redundancy; it's a plane that can fly on almost nothing. I knew this, even as the fog filled the entire windscreen of the cockpit.

Then there was a large, terrifying alarm sound. 'DUAL ENG FAIL' came the control voice. Captain Meredith and I shot each other a quick glance. Very few things on an aeroplane can scare me, but both engines failing ... Imagine driving down the motorway and a loud voice starts shouting in your ear that you are speeding and going too fast and the wheels might fall off the car. At the same time, an equally loud voice is telling you that you're too slow and are about to stall – and you're in the outside lane. Your job is to try and think through that and drive at exactly the right speed. It is deadly.

Meredith held the plane at its speed while I reworked all the controls in order to try and find out exactly what was going wrong. We spoke to ATC and levelled off as I frantically waited for the reboot. There was nothing obvious. I stayed calm, but I will tell you, when you get an unreliable airspeed warning, you don't think about being in a simulator. You just think about figuring out which of the nine thousand separate systems might be wrong with your damn plane until it can tell you exactly where you are and where you're going before you overcompensate on the thrust, burn out an engine and flip a spin. Meredith's gaze was fixed on the altimeter, desperately trying to keep the plane dead level however fast we were going.

The beeping continued.

'Can you get a visual on anything?' said Meredith calmly. 'Just make double sure we're not flying upside down.'

I peered out of the cockpit but there was still thick fog. We could have been going straight down for all I knew, as now we couldn't trust the instruments. On the other hand, we could be about to break through the cloud fifty feet above a mountain. You think I'd know, that you can tell when you are going up or down. I am here to tell you that you absolutely can't. Close your eyes in a lift if you don't believe me. The fluid that spins in your ears to tell you which way is up doesn't keep up with real time – that's why you can get dizzy when you whizz yourself around and the fluid keeps going. In the air, you can think you're perfectly level when you're actually plunging towards the ocean; you simply won't suspect a thing.

But I was there. I was present. I wasn't terrified, or panicking, or worried. I knew what to do.

The fog was all around. 'Reset?' I said to Meredith, and she nodded. I performed the flying equivalent of turning the aircraft off and back on again. For a few terrifying seconds, we flew in silence, on course into nothing, holding our nerve, waiting for the lights to come back on.

'Reboot complete,' I said, and then I saw it. The small red warning light, blinking overhead. Making out a small prayer, I flicked it off and back on again and the alarm, thankfully, stopped and the mileometer blinked into action as the plane settled down. We knew suddenly where we were, and where we were going and, most crucially, how fast, and I could correct our course.

We tried to keep our smiles off our faces as Mo ordered us to turn around and make an emergency landing at Birmingham – you never actually get to where you're going in a simulator. The landing was protocol, talking to ATC and carefully setting down a plane full of fuel on a runway that was designed for empty aircraft, but we knew what we were doing, and now, working as a team that fully trusted one another, we managed it perfectly. Mo obviously was trained to give no reaction, but we knew we'd done well, even if it took until taxiing to remember that in fact we had not just saved four hundred and seventy-two souls, but were sitting in a perfectly safe tin can in Hounslow.

'Nice work,' said Meredith. 'Are you going for captain yourself one day?'

'Maybe,' I said.

I turned on my heel in the corridor, pulling down my uniform jacket. My phone was ringing. It was Gramps, and I picked it up.

'Ah, bad news from the insurance company,' he said.

'What?' I said. 'What do you mean?'

'Apparently I ... uh ... well, we didn't pay the right premium ...'

'You didn't pay the *insurance*?'

'Turns out we insured the passengers ... but the plane, uh ...'

'... not so much?'

'It's an antique, apparently. Morag? Are you there?'

'Let me have a think,' I said.

It felt like the end of everything. No insurance. No hope except that awful guy.

And, I supposed, barring surprises, a newly qualified senior pilot. Who was beginning to work out – albeit a little late – exactly what she wanted.

Hayden was waiting there, passenger side; he no longer had airside clearance. But he was looking around the airport as if totally at home there, casually leaning by the entrance.

Oh God.

Everything there. Within my grasp. A man. A future. Money. Excitement. A cool job, long haul. Everything anyone could ever dream of. I genuinely couldn't believe what I was going to do.

We ended up in a coffee shop, one in a long line of sterile, identical chains that looked and tasted the same all over the world in the same glass and white airports, the same climate-controlled nineteen degrees, with the same smell of duty free in your nostrils, and coffee, and toilets and low-level anxiety.

'Something happened,' I said.

'I know,' said Hayden. 'I totally get it. It's been such a huge experience for you. Take as long as you need, Morag.'

He looked me right in the eye. Falling in love with this man had been the easiest thing in the world.

'No,' I said. 'Not that.'

And then I told him what I had heard.

His face went white. I could see, slightly dispassionately, the thoughts running through his head ... whether to deny it, or claim I'd been mistaken or had called the wrong person or ... they all went through his brain, I could see, clear as day.

Then he squared his shoulders and took a deep breath.

'I have been such a fucking idiot,' he said quietly.

I had been, I realised, expecting denials, or cover-ups, or stuttering half-truths.

Instead, he stared at his cup.

'It's true,' he said. 'I always wanted to be a pilot.' He shrugged. 'Can't think in three dimensions. Failed every single aptitude test.'

He picked at the paper cup, and I was reminded of my dad, who of course had also gone into a flying adjacent job. Dang.

'But why ... ?'

'You ... you're so amazing, Morag,' he said. 'What you do. It's astounding. I mean, my God. Landing those birds ... It's just fabulous.'

319

'But ... why did you take it as yours?'

He sighed. 'Because ... I'm so boring, Morag. I'm so dull. You even said it yourself.'

'As a compliment!'

'*How* is that a compliment?'

'You have a high-flying job that takes you all over the world!'

'Yes, but it's not *actually* high-flying, is it?' he said with bitterness in his tone. 'I just ... I just wanted to feel what it would be like.'

'Yeah, to chat up a girl.'

He squirmed.

'Did it work?' I said. 'How did you spend the rest of the evening? Joining the mile-high club? Oh no, I forgot. You can't take a plane up.'

'Nothing happened! I promise! I just ... I just wanted to sound impressive. I'm ... I've been such a dickhead, Morag. Such a dickhead.'

I looked at him. 'But that's ... I mean, that's just one time, one coincidental time you happened to sit on your phone. So I have to take from that that it could be loads of times. Any time. Was that the very first time?'

His silence told me everything.

'And all the time you were so interested in me, so interested in my job ... that was just research for your secret fake life?'

'*No!* Morag, I promise. At first, it was kind of interesting but, no, Morag: it was you. It was. I did want us to build a life together. I just ... I just wanted to be a more interest-ing person.'

'The person you were, that dull person,' I said, 'was fine. Better than fine. Perfect, in fact. Or so I thought. I really did.'

'You can't throw it away then,' he said, his face a mask of

anguish. 'You can't, Morag. What we have is ... it's been really good, hasn't it?'

'Really good,' I agreed. 'Really good. I wish ... I wish you were that guy. The guy I thought you were. The guy who was happy in his own skin. Who ... was nice to my mum and nice to kids and called when he said he would and didn't mind going round IKEA on the weekends.

'God, I really, really liked that man. I had so many plans with that man. But you would mind. You would. Deep down. And eventually it would start to show. And if I've learned one thing ...' I couldn't stop thinking, now, of a strange man standing in a clearing, utterly quiet, utterly still, holding up his hand so he could be trusted by a hawk. 'if you can't be deeply, wholly true to yourself ... you can't be happy. You just can't. We couldn't be happy. Not in the long term.

I stood up.

'And I think I'm the same. I don't think I can be Dubai Girl. I'm not sure I ever could. I think there was always something inside me holding me back. Not just the near-miss. Something deep inside that knew it wasn't right. However much I wanted it to be. And, Hayden, oh God, I wanted you. *That* you ...'

I tried to smile, but I was feeling so sad.

'Please,' said Hayden. 'Please give us another chance. Please.'

He stood up too, and I looked at him with so much regret. All the things I had thought he might be ... The handsome man smiling at the end of the church aisle one day. The funny dad, picking the kids up from football in his chinos, having Sunday barbecues. Joking at parents' nights. Everything I had seen in him. Everything I had imagined and wanted so badly, just as he had imagined and wanted so badly things he thought he saw in me. As ephemeral as a cloud on your starboard side on a summer's day – a wisp.

I shook my head.

'I'm sorry, Hayden,' I said. 'I have a flight to catch.'

Chapter Thirty-two

It was a bright, cold morning in Carso. All the neat and tidy gardens of the town were springing to life. Every last one of them was engineered to be a suntrap, out of the wind, no shade at all, designed for when, on a nice day, even if the cold winds still blew off the sea, you could sit out, take it all in and enjoy every single bit of the day. I smiled to see the hardy perennials planted in rockeries; tiny, star-shaped flowers of purple, white and yellow, fighting against the odds to thrive.

But I didn't stop. I didn't even tell Nalitha that I was there. I told nobody. If I did, I would lose my momentum, lose what I planned to do, back out. I couldn't tell anyone anyhow. It was totally unlike me.

I was not doing what my family told me: going to flight school because it was expected. I wasn't falling in with what my boyfriend wanted, living somewhere I didn't like, taking jobs I didn't want, always looking for the next thing. I wasn't straightening my hair, dieting, always looking for the next step, the next big thing.

I marched straight to the hangar and took what I needed. Then I popped into the dodgy pub, as opposed to a nice pub, hoping nobody would spot me and grass me up to Gramps, to grab a sandwich – and ran into the actors.

'WELL MET, AERONAUT,' boomed a voice.

'Uh, hi there,' I said. Then I frowned. 'What are you up to? Why are you all still here?'

Leopold eyed me severely. 'They've asked us to extend the tour.'

'That's great news.'

'Well, it would be if you could get any milk other than cows' up here,' said the pretty young guy, pouting. 'You know, some of us are lactose-intolerant?'

I thought about pointing him in the direction of Frances the goat, but decided against it.

'We were meant to be going to Mure,' said Boona. 'But they have no power at all. We're giving them another day.'

'Okay,' I said. It occurred to me that they had no idea I wasn't the regular pilot, that I didn't live up there. Then something else occurred to me.

'It's *Peter Pan* you're doing, isn't it?'

They nodded.

'The boy and girl who could fly?'

I rubbed my chin. Actually, this would be very useful for what I had planned.

'Ferry leaves in twenty minutes. Fancy doing a private performance? There will probably be a very good lunch in it for you.'

I have to say, for a bunch of people who weren't getting any extra cash, they were amazingly keen. It was a glorious day, I suppose, and to be fair the dodgy pub was not exactly somewhere you wanted to hang around for longer than you absolutely had to.

We headed down to the ferry. Boats weren't normally my method of getting about the place but in a gentle, lilting day like today, the eddies on the water were purely pleasurable, and the putt-putt of the engine was relaxing as we edged out of the harbour.

Jimmy landed us on Inchborn – we were the only guests, as most people were still getting over the wreckage of the storm, and it wasn't an official school visiting day – and I now confidently strode up the hill.

I'd only been down south for a few days but the air felt sweeter, and it seemed like the wildflowers and machair grass had grown in the meantime. The island buzzed and hummed with life, birds in the distance circling and cawing over the cliffs. The wind was rifling the long stalks as we walked up, full of nerves and anxiety, to the little gate at the bottom of the old stone house.

Gregor was round the back, standing by the copse of trees, staring into them. His hand was empty.

'What's he doing?' boomed Leopold, but the others shushed him. Frances, who was at Gregor's side, immediately came galloping up to me in a ridiculously dog-like fashion, her goaty smile as enigmatic as ever. I scratched her ears as she butted me gently.

Gregor turned round, looking initially furious at the intrusion. There was no sign of his hawk at all.

'What—?' He marched towards us, only gradually recognising me. Maybe he did need those glasses after all. I beamed at him.

'Surprise!'

He shook his head.

'Goodness. You really do just appear out of nowhere.'

'And this time I brought friends!'

Then he just looked puzzled.

'But what are you doing here?'

'Well, I have some work to do.'

'Busy busy busy,' he said, but his mouth was twitching.

'And also,' I said, 'I brought you . . . a thank you present.'

'That you got for free!' boomed Leopold. The others shushed him again.

Gregor frowned.

'I didn't need a thank you present.'

'Well, that's the point of presents. Look!'

'What's that?'

I handed him a hastily assembled picnic basket filled with Tunnock's tea cakes and caramel wafers. They were the best I could do at short notice. He peered in it.

'I'm not saying I have any objection to a tea cake,' he said, 'but if you like we could—'

'Have you cooked? Good, let's have that instead,' I said before he could change his mind. He smiled properly for the first time.

'Did you just come back for my cooking?'

'Yes,' I said without hesitation.

'Okay,' he said. 'But you have chased away my hawk.'

'Maybe you're not very skilled at falconry.'

326

'To eat my food and insult me . . . ' he said.

'Admit it,' I said. 'You missed me.'

And his mouth twitched again.

He brought out a collection of goat's cheese tartlets. I didn't really want to think about having a pet you also milked but the lactose-intolerant young actor somehow managed to eat them without worrying about it, as well as some rich amazing coleslaw, cold clear water and a large pot of tea.

'Where's the . . . ?'

'Bread, yes. Let me just go and get it, madam.' He bowed.

Then he looked at me.

'There's something different about you,' he said.

'I'm not dripping wet?'

'That's not it,' he said. 'You look like something has been lifted. How was the exam?'

'It was fine,' I said, quickly looking away. 'Anyway, I brought you something.'

'Lots of people. I see that.'

'No!' I said. 'They're going to perform a show.'

'They're what?'

I went and fetched a chair out of the kitchen.

'Sit down,' I said. 'Do you need your glasses?'

'Only if I read all through whatever this is,' he said grudgingly. 'Which isn't out of the question.'

'No, it's going to be cool,' I said, crossing my fingers.

'Why is there only one chair?'

'I have to . . . do something,' I said quickly.

327

'Does it involve annoying the guillemots?'

'Nope!'

He frowned, but it was too late; Leopold had already advanced, booming.

'Welcome, visitor,' he said, more or less pushing Gregor into the chair, 'to this, the Isle of Neverland.'

I blinked. It did feel a bit like that.

'Sit back and you will believe a boy will fly like a bird.'

'And me!'

This was Boona but, to my incredible surprise, she no longer looked like the slightly anxious mum who didn't want to get on my plane. Wearing a blue nightie, hair in a long braid down her back, anxious expression on her face, she looked ... well, she looked like a young girl. It was so strange.

'I want to fly too!'

'Oh, Wendy, well I don't know about that!'

'But, Peter, where's your shadow?'

Gregor looked at me.

'It's about a boy,' I said quietly, 'who gets lost. But has the most wonderful adventures.'

He nodded and stiffened suddenly, realising that I knew.

'Luke,' he said eventually. 'His name was Luke.'

I wanted to stay, I found. I wanted to sit out on this bright sunny day, on this strange, magical island and watch amazing actors weave a spell from nothing more than some blankets and old clothes.

But I had work to do.

I heaved my bag onto my shoulder and disappeared over the ridge, the voices fading into the distance as I scrambled once more down the dunes.

There she was, no longer at the end of the beach, but looking no better for that; scoured out, sand all over her windshield.

I strained my eyes and looked out at the sky; it was as calm and clear a day as you ever got here. Visibility easily for ten kilometres. Not a breath of wind. The kind of day that is incredibly rare. My stomach lurched. If I was going to do it, it would have to be now.

I bent down and took out my tools, including the absurdly heavy jack, found what I needed on the beach – a huge flat piece of driftwood – to give us stability on the sand. I was nervous, but I knew how to do this. I'd seen Gramps do it, and he'd shown me and made me do it. I was fine. I was competent.

Sure enough, with only a bit of swearing and mild annoyance, I managed to change the dang tyre, even as I could just about hear fragments of a jolly pirate song floating over the dunes.

Okay. I took a deep breath and pulled open the door.

The smell was horrible, like washing that has been left in the machine for too long. But, though it was unpleasant, it was not rancid. Liveable with. And the plane itself was dry.

I closed the door behind me, pushed open the cockpit door, and picked the crap up off the floor.

There were no lights on, of course, but the sun was shining on this bright day. I swallowed hard. What I was going to do – while not technically illegal – was so far from normal strictures and regulations I would lose my pilot's licence if anyone ever found out about it.

Having checked the fuel which, thank God, appeared unharmed, I closed my eyes, took a deep breath and put the key in the ignition. It choked, coughed, sputtered. Nothing. I took a deep breath, told myself to be calm, turned the key again – and it caught. I heard the engines, but more than that, I felt them at the very depths of my stomach: the familiar roar as the propellors started to turn. I glanced around me. Nothing in the cockpit was working – no speedometer, altimeter, onboard computer and gyroscope. None of it. I manually pulled up the flaps. Okay, they were still working. Check. That would be fine.

I looked out of the window. When did we ever get a day like this? So clear and bright? Never. If I was ever going to fly instrument-blind – do the thing you were never ever supposed to do – it was today.

We had an hour. One exact hour to make a twenty-minute flight when there was nothing, absolutely nothing in the air. Nothing scheduled, no overheads, no jet liners twenty thousand feet up en route to Iceland or Canada. For this tiny space in the afternoon, we had a completely clear sky.

But that's what Luis and Serenata had thought. They thought they had a whole blue sky that belonged to them alone.

I thought about it once more. I didn't have to do this.

But it would be the end of everything. Gramps's business. The entire dream of the family. My great-grandfather's heroics; the lifeline to the little islands of the archipelago; the Christmas presents delivered; the happy plane-spotters, the holiday-makers, the brides, the new mothers, carefully flying home from the mainland hospital with their new babies; the papers bringing news from all over the world; the soldiers, returning from the war; the family reunions, the great escapes.

Everything *Dolly* meant would be lost, and that ridiculous man would come in with his huge planes that couldn't land on the tiny airstrips. They would turn the most astonishing, miraculous thing – the ability humans had dreamed of for as long as there had *been* humans to soar above the clouds and break the earthly bonds like birds – into a grim, miserable processing facility.

'No,' I said to myself. 'No.'

I slipped out of the cockpit. Back at the house, sneaking in the back door, I noticed through the window that the young boy was now the beautiful princess tied to a rock. Both Gregor and Frances seemed entranced.

'Bork,' said Barbara, who had followed me into the house.

'Sh!' I said.

I crept into the little pantry and felt in my pocket for fresh batteries. Sure enough, there it was: the Morse decoder. I'd briefed Donald and sworn him to complete secrecy. Obviously he should have said no, but he didn't want to lose *Dolly* any more than I did. There was not a thing scheduled that afternoon, nothing that would be in the air, and anything that as much as tried, he was ready to deny them.

I started on the button.

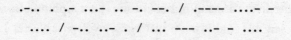

```
.-.. . .- ...- .. -. --. / .---- ....- -
.... / -.. ..- . / ... --- ..- - ....
```

LEAVING 14H DUE SOUTH

It took so long to come back that I thought I'd made a mistake; that Donald wasn't there or he'd changed his mind and called the Civil Aviation Authority.

Finally, as I was getting very anxious and not sure how long I could distract Gregor for, through it came.

```
-.-. .-.. . .- .-. . -.. / ..-. --- .-.
   / - .- -.- . -....- --- ..-. ..-.
```

I closed my eyes.

CLEARED FOR TAKE-OFF

I walked back to the plane, knowing that this was it. My stomach was lurching. But I couldn't stop, however jangled I felt. Barbara fluttered and hopped next to me but I couldn't worry about her just now.

I got back to the plane, clambered up the steps, my heart in my mouth, and got into the cockpit. Now or nothing. Barbara didn't take well to not being allowed on board and borked at me crossly as I shut the door behind me.

I turned the key and this time the propellors were happier to fire themselves up. Breathing deeply, I put my hands on the yoke and started moving her to the end of the beach, where I could head straight across the glittering sand, its strange ripples both timeless and temporary, and take off to the east. Making an immediate turn south, I could see the mainland coastline. I would see it, I told myself. Just keep level. Just check. I knew this land like the back of my hand; I had been raised as a part of it. I knew exactly where I was going.

I couldn't help my eyes straying to where the gyro should be, where the altimeter should tick. I didn't even know how fast I was going.

I taxied to the cliff where we'd had such an unsightly time of it, then turned round to give myself the full run of the beach. It was such a beautiful day. The sun danced across the sea, creating diamonds all the way to the shore. The waves were tiny and inviting; not the crashing monsters they had been that night.

It had to be now. I even nearly spoke to my co-pilot – the usual checks – before remembering that of course I didn't have one. Or a radio. Or a mobile phone signal.

Think Amelia Earhart, I told myself. Think Aida de Acosta. Think of my great-grandfather Ranald and all of those brave flyers who came before GPS, who came before redundancy and computer systems and flying by wire.

I didn't like to think about what had happened to a lot of those pilots.

I wouldn't know where I was, what direction I was heading, which was up.

I pulled back the throttle.

'STOP! STOP!'

A tiny figure was running out on the beach. A tiny figure with a furrowed brow and thick eyebrows and a worried expression, closely pursued by a goat.

I pulled up crossly, the plane's propellers whinnying as they slowed down again, and opened the door. I didn't come down.

'I have to go!' I said. 'I have a tiny window, a *tiny* window where there's nothing else in the sky! Get out the way.'

'I know,' he said, panting. He turned round. Behind him were the actors, lugging something that looked heavy.

'I came,' he said, 'as soon as I realised what you were doing.'

'Well, you can't stop me.'

He frowned. 'I don't want to stop you. I want to come.'

'Well, you can't.'

'I absolutely can! I just watched that play.'

'All of the play?'

He looked at me, and somehow the broodiness was gone, or at least, lightened; his face even had an impish look about it.

'Well, apparently to die,' he said, 'would be an awfully big adventure.'

'Oh, for God's sake,' I said. 'It was meant to be distract you while I got *Dolly* off, not *inspire* you.'

'I thought it was to comfort me.'

I met his gaze.

'That too.'

'Thank you. It did. Very much.'

He cleared his throat and changed his tone.

'Anyway, you need me,' he said.

'I very much doubt that. And you're terrified of flying!'

'Yeah,' he said. 'But I hear you're quite good.'

The actors arrived across the beach and put the heavy box down.

'Well, you lot aren't coming,' I said.

'We'll catch the ferry, thank you,' said Boona, eyeing up the carcass of the Twin Otter. 'God, if I thought that plane was bad *before* . . .'

They hoisted up the box. I recognised it: it was the one we had dropped off, what now seemed like a long time ago. But it wasn't, really.

'What *is* that?'

'It's a gyroscope,' said Gregor. 'I got it to accurately plot migratory patterns. Compasses are—'

'Not much use, no,' I said, staring at it, astounded.

'So?'

He looked at me hopefully.

What he had was the potential difference between life and death.

'Get on,' I said. 'Be quick.'

The actors retreated to a safe distance on top of the machair. I turned the plane round yet again, wondering how long she would keep going or whether something would short her out at the worst possible moment. Gregor buckled himself into the co-pilot seat and busied himself taking out the instrument.

'I can't believe you're being practical!'

'And you're being spontaneous,' he said back.

He looked out on the sea.

'How dangerous is this?'

I didn't answer.

'Prepare for take-off.'

We ran the full length of the long beach, the sand rumbling underneath the plane's wheels, then – just as it looked as if we were running straight into the sea, just as it looked like we would just keep going into the water and drown in our seat belts – as Gramps had taught me, I gently but firmly pulled back on the throttle, and slowly, but with increasing confidence,

Dolly trundled and clattered along the sand and then one inch, two, and we were airborne, lifted up from Inchborn, lightly flying into the blue. I could see out of the corner of my eye the actors on the machair bouncing up and down, delighted.

'We need to be going south-south-east,' I said. 'And if the flaps on the wings don't lie entirely flat, tell me *immediately*.'

As we banked, the sea filled the entirety of the starboard window. Normally I would check my route plan at this point, make sure the onboard computer knew we were following the right schedule. Not knowing how far and fast I was climbing was worrying.

But I could do it, I told myself. I was a pilot. With a pull, we were suddenly in a small cloud, and everything around us became white with no clue as to where we were. I wasn't looking at Gregor but I could sense his tenseness. It felt like we were in there for ever, with no idea which way was up. My throat was dry.

Suddenly from the back of the cabin came a loud borking noise.

'You are kidding,' said Gregor.

'We have a stowaway,' I said. 'Oh great. Three souls on board.'

But just as I said that, we burst through the cloud cover and suddenly could see – could see everything: Inchborn below us, with the three actors waving even more furiously, tiny dots on the top of the dunes; the house just visible – Gregor swore under his breath – a minute brown flash surrounding it. His hawk.

And, in direct line with the gyroscope, over the light washed-blue spring sky – the mainland. Everything was spread before us. The very northern tips of the world I knew. And beyond it, England, Europe, the Middle East – the whole world all within my grasp.

336

But I just wanted to go home.

'Nose right a bit,' Gregor would say occasionally, or 'Just left' or 'The water is listing down' to keep me steady. It was unfathomably comforting.

I flew on, closer and closer; nervous more than ever of flying over land though. Flying over where other people lived.

Dolly coughed and stuttered, which alarmed Gregor, but she didn't stop. This old plane, which had nearly sunk to the bottom of the sea, had risen again, and it felt so good to feel the sun on my face through my sunglasses.

'Is she all right?' he said.

'Never better,' I said, and I meant it. We were going to make it! We were.

Chapter Thirty-three

It was overconfidence that did it. As we stuttered into view of Carso, I felt my pulse beat faster. We were nearly there. I found the airfield without difficulty. Then I instinctively went to tell ATC that we were coming in and of course I couldn't do it. Normally they'd tell you what height to descend to, and I would know what height I was at anyway. Not knowing – the gyro had been invaluable in telling us we were level, and what direction we were going, but it had absolutely no idea how high up we were – threw me.

I tried to calculate the speed I would need to be coming in at, but that didn't matter – the plane had no idea how fast I was going. I had thought so endlessly about how to take off safely that I had just assumed I could figure out landing if we got that far.

Then I saw something on the airfield.

It was enough to distract me as I was gradually trying to descend. We were going far too fast, ridiculously so; we were

338

going to smash straight into the runway. The town loomed absurdly quickly in front of us. Gregor didn't panic, to his absolute credit. But he might have closed his eyes. Barbara was borking furiously.

I descended, then immediately aborted when I saw how impossible it was. We soared up again, roaring into the air. So much for our inconspicuous landing; you'd be able to hear us from Wick.

Sure enough, when I went round again – no flight path, no height warnings – there were several figures lining the runway, shading their eyes. Obviously they were looking at us. Oh God.

This time, we were so slow I thought we were going to stall. If we stalled, we would immediately turn from a plane into a pile of metal that couldn't withhold gravity any more than I could.

I pushed up the power and off we went again, this time nearly skimming the roof of the hangar. Gregor was white.

I closed my eyes. Thought of my grandfather, my great-grandfather, my training. The plane itself, and the blood of her running through my veins.

I could do it. I *could* do it. We weren't going to be a statistic, or a psychological investigation or a warning lesson to other kids in flight school.

Then I felt a warm hand on my hand, and a voice whispered, 'Second to the right, and straight on till morning.'

I pulled back for one more go-around, praying that this wouldn't be another missed approach. I remembered my grandfather. Balance, balance, he would tell me. Balance on the wind like a bird on a finger. I thought of Gregor holding up the hawk. I found the biting point. Between how the speed felt if you could not see it, between how the wind responded if you did not know it. To bring us down safely.

339

I surfed a gust I felt on the back of the plane, brought our speed down, slow and steady, and felt our altitude through the floor, through my body.

And the wheels gently kissed the tarmac, and we landed like butter.

Chapter Thirty-four

There was a line – Gramps, Peigi inevitably, Donald of course and another, familiar tall figure. They clapped and clapped as I emerged rather shakily from the cockpit.

'What the *hell* is that?' I said, indicating exactly what had distracted me so badly on first approach.

Callum Frost stepped forward.

'I thought you'd be pleased.'

It was a carefully restored, absolutely beautiful, replica of *Dolly*. A Twin Otter, sixteen-seater ... designed to land on a beach.

'No way!' I said, astounded.

'Turns out,' he said, 'your grandfather doesn't think quite as poorly of me as you do.'

I looked at Gramps who raised his hands.

'I thought I'd never see *Dolly* again.' He shook his head. 'My girl!'

'What about your big buses?' I accused Callum, even

though I was desperate to go explore the sixteen-seater; she looked a beaut.

'Ah yeah, maybe we can talk about some of them too,' he said. 'Now you have the chance to be a great big airline magnate with two planes.'

Everyone paused as something pushed past me on the steps.

'. . . and a chicken, apparently,' said Callum Frost.

I blinked.

'I've sold him the route, my girl,' said Gramps, beaming broadly. 'Thanks for being so cross on my behalf though.'

'I might have said,' interjected Callum Frost hastily, 'that it's rather dependent on you flying it.'

There was a small cough from the depths of the cabin. Oh my God, Gregor. He must have thought he was about to crash. He would want to rush back to hide himself on his island again, having realised that in fact real life absolutely wasn't for him. I could hardly blame him.

Indicating to the people on the ground to give me a minute, I dived back into the cockpit.

'I am so, so sorry,' I said. 'I dragged you too far out of your comfort zone. I really am.'

'You really did,' he said, looking rather pale and standing up on slightly wobbly legs.

'Good God,' he added. 'I cannot even begin to tell you how much I needed it.'

He looked at me for a long time, brow furrowed, his strong mouth hesitant.

'You . . . you came back.'

I nodded.

'For the plane?'

'Not just the plane,' I said.

'Also Barbara,' he said.

'Also Barbara.'

I found, somewhat to my surprise, that we were holding hands. His face still looked shocked.

'I have to tell you,' he said, 'I'm ... I'm a bit messed up.'

'I know,' I said. 'Me too.'

'The night you arrived ...' His mouth twisted into what might have been a smile. 'I was so wretched. So lonely. And I ... I wished for someone. Someone to come. And then ...'

'A bog monster turned up.'

'Well, basically. You can see why I was a little startled.' He looked at me. 'I ... I changed my mind about you though.'

'When I ate your bread?'

'No, not then.'

'When I fell out with your chicken?'

'No, actually not then either.'

'Bork!'

'Be quiet, Barbara.'

He rubbed his mouth.

'What about when I melted your kett—?'

He cut me off.

'When you dived into the freezing water to save a stupid rusting hulk just because of your grandfather ... when you were wild and free and brave and clever ... that wasn't bad.'

I smiled and moved closer to him. He looked down at me.

'Is this just because you feel sorry for me or think I'm all tragic and stuff?' he asked.

'Eh,' I said. 'We all have excess baggage. Anyway, no, it's nothing like that.

'It's because I've seen you in your underpants.'

He burst out in surprised laughter and I found in myself an

unusual feeling: wanting to do something for solely the pure reasons that I wanted to do it. Not because I thought I ought to, or other people wanted me to do it, or because it felt like the right age to be doing things, or because it would lead me up the ladder.

Because I absolutely couldn't not.

'I was thinking, if we did crash,' he said, 'I would have one regret.'

'Oh yes?' I said.

And he took me in his arms and kissed me wonderfully. His lips were soft, the bristles on his chin felt gentle; in fact, he felt entirely and absolutely perfect, soft and hard all at once. Then all of a sudden he pulled back.

'What?' I said, worried.

'Well, it's just in this plane . . . ' he started. 'I'm worried we'll make the wings fall off or something?'

'Shut up!' I said, hitting him lightly on the arm. He grinned broadly.

'I mean . . . I don't want to join the mile-low club.'

I looked into his eyes. 'I don't remember inviting you.'

'Also,' he said, 'Barbara will peck me on the arse.'

'Bork,' said Barbara.

'Okay,' I said. 'Well, I guess we should get off this plane.'

'Thank you,' he said. 'I would like that very much.'

And he took me by the hand, and I put the cabin doors to manual and opened up again to the fresh blue sky and the crisp flowing air. As we descended into the sweet-scented evening, I realised, somewhere deep inside, that around about six million miles after I started, I had finally come home.

Epilogue

It's kind of a hobby but it keeps us busy. Dad is bursting with it. It's a labour of love for him: sourcing original, ancient parts and speaking to fellow plane enthusiasts all over the world. And Gramps, easing himself into retirement, is very content with a spanner in his hand. Gregor is, technically speaking, useless, even though I did get him to design a new logo and he did. It's beautiful – a guillemot, taking off. And slowly but surely, *Dolly* will take shape again. She'll never be fit for commercial flying, but she'll do as a rickety old hop-around for us.

Plus, I also like to go home at night.

We can't live on Inchborn for ever, of course: the house, the island belongs to the nation; it belongs to everyone.

But we have time. This is our summer to dabble our feet in streams, to explore the nesting cliffs, to fish and walk the long machairs. When the tourists have gone back on the ferry, the island is ours. On hot days ... well, we don't wear very much. The first time I did it, I slightly shocked myself, and Gregor laughed and said how on earth did I ever think I was going to manage holed up in a glass-walled apartment in Dubai and I stuck my tongue out at him for rudeness and he chased me into the little copse, which might have been what I had planned all along.

Frances and I are great friends, which makes Barbara very jealous, but the hawk is Gregor's alone. He spends time, stock-still, communing only with this perfect, fierce creature, and I understand and respect his need to do so.

Callum Frost video-calls me and Nalitha and Indirah – I figured if we were getting another pilot we might as well keep it a female affair, seeing as there weren't any relatives handy – every couple of weeks and complains about overrunning schedules and pausing too long to drop people off and carrying not-strictly-paid-for baggage allowances, and we fold our arms and stare at him like we're the hardest girls in school and he always backs down. I think he quite enjoys it, so we're holding our peace.

Gregor is trying to teach me to cook. I am awful. But, it turns out, I am a good baker. 'I'm not surprised' was his only com-ment. 'Doing very precise things exactly following instructions over and over again is very you.'

And beyond that we have no future plans – not a one – except that I will love him and my life as hard as I can because I know all things are fragile as a bird's wing, as an egg's shell, as a dam-aged heart.

Acknowledgements

Thanks: Jo Unwin, Lucy Malagoni, Rosanne Forte, Nisha Bailey, Kate Burton, Matilda Ayris and César Casañeda-Gámez, Joanna Kramer, Hannah Wood, David Shelley, Charlie King, Deborah Schneider, Rachel Kahan, Gemma Shelley, Stephanie Melrose, Fiona Brownlee and all at Little, Brown and JULA.

Thank you also to the people of Barra, particularly Kursty, and to the National Museum of Flight, Scotland. And thank you to Captain Colin Rutter; Flight Training Captain Alastair McKinnon; Captain Laura Savino and Captain A. N. Other ☺. Once again, please do not use this book as a pilot manual; bad things will happen ☺.

Escape with
JENNY COLGAN

In a quaint seaside resort, where the air is rich with
the smell of fresh buns and bread, a charming bakery
holds the key to another world...

'Deliciously warm and sweet'
SOPHIE KINSELLA

Escape with
JENNY COLGAN

Escape to a remote little Scottish island and meet the charmingly eccentric residents of Mure…

'Charming, made me long to escape to Mure. Total joy'
SOPHIE KINSELLA

Escape with
JENNY COLGAN

Nestled amidst the gorgeous Scottish Highlands lies
a magical world of books and romance…

'Gorgeous location, dancing dialogue and
characters you'll fall in love with. Irresistib[le]'
JILL MANSELL